Antonio de Trueba, Henry Joseph Gill

The Cid Campeador

Antonio de Trueba, Henry Joseph Gill

The Cid Campeador

ISBN/EAN: 9783337422882

Printed in Europe, USA, Canada, Australia, Japan

Cover: Foto ©Andreas Hilbeck / pixelio.de

More available books at **www.hansebooks.com**

THE
CID CAMPEADOR

A HISTORICAL ROMANCE

BY

D. ANTONIO DE TRUEBA Y LA QUINTANA

Translated from the Spanish

BY

HENRY J. GILL, M.A., T.C.D.

LONDON
LONGMANS, GREEN, AND CO.
AND NEW YORK
1895

PREFACE

THE "CID CAMPEADOR" has been for centuries the great popular hero of Spain. He takes the same place in that country as King Arthur does in England, Roland, or Rolando, in France, and William Tell in Switzerland; and, like them, his life and exploits are, to a great extent, founded on popular traditions. In English-speaking countries there is very little known respecting him, and the translator ventures to place before the public a work which is considered by Spaniards to be one of the best historical romances in their literature. It is founded on a large number of ballads and other poetical pieces, extant in Spain for centuries, and on a very old work named "The Chronicle of the Cid."

The Author writes in his Introduction: "The Cid is the most popular of the Castilian heroes, and not without reason, for in him are personified all the virtues of the citizen and of the soldier. A good son, he avenges the insults offered to his father by bravely fighting with the Count of Gormaz: a good cavalier and faithful lover, he gives his hand and heart to the daughter of the man whom he had slain in fair combat: a good monarchist, he risks the anger of King Alfonzo by compelling him to take an oath that he was not guilty of a crime which would stain the throne of Fernando the Great: a good soldier and a good vassal, he conquers, with his invincible sword, hostile realms and Moorish kings, and lays at the feet of his sovereign, who had unjustly banished him, the spoils which he had won and the countries of which he had made himself master : a good patrician, loving the glory and the preponderance of his native land, he proceeds to Rome, enters the Church of St. Peter, and seeing in the place of honour the seat of the representative of France, he breaks it in pieces, filled with indignation, and puts in its place that of the representative of Spain : and finally, a good Christian, a good husband, and a good father; before entering into the combats, when calling upon God, he also uses the names of his wife and children, over whom he had wept when parting from them,—he who, in battle, showed a heart more hard than the armour which covered it."

CONTENTS

CONTENTS

THE CID CAMPEADOR

CHAPTER I

WHICH TREATS OF SOME LOVE AFFAIRS WHICH COMMENCED
ALMOST WHEN OTHERS END

JOYOUS festivities were being celebrated at the Court of Leon in the spring of A.D. 1053. Don Fernando I., King of Castile and Leon, had journeyed to Najera to visit his brother Don Garcia, King of Navarre, who was sojourning, in bad health, in that town; but, having learned that Don Garcia desired to take him prisoner, on account of certain matters which were pending between them, regarding the partition of their late father's kingdom, he quickly withdrew to a place of safety. Don Garcia having gone, in his turn, to visit his brother, was incarcerated in the Castle of Cea. However, having succeeded in escaping from it, he summoned the Moors to his aid, and entered Castile, determined on revenge, and committed horrible atrocities. Don Fernando sallied forth to meet him, engaged with him at Atapuerca, not far from Burgos, and the invading army was completely routed. Don Garcia was killed by a lance-wound inflicted on him by a soldier named Sancho Fortun, who had gone over to the service of Don Fernando.

This, then, was the occasion of the festivities to which we have alluded, festivities which had attracted to the Court great numbers of ladies and cavaliers, not alone from Castile and Leon, but also from the other kingdoms, into which, at that time, Spain was divided. There had been various games, and a splendid tournament had taken place, in which Don Fernando had broken lances with the bravest and most polished cavaliers of the period—a period so celebrated for skilful jousters and valiant warriors.

Night having come on, the dances, games, and jousts ceased, and great bonfires were lighted up in the open places of the town and in the surrounding fields, where the people continued the rejoicings until the approach of morning. They mingled their songs and acclamations with the continuous clanging of the bells and the sounds of the rustic musical instruments used in those times, until the ladies and cavaliers filled up the halls of the royal Alcazar. In them was to be celebrated a ball well worthy of the festivities that had taken place on that memorable day, the remembrance of which both Castilians and Leonese preserved for long years after, on account of the favours which their king dealt out to them with a generous hand.

If we were to paint with rich and vivid colours the halls in which was assembled the Court of Don Fernando, we should perchance please readers fond of the maryellous and magnificent. The picture would indeed be very effective, but we should fail in strict adherence to truth, and in our intention to sacrifice everything for its sake, during the long course of events which we are about to describe. The spirit of independence which reigned at that period in Castile had driven out the Eastern luxury which the Moslims were in the habit of displaying, during four centuries, in the southern parts of Spain. The contemporaries of the Cid were as brave and manly as the heroes of Covadonga, but also as rude and simple-minded as the first champions of the Holy Crusade, who had succeeded in driving back into the African deserts the impious followers of the Crescent. Light and flowers were the riches which abounded in the halls of the Alcazar of Leon—light and flowers which are the riches of the fields, the luxury of nature. However, if any discontented person found those decorations too insignificant, he must have found compensation in the beauteous dames and brave knights who moved about in all directions, evidently well pleased and content. All were impatiently awaiting the arrival of the king, which was to be the prelude to the dancing and to the other amusements proper to the occasion and to the period, when the voice of a page was heard above the buzz of the crowd, announcing the approach of Don Fernando and his family. A profound silence reigned throughout the saloons, and all looks were fixed on the door which communicated with the royal apartments. And, indeed,

Don Fernando immediately appeared, accompanied by his queen Doña Sancha, by his daughters Elvira and Urraca, by his sons, Sancho, Alfonso, and Garcia, and by some grandees who, during the day, had had the honour of accompanying him, and whom the king had invited to his table. Amongst these last universal attention was centred on an old man of noble appearance, to whom Don Fernando directed his conversation frequently and with great kindness. That old grandee was the noble Diego Lainez, lord of Vivar.

We have said that all looks were fixed on the royal family, but for our credit sake, as true and accurate narrators, we must make an exception. At one end of the principal hall a gentle maiden, who might count perhaps twenty summers, was conversing, without paying attention to their arrival, with a handsome youth not much more advanced in years. The importunities of a rather ancient dueña, who evidently feared that they might be noticed, judging from the terrified way in which she frequently gazed around, did not succeed in interrupting their confidential chat, which to all appearance was of an amatory character. The two young persons were Ximena, daughter of the Count de Gormaz, and Rodrigo, son of Diego Lainez; the elderly lady, who showed herself so uneasy, was Lambra, the dueña of the young girl.

The conversation between them was indeed of the nature mentioned above, for Rodrigo and Ximena loved each other from the years of their childhood, and love was always the subject of their conversations. Let us tell how the son of Diego Lainez and the daughter of Don Gome de Gormaz first became lovers. Bonds of friendship and relationship—the latter, however, rather distant—had united for very many years the two families. On the occasion of the celebration of certain famous tournaments at Vivar, Don Gome and his family repaired thither, and were hospitably lodged in the house of Diego Lainez. Rodrigo at that time was four years old, and Ximena, whose parents had brought her with them to Vivar, but little younger. Diego Lainez, to do honour to his friends, gave a banquet sufficiently splendid and abundant, when the traditional frugality in his household is taken into consideration. On this occasion the two gentlemen renewed their pledges of friendship.

Teresa Nuña, the noble wife of Diego, loved her son with a tenderness only to be compared with that with which the wife of De Gormaz loved her daughter. The children rivalled each other in beauty and grace, and the two mothers started a friendly and praiseworthy discussion on that subject, after the termination of the banquet. We call it praiseworthy, because maternal pride is noble and holy, although it may appear unreasonable to those who judge it dispassionately. That controversy ended by all those present, including the fathers of the children, agreeing that they were equal in beauty and grace, as they were almost equal in age.

"They seem made for each other," said Teresa Nuña. And from that opinion a thought took birth which was received with enthusiasm by both families—to enlace more and more their interests and friendship by the union of Rodrigo and Ximena. The realisation of this project was arranged for the time when the two fair scions of those noble families would have completed their twentieth years; for in that iron age all the risks to life and health attending the too early marriages of young girls were, with good reason, avoided.

Love, and above all the love of a mother, is the source of the most beautiful and poetic thoughts; thus it was that Teresa was inspired with a very beautiful idea. It was, that the children should consecrate this arrangement for their future union with a kiss, which also should be the pledge of a love that commenced on that day. Teresa Nuña, therefore, took Rodrigo by the hand and led him up to Ximena; he then sealed with his pure lips the blushing cheek of the girl, who, in her turn, kissed that of Rodrigo.

This compact was a bond which made the intercourse of the two families more close than it had been before, and the two children grew up like two flowers on one stem—brother and sister in their education as they were also in their souls.

Many years passed, and nothing had disturbed the warm friendship of the two noble families; however, some special privileges conferred on Diego Lainez at the Court of King Fernando, with whom the two grandees had enjoyed much favour, irritated De Gormaz, whose nature, to judge by some circumstances which had arisen anterior to those which afterwards took place, was widely different, in nobleness and generosity, from that of Diego. Indeed, thanks to the prudence of the latter, a complete estrangement had been avoided until a short time before the events which we have narrated at the beginning of this chapter; but at last De Gormaz took the initiative by ordering his daughter to have no communication whatever with Rodrigo, threatening Lambra to expel her from his household if she permitted such.

On the day of which we are now treating the exasperation and the anger of De Gormaz rose to their highest point, on account of the kindness shown by the king to Diego, and, on the other hand, by the coldness with which he himself had been received, and above all, by the slight which he considered had been cast on him, by his not having been invited to the royal table, as had been Diego Lainez, to whom he attributed his disgrace with the king. Certainly Diego was very far indeed from meriting such an accusation on the part of his former friend, for on that very day he had done his utmost to rehabilitate him in the eyes of Don Fernando; the king, however, had just motives for complaint against the count, and the good offices of De Vivar had been unavailing.

At the moment when the entry of the royal family into the saloons of the Alcazar was announced, Don Gome was passing through them, accompanied by his daughter. Although feeling much resentment, on account of the coldness of the king, he did not wish to renounce all chance of recovering the favour of Don Fernando, provoking afresh his resentment by abstaining from joining his suite, and thus acting differently from all the other cavaliers who were passing through the saloons. It so happened that, charging Lambra with the care of his daughter, he advanced towards the royal family. Rodrigo, who was watching for an opportunity to speak to the young girl, saw heaven opened when he perceived that she was free from the presence of her father, and flew to her side despite the anxiety which he knew it would cause the dueña.

Many days had passed since Ximena had seen him, and it is easy to imagine what was her pleasure, taking into account the tender and old love which united them.

"Ximena!" murmured Rodrigo in a low voice, trembling with emotion.

"Rodrigo!" whispered the girl, without being able to add another word.

"By all the saints of the heavenly court," said the terrified dueña, directing an entreating gesture to Rodrigo, "I ask you to depart hence, for if the count sees you it will go ill with my lady and with me. You doubtless do not know that he has threatened to cut my skirts short, in order to disgrace me, if I allow my lady to hold any converse with you. I beseech you to do nothing to increase his anger, as things have not gone well with him to-day."

"Fear nothing, honoured dueña," replied Rodrigo, "for if the count cuts your skirts short I shall give you others made of the richest cloth."

"I know well that you are a cavalier, and it is the prerogative of cavaliers to be generous. Speak with my lady; but be brief. I shall meantime keep watch, and say my beads that my lord may not see ye."

Rodrigo and Ximena were already conversing, not paying the slightest attention to the words of Lambra.

"Rodrigo," said Ximena, "whither have gone those happy times when the houses of De Vivar and De Gormaz were as one trunk with two branches; when no cloud obscured the bright sky of our loves; when we saw the distant horizon rosy and beautiful before us; when I found in your parents the love which you found in mine? Vain have been your efforts, vain have been mine, and vain also have been those of your friends and mine, to appease the enmity which now separates our noble parents."

"That time, Ximena, has not, perhaps, passed away never to return. My father, the son of Lain Calvo, although old, preserves, in youthful luxuriance, the noble pride of ancestry, and it would not correspond with such dignity if he were to bear with patience the unjust suspicions with which your father has responded to his friendship. For a long time he has borne them, Ximena. I indeed might humiliate myself before your father, without such humiliation casting a stain on me, for I would do it for your sake, and no reproach could be directed against him who humiliates himself for a lady. What does your father desire? Honours; riches; a kingdom; a throne for his daughter? You shall have all that, Ximena, I swear it by our love and by the honour of my ancestors. My arm is strong and my heart full of courage. Even to-morrow I shall set out for the country of our enemies. I shall enter the territory of the Moors, I shall fight as Bernardo fought at Roncesvalles, and I shall be victorious; for that love, which I have cherished for you during so many years, will make me invincible; and I shall lay all at the feet of your father, demanding, as a recompense, your hand and the return of the friendship which, at one time, was equal to ours for him."

"Good heavens!" said Doña Lambra, "my lord is just coming, and you, Don Rodrigo, will be the victim of his anger; and if he cuts my skirts short, good-bye to those of rich cloth!"

The two lovers paid little attention to the inquietude and the ridiculous words of the dueña.

"I know well, Ximena," continued Rodrigo, "that your father will use every means in order to avenge his supposed injuries on mine, and perchance I, the idol of Diego Lainez, shall be the first victim of his attempts; for, in order to wound the heart of the father, he will wound that of the son, by taking from me the hope of gaining the sole object of my ambition, which is yourself, Ximena. However, if the love which you often have sworn to me is real, if you hold in any account the happiness, the hopes, the life of the companion of your childhood, of him who has dreamed of such felicity with you, you will know how to resist his endeavours until the day shall come when Rodrigo will return to Castile, worthy of the daughter of a king. Then pride will compel him to grant that which his ambition, thwarted in its hopes, now denies to me."

"I swear to you," answered Ximena, in one of those bursts of enthusiasm in which, without taking reason into account, all things appear possible to us,—"I swear to you that nothing in this world shall be able to conquer my resolve,—I shall be the wife of Rodrigo or of none other. My father may be able to extinguish the breath of my lungs, but never the love of my heart."

"Ah!" exclaimed Rodrigo, "blessed was the day when my eyes first looked on you! Perhaps, without the love of Ximena, Rodrigo Diaz would be one of those plants which spring up, live, and die, without having borne any fruit; one of those men who pass through the world without leaving a trace which might point out his path to those who come after him; your love, however, will immortalise his name; by him the plains of Castile will be stained by Moslim blood; through him the standard of Mahomet will be trampled under foot by the Christian kingdoms; in him the weak and the oppressed shall have an arm to sustain and defend them; and through him the race of the Counts of Castile shall wear the royal purple."

Whilst thus speaking, forgetting where he was, the cheeks of Rodrigo flushed, his broad and noble brow lit up, and his eyes sparkled, as if all the fire that inflamed his heart flew to his head. The eyes of Ximena shone also with joy, and her heart beat with violence, agitated by love and pride,—by pride, for the daughter of a king would have felt it, knowing she was loved by such a generous and brave youth, to whom she desired to return, in her ardent glances, all the treasures of love which were shut up in her soul.

The anxiety of Lambra was increasing every moment, and not without cause; for the crowd which had collected around the royal family, curiosity being satisfied, was moving off and distributing itself through the saloons; and the honoured dueña feared the return of her master, or that someone might notice her complacency and report it to him.

"Ah! my skirts!" she said, moving in between Ximena and Rodrigo, "my master is coming, and he will cut them short without remedy!"

A group of cavaliers came from the farthest end of the hall, and Rodrigo thought he saw amongst them Don Gome.

"Adieu, Ximena," the young man hastened to say; "either everything or nothing, either death or Ximena!"

"Either Rodrigo or nothing!" replied the young girl, following with her glances her lover, who was just issuing from the halls of the Alcazar at the instant that the count was returning to the side of his daughter.

An unusual joyous expression could be noticed on the visage of Don Gome, which but shortly before was gloomy, and frequently contracted by anger. The cause of this was, that the Count de Gormaz, far from receiving, as he feared, a fresh slight from the king, had met with a kind reception, which, as he had not anticipated it, doubly pleased him. To what was due this sudden change in the feelings of the monarch? It was caused by the endeavours which Diego Lainez, taking advantage of the mood in which the king was on that day to grant favours, had used, with the object of restoring his former friend to the royal favour. The monarch ultimately had yielded to his solicitations, promising to show marks of kindness to the grandee De Gormaz, in the presence of the entire Court. And indeed the king had done so; when Don Gome had approached him in the saloons of the Alcazar. Don Fernando had succeeded in concealing his resentment, and received him with the same kindness which he exhibited towards Diego Lainez himself.

"Ximena, my daughter!" exclaimed the count, pressing her in his arms, for he required some means of showing his content, "the king, despite my calumniators, has remembered my services, and restored me to his favour. Don Fernando, who knows how much I love you,—that you are the dearest thing that your father possesses, and that honouring you he honours me,—desires to see you, and has commanded me to lead you to him."

Pleasure, in turn, shone on the countenance of Ximena; it was not, however, the same kind of pleasure which her father experienced; it was not that joy which proceeds from satisfied vanity. The reason for it was, that Ximena loved her father, although she was well acquainted with his defects, and desired his happiness, whatever might be the occasion of it. A ray of hope now brightened up her heart—the hope that the old friendly relations between the two families might be renewed, the consequence of which would be the return of those happy times when no obstacle was interposed between her and her lover. Pure and loving souls are as much inclined towards hope as towards despair; Ximena, therefore, ran over in her mind, in a brief space of time, those conflicting sentiments, and passed from darkness to light, from death to life.

Her father then led her into the presence of the king, from whom, as well as from the queen and the royal children, she received a most kind reception. The many different experiences, which she had passed through on that day, had in no way rendered her less beautiful than usual, and a murmur of admiration arose amongst the ladies and cavaliers who were accompanying the royal family when Ximena approached. De Gormaz smiled with satisfaction and pride; and Diego Lainez, contemplating for the thousandth time so much beauty and nobleness of expression, could not help thinking, " My Rodrigo will be a hero if she commands it; he will gain a throne if she asks him for one!" And a similar thought most likely came into the minds of many others, for no one connected with the Court was ignorant of the old love that united Ximena and Rodrigo, nor of the influence that the maiden exercised on the soul of the valiant youth who was the pride of the family of De Vivar, and the hope of the good Castilians and Leonese.

CHAPTER II

IN WHICH CERTAIN FESTIVITIES ARE DESCRIBED, WHICH ENDED WITH A BLOW ON A FACE

THE numerous guests who occupied the saloons of the Alcazar were devoting themselves, joyously and noisily, to the various amusements which the magnificent festival provided; whilst the king and the royal princes were familiarly conversing with the group of cavaliers that surrounded them; and the queen and princesses, amidst another group composed of beautiful women, were amusing themselves also with pleasant conversation. It could be easily seen, however, that if the queen devoted most attention to Ximena, the father of the latter was not obtaining similar favour from the king, notwithstanding the apparent kindness with which he had been received only a very short time before. Affection which does not proceed from the heart cannot long sustain its fictitious semblance, and, in a moment of forgetfulness, the mask which conceals it falls off, and the cold visage of indifference appears. Such was the case with regard to Don Gome, and, on the other hand, the sincere and wise monarch was openly showing the real affection which he felt for De Vivar.

"Gentlemen," said the king, addressing the cavaliers who surrounded him, "as a brother I have lamented the death of Don Garcia, but as a king, obliged to sacrifice the warmest affections of my heart to the good of the kingdom, which God has entrusted to me to rule over and govern, I must rejoice at the victory obtained by the Castilian and Leonese arms at Atapuerca. In celebrating that glorious triumph I have given proofs of my munificence to the commoners, my vassals. It would not be well that the cavaliers who assist at my Court should be debarred from participating in my favours, according to their merits. You, noble and loyal Peranzures, I appoint major-domo of my Alcazar; as you have served my State so well, with your sword in battle and with your wisdom at the Court and in the councils, I know you will also faithfully serve my household. To you, honoured Arias Gonzalo, I entrust my treasures, feeling sure that they will increase under your supervision. To you, noble and prudent Diego Lainez, I confide the care and education of my sons, as I feel sure that, having instructed your own son so well, you will act similarly with regard to mine. You well know how I love the princes; placing them in your charge is the greatest proof of friendship and confidence that a king can give to a subject, and I now tell you that if I could give you a greater proof I would heartily do so. You, the most faultless cavalier and the most honoured and prudent of the grandees of Castile, will cultivate the talents of my sons, so that the crowns which one day shall encircle their brows may sit well on them. God gave me three kingdoms, and I shall leave one to each of them. You, brave Count de Gormaz, shall be, from to-day, the General of the Leonese and Castilian troops, in the place of Diego Lainez and Peranzures, whose arms have been weakened by age and by the constant wielding of the sword and lance. You have given me proofs of your courage, fighting against the Moorish power, and I doubt not but that you, and the cavaliers who surround you, will serve me well, some by their valour in battle, and others by their loyalty and wisdom."

Peranzures, Arias Gonzalo, and Diego Lainez bent their knees and kissed the hand of the king, in order to thank him for the great favours which he had conferred on them, as was their duty as good and grateful subjects; De Gormaz, however, when his turn came, gave loose reins to the anger which had been accumulating in his heart whilst the other cavaliers were being thus addressed, especially De Vivar, who appeared to him to have been unjustly favoured by the king, whose coldness towards himself he attributed to the evil counsels of the honoured old man, who indeed was far from deserving such a suspicion.

"Sire," he said to the king, directing his glances from time to time towards Diego Lainez, "the Count de Gormaz would be a fawning courtier, and not an honourable cavalier, if he were to thank the king for favours which he does not receive. If flatterers alone please you, do not hope to find one in me."

Another monarch, less prudent than Don Fernando, would have punished the audacity and ingratitude of Don Gome, and would have put a bridle on the tongue which had so rashly spoken; Don Fernando, however, restrained his vexation, and allowed De Gormaz to express his resentment, even though it were unjust, and even though he did it in terms unfitting a subject in the presence of his king.

"You entrust, sire," continued Don Gome, "the education of your sons to a feeble old man, as if they should be reared up to be monks, or as if you should desire them to be as effeminate as women ; and, to favour a debilitated flatterer, you forget, sire, my services and the valour with which I have always served you ! If you desire that the princes should be good cavaliers, skilful in breaking a lance in a joust, and daring and prudent in attacking a squadron of Moors, to whom should you confide their training? Is it to an old man, whose hand can scarce hold the staff which supports him, or to me, who have valour in my heart and strength in my arm to brandish a sword, not only against the infidel, but against all who dare to doubt the truth of what I say? If there is any such, I stand prepared to meet him !"

Speaking thus, Don Gome advanced insultingly towards Diego Lainez, provoking him by his look as well as by his words.

The old man looked towards the king and curbed his righteous indignation, which, if it had not been restrained by the presence of his sovereign, would have burst forth in rage ; if not indeed with the aid of the sword, which his aged hands could not wield, yet with the voice which could be still energetic and terrible in defence of an honour which nobody but the Count de Gormaz had ever dared to cast a slur on ; he then said—

"Sire, pardon me if in defending my outraged honour I pass beyond the limits of the moderation which I should adhere to in the presence of my lord and king." And he continued, fixing his gaze on De Gormaz : " Don Gome, you are unjust in the highest degree if you think that I am a flatterer and calumniator. Diego Lainez is grateful for the favours which he receives from his king, but he never tries to win them, much less by means of flattery and calumny. If the reasons which you have brought forward, in order to prove that the king should have entrusted to you, instead of to me, the education of the princes, have convinced him, to whom I owe this mark of confidence, I shall renounce in your favour so great an honour, although I consider it the most signal one which has been conferred on me during my long life, consecrated almost entirely to the service of my country. However, I do not think that those reasons weigh much with the king. That weakness which you see in my hand, those grey hairs which you see on my head, and those scars on my face, only prove that I have lived longer than you, and that I have not spent my life entirely in the saloons of the Court. If I can no longer break a lance at a tournament, or enter into close quarters with a hostile army, I can teach how to do both one and the other; you, who learned those things from me, should be able to certify to that, and respect me, if no longer as an old man, at least as your instructor."

The king recognised the unreasonableness of the count and the prudence and moderation of De Vivar; he did not wish, however, to decide publicly in favour of the one or of the other, for he knew the evils which a complete rupture between those two noble families would cause to the State, as both of them were powerful on account of their wealth and the number of their partisans; therefore, to make the Count de Gormaz an enemy was a thing which even a monarch might shrink from. Thus it was that he thought it best to use his influence with a view to reconciling both opponents, and thus continue in friendly relations with them.

"Leave aside," he therefore said to them, "those sad contentions, and think only of renewing the friendship which, in times not far remote, united you, and of serving your country and the religion of your forefathers, now continually menaced by the Moors, for by no other means can good Christian cavaliers give proof of their loyalty. Both of you are strong pillars, to support our faith and my throne, and it would never enter my mind to favour one of you to the prejudice of the other; indeed, in order to recompense your merits I have desired that each of you should fill the position which circumstances necessitate. When De Vivar was robust and strong enough to wield a lance, he commanded the Christian armies, and now that he can only serve me by his wisdom and experience I confide to him a task for which those very qualities are most necessary. You, Don Gome, are the most capable of commanding my troops, and therefore I make you their leader. Some future day you will be old, as Lainez now is, and then the king will utilise your wisdom and loyalty in his household. Knowing that you are valiant and take pleasure in the chances of war, I believed that it would not be pleasing to you if I appointed you to a position in my Alcazar which only old men, as Arias, Peranzures, and Lainez are, can properly fill; or, if not they, only those cavaliers who, on account of a peaceful nature, are ill suited for battlefields. Lainez, stretch forth your hand to Don Gome and he will willingly clasp it."

The old man then held out his feeble hand, as if to seek that of the count, desirous of pleasing the king, and of sacrificing his just resentment for the sake of a reconciliation which might prevent many evils to the State, and which might restore tranquillity to his household. Perhaps, at that moment, he was also thinking of Rodrigo, whose happiness depended on the renewal of friendly relations with De Gormaz. Judge, however, of his surprise and indignation when he saw the count draw his hand away, and heard him say in accents full of disdain—

"The hand of the Count of Gormaz never has clasped and never shall clasp that of a culumniator."

"Don Gome!" exclaimed the honoured old man, assuming the haughtiness of a cavalier deeply outraged, "before extending my hand again to you I would cut it off. You—you are the culumniator, whose hand would have stained mine if it touched it!"

"If it has not stained your hand," exclaimed the count, "take this, old dotard; it will stain for ever your visage."

And with a blow on the face of the venerable old man he drew blood—the blood of Diego Lainez, of him who in former times was the terror of the Moors, the bravest cavalier of Castile, the son of Lain Calvo!

"Justice of God!" cried the outraged old man, vainly endeavouring, such was his weakness, to return the blow of the coward and avenge the insult which he had received; anger, however, stopped his voice, clouded his visage, and made his head so dazed that he fell to the floor.

"Traitor! unworthy knight and bad subject!" exclaimed the king. "In my presence you dared to raise your hand against an aged cavalier, who, old as he is, is worth more than your entire race! As God lives, my executioner shall cut off, to-morrow, in the public place of Leon, the hand which has acted in so dastardly and cowardly a manner! My guard here! My guard here!"

The voice of Don Fernando, however, was lost in the noise and uproar which arose throughout the saloon. The ladies uttered terrified cries and fled precipitately into the inner apartments of the Alcazar, believing that they would find in them a refuge from the tumult; and the cavaliers, divided into two parties, one in favour of Don Gome and the other for Diego Lainez, placed their hands on their swords and broke out into loud imprecations and threats, without paying any attention to the presence, to the words, or to the authority of the king or of the princes. At last Don Fernando succeeded in allaying the tumult just at the moment when the old man was rising from the ground. He then clasped him in his arms and pressed his lips on his cheek, as if to remove from it the stain which the blow of De Gormaz had imprinted thereon. His anger being calmed for the time, he was able to reflect, and the prudent monarch thought that, if he insisted on arresting De Gormaz then and there, torrents of blood would flow in the Alcazar and that inextinguishable feuds would blaze up amongst the flower of the chivalry of Leon and Castile. He remembered that the grandee De Vivar had numerous champions, on whom he could rely to avenge such an affront, and he considered it more prudent to defer the punishment of the count to a later time. The voice of Diego was then heard in support of such a decision.

"To Vivar, to my castle!" exclaimed the old man, tearing his hair, and shedding the first tears which came from his eyes since he had girded on the sword and buckled on the spurs of a knight. The outrage inflicted on him had not disturbed his mind so much that he could not remember what was due to the dwelling-place of the king, in whose presence no honourable cavalier could draw his sword to avenge personal insults.

Diego Lainez was obeyed: a few minutes later he was journeying, in a litter, on the road that led to Vivar, accompanied by many followers, both on foot and on horseback; and the halls of the Alcazar became deserted.

The Count de Gormaz had many partisans in Leon, as was proved by the large number of cavaliers who thronged to his side when the friends of De Vivar grasped the hilts of their swords, enraged by the vile offence inflicted on the old man. However, when the tumult had been appeased, when reflection forced them to realise on whose side was right, Don Gome could scarcely have found a cavalier to draw sword in his defence. It might be said on the following day that, in a few hours, the count had lost all his friends, for those who had been hitherto firmly attached to him were now content to remain neutral with regard to the matter of which everyone was speaking.

———

CHAPTER III

IN WHICH THE READER WILL SEE WHAT HAPPENED TO RODRIGO AND HIS SQUIRE BETWEEN LEON AND VIVAR.

WE have seen Rodrigo quitting the Alcazar precisely at the time when the pleasures of the ball and the fact of finding himself amongst the most beautiful women of Leon and Castile should have made his remaining there exceedingly agreeable. And whither was he going? What was his object in departing from the centre of joyousness and pleasure? The chronicles do not give much information on this occasion, as on many others, as to the actions of our hero.

The tumult and bustle of the Court were insupportable to him; his uneasy soul required calm and solitude; he desired to concentrate his thoughts on one subject alone, on the love which, the more it was thwarted, the more it became strong and burning in his heart. What were all those beautiful women to him, all those elegant and noble cavaliers, all that delicious music, all those amusements and dances, all that animation, that life, that gaiety of the Court, if he could not continue his sweet converse and his love-whisperings with Ximena—his love-dreams of love and happiness of a former time? He had reflected that if he had gone to take leave of his father, he could not do so without also taking leave of the king and of the cavaliers who surrounded him, and in that case they would all have endeavoured to prevent his abandoning the pleasures of the ball, as it would be impossible for them to understand his desire and the necessity he felt to be alone. He therefore returned to the house in which he had apartments, and mounting a spirited steed, he rode out from Leon, followed by Fernan Cardeña, a squire, who had formerly been that of his father and now was his, for the prudent Diego had transferred him to his son on the eve of the battle of Atapuerca, in which Rodrigo fought for the first time. He knew that Fernan, on account of his valour, his joyous and sprightly disposition, his experience, and above all, his loyalty, was, amongst all his vassals, the most fitted to accompany and serve the youth. Speaking strictly, the name of squire could scarcely be given to Fernan, considering the functions he performed with regard to Rodrigo, and the duties which were usually fulfilled by those that bore that name. Fernan was in reality a companion to Rodrigo; he might be considered as his military tutor rather than as his squire; and judging by the arms, both offensive and defensive, which he carried, he might almost have been mistaken for a cavalier.

The night was calm and beautiful, and a brilliant moon illumined the country lying around Leon, which was also enlivened by the shouts of the peasants, still engaged in their dances, and by their songs and acclamations. Some excited by the light of the bonfires, some by that of the moon, and some indeed by the abundant draughts of the juice of the grape, which they had indulged in, drinking to the health of Don Fernando, who had shown himself so liberal to everyone on that memorable day.

"By Judas Iscariot!" said Fernan to himself, "it appears to me as if they were a band of witches, celebrating their Sabbath around those bonfires, having bewitched my lord and master. He, who was always in good humour and fond of conversing with me on assaults and battles, and of the Moorish dogs spitted on my lance, does not now seem to care a pin where he goes or what he sees, and rides on as silent as the dead. However, it is my opinion that it is that Ximena who has bewitched him, she whom he intended to marry before the falling out of Don Gormaz—may God confound him!—with De Vivar, whom I pray God may bless. Certainly that maiden is a dainty bit, not alone for a hidalgo, but for an emperor; notwithstanding, I don't see why my master should so put himself about for any woman, be she noble or simple. There are many more women than men, for, whilst we go to the wars and half of us are left there, they, the minxes, remain peaceably in their homes, waiting till God, who created them, takes their lives, and the numbers that there are of them everywhere is becoming a regular plague. Then, if there are two women for every man, is it not simple nonsense and foolery to make such a fuss about losing one of them. Oh, how little would the son of my mother be troubled if he were to lose the two that fall to his share, for neither of them will let him enjoy her love, with their jealousies and quarrellings. We shall arrive at Vivar to-morrow morning, if the pace at which we are going does not kill our horses, and I swear by the name I bear, that I will not let Mayorica, the maid of my lady Doña Teresa, ill-treat and persecute me by her jealousies. For, if two women fall to the lot of each man, why must one of them get enraged if he should love the other? By the soul of

Beelzebub, why should I get out of temper on account of such unreasonable conduct on the part of women? But the selfishness of my master gives me much pain, and I feel it on my conscience to divert him a little, for the mind must be distracted if this tedious journey is to be made any way bearable. These roads are rougher than those of glory, and this continuous trot does not conduce to bodily comfort."

Thus reflecting, Fernan applied his long rowelled spurs to his horse and soon joined his master.

"We have a fine night, sir," he said to him; but Rodrigo still continued pensive, urged on his steed without intermission, and did not make any reply.

"We have not yet heard the cock crow at the inns we are leaving behind us, and our journey is half over; it appears to me that we might somewhat slacken our pace, for, without killing ourselves or our horses, we can easily arrive at Vivar before midday."

Rodrigo did not seem to hear, and Fernan continued—

"This night reminds me of one on which, being in the service of your father, we gave good account of a squadron of Moors who were about setting fire to the harvests in the country of the Christians."

Rodrigo still continued absorbed in his meditations, but Fernan was not yet vanquished. He had just touched, without effect, one of the chords which most easily vibrated in the heart of his master—that of war; he now made up his mind to touch the other—that of love.

"We shall spend much less time to-night in the journey from Leon to Vivar, than when you, your father, and I journeyed from Vivar to Leon, accompanying Doña Ximena."

Rodrigo started on hearing the name of his beloved; and Fernan, whom the movement did not escape, said to himself—

"It is certainly Ximena who has bewitched him with those eyes of hers, which are bright as the morning star. May Mayorica tear out my eyes when we arrive at Vivar, if it is not of that maiden he is thinking!"

The good squire was not wrong; the enamoured youth was thinking of his Ximena, was reflecting on the happiness which he had enjoyed when at her side, and was considering what were the probabilities of its being renewed, and of his securing her for himself.

"How happy," he reflected, "were the days which we passed near each other, sometimes in my father's mansion at Vivar, sometimes in that of her father at Gormaz! When we were children we believed that a tightly tied knot bound us together, although we were ignorant of its nature; we only knew that we loved each other and could not cease from loving each other; we grew up, and with our growth our love increased, and then we began to feel that we knew the names we should have to call each other by on some future day. Who could have told us then that a day would come, when the union which our dearest hopes and those of our parents looked forward to, should become little less than impossible? We were at a tournament once, and when a knight splintered the lances which he had to break, in order to be proclaimed victor, Ximena said to me, 'Rodrigo, when you bind on the sword of a knight, you will combat thus, you will conquer thus; and thus shall you receive the prize,—then your glory shall be mine!' And when the queen of the tournament, seated on a throne, gilt and adorned with garlands of flowers, presented the prize to the victor, who knelt at the feet of her whose beauty was extolled by the noblest and bravest cavaliers, I said to my Ximena, 'Some day you will be the queen of the tournament and I the victor, to whom you will hand the prize; all will applaud you and admire your beauty, and your glory will increase that which the victory shall bring to me.' At other times, swift as the butterflies and joyous as the birds, running through the gardens which surrounded the castle of your father or of mine, or seated under the shade of the trees in the woods, casting flowers into the stream which rushed by them in its rapid course, or standing together on the ramparts of the castle, gazing on the clear azure of the sky, and breathing the perfume of the fields which the fresh breezes of the night bore towards us, we dreamt of a life of love, of glory, and of almost heavenly happiness."

At this point of his reflections Rodrigo Diaz had arrived, when Fernan interrupted him, pronouncing the name of Ximena. They spoke for some moments of the day to which the squire referred; however, as the youth did not consider it prudent to give him any explications regarding his love affairs, and as he could not well talk of matters therewith connected, without having to refer to them, he changed the conversation. Finding that he had to talk of something, as he saw that the squire was resolved not to remain silent, he reverted to the subject which he thought would please him, and began to talk of the wars.

Fernan, who of the six-and-thirty years which he counted had passed twenty on fields of battle, distracted the attention of his master completely from his amorous meditations. He related to him many wonderful events, which the chronicler, to whom we owe much of what we are relating, considered, for the most part, pure fables, but which Rodrigo evidently believed, becoming at times very enthusiastic, and breaking out into such exclamations as — "Ah! Moorish dogs! . . . By St. James! that lance thrust was worth a king's treasure! . . . God's anger! what a caitiff was that knight!—Oh that some-one had been there to cut off the wretch's head!"—and others of a similar kind.

About this time morning began to dawn, and the birds to sing in the trees which overhung the road. Our travellers arrived at an inn, called the Sign of the Moor. Fernan advised his master to dismount there, with a view to strengthening a little the stomachs of both riders and horses. Rodrigo assented, as he considered that, if love had taken away his appetite, the case was different with regard to his squire and the tired beasts.

They were just dismounting when they heard a noise, as of horses, in a dark grove which was opposite the inn, and almost at the same time they heard a voice which called out to them—

"To my rescue, cavaliers!"

"Halt, villains! for such ye are!" cried Rodrigo, grasping his sword and preparing to attack the strangers.

"By the soul of Beelzebub!" shouted Fernan, "do not touch them; your sword should not be used against this crew of bandits, for such they must be, and moreover rustics from this neighbourhood. You shall see what my lance can do with them."

Saying this, Fernan rushed on the men who were in the wood. His master did not accompany him, as he felt that he should not use a knight's sword, for the first time, in a fight with miserable highway robbers—the sword with which he had been girt, only the day before, by the King of Castile and Leon.

Whilst Fernan was fighting in the wood with those whom he considered bandits, overthrowing each with a thrust of his strong lance, one of them separated himself from his companions and rode rapidly to the inn. When he reached it he dismounted hastily, gave a terrible blow to the door, which caused it to fly into fragments, and entered, issuing forth, an instant after, carrying another person, who appeared to be a woman. He leaped on his horse with her, spurred it violently, and just then, Rodrigo, who stood observing the scene, heard a voice which cried out—

"For the sake of God, sir knight, save a maiden who has been torn away from her parents by those miserable ruffians!"

Rodrigo believed now that the occasion had arrived, when he could fulfil one of the duties imposed on him by the oath he had sworn when he was made a knight, which was to defend the weak and oppressed; and, placing his hand on his sword, he closed with the abductor, who, in his turn, drew his weapon, holding with his left hand both the bridle of his horse and the young girl. The combat was fierce and obstinate; the disadvantage caused to the unknown by having to hold his prey was equalised by the caution which Rodrigo had to use, in order not to wound her whom he was endeavouring to save; and, moreover, the leafy trees dulled the early morning's light. The gallop of a horse was then heard, which was coming in the direction of the combatants; the bandit turned his head by an instinctive movement, doubtless to see if it were one of his companions coming to his aid, and just at that moment the brave youth thrust his sword through the neck-piece of his armour, causing him to fall to the ground, pouring forth a stream of blood, and dragging down with him the maiden, who had just fainted.

At that moment Fernan arrived, brandishing his heavy lance.

"Well done, sir! well done, I swear!" exclaimed the valiant squire, when he saw that his master had triumphed over his adversary. "You are worthy of your father, and have given good handsel to your sword; for, as far as I can see, those traitors were abductors of women. Be off to hell, villain," he continued, turning towards the vanquished man; "in the wood two of your comrades lie biting the dust, and you will be able to make the journey in love and good fellowship."

Thus speaking, both the knight and the squire dismounted, in order to aid the girl. She was, to judge by her dress, a country maiden, and very beautiful. They bore her to the inn, the owners of which were much rejoiced to see her free from her persecutors; for, even though they were not strong enough to succour her, they knew that she must have been carried away by force. Thanks, now, to the cares lavished on her by the innkeeper and his wife, the knight, and the squire, she regained consciousness in a short time, and falling on her knees before the brave youth who had rescued her, she warmly expressed her gratitude, shedding tears all the time. They did their utmost to console her, and, as it did not appear prudent to Rodrigo to leave her in the inn, exposed to the danger of again falling into the hands of those of her abductors who had escaped the lance of Fernan, he made up his mind to bring her to Vivar, where she might recruit her health, which had been seriously impaired in a few hours. The maiden willingly assented, and when the squire and the horses had partaken of a hasty meal, they assisted her to mount on the steed of the man who was lying there, apparently dead, and they all set out on the road to Vivar, just as the sun was rising in the east, and the labourers and muleteers, coming from all quarters, were lending life and animation to the country, solitary till then, with their joyous songs and friendly talks.

CHAPTER IV

IN WHICH THE MAIDEN, IN ADDITION TO HER OWN STORY, RELATES CERTAIN MATTERS, WHICH WILL ROUSE THE ANGER OF THOSE WHO READ OF THEM

"My master will be glad to know how you happened to fall into the power of those ruffians," said Fernan to the girl, when they had rode a short distance from the inn, not being able to restrain the curiosity, which was also felt by Rodrigo, although the image of Ximena was not for a moment absent from his mind.

"I shall do so with much pleasure, courteous squire," replied the maiden; "for if the knowledge that I was forcibly carried away has been sufficient to induce this good knight to run to my succour, he will feel better pleased for having performed that kind action when he shall have learned more of my misfortunes."

"Relate them to us, relate them to us," said Rodrigo, impatient to hear the adventures of his protégée, whose gentleness and beauty had much struck him.

The young girl hastened to comply, saying, "God gave

me very honourable parents, although their position was only that of peasants, and I always dwelt with them at Carrion, in this neighbourhood. They were vassals of Don Suero, and although continually crushed down by the exactions of the count, demanding constantly contributions from them, in which went the greater part of the fruits of their toil, they nevertheless lived contented; for the love which my parents had for each other made all their troubles bearable, and even sweet. I was born, the sole fruit of their marriage, and they loved me with such tenderness that, if I were removed from their side, life would have no charm left for them. To relate all the care they lavished on me, until I completed my fourteenth year, would be a never-ending story; I believe that the poor love better than the rich, for, since love is one of the pleasures, and perhaps the only one, which is not forbidden them, they devote themselves to it with all the strength of their souls. Poor as they were, my parents managed to give me an education much better than is usually received by girls of my position. Whether it was for that reason, or on account of the great care with which my mother guarded me, it is certain that I was always preferred to my companions by the young men, when we danced on the threshing-floors on Sunday evenings, when they sang in our praise under the windows, and when they returned from the woods with branches covered with May bloom, which they stuck in the ground near the doors of the houses. Near our house lived a young man, named Martin, who, amongst all those of his age, distinguished himself by the affection which he manifested for me, and by his many good qualities, especially by his kindly disposition and his valour. For my part, I grew to love him very much, as also did my parents; having demanded from them my hand, as he knew that my heart was his, they willingly assented, and the day of our marriage was arranged. You cannot know how much Don Suero was hated in the district, both by the nobles and by the country-people, on account of his tyranny as well as of his evil life, the report of which more than once reached the ears of the king. He, however, had not found an opportunity to punish him, as Don Suero is as powerful as he is cunning and daring. Not far from Carrion, in a valley covered with gloomy woods, there is a sanctuary to which, every year, the inhabitants of the country, for twenty miles round, go on a pilgrimage; and there they indulge in dances, banquets, and other amusements suitable for such festivals. This pilgrimage takes place in the pleasantest part of spring, and the rustic festivities render the joining in it very delightful. Early in the morning my parents, Martin, his parents, and I set out from Carrion, and, having arrived at the sanctuary and visited it with devotion, we retired to refresh ourselves by taking a meal and a rest under the shade of the trees, seated on the grassy sod, that was sprinkled over with flowers, which delighted us with their beauty and perfume. When our frugal but savoury repast was finished, a poor blind man approached us, playing a lute. We gave him what remained of our meal, which he thankfully accepted, also a draught of wine, which put him in good spirits. We then asked him to play his instrument, in order that Martin and I might dance to its music. The blind man did as we requested him, and we danced with much pleasure both to ourselves and to our parents, who warmly applauded us. Many persons approached, forming a circle round us; but suddenly the trampling of horses was heard, and all turned towards the path from whence the sounds proceeded, and then we all trembled when we saw the Count, Don Suero, who was riding on, not far from us, with a brilliant company of pages and cavaliers, and who kept his gaze riveted on me with an attention which terrified me. The blind man let his instrument fall on the ground when he heard the name of Don Suero, and began to tremble in such a way that those who were standing around felt compassion for him. He endeavoured to conceal himself amongst them, as if the eyes of the count were those of a basilisk, and he feared lest they might gaze on him. The crowd dispersed as soon as the music and the dancing, which had attracted them, ceased; Don Suero and his attendants continued their way, and shortly after our inquietude had almost disappeared. But not so with the blind man, who remained there full of terror, listening to the slightest noise which could be heard about us. We asked him what was the cause of his inquietude, and this is the lamentable story which he related to us, from time to time shedding copious tears: 'God, when He took my wife from me, left me a daughter, and also my eyes, with which I could gaze upon her beauty, for you cannot imagine how beautiful my Sancha was! Poor and rich envied me my treasure, for gold and silver and palaces could not be of so much value to me as my daughter. "Father," she used to say to me, "you are the centre of my affections on earth." "Daughter," I used to say to her, "you will be my glory in this world." Such was I to her, and such was she to me. One day we saw from our window a cavalier, who, riding across the fields which I cultivated, was directing his way towards our happy abode. He came up to the door and asked for a drink of water, for it was the month of July and the sun was so burning that Sancha and I had returned home from our work, in order to escape his rays. My daughter handed the water to him, and we invited him to rest beneath our roof. The cavalier thanked us, but did not accept our offer. "You have been hospitable to me," he said, "and I desire to show you that I am grateful; in exchange for the kindness you offer me I ask another from you; if at any time you should go to Carrion, where my estates are, come to the castle which I have there, and I shall be well pleased to see both of you and extend my hospitality to you; if you do not so, I shall be much vexed, for it will prove that you do not trust in my goodwill, as I do in yours." We promised to do as he requested, if the occasion should arise, and the cavalier went off by the way he came, leaving us delighted with his courtesy, and resolved to comply with his wishes, if ever we should be in the vicinity of Carrion. The opportunity came, and it appeared to us that it would be an act of discourtesy if we were to return home without seeing the count, for the offering of a favour is of more worth than the acceptance of it. We proceeded to his castle, and Don Suero received us and entertained us, not as peasants, which we are, but as if we were kings. He showed us his magnificent apartments, his richly - wrought furniture, brocades and tapestries worthy of an emperor, gold and silver vessels, and beds covered with silk and gold. My Sancha saw damsels there clad like queens. None of them were as beautiful as she was, but appeared so on account of the richness of their apparel and the fairness of their faces, not browned, like hers, by the rays of the sun in summer and the cold blasts of winter. When so great riches and such luxuries had made us lament secretly the misery in which we always had lived, without noticing it until then, the count asked us if we would like to remain in his palace, where a happy life would await us, compared with that which we had experienced, and which we should in future experience, working in the fields. Little would have made us accept his proposal, but my Sancha and I had heard that ambition, flattery, and calumny, which destroy both body and soul, reside in palaces, and we resisted the temptation and the importunities of Don Suero. We took leave of him, expressing our thanks; but, on reaching the gate of the castle, we found it shut, and when we were about to call out for someone to open it, two servants of the count seized on me, and two men on my daughter, and separated us, carrying us off with violence, Sancha I know not whither, and me into a dark prison cell. In vain I implored them, in vain I called the count by the name of traitor, in vain I questioned my jailers, for I remained many months in my cell, separated from the world, and without a ray of light falling on my eyes. From time to time I heard the bolts of my dungeon, and a person—I know not whether it was a man or woman, for the darkness was always complete, and no voice, except my own, ever sounded— brought to me the meagre food which prolonged my sad life. One day I took up the vessel in which water was left for me and raised it to my lips; I found in it a sweetish liquor, which I drank without distrust; in a short time I felt a great heaviness coming over my entire body, my senses were numbed, my eyelids closed, and in a few moments I fell into a heavy sleep. That sleep must have lasted very long, or at least so it seemed to me, on account of the torments I suffered during its continuance; at first there was a horrible nightmare, during which, at one time, my daughter appeared calling on me, in her desolation, to deliver her from the count; at another, weeping, in despair, over her lost honour; after that I felt an acute pain in my head, as if my eyes were being torn out, and I thought I heard footsteps of persons moving about me. At last I shook off that infernal sleep; my senses recovered their activity, and I only then felt a great weariness over my entire body, and an agonising pain in my eyes. I raised my hand to them and found my face bathed with a liquid, which I thought was sweat. A terrible suspicion seized on me at that moment : I feared that they had deprived me for ever of the light, and the pain which I felt in my eyes for some days confirmed that idea. From that time forth I desired more ardently than ever to be able to leave my prison, in order to find out if my suspicions were correct, if I were condemned to live for ever in darkness; and I incessantly demanded my liberty from my jailer, who at last, speaking to me for the first time, informed me that I was about to receive my liberty. He then took me by the hand, and guiding me through some winding passages, left me in a place, which appeared to me to be a field, for the air was circulating freely; the rustling of the leaves, moving over the ground, could be heard; my feet trod on a soft substance, which I knew to be grass; and the murmurings of the fountains and brooks arrived to my ears. Then—ay, then! a despairing cry escaped my lips; there was no longer any doubt, the Count of Carrion had condemned me to perpetual darkness; the sun, the sky, the verdure of the fields, and above all, the dangerous beauty with which God had endowed my daughter—my beloved Sancha—could never again be seen by me! "But what has become of her, my God!" I exclaimed. "Where shall I find her? Where is she, that she does not come to guide her poor blind father in the darkness which will perpetually surround him?" And from that time to this I seek my daughter everywhere, in the villages and in the cities, in palaces and in cabins—and nowhere can I find her. A hundred times have I gone to Don Suero to demand of him where she is, and he has always ordered his servants to drive me with blows from his palace, and now I fear to go near him again, for he would kill me, and I do not wish to die until I have clasped my daughter in my arms, and found a cavalier who will avenge the terrible injuries which have been inflicted on us.'"

"God's anger! what a wretch that count is!" exclaimed Rodrigo, when the girl had related thus far, and to whom he had listened with visible emotion. "I would give my life," he continued, "to prove against him the temper of my sword; and I pray God to grant me an opportunity of doing so."

"In such a way did Martin cry out," continued the maiden, "when the blind man terminated his sad history. You could have seen him, sir knight, clenching his strong hands, brandishing the stout stick which he used as a staff, and following with his eyes the road on which, but a few minutes before, the count had disappeared, as if seeking that infamous cavalier, in order to crush him with his righteous anger."

"I vow by Judas Iscariot," exclaimed Fernan, not less indignant than his master, "that if I can get my lance near that villainous wretch, I will spit him on it like a hen, not alone in the presence of the King of Leon and Castile, but even in that of the King of Heaven Himself. But continue your narrative, fair maid, for both my master and I are most anxious to hear the conclusion of your own adventure."

The maiden then returned to what concerned herself, and the knight and the squire approached their steeds as near hers as they possibly could, so as not to miss a word of what she might say.

"The sun was about to hide himself behind a distant hill; and the birds were bidding him farewell, singing plaintively in the trees which surrounded us; and the pilgrims were beginning to leave the sanctuary, as their songs and their joyous cries could be heard on the various roads which branched off in all directions. We took the one which led to Carrion, and the blind man with the lute was to get a night's lodging in the hermitage. His story had taken gladness from our hearts, and we were walking on, silent and uneasy, as if we foresaw some misfortune. Night had come on, and the moon was alternately lighting up the landscape and hiding herself behind the large black clouds which were moving across the sky. On entering a narrow road, bordered by thick trees, we perceived, in the obscurity, some dark objects which appeared to us to be men on horseback, and we were not wrong, for just then they advanced to meet us, calling out to us, 'Halt, ye rustics, or whoever ye are.' Martin recognised the voice as that of one of the servants of Don Suero, and told me so, placing himself before me, as if to protect me from a danger which he believed was threatening me. Two of the horsemen dismounted and came towards me with drawn swords; the moon then concealed herself behind a dark cloud, and a terrific fight took place between the ruffians and Martin, whose father, together with my father, ran to his aid, although they were armed even worse than he was. At last, however, the combat ceased; but the darkness prevented me from seeing what had happened to Martin and our fathers. One of the ruffians then lifted me up in his strong arms, without my being able to resist him, as terror had deprived me of all strength, and placed me in those of one of the men who had not dismounted; he then, placing me before him on the horse, gave it the spurs and galloped off, followed by his comrades, not, as I judged, by the road towards Carrion, but to a castle situated at the boundaries of the district.

"He who had carried me off was Don Suero, whom I afterwards saw lying insensible before the Inn of the Moor. An hour before your arrival we all dismounted at that hostelry, for the ride had been rapid and long, and both riders and horses were almost exhausted by hunger and fatigue. However, when they were about to resume their journey, the footsteps of your steeds were heard, and Don Suero, shutting me up in a room, sallied forth with his followers to meet you. You know now, sir knight, how grateful I should be for the service you have rendered me ; but, even if saved from my abductor, I cannot but weep for my father and for the brave youth to whom I was to have been married, and of whose fate I am ignorant, as they are of mine."

Thus speaking, the girl gave vent to her tears, which even the kind words of Rodrigo and his squire were unavailing to restrain.

Not long after this the battlements of the Castle of Vivar were seen in the distance, and when the sun had about half finished his daily journey our travellers arrived at the end of theirs.

CHAPTER V

HOW RODRIGO AND HIS SQUIRE WERE RECEIVED AT VIVAR

THE first care of Rodrigo on entering his paternal mansion was to entrust the young girl to the care of his mother's servant-women, and they, knowing how necessary rest was for her, prepared a comfortable bed, in which we shall leave her to her repose, in order to describe the reception which his mother gave to the newly-made knight, and which his sweetheart gave to Fernan.

Rodrigo had now been separated from his mother for many months. Being ignorant of the customs of the Court—as he had scarcely ever been absent from Vivar, except when visiting the estates of Don Gome or attending some tournament in the vicinity—his father brought him to it, in order that he might become acquainted with its usages and learn all that a young man, who would soon, most likely, be made a knight, should know.

Teresa Nuña was a lady in whom were to be found all the virtues and good qualities that one could desire in a woman. The nobility of her race, and her prudence and beauty gave her a right to shine in the royal Court, but her ambition from the time she was a child was of a different kind. All the glory and all the delights of the world were, for her, only to be found at the domestic hearth; to love her family, to be loved in return, and to be the guardian angel of the weak and of the poor—these were the objects of her ambition, these were her greatest delights, these were her supreme desires. At the time when she was born it was usual for girls who, like Teresa, looked with disdain on worldly riches and the pleasures of love, to bury themselves in a cloister; nevertheless, although her faith was as pure and as holy as that which, five centuries later, inflamed the soul of another Teresa, the singer of divine love,—even though she may not have participated in the same religious ecstasies as that saint,—Teresa Nuña entertained different views. She considered that the cloister should be the asylum of the unfortunate, a refuge for hearts which looked for nothing but heaven, the dwelling of those who could do but little for the cause of humanity. To make the happiness of an honoured husband, to give to her country sons who might be an honour to it and defend it, to cover with the mantle of charity and mercy the nakedness and the misery of the unfortunate—these things were in her mind the holiest duties of a woman. For something more than singing to heaven the psalms of the poet-king, through the bars placed across the window of a cell, did God place the woman by the side of the man,—woman, that weak, beautiful, sweet, persuasive being, full of charity, all spirit, all poetry. God, who causes sweet-smelling flowers to spring up in the midst of the foul marshes, and the herbs to grow on the hard rock, in order that the odour of their flowers may neutralise the fetid smell of the marsh, and the soft leaves the asperity of the stone; God, we repeat, has placed the woman at the side of the man in order that the sweetness of the one nature may neutralise the asperity of the other. When a woman's heart is broken by a man, or when he refuses her the shield which should protect her weakness, let her seek in God that which he has taken from her or refused to her, and woe to them that deny to her such a refuge; however, where reasons for shutting herself up in a cloister do not exist, let her fulfil in the world her glorious destiny. Thus thought Teresa Nuña when the brave and honoured Diego Lainez besought her hand; she gave it to him with joy, for by doing so the honour of her house would be increased, and, above all, her noble aspirations would find their realisation. From that time forward she was, more than ever before, the mother of the unfortunate; and when nature gave her another right to that sweet name, when she was called such by the rosy lips of her child, she considered herself the happiest woman in this world. It is easy, then, to imagine the love she felt for Rodrigo, she whose heart was a treasure of love and tenderness for all, and the pleasure she would feel in again clasping to her heart that handsome and gentle youth after some months of separation from him. He had scarcely dismounted in the courtyard of the castle when she ran to meet him, and both were reunited in a close embrace.

"How is it, my son," asked Teresa of the youth, "that your father has not come with you, for had he done so my happiness would be complete?"

"Do not be uneasy, dear mother," replied Rodrigo; "last night I left him well, and much honoured by the king, at Leon, to which city Don Fernando has returned."

"I am rejoiced, son of my soul, on account of the affection which Don Fernando feels for your father, and the favours which he confers on him; however, I would be more rejoiced if I could have him always by my side, for if the love which I always had for him made me weep during his absence when he was still vigorous and young, it makes me doubly sad when he is away from me now that he is feeble and old. I fear that the disquietudes of a Court life may injure his health, or that he may be injured by the plots which his rivals and enemies get up against him."

"As to that, have no fear, mother. Our rivals know that, even if the hand of Diego Lainez is weak to avenge injuries, it is not so with that of his son. Who will dare to insult Diego, now that a knight's sword has been girt on Rodrigo?"

"Oh, my son!" exclaimed Teresa, again embracing the youth, full of delight, as much for the generous impulse which the words of her son manifested as for the news that he had been made a knight. "How is it that the eyes of your mother did not sooner notice your sword-belt? When, my son, were you so honoured?"

"Only yesterday, dear mother, and much honoured indeed, for the king girt on my sword, the queen gave me my steed, and the Infanta Doña Urraca buckled on my spurs."

"Oh, how great an honour you will become to the order into which you have been received!"

"Such, I trust, shall be soon, mother; for I only come to

take leave of you before setting out for the frontiers to fight against the Moorish power; for oh, my mother, I want riches, I want a throne!"

"I well can understand those noble aspirations, as the blood of the Counts of Castile flows in your veins. Proceed, then, to the war, even though parting from you will make your mother's heart bleed, as I would wish to keep you always near me. However, let no ambition dazzle you, beyond that of serving your country and the faith of your forefathers. You say that you desire riches, that you desire a throne. Why do you desire a throne, my son?"

"I desire it, dear mother, in order to raise myself above that ambitious count, who looks on me as one too poor and humble to merit the hand of his daughter."

"Ah, my son, you have then not yet conquered that love, the realising of which has become almost an impossibility, and which has caused such inquietudes both in your soul and in those of your parents? You have not yet forgotten Ximena?"

"Forget her? forget her? Never, my mother! In vain have I tried to do so; in vain have I sought to erase her image from my heart; in vain have I tried to think that to love Ximena was almost the same as to humble myself before her father, a humiliation unworthy of the race of Vivar; but this love still dominates me, stronger and more vigorous than ever. Forget her? forget her? Had I but loved her a day, a month, a year, and not almost during my whole life; were Ximena and I the maiden and the youth, whose union might appease paternal rancours or satisfy paternal ambitions, and in which love had little part; were she less beautiful, less discreet, less honoured than she is—then perhaps I could forget her; but you, my mother, know how deep is the love which unites us; for you, whose eyes were ever fixed on us, have seen it spring up and increase, and you have even fanned its flame by keeping us ever near each other, and by letting us see the pleasure and the pride which a similar love caused you. I promised you, indeed, when I left your arms to betake myself to the Court, that I would endeavour to forget her, and I even said to you that I had hopes that I might be able to do so; but I was mistaken, dear mother. Many days passed without my seeing her, but none that I did not think on her; and that day on which my father brought me with him to the Court was the happiest of my life, and proved to me that separation had only made our love stronger. Had you seen her eclipsing with her beauty that of the fairest dames of Leon, and receiving the homage of the bravest and best cavaliers, you could not ask me, mother, Have you forgotten her?"

Teresa was now convinced, if indeed she had not already been so, that the love of her son was above all reasonings, and she did not try to overcome it with hers. She thought it better, therefore, to endeavour to remove the pain from his burning heart by pouring on it some drops of the balsam of hope.

"Do not forget her, then, my son," she said to the excited youth, caressing him with her hand, and with a look full of love and tenderness. "This love will elevate your soul and strengthen your heart. Summon our friends and vassals, and go fight against the infidel, for the glory and the power which you will achieve shall throw into the shade, as you have said, the ambitious Don Gome, and Ximena will become your bride. The contentions which separate her family and ours are not of that kind which, between honourable rivals, cannot be terminated without honour being stained. Go, my Rodrigo, go to your repose, for indeed you require it after so long a journey, and to-morrow we shall see what can be done to promote your happiness; for your mother, more experienced than you in the affairs of this world, will aid you with her love and advice."

Teresa and her son again lovingly embraced each other, and the youth retired to take off his armour in order to seek repose; not, however, without having related to her the adventure at the Inn of the Moor, and having recommended to her care the maiden who had sought the hospitality of the castle.

Having described the reception which was given to Rodrigo at Vivar, we must also describe that which Fernan received.

Almost at the same time that our travellers rode into the courtyard of the castle, there entered after them a large number of girls and young men, vassals of the grandee of Vivar, who, having seen Rodrigo arrive, and having recognised, by his armour, that he was now a knight, came to welcome him and offer him their congratulations on account of the order of chivalry which he had received, playing rustic instruments and singing joyous songs. As soon as Rodrigo dismounted he ascended to the upper apartments, leaving the young girl, his guest, with his squire, in order that he might place her under the care of the servants of his mother, as we have already mentioned. Fernan then proceeded to the stables, to see that the horses were properly attended to. When he returned to the courtyard the male and female peasants began to pour in, and amongst the latter he saw one so graceful and pretty that he would have fallen in love with her at once, if his heart had not been captured beforehand, by her charms. As it was a long time since he had seen her, he forgot where he was, and running up to her, gave her a warm embrace, which the girl did not try to avoid, as she was rather fond of the brave squire, and love, particularly amongst country-people, often goes beyond the bounds of decorum. At that very moment Mayorica heard the music and the cheering in the courtyard; she ran to her window, which looked out on it, and was much enraged, with good cause, when she saw Fernan so warmly embracing the peasant girl. "Ah, traitor!" she exclaimed; and when he heard that cry, the squire let go the girl, who, uttering another cry, suddenly ran off from her companions and from the castle, not without threatening both with her look and hand the unlucky Fernan, who did not notice this, however, on account of the perturbation of his mind.

The good squire remained as if thunderstruck for some moments, but he soon recovered his habitual serenity, and began to consider, whilst ascending the stairs, what he should do to escape the strong language and, perhaps, the nails of Mayorica.

"What a fool I am," he said to himself, "not to be able to restrain my impetuous feelings, when prudence should counsel me to do so!" and he tugged at his hair out of pure vexation with himself. "A fool, and ten times a fool," he continued, "not to remember the unreasonableness of women. O ye women, cause of all my troubles! but it was I myself, donkey that I am, that was the cause of the present one. Why do I not cast both of you off, or turn Moor, so as to have three, and none of them to tear my beard if I love the others. But I am an old Christian, and have fought long years against the law of Mahomet and must fight against it still; however, for all that, I cannot deny that Mahomet was a wise man, in one thing at least—permitting a man to have three wives. I would not only allow three but three hundred, so that none of them could claim more than the three-hundredth part of a man's love. A man returns home, after a long journey, sore and weary, and instead of finding a woman to welcome him with open arms, he finds a regular fury, who receives him with abuse and with scratches enough to blind him."

With these wise reflections Fernan ascended the stairs, and, entering the chamber of Mayorica, he found her, bathed in tears, sitting on a chair, in such a condition that it awoke compassion to see her. Such, then, did our squire feel, and as pity is said to be akin to love, his returned in such a degree that his angry thoughts were well-nigh forgotten.

"Who has offended you, Mayorica of my soul?" exclaimed Fernan, approaching the damsel with open arms; but she suddenly arose, and seizing, with great fury, the squire by the neck, cried out—

"Ah, traitor, and worse than traitor! I will choke you, so that you may never more deceive honourable girls who are worth more than your whole race."

"I vow by Judas Iscariot! by the soul of Beelzebub!" muttered Fernan with stifled voice, struggling to get free from his enraged sweetheart. "Let go, let go, you vixen, or I shall make you do so, even if I have to strike you."

And making a violent effort, he found himself free from the young woman, whom he pushed from him across the floor, though he did not do so before getting some scratches on his face.

Mayorica, knowing that her nails were insufficient weapons to fight against so robust a lover, had recourse to the usual one of women, that is, to her tongue, and Fernan to a similar one, as he considered it was not courteous and honourable to fight with stronger weapons, especially when his adversary was a woman.

"Woe is me! who, having refused the love even of hidalgos, have kept my honour intact for the sake of such a low-born squire, a greater traitor than Judas himself!" cried Mayorica, bursting out again into torrents of tears, that would have softened a stone.

Fernan laid aside his annoyance and endeavoured to conquer the anger of his sweetheart with mild reasoning, for his heart was as soft as wax when dealing with women, as it was hard as flint before his enemies on the field of battle. And besides, what should a man do but humble himself before a woman who at thirty years of age—for Mayorica was not a day younger—comes with unstained honour to a man, in order that he may claim her as his own?

"Be quiet, be quiet, Mayorica of my soul! I always look on you as my own, and I have always loved you, and ever will love you," he interrupted, with endearing accents and an affectionate gaze.

"Ah, you villain!" replied the young woman, "it was not enough for you to act the traitor but you must also come to me with lies in your mouth. You then want to deny what my very eyes have witnessed?"

"Let not that pain you, Mayorica; with my arms I did not give my heart to that peasant girl, Aldonza; I keep it always for you."

"Be off, traitor! your ridiculous excuses enrage me more than they appease me. Depart from me, and never, as long as you live, dare to look on me again with eyes of affection."

It appeared to Fernan that the anger of Mayorica was lasting much too long; thus it was that, his patience failing him, he determined to make use of his arithmetical argument, and if he could not succeed in convincing her with it, to renounce the attempt, and even, if necessary, his love itself.

"Well, then," he said, "I am fond of Aldonza, but, I swear to you, of no other but you and her. I have told you a thousand times that, according to my calculations, there are two women in Spain for every man. Is it not nonsense, then, to blame me for only claiming what belongs to me, when I go no farther?"

"Be off with you, shameless wretch!" exclaimed Mayorica, at the height of her exasperation.

"Yes, and at once," said Fernan; "for Aldonza is awaiting me, in order to repay with interest the embrace I gave her."

Saying this, he quitted the chamber of Mayorica and went off to his own, muttering on his way—

"By the soul of Beelzebub, how this nonsense, this obstinacy, this absurdity of women, makes my blood boil! I will rest myself to-night, for I need to do so, and to-morrow I will compensate myself with Aldonza for the ingratitude of Mayorica. That girl is affectionate and not cross and quarrelsome, like the vixen I have just left."

CHAPTER VI

HOW FERNAN DESPAIRED OF GETTING WOMEN TO UNDER-
STAND REASON, AND HOW DIEGO LAINEZ HOPED THAT
HIS HONOUR WOULD BE AVENGED.

MORNING began to break when a cross-bowman, who was keeping watch on the battlements of the Castle of Vivar, heard the trampling of horses at a short distance from the fortifications, and a moment after he saw advancing a body of horsemen and also men on foot, who seemed to bear a litter. He put to his mouth the speaking-trumpet which hung from his neck, and cried out, "Who goes there?" Those who were approaching answered by a signal, which he evidently understood, as the bridges and the portcullis were at once lowered, and the cortège entered the courtyard.

A short time before Fernan had left the castle by an iron-bound door, which led to the stables and which was used for the egress and ingress of the servants of the lords of Vivar, especially in the night-time, when the principal entrance was defended by a double portcullis and a gate, too heavy to raise frequently.

Whither was the squire going so early in the morning? It is easy to guess, if we remember the last words he used when retiring to rest a few hours before. Notwithstanding his quarrel with Mayorica, he had slept that night like a dead man, until an early hour of the morning, at which time he awoke, as was his custom, and hastened off to the dwelling of Aldonza, for she lived at some distance, and he had to be back in the castle before his master arose, when he should have to be in attendance on him. We must, however, tell who the girl was whom he was about to visit, and also who the old woman was with whom she lived. To do this it is only necessary to copy literally the words of the chronicler, who writes: "The girl was named Aldonza, and was very pretty and attractive, so that there was none like her in those parts. Many gallants sought her affection, but it was of no avail, as she was in love with a gentle squire named Fernan, who belonged to the house of the honoured Diego Lainez. There lived with her an old witch, by name Mari-Perez, whom all the maidens and youths that were in love went to consult."

Far be it from us to question the text which we have just

quoted : the reader can do it if he so desires.　If the occupation of Mari-Perez may not be considered a very honourable one, let the blame rest with the chronicler, and let it be put down to malice, for it looks as if he harboured such against her, to judge by the way he expresses himself.　All we shall add is that Aldonza called the old woman with whom she lived "mother," but we are certain that she was not such, for if she were so, that fact would have been mentioned in the chronicle, which goes into much detail regarding the persons who figure in it.

Aldonza and the woman she called her mother resided in a cottage situated amongst the trees of a lonely glen, through which rushed a torrent, whose roar contributed not a little to increase the superstitious dread with which the inhabitants of the country surrounding Vivar approached the dwelling-place of the witch, for by that name Mari-Perez was commonly known.　Fernan, however, who did not trouble himself much about witchcraft, knocked at the door of Aldonza, consoling himself with the thoughts of the good reception he would receive from Aldonza, compared with the scratches which Mayorica had inflicted on him.　The girl appeared at the small window above the door and asked who was there.

"It's me," answered the squire; "open the door, for this mist that's rising from the brook is freezing me."

"Wait," said Aldonza, and taking up a jug of water, she threw it out on the unfortunate Fernan, exclaiming—

"You will die here, traitor, villain, ruffian, blackguard! Do you think you can deceive me any longer?　It is you that are tricked now!"

And not content with having wetted him to the skin with the water and nearly broken his head with the jug, she began to hurl down on him such a quantity of tiles, stones, and other projectiles, that if he had not sheltered himself at once behind the trunk of an oak tree, which luckily happened to be near, she would have nearly killed him, considering her fury and the accuracy with which she aimed.

"Halt, you minx!" exclaimed Fernan, soaked through not only with water, but also with blood.　"As sure as I catch you, I'll take every inch of skin off your back with lashes.　Is it thus, you vixen, that you treat so faithful a lover as I am? Would that I had never set my eyes on a jade like you!　May I lose my strength if at this very moment I do not, with blows and lashes, half kill both you and the witch who lives with you!"

Thus speaking, the squire rushed at the door and gave it a furious kick, in order to break it in; but his own head narrowly escaped being broken in by another jug and more tiles and stones, which made him return to his tree more quickly than he could have wished.

"What did I do to you? what did I do to you, that you should attack me with such fury?"

"Be off, traitor!" replied the girl; "be off to the castle, and tell her who awaits you there that from this day forward you are hers alone."

The enamoured Fernan came now to the conclusion that Aldonza had discovered his love for Mayorica, and he began to think of using his eternal arithmetical argument; he remembered, however, the little good it had done him with Mayorica, and recognised that Aldonza was not then in a condition to listen to reason. He thought, therefore, that the best thing he could do would be to return to the castle, which he did, cursing the unreasonableness of women, and swearing by all the saints in heaven that, in future, he would have nothing to do with any of them as long as he lived, even if a war took place in which so many men should be killed, that there would be a hundred women left for every man that survived.

Let us return with him to the Castle of Vivar and discover who were those that we saw arriving there, and what was taking place in it, even though the reader has most likely guessed that they were Diego Lainez and his friends and servants, who had set out from Leon only a short time after Rodrigo.

It was pitiable to see the state of affliction into which Teresa was thrown when she saw her husband, whom she, full of love and tenderness, ran to receive and clasp in her arms. The honoured Diego Lainez, though he knew his wife would be deeply pained, did not conceal from her the affront he had received, for it was a matter of necessity for him to unbosom himself to some beloved being, who would help him to support such a trial. Teresa Nuña, although the most tender and sensible of women, was endowed with great strength of character to bear tribulations; she was one of those beings whose presence and words strengthen the weakest, and infuse confidence and hope into those who have almost lost them. Thus it was that she succeeded in consoling Diego to a considerable extent, particularly when she repeated the words which Rodrigo used when expressing his determination that no insult to his house should go unavenged. At that moment

Diego conceived the idea of finding out for himself what he might hope for from his son.

Scarcely had Rodrigo risen from his bed, when he was informed that his father had returned to the castle ; he hurried to visit him, and entered Diego's chamber a very short time after Teresa had quitted it.

"Father and lord, embrace me," he said, without noticing the affliction which was clearly stamped on the features of the old man. His father clasped him to his breast, and taking his hand, pressed it between his with such force that little more would have disjointed the fingers, for it seemed that Diego, with the strength of his will, had concentrated in the hand with which he squeezed that of his son all the power that the remainder of the muscles of his body retained.

The youth started back, trying to disengage his hand from the grip of his father ; pain coloured his cheeks and injected his eyes with blood.

"Let go, father," he cried out, "let go. Anger of God ! if you were not my father, you should pay for that squeeze you have given me."

The old man let loose the hand of the youth, and pressing him again to his breast, said, weeping, not indeed with despair but with joy—

"Son of my soul ! that indignation was the comfort which your father needed. Use that fiery spirit in avenging my honour, which is lost if your arm does not save it."

"Justice of God !" cried Rodrigo, rising erect like a viper disturbed by a wayfarer. "Who is the traitor who has dared to attack your honour—which is mine also? Tell me, father, for neither you nor I can live, if the honour is dead, which no person till now has ever dared to stain. Who, who is the coward that has affronted you ? "

"My son, the Count of Gormaz has struck me on the face with his hand, has covered my cheek with blood in the sight of the king and the grandees of Leon "—

And sobs smothered the voice of Diego.

"Anger of God !" exclaimed the brave youth, convulsed with anger even greater than that which his father felt in his grief and old age. "Do not weep, father ; for I swear to you that I shall cut off the hand which has stained your visage, even though the cowardly felon should hide himself in the bowels of the earth."

"Go, my Rodrigo, go and challenge him to single combat.

The king will oppose no obstacles to it, for God, who cannot consent that an old man should be outraged, and an honour thus stained which was gained by fighting for the faith during four centuries, will put valour in your heart and strength in your arm. Public was the offence, public also must be the vengeance!"

Speaking thus, Diego Lainez went to a large press that stood in the chamber in which they were, and contained various kinds of arms. He took down a sword and handed it to Rodrigo, with these words—

"Take and bind on, my son, the sword of Mudarra; go and avenge with it your father."

Rodrigo took the sword, kissed its cross-shaped hilt, and exclaimed—

"Glorious sword, whose blade was tempered with the blood of Ruiz Velasquez, be thou tempered again with that of the cowardly Count of Gormaz, and bring honour to the arm of the son of Diego Lainez, as the son of Gonzalo Gustios brought honour to thee!"

The high price at which he valued his honour and the magnitude of the insult he had received had caused the old grandee to exaggerate his impotence to take vengeance on the count; it is true that he had scarcely had an opportunity of proving the bravery of his son; however, it was not so with regard to many other cavaliers of his family and of his acquaintance. Thus it happened that, on the same day that he acquired the certainty that his son would proceed to fight for the honour of their house, a great number of his friends and retainers presented themselves, offering the aid of their arms, of their riches, and of their men-at-arms, in order to wash out the stain which he grieved over. When Rodrigo, therefore, set out for Leon, having received the blessing of his parents, he was followed by the good wishes of a multitude of lords and cavaliers, and also by many of them in person, who desired to be present at the reparation of the honour of De Vivar, and even to defend it with the strength of their arms, in case the youth should succumb in the combat.

CHAPTER VII

HOW RODRIGO FOUGHT WITH THE COUNT OF GORMAZ

THE principal gate of the Alcazar led out on a broad square, bounded on all sides by the magnificent mansions of the noblest families of the city. Amongst them was that of the Count of Gormaz, who, although he had a very large and strong castle in the country, with appointments worthy of a king, resided usually in the Court city, since death had deprived him of his wife at Gormaz.

Don Gome had loved his wife as Diego Lainez did his, for she had been equally worthy of being loved. Whilst he enjoyed her affection and caresses, ambition had never come to disturb his happiness, and he cared but little for the Court, at which he was scarcely ever seen. However, from the time he fixed his residence in Leon, whether it was that the death of his dear companion had left a void in his soul, which had to be filled up in some way, or whether it was that the glitter of a Court life had deteriorated and darkened his heart, formerly free from evil passions, it is certain that he became entirely changed. Envy overmastered him, as a consequence of a boundless ambition for honours and riches, which indeed he had no need of, for the count was of very noble origin, and his family one of the richest of Castile. He certainly loved his daughter, and was loved by her; it is also certain that Ximena had united in herself sufficient beauty, discretion, and other good qualities to make her the pride and glory of her father; all this, however, was not sufficient for Don Gome, and his daughter filled but a small portion of the void left in his heart by the death of his wife. There are in men certain physiological phenomena which do not admit of satisfactory explanation; in the case of the Count of Gormaz these were very numerous.

Let us leave, however, this digression, and see what was taking place in the palace of the count. In one of the apartments, which overlooked the square of the Alcazar, was the sweet, the beautiful, the loving Ximena, reclining on a couch, and drying up with her handkerchief the abundant tears which flowed from her eyes. She was thinking deeply, and her meditations must have been tortures to her soul, to judge from the agony which could easily be seen on her countenance.

Not far from her, Lambra was occupied, much less with the work which lay upon her lap, than with drying up the tears which the grief of her mistress caused her to shed.

The honoured dueña deserves that we should say a few words about her, for the part which a dueña performed with regard to a young girl was not an insignificant one, especially when the maiden is in love and has lost her mother. Lambra was one of those women whose case would almost give one a right to speak strongly against nature, if nature were not the work of God—of God who has a heaven, with which to compensate people for the privations which they have to bear on earth. She was one of those women to whom nature had given a superabundance of love and, at the same time, had denied them the privilege of lavishing it on men, for, as far as she was concerned, her countenance was cast in such a mould that the more she might desire to approach men, the more would they fly from her. Women of this kind devote their love to the first being that crosses their path, for if they did not do so their hearts would burst with the affection which fills them. In this condition was Lambra : Ximena was the being who had crossed her path and on whom she had poured out all the love of her heart; she was present at her birth, and had witnessed her physical and moral development from day to day without ever losing sight of her, thus filling up her soul with her, if we may so express ourselves; and it may be said indeed that the maiden formed part of her being. Thus it was that she wept or smiled when Ximena wept or smiled, and almost hated or loved according as Ximena did the one or the other.

" Do not weep, my darling," she said to the young girl, affecting a calmness which she did not feel ; " do not think any more of your unfortunate love affairs, for if you keep brooding over them you will be in your grave before three days are past, and that would be neither good nor Christian on your part. Let God, who created us, kill us, and let us not kill ourselves."

" But of what use is life to me ? " replied Ximena, rousing herself from her meditations.

" Ave Maria ! what a mad question ! For what do we preserve our lives but to be happy ? "

" Alas, Lambra, you cannot understand that my happiness is now impossible in this world. How can I be happy without Rodrigo ? "

" Have you then lost him ? "

" I have lost him, Lambra.   If I feared that I had lost his love, when no really serious matter justified the hostility between my father and his, how much stronger are now my reasons for fearing it, when my father, the Count of Gormaz, has imprinted on the face of his father a stain which only can be washed off with blood ?   The hand of my father has opened an abyss between both our houses."

Lambra knew that what Ximena said was only too true, and felt almost dismayed by the task that was imposed on her— that of consoling and cheering up the maiden ; notwithstanding, she did her best to conceal her inquietude, and asked—

" Do you feel confident that Rodrigo loves you ? "

" I have never doubted it."

" And have you not often heard it said that love conquers all things ? "

" Yes, Lambra."

" Then do not be disquieted, and trust that the love of Rodrigo may be able to throw a bridge over the abyss of which you have just spoken, in order that your house and his may be reconciled and form again but one family."

This reflection, although it was rather sophistical, shed a drop of balsam on the wound which was torturing the soul of Ximena, into whose mind flashed, at that moment, a ray of light : " I shall throw myself on my knees at the feet of my father," thought to herself the daughter of Don Gome, " and I shall beseech him to repair the offence which he has committed against Rodrigo, and if he loves me, he will comply with my wish."

Whilst Ximena was still formulating this request, her father entered the chamber.   By the appearance of his daughter, whose face was still stained by tears, Don Gome divined her feelings.   Such were the marks that grief had imprinted, in two days, on the visage of Ximena, that the count could not prevent himself from being deeply moved ; for he loved his child very much, notwithstanding the fact that the evil passions which had taken possession of his heart were causing her the deepest misery.

' My daughter ! " he exclaimed, pressing her tenderly in his arms, " you weep, and do not try to find consolation and alleviation of your troubles in me.   Do you perchance doubt of the love of your father ? "

" Ah no, my father ! " answered Ximena, bathed in tears.

"Do you not know," continued the count, with endearing accents,—"do you not know, daughter, that, from the time I lost your mother, you have been the sole being in this world that I have loved? Do you think that I have no care for your happiness because I have sworn that you never shall be the bride of the son of De Vivar?"

"But, father," said the young girl timidly, "you know that such an oath destroys my happiness during my entire life."

"It will destroy it, if you do not forget Rodrigo."

"And do you believe that I can forget him? Do you believe that a love can be forgotten that had its birth almost at the same time that we had ours? Do you believe that it is possible for a woman to forget a man like Rodrigo?"

"Nothing resists time and injuries received. Those which Diego Lainez has inflicted on your father are such that your union with his son would be an unbearable humiliation, not alone to a race like that of De Gormaz, but even to that of a low-born peasant. He who has so vilely calumniated me at the Court; he who, for his own aggrandisement, has lowered me so much in the eyes of the king; he who has robbed me of the favour of Don Fernando; he who has been so treacherous to his most loyal friend, deserved that your father should refuse to his son your hand, and even should strike him in the face before those in whose eyes he had so humiliated me."

"Consider, my father, that a fatal error may have blinded you. If you do not wish to commit an unjust act, if you do not desire to enter into a contest in which both of us may die, you by a lance or sword wound, and I by the grief which your loss would cause me, make good the insult which you offered to Diego Lainez in the saloons of the Alcazar, and forget for ever those which you imagine that you have received from him "—

"Ximena!" exclaimed the count in a severe tone, "what advice is this you dare to give me? If it were another who so counselled me, I would tear out his tongue. Do you value so little the honour of your father, and do you consider him such a coward, as to think that he should ask pardon of him in whose face he would rather spit?"

The anger which the count exhibited whilst speaking those words discouraged Ximena, and deprived her of her last hope. The daughter of Don Gome answered her father with tears alone. He, feeling compassion for her grief, repented of his sudden burst of indignation, and clasped her again to his heart, pressing with his lips her pale brow. He felt, doubtless, that his pride was yielding in presence of his child's grief, and in order not to desist from his intention of responding with fresh insults to the reparation which he felt would soon be demanded from him by De Vivar, he went off from Ximena, who followed him with her eyes to the door of the chamber as sadly as if it were the last time she should ever see him.

The king, who desired to bring about the reconciliation of the count with Diego Lainez, fearful of the fierce strife which otherwise would blaze up between the partisans of the two noble families, summoned Don Gome to the Alcazar. At the moment when the count left his house in order to obey the order of the king, there rode into the square a body of knights who, apparently, were also proceeding to the Alcazar. Amongst them was Rodrigo Diaz de Vivar, who, as soon as he perceived the count, separated himself from his companions, and made his way hastily towards him.

"Listen, traitrous count, ignoble cavalier!" he said to him. "I, Rodrigo Diaz de Vivar, son of Diego Lainez, whom you wounded on the face, as he is old and cannot wash away with your blood the stain you put on his honour, do now challenge you to single combat, in which you will fight against me; and five knights from amongst my friends shall sustain my rights against five chosen from your friends, in case either you or I should fall in the battle. I am about to demand permission for this from the king."

"Be off, then," answered the count, turning his shoulder on the young man with haughty disdain; "the Count of Gormaz fights with giants, and not with boys like you."

"Infamous count! boys have conquered giants," responded Rodrigo, with much difficulty keeping down his anger. "Remember that David was very young when he overcame Goliath. If I am a youth in years, I am a giant in the valour which my outraged honour and your cowardice instil into me."

The count gazed on him with contempt, and proceeded a few steps on his way. The youth, however, intercepted him, becoming more and more enraged.

"Leave me," exclaimed at last Don Gome, also filled with anger, "leave me at once; for if I wounded your father's face with a blow of my hand, I shall chastise your insolence with kicks."

Those words, and the tone in which they were spoken,

exasperated Rodrigo to the highest pitch, and he exclaimed, placing his hand on his sword—

"Defend yourself, villain, defend yourself, or I shall kill you behind your back, like a traitor and coward as you are!"

"You shall not do so, but you shall pay dearly for your audacity," replied the count, unsheathing his sword, and rushing on Rodrigo with such fury that the young man had scarcely time to place himself on his guard.

The count was robust and of enormous strength, so great that on account of it he had gained the name of *Lozano*,[1] by which he was commonly known, and which both history and tradition have brought down to us. Rodrigo was of high stature, but very thin, and his strength was not yet developed. Thus it was that, the physical powers of the two combatants not being equalised by defensive and offensive arms,—as was usual in solemn combats, when there was great disproportion in the strength of the two parties,—the spectators considered the victory of the count as certain. Those present consisted not only of the retinue which had accompanied Rodrigo, but also of a large number of persons whom the clashing of the swords had attracted to the windows and balconies of the buildings which surrounded the square, or who had flowed in through the streets that led to it. Amongst those spectators was the king, Don Fernando himself, who appeared on a balcony of the Alcazar just as the fate of the combatants was about to be decided. They were fighting with a fury not often seen; the strokes of the count were terrible from the force with which they were dealt, but Rodrigo avoided them with an agility and dexterity that could scarcely be expected from him, considering the limited practice he had had in warlike exercises, which only consisted in his having broken a few lances at tournaments; moreover, he did not for an instant lose the calmness and presence of mind so necessary in a fight. At last Don Gome aimed a terrible blow at his adversary, which the sword of Rodrigo did not altogether succeed in warding off, and he felt the blood running down his face. This advantage gained by his enemy, far from discouraging him, only inflamed his anger more and more, and lent new strength to his arm, new breath to his lungs, and increased agility to his limbs.

At that moment a cry of agony was heard from the mansion of the count, a cry which the clashings of the steels, increasing

<hr>

[1] Strong, lusty.

in rapidity and force, fortunately prevented Rodrigo from hearing. We say fortunately, for if he had heard it, his heart would have become so troubled, that the good sword, which he had consecrated by a reverent kiss when he received it from his father, might have fallen from his hand. Yes; such would likely have happened to Rodrigo, for it was Ximena who had uttered that agonised exclamation, when, having gone to the window of her chamber, she saw her father and her lover fighting so fiercely; when she saw the visage of Rodrigo bathed in blood, and perceived with the eyes of her soul that her hopes of happiness had now indeed vanished for ever; for her misery was certain whichever succumbed—her father or Rodrigo. Of what use would life be to her without the latter? And if her father fell, how could she marry his slayer? Not in vain had she said, but a short time before, that an almost impassable abyss had opened between her house and that of Diego Lainez.

The combat, in the meantime, was raging even more fiercely than before, and its end was evidently approaching, as the combatants, panting and covered with blood, instead now of defending themselves, were endeavouring, to their very utmost, to kill each other. Don Gome then suddenly drew his dagger, and with it in one hand, and his sword in the other, blind with rage and desperation, rushed on Rodrigo, parrying with his sword the strokes of his adversary, and doing his best at the same time to pierce him with the dagger.

" Back, felon, traitor, back ! " exclaimed Rodrigo, indignant at the perfidy of the count. He, however, neither heard the words nor listened to the voice of honour, which reprobates every cavalier who has recourse to a vile stratagem in order to conquer his enemy; Rodrigo fell back a step, and received on the point of his sword Don Gome, who fell, pierced through, to the ground, uttering a cry of rage and agony.

Loud applause resounded on all sides; cavaliers and citizens rushed towards Rodrigo to carry him in triumph to where his wounds could be dressed, for abundant blood was streaming from them. Numerous flowers, which had adorned the windows and balconies, fell at the feet of the brave youth, and formed the victor's crown.

CHAPTER VIII

HOW XIMENA DEMANDED JUSTICE FROM THE KING AGAINST RODRIGO DIAZ

SOME days have passed since Rodrigo avenged his father by killing Don Gome, Count of Gormaz.

He had almost recovered from the wounds which he had received in the combat; but there was another wound in his soul which science could not cure. His sword had deprived of life the father of his beloved: would she ever accept the hand of him who had wounded her parent to the death? Could the slayer of the Count of Gormaz hope for the love of Ximena Gome? Nothing could console Rodrigo; no hope of happiness remained to him. An invincible sadness over-shadowed him, which could not be driven away, either by the joy of his parents when they saw the stain washed away which had sullied their honour, or by the caresses and care which they lavished on him; for Diego and Teresa had proceeded to Leon immediately on learning the condition of their son, in order that they might assist at the healing of his wounds.

One morning the king, Don Fernando, was amusing himself in the company of his family, which he dearly loved. What more pleasing sight than that of a powerful king, of a warrior, as skilful as he was wise and brave, surrounded by his children and his wife, forgetting the triumphs of his arms and the cares of state, in order to give himself up completely to the joys of the domestic hearth, with the same simplicity and effusion which the humblest subject exhibits? At his side was his wife, a noble and honoured matron, all the pleasures of whose life were found where her husband and children were. Don Fernando saw her, at the height of her contentment and maternal pride, sharing with him the affection of their sons and daughters, brave youths and beautiful maidens; his heart participated in the satisfaction and pride of hers, and the happy monarch considered as trifling the pleasures he enjoyed surrounded by his courtiers, compared with those he tasted surrounded by his family. There are in *The Chronicle of the Cid* a few words which form the greatest eulogium on Don Fernando as the head of a family. Those are: "He made his sons read that they might be the better instructed; he taught them the use of arms, how to fence and combat; also

4

to be hunters.　And his daughters he caused to pursue their studies under dueñas, that they might be accustomed to, and instructed in, all that was good."　If history had not distinctly made known to us that Don Fernando I. was a tender and affectionate father, as well as a faithful lover and husband, the facts would be demonstrated to us by his having had no illegitimate child, which was a very common thing amongst the princes and lords of the period.

"Father," said Don Sancho, who was the eldest of the princes, "you have spent very much time in camps, you have often exposed your life to the swords of your enemies; live henceforth more for your family, and do not go away from my mother and my brothers and sisters.　I, although unworthy of so great an honour, will take your place in war; if it is necessary to fight against the infidels and the other enemies of Castile and Leon, do not think, my father, that fear would cause me to vacillate or draw back, for not in vain does your blood flow in my veins."

"O my son!" cried Don Fernando, feeling tears of joy coming to his eyes, and clasping Don Sancho in his arms, "I do not now fear death, for Leon and Castile will have in you the best of kings!　Secure of leaving behind me such a successor, I shall care not should I lose my life in the wars."

"Not care for your life?" exclaimed at the same time the queen and his children.

"How would it be with us should you die, dear father?" said Urraca, the eldest of the princesses.　"Grief would kill us also!　Sad is the lot of daughters who love their father very much and lose him!"

Just then it was announced to the king that Ximena Gome requested an audience.　Don Fernando, who never refused to hear his subjects, now felt, more than ever, the desire of consoling the afflicted, and believing that the daughter of the late Count of Gormaz was very unhappy, he ordered that she should be conducted before him.

"Justice, my lord, justice!" exclaimed Ximena, casting herself at the feet of the king, and unable to articulate other words, for sobs were almost choking her.

The noble maiden was completely changed, a fearful pallor covered her emaciated face, which was wet with tears, and even the disorder of her garments and hair showed her grief.

"Justice, my lord, justice!" she repeated, as if she were

about to lose her reason, and as if the idea which those words conveyed was the last glimmering light of her mind.

The king, the queen, and the princesses endeavoured to calm the excitement of her mind with affectionate words, and their efforts were not unavailing, for in a short time she was able to express the feelings which overmastered her, and the desire which had led her thither.

"My lord, an audacious youth, the son of Diego Lainez, slew my father, the Count of Gormaz, a few days ago, as you already know. Grief has kept me prostrate on my bed until to-day, when I come to demand justice from you. Grant it to me, my lord, by punishing the slayer of my father, for if good kings represent on earth the authority of God, you, my lord, must punish a murderer, under pain of incurring the displeasure both of God and of men. During the fever which has been burning in my brain since the day on which the hand of Rodrigo made me an orphan, I have seen the spirit of my father, rising from his sepulchre and demanding vengeance, and I promised it to him, counting on your justice. If you do not grant it to me, my lord, cavaliers are not wanting amongst my kinsmen who will respond to my request; I shall go through your states of Leon and Castile, demanding the aid of all good men, and both friends and strangers will hearken to my call, and the horrors of war will avenge your injustice and the perfidy of De Vivar."

"Calm your grief and your resentment, Ximena," answered the king in a kind voice, "for I promise to do you justice. If Rodrigo Diaz treacherously killed your father, justice shall bring down her inexorable sword on his head, just as if he were the humblest of my subjects."

"My lord, I trust in your promise. Ask the princesses, what they think is the grief of a daughter who loses her father, and the anger she should feel against the man who killed him. Those who love you as I loved my father can well understand what I suffer, and will make you also, my lord, understand it."

"I have been informed that Rodrigo killed your father in fair and honourable combat, and for my own part I can assure you that your father had his sword, and also his dagger, unsheathed. That he was not attacked unarmed is proved by the dangerous wounds which he inflicted on Rodrigo."

"Ah! dangerous wounds!" exclaimed Ximena, her face again becoming pale, which had coloured up with excitement whilst she was addressing the king; and then she felt her impotence in trying to conquer love with feelings of revenge. What would she not have given, at that moment, to be able to tear from her heart that undying affection which, in her mind, was a crime against the dead body of her father, whose wounds were still dropping blood and crying for vengeance !

That exclamation was also a revelation to the king, who, not being ignorant of the love which had formerly united Rodrigo and Ximena, doubted whether it could have been completely extinguished in her, and changed to hatred, as the demand she made of him seemed to testify. Don Fernando, however, knew human hearts, especially the hearts of women, too well, to openly oppose her feelings, especially when he felt almost sure that they were but transitory; he knew very well that when a sentiment is rooted in the core of the heart, it goes on increasing, of itself, until it is powerful enough to drive away all others which had been pressing it down, in the same way that the sun drives off the clouds that for a time obscure his brightness, showing himself soon again with the glory of the conqueror. The wise monarch also knew that the weakest and most superficial caprices change, when strongly opposed, into strong and deep determinations, and for that reason he resolved to temporise with Ximena, trusting that time would make her desist from her complaints. He knew the Count of Gormaz and Rodrigo well enough to feel certain on whose side was the right, and he had not forgotten the grave offence by which the former had given the latter just excuse to kill him, even if the fight had been with equal arms, much more so when perfidy was resorted to, for Don Gome had acted in a perfidious manner, striking on the face an honourable and feeble old man who had held out his hand generously to him.

"Ximena," he said to the maiden, "I repeat that you shall receive justice from me; if Rodrigo acted treacherously he shall be punished, and you know that in my realm there is justice for all, and no one can escape it, be he ever so powerful."

Ximena returned to her dwelling. Notwithstanding the promise that the king had given her to punish Rodrigo if he were guilty, her inquietude, her grief, and her despair had increased rather than diminished. That night her sleep was a delirium in which was epitomised an eternity of torments; a horrible nightmare pressed on her for long hours; she saw a man, exhaling his last breath, and calling out her name, the name of Ximena.

And that man was not he whom she had seen during the nightmares of preceding nights, that man was not her father.

He was Rodrigo Diaz!

When she awoke, when she succeeded in shaking off that terrible nightmare, at the very instant in which she was struggling to get near the dying man, in order to infuse new life into him with her breath, calling him by the sweet names which she had lavished on him in other times, when they wandered through the fields of Gormaz, or those of Vivar, happy and joyful as the birds and butterflies, then,—ah! then, she became enraged with herself, tore her hair in terrible despair, and rushed to the window of her chamber in order to throw herself from it; and she would have done so, if Lambra, who watched constantly by her side, disconsolate and despairing like herself, had not pulled her back, despite her struggles, which were but feeble, as her strength had been much reduced by grief and by fever.

And when she recognised her impotence, not alone to crush down her love, but also to find death as an end to her sufferings, she fell on her knees, and, raising her eyes and hands to heaven, she exclaimed—

"O my father, pardon, pardon! Mother, why did you not smother me in your arms when you brought me into the world?"

She then fell on the floor, like an inert mass, and the voice of Lambra resounded through the mansion, summoning assistance for her mistress.

.   .   .   .

On the following morning Ximena rose from her bed very early, notwithstanding her strength being so reduced that she could scarcely walk a step without stumbling, and began to make preparations for a journey.

"But, my lady," said Lambra, "would you not be better at Gormaz, where all love you, and where you would have your own house and the recollections of your childhood?"

"It is from those very recollections that I desire to fly, for you well know that Rodrigo and I passed our childhood partly at Gormaz and partly at Vivar."

"You are right; I did not think of that; but, however it may be, it would be a sad life in a desert like"—

"My life must be a sad one wherever I may be; and as

my only hope is now of heaven, I desire to make myself deserving of it whilst I live on earth. If the king will not do me justice, the friends of my father will do so; but I have not courage to hunt down him who shed my father's blood. . . . I will not persecute him, but I shall forget him for ever."

Ximena and Lambra continued to get together all the articles necessary for a long journey.

"Do you intend to bring these trifles with you?" asked the dueña, showing to her mistress a casket which, with other things, she had taken from a drawer.

"Yes," answered Ximena; "for that casket contains many souvenirs of my mother. . . . But oh!" she added, "it also contains some of Rodrigo. Give it to me, give it to me. I will keep for ever those of my mother, but I shall burn those of that traitor."

And taking the case in her hand, she began to turn over the things which it contained. They were, for the most part, ribbons, flowers, rings, and children's toys. The first she drew out was a wreath of flowers. "Ah!" she said, "with this wreath he adorned my brow on my fifteenth birthday!"

She was about to pull it to pieces with her hands, but she feared to touch the flowers, as if they were covered with thorns. She then drew forth a black curl bound with green ribbon, and said, "Here is a lock of his hair which he gave me the last time we were together at Gormaz, as a pledge of a love which he himself has destroyed!" And she raised her hand to cast it far from her; but she stopped, pensive, and apparently struggling with opposing feelings. Suddenly tears gushed from her eyes, and she cried out, placing the wreath and the curl again in the casket, "Leave them there, Lambra, leave them there; and let this wreath and this curl be the haircloth to torture me in my solitude."

The maiden remained motionless for a short time, during which she ran over in her imagination the story of her love—the story of her life—for they were both but one. The purest love,—ardent, surrounded with heavenly illusions, with gilded dreams, with light, with flowers,—the beauty of which can only be understood by certain enamoured souls,—had entirely made up the life of Ximena. And at seeing her hopes blasted, at seeing parched up, never to sprout forth again, that flower of paradise which perfumed and inebriated her soul, she felt her heart torn with the profoundest sadness, with an immense despair, with an agony that cannot be described. The youth or the maiden who has consecrated entire years to a love which holds its mastery in dreams as well as in waking hours, always sweet, always beautiful, always surrounded by an enchantment superior to all other enchantments of this world, and in a day, in a few hours, loses, without hope of recovering it, the object of that love—such a youth or maiden only can comprehend the grief of Ximena. In those moments of terrible despair the sole comfort that can be found is to have a mother, a father, a brother, a friend—some being sufficiently good and sensible not to laugh at our tears, so that we may cast ourselves into his arms and weep on his breast, saying, "My heart is pierced; give me, for the sake of God, a little love, with which I may calm my grief; fill up, as much as is in your power, that deep void which is left in my soul; make less bitter the transition state from hope to despair!"

And it was granted to Ximena to enjoy that comfort: she had Lambra beside her, plain and homely, perhaps, but affectionate and good, and she threw herself into her arms and solaced herself with copious tears.

On that same day the disconsolate girl set out for Castile, accompanied by the dueña and a few of her servants; and tradition affirms that, after them, a youth went out from Leon, who stopped on an eminence near the city, and followed with his gaze the daughter of Don Gome, until a distant turn of the road removed her from his view.

CHAPTER IX

HOW A MOORISH PRINCESS WAS CONVERTED, AND HOW A SOLITARY CEASED TO BE SUCH

AT that time the Moor Almenon was King of Toledo, and with him Don Fernando the Great, King of Castile and Leon, kept up a cordial friendship. This Moorish monarch had a daughter, very beautiful and tender-hearted, named Casilda.

In the vicinity of the gardens which surrounded the Alcazar of Almenon, there were gloomy dungeons in which wept, half-starved and loaded with chains, many Christian captives.

One day, when Casilda was walking in her father's gardens, she heard the sad wailings of those captives : her kind heart caused her to weep for their sufferings, for she liked Christians from the time when, in her girlhood, a Castilian female slave told her that the Christians loved God, their king, and their families ; that amongst them the weak and oppressed were protected ; that they rewarded the good and punished evil-doers.

The princess then returned to the palace, with her heart full of sadness, and knelt at the feet of her father, saying—

"My father, in the dungeons near your gardens a large number of captives are suffering. Remove their chains from them, open the doors of their prisons, and let them return to their own country, where await them, sad and weeping, their parents, their brethren, their wives, or their lovers."

Almenon blessed his daughter in the depths of his heart, for it was naturally good, and as Casilda was kind and beautiful, and his only daughter, he loved her as the apple of his eye. What loving father does not rejoice when he sees that his children are good and tender-hearted?

The King of Toledo, however, far from complying with Casilda's request, considered that he was bound to punish her rashness, for to compassionate Christian captives and plead for their liberty was a crime, according to the traditional belief of those of his race and religion.

For this reason he concealed the contentment of his soul; for this reason he said to Casilda, with a stern look and threatening voice—

"Depart, unbeliever! be silent, unworthy princess! Your tongue shall be cut out, and your body cast into the flames, for such is the punishment merited by the Moslim who pleads for the Nazarenes."

And he was about to summon his executioners, in order to hand his daughter over to them.

Casilda, however, fell again at his feet, asking pardon from him by the memory of her mother, the late queen, whose death Almenon had now wept for a year.

And Almenon felt his eyes wet with tears, and he pressed her against his breast and pardoned her, kissing her at the same time ; he said, however—

"Take care, my daughter, not to plead again for the Christians, nor even to feel pity for them, for then I shall have neither pardon nor compassion for you."

The maiden, nevertheless, walked again in the gardens, and the wailings of the captives came again to her ears; charity strengthened her heart and illumined her soul.

The princess bribed with gold one of the guards of the dungeons, and from that time she went every day, bringing food and consolation to the poor captives.

One day she was carrying food concealed in the folds of her garments, when she suddenly met her father on a winding path, bordered by rose-bushes.

It was a morning in springtime; the roses were expanding their blooms all around; the birds were singing in the branches of the trees; the sun was just beginning to cast his rays on the limpid jets of the fountains; and the air was sweetened with the most delicious odours.

"What are you doing here so early?" asked Almenon of the maiden.

"My father," answered the princess, becoming as red as the roses which the morning breeze was agitating by her side, "I have come to gaze upon and enjoy the odour of those flowers, to hear the carols of the birds, and to see the sun's rays sparkling in the fountains."

"What are you carrying in the folds of your dress?" asked the king in a stern voice.

"Roses which I have gathered from these bushes," replied Casilda, imploring from the bottom of her heart the aid of a holy being named Mary, of whom, when she was a child, she had heard the Christian slave speaking.

And Almenon, doubting her answer, opened the folds of her dress, and a shower of roses fell upon the ground.

From that day the princess redoubled her assistance and her consolations towards the captives; from that day she was more loved by her father; from that day she adored, on the altar of her heart, the Nazarene Divinity, and felt an ardent desire to adore Him in the Christian temples. God, who sometimes leads His creatures to their good by the strangest paths, struck down the bodily health of Casilda by a disease, which withered the roses on her cheeks and filled Almenon and his Court with uneasiness and fear.

The most famous physicians of Seville and Cordova were summoned to Toledo; but they exhausted their science, and could not restore the princess to health.

Almenon then wrote to the King of Leon and Castile, asking him to send the best physician at his Court, and Don

Fernando hastened to comply with his request, for he also had daughters whom he loved, as Almenon loved his.

The Leonese doctor came to the conclusion that the only chance of saving the princess was by sending her to Castile, in which there was a lake, the waters of which had great curative virtues, especially regarding the disease from which Casilda was suffering.

And she went to Castile, entrusted by her father to the care of Don Fernando, and having bathed in the lake of San Vicente, which is in the province of Briviesca, she recovered her health, and the roses again bloomed on her cheeks.

However, when the waters of the lake of San Vicente had healed her body, Casilda desired that the waters of the Jordan should heal her soul, and she received baptism, her godfather and godmother being the King and Queen of Castile and Leon.

Her father learned soon that she had embraced the faith of the Nazarene, and sent her word that he wished to see her no more. Casilda wept, for she knew that her father also wept; but Jesus, who had restored to health the daughter of Jairus, who had suffered as she had done, said, "There is no man, that hath left house, or brethren, or sisters, or father, or mother, or wife, or children, or lands, for My sake, and the gospel's, but he shall receive an hundredfold now in this time, houses, and brethren, and sisters, and mothers, and children, and lands, with persecutions: and in the world to come eternal life." And Casilda desired to follow the Nazarene.

She then determined to consecrate her life to penitence, where the tumult of worldly passions could not interrupt her in her holy task, and where, at the same time, she could practise charity towards all who might be in need of it.

The lake of San Vicente was situated in a lonely, rugged country, and thus the poor invalids who went to seek health in its waters could find no person to extend hospitality to them, and very many died from the cold of the winter, or the heat of the summer, both of which were excessive in that region.

Casilda erected there a hermitage, and resolved to pass her life in it, dedicating herself to the service of God, and to the care of suffering and despairing human beings.

One day she saw a number of persons, some riding and some on foot, who were making their way towards her humble abode, situated on the margin of the lake. A litter, drawn by a horse, came on in the rear, in which she thought she perceived two women. She believed that some invalids were coming in search of health, as frequently happened, on account of the beneficial qualities of the waters of the lake, and she hastened to meet them, in order to offer them her charitable care and the hospitality of her dwelling. Indeed, one at least of the two women who occupied the litter appeared to be in a very weakly state, to judge from the pallor and emaciation of her face. Casilda had arrived within a short distance of the litter, and seeing that its drivers were in doubt as to the way they should go, for the ground was very rough and covered with brambles, amongst which it was difficult to discern the paths that led towards the lake and the hermitage of the solitary, she said to the strangers—

"If you are coming to my dwelling-place, where I shall willingly receive you, I shall guide you to it by the shortest and easiest path."

"Yes," replied the pale woman in the litter, "we were proceeding to your dwelling, and may God recompense you for any kindness and hospitality you show us."

Casilda then walked on towards her hermitage, and the litter followed.

When all had arrrived at the door, the women descended from the vehicle, and Casilda recognised the younger of the women, who also knew her. They embraced each other warmly.

"Ximena!" exclaimed the daughter of Almenon, "you in those solitudes! Why, notwithstanding the emaciation of your face, did I not at once recognise you—you to whom I was offering hospitality, as if to a stranger, rather than to one whom I hold deep in my heart?"

"You see me here, Casilda," said Ximena,—"you see me here, seeking, not the health of my body in the waters of this lake, but that of my soul in solitude, in mortification, in prayer, and in charitable works; I therefore desire to be your companion in this holy and peaceful retreat."

"You are indeed welcome, friend of my soul! who thus abandons the pleasures of the Court, in order to serve God and humanity in this desert. Come into my dwelling, which is yours also, and take some repose, for you have indeed need of it, as has also this worthy lady, after the fatigues of your journey."

In truth, Ximena and Lambra, for now we know that they were the travellers, were almost dead with weariness, for they had been obliged to go a considerable portion of the way on foot, as some of the paths were so rugged and bad that it would have been dangerous to remain in the litter.

Immediately afterwards, Ximena sent away the vassals and servants who had accompanied her, and entered the hermitage with Casilda, opening her heart to her, as she would have opened it to her mother, if God had left her by her side to strengthen her soul in the violent storm through which it was passing.

We have seen that these two noble maidens knew each other formerly. Ximena indeed had several opportunities of meeting Casilda during the time she had spent at the Court of Don Fernando, previous to her baptism, and two good and generous souls need but a short time to understand each other. They understood and loved each other in a few days.

Let us now leave them together in that solitude, which worldly cares did not disturb, for other sad souls, like that of Ximena, call upon us to reveal their griefs to the world.

CHAPTER X

HOW MARTIN SET OUT TO AVENGE HIS FATHER

Not far from the river Cea lived an old peasant named Ivan, who had been a crossbow-man, in the time of the last Count of Castile, afterwards lance-page, and finally squire. Tired of the dangerous and agitated life which those of his profession had to go through, and being the possessor of a little money, which, by economy, he had saved during several years, he bought a cottage, with a few acres of land, retired to it with his wife and children, and had lived there for some time, quite ignorant of what was passing in the world, for his dwelling-place was in a lonely valley, the quietude of which was only disturbed once a year by pilgrims who passed through it on their way to the shrine which was near it.

On the night succeeding the day on which the annual festival was held there, Ivan was sleeping tranquilly, for he had taken part in the pilgrimage, when, at the first crow of the cock, someone knocked and called out loudly at the door.

The farmer awoke, went to his window, and asked, by no means in a good temper—

"What drunken fellow is thumping at my door? By St. James! this is a nice hour to disturb from their sleep people who have to get up early to go to their field-work."

"Anger of God! what a churl you are, Señor Ivan!" answered the unknown person, who did not appear to be in better humour than the farmer. "Open the door at once, and cease your chattering, for there is no drunkard here, or anything like one. Don't you know me?"

"May God forsake me if it is not that fool Martin!"

"The very same, confound you! Open at once, if you don't want me to break in the door."

The farmer hastened to light a candle, and to let the stranger in. On seeing him he started back, horror-struck: everything showed that the newly arrived had been engaged, a very short time before, in a fierce fight; his hands, his face, and even his clothes were covered with blood.

"Glorious St. Isadore!" exclaimed Ivan, "what is the matter? You are wounded?"

"In the soul!" replied the young man. "The wounds on my body matter little, for they are only scratches that can easily be healed."

"Let me examine them for you."

"It is useless, Señor Ivan. Those which it is important for me to heal are the wounds of my soul; the medicine you have to supply me with is a lance, a crossbow, a sword, some arm or other, for I come to ask nothing else of you."

"I shall give you one with pleasure, for there are plenty of arms in my house, thanks to my old profession, and also to the need I have of them in this lonely place, where I have often to defend myself against bandits."

Ivan approached the light to one of the walls, on which were hung various arms, and added—

"Take whichever you please, for the bravest knight of Leon or Castile does not possess better tempered ones."

The young man took down a lance and also a sword, which he girt on with as much skill as the most experienced cavalier could have used, and said :—

"Thanks, Señor Ivan. God be with you and do not tell anyone that you have seen me to-night."

"But, Martin, won't you tell me what you are going to do? What has happened to you?"

"Some day you shall know, Señor Ivan."

"But where are you going, my son?"

"To avenge my father, who lies dead in the wood; and Beatrice, who has already perhaps been dishonoured by Don Suero—may God curse him, and may this lance soon pierce him through!"

"May it be so!" replied the farmer, embracing the young man, who, throwing the lance across his shoulder, went forth from the house and disappeared in the darkness.

Martin walked a long distance through the dark woods, until he came to another house, situated in the midst of large and fertile meadows.

This house, or rather stable, belonged to Don Suero, and in it was kept a magnificent stud of horses, the property of the count, which also had the use of the meadows, and of which a single groom had the care.

Martin struck a heavy blow on the door of the stable.

"Who is there?" called out the groom.

"Open, if you do not wish me to break in the door, and your head as well."

The groom considered himself too weak to resist a man who spoke in such a way. He opened the door, trembling, and said—

"Pardon, sir cavalier."

"I am not a cavalier," interrupted Martin; "but I want to be one. Get out the best horse you have in the stables."

"I would be delighted to please your honour, but"—

"'Fore God! he addresses me with 'buts'!" exclaimed Martin, placing his hand on his sword.

"Pardon me, sir cavalier," the groom said, terrified, going into the stalls and unloosing one of the best horses; "I only wished to tell you that my master will almost beat me to death when he finds that I have let one of his best horses be sto— I mean taken away. Does this one please your lordship?"

"Yes," answered Martin; "put that saddle on it, which I see hanging up there."

"Sir knight, that saddle is the one which is used in trying the paces of the horses when my master comes to select one, and if you take it what will become of me?"

"Be quick, I tell you; it will be only a few blows more or less," said Martin in a threatening tone.

The groom saddled the horse without further reply. Martin buckled on a pair of spurs, which he demanded from him, and, persuaded that the man had not recognised him, he thought it most prudent to say no more. He then sprang upon the horse, and giving the excellent steed a sharp stroke, he disappeared through the adjacent fields.

Not far from the road which led from Burgos to Leon there was a hill, situated so near it that its course could be seen from it for a long distance ; this hill was the resort of a band of robbers who at that time were the terror of travellers who journeyed through that district. Martin rode on to it, and arrived there shortly after daybreak. He advanced a little into a wood which grew on the hill, and cried out, making a kind of speaking-trumpet of his hand—

"Hallo, bandits !"

The look-out, whom the robbers had stationed not far from the place where Martin stopped, had perceived him a short time before he spoke, and as he saw that he came alone he did not think it necessary to give the signal of alarm to his companions.

"Where is the cavalier going ? " he cried out in his turn.

"To ask that I may be admitted into your honourable band."

Martin knew that honour is such a fine thing that even bandits like it to be attributed to them.

"If such is your intention," said the look-out, "follow the path you see then, and at the end of it you will find the entire band, whose chief will, perchance, concede to you the honour which you solicit."

The young man then advanced, and in a short time discovered the bandits, who were about twenty in number, and who were lying under trees, to the trunks of which their horses were fastened. Martin could scarcely forbear from shuddering and feeling a sense of repugnance, when he saw the ferocity which was stamped on their visages, and when he heard the filthy language they were using. On perceiving him, one of them arose, who was distinguished from the others by his garb and by the large scars which were on his hands and face. Martin began to make known to him the object which led him thither, but the captain of the bandits, for it was no other, interrupted him, saying—

"Brother, do you think we are deaf? We have heard you and we now know for what you come. Tell me, however, what is it that entitles you to be admitted into the band of the Raposo,[1] for by that name the son of my mother is known ? "

---

[1] A fox.

"Anger of God, Don Raposo, if it were any other but you who asked me that question, you should soon pay a visit to your friend Señor Lucifer. Do you not see, confound you, the blood which I have on my hands and garments, and the wounds on my face. This blood does not come from slaughtering cattle, nor those scratches from a jealous sweetheart. Go to the place I shall mention to you, and you will find the body of the cavalier whose life I have taken, in order to provide myself with these arms and this steed, and when you are coming back fetch me the dagger which I forgot to draw from his breast."

"You don't waste much respect on him who is to be your captain," said the Raposo; but I desire to be indulgent towards you as a reward for the good work you have done. I believe what you say, for you could not have become possessed in any other way of these arms and that splendid horse, for your dress and your manner shows me that you are just as much a cavalier as I am a bishop. However, if you wish to become a member of our honourable brotherhood, you must take the usual oath."

"I will take a hundred of them if you like," answered Martin, dismounting.

The captain of the bandits walked over to a tree, at the foot of which were heaped up a great number of sacred vessels and ornaments, which they had stolen that night from a neighbouring church, and taking up a crucifix of considerable value he held it up before the youth, and said—

"Will you swear fidelity to your brethren? Will you swear to carry off women, to enter and plunder houses and churches, palaces and huts? Will you swear to rob and kill priests the same as laymen, poor the same as rich, women the same as men, children the same as grown-up people?"

"Yes, I swear!" replied Martin, firmly resolved, however, not to keep so sacrilegious an oath, for he did not consider himself bound to do so, taking it only with his lips and not from his soul.

"Salute our new brother!" said the Raposo, turning towards his companions. They went up to him and embraced him one after the other.

"Brother," continued the captain, when this ceremony was ended, you now must know that he who is honoured by being received into our band, is obliged to celebrate his admission by giving a skin of good wine to all the members of the confraternity. I suppose that the late owner of your arms and steed had also a well-lined purse, full of gold coins, and therefore, I expect that you will be generous towards us."

Martin was rather perplexed at this requirement, for he had no money whatever; knowing, however, that with such people he must show himself a braggart in every way, he replied—

"If another had expressed a doubt of my generosity, he would lose his tongue for it. I have not a single miserable coin about me; what do I want with money? By all the saints in heaven and all the demons in hell, do you imagine that I am one of those honest peasants who only drink when they can pay for it?"

All the bandits pulled out purses full of gold, and exclaimed—

"Brother, take as much money as you want; we will lend it to you until we make our next haul; you can then pay us back out of your share of it."

"I thank you," replied Martin; but I won't take it, for I don't want it. You will see, by Señor Noah, that I'll manage to get wine enough to make half Castile drunk, even if, to procure it, I have to send to the devil all the innkeepers within ten leagues round us."

Thus speaking, he gave spurs to his horse, rode through the thick wood, and disappeared, light as the wind, in the direction of a lonely hostelry, which could scarcely be distinguished on the distant horizon. He paid no attention to the voices of his new comrades, who called after him, cautioning him of the risk he ran of falling into the hands of a patrol of the Salvadores,[1] bodies of armed horsemen who, by command of the king, requested to give it by the Count of Carrion and other grandees, wandered through that district for the purpose of protecting travellers from the attacks of the highwaymen.

We know not how Martin arranged matters with the innkeeper, but two hours had scarcely passed when he returned, bringing, thrown across his saddle-bow, a large leather wine-bag, which contained fully twenty gallons, according to our modern measures. Shouts of joy and loud applause received him on his return.

"He is a good comrade, and will be the pride of the band of the Raposo."

"What an aroma that wine has! It is three years old, at least."

---

[1] Saviours, deliverers.

"I'd like to have some of those Moorish dogs here, to see if they would turn up their noses at that gift of God."

"The monks of Sahagun never taste better."

"Thunder and lightning, what a night we'll have with it!"

"I'd turn Moor at once if Mahomet were only as good as it is."

"The innkeeper was a heretic, and kept it without baptizing it."

"Yes, yes, the wine-bag is a Moor—it is a Moor!"

"Then let us attack him.　To arms—to arms!　War, war!"

"War to the Moor!　Up for St. James and Spain!"

Such were some of the exclamations which followed the arrival of Martin.

Having uttered these cries, the bandits took several sacred vessels from the heap whence the Raposo took the crucifix on which he had administered the oath to Martin, and the sacrilegious ruffians filled them with wine and lifted them to their impure lips.

Martin shuddered at the sight of this impious profanation and did not take any part in it.

The Raposo noticed this, and said to him—

"Brother, you would make a bad priest if you can't drink out of a chalice.　Is it because you have not taken orders?"

"By Lucifer!" exclaimed Martin, placing his hand on his sword, feeling persuaded that he was lost if he did not put on a bold face.　"Know, Don Raposo, or Don Villain, that if I have not orders I at least have a sword, and that if I do not drink wine, I'll drink the blood of anyone that insults me as you do."

"So, low peasant," replied the Raposo, also placing his hand on his steel, "you dare to speak thus to your captain!　I'll resign my honourable position if my dagger does not teach you to be respectful."

The two opponents held their naked swords, and were about to rush on each other; all the bandits, however, hastened to make peace, trying to persuade the Raposo that their new comrade, instead of meriting punishment, deserved praise, since by his audacity he showed what might be expected from him when occasion should arise.　These reasonings appeared to be satisfactory to the Raposo; he laid aside his vexation and stretched out his hand to Martin, saying—

"Pardon, brother; I only wished to try your mettle, and I am satisfied with it."

"You, señor captain, must pardon me," replied the young man, clasping the rough hand of the bandit; "but know that I cannot bear being calumniated, by being supposed incapable of doing what my comrades do. Do you think that it is scruples of conscience that prevent me from using these vessels? I want a big draught of wine to satisfy my thirst, and I shall not drink it from a nutshell, as you do."

Thus speaking, Martin took the helmet from the head of one of the robbers, poured wine into it and emptied it at a draught, amid the applause and acclamations of the bandits.

They continued without ceasing their libations, the wine-bag was getting emptier and emptier, and drunkenness was overmastering all of them, including the captain. Notwithstanding, Martin kept his head clear, whether it was that he was more accustomed to wine, or, which is more probable, that he drank very little, although he lifted the helmet often to his mouth, taking advantage of the condition of his companions.

The state in which they then were was horrible to see; their lips only uttered blasphemies, obscene expressions, and disconnected phrases; and in the end sleep took possession of the greater part of them. Even the look-out had abandoned his post, seeing that his comrades did not come to relieve him, and as he was desirous of participating in their libations and uproarious merriment.

It appeared to Martin that he heard the sound of the footsteps of horses in the direction of the main road, and, turning in that direction, he cried out—

"The Salvadores! Up, comrades! the Salvadores!"

Five or six of the bandits arose on hearing that cry, and, following the example of Martin, hastened to mount their horses. Some of the others, including the Raposo, were fast asleep, and the rest, having tried to rise, fell back again on the ground.

The danger was imminent, the situation was desperate; the hill extended in its entire length only about fifteen hundred paces, and was surrounded on all sides by an extensive and bare plain. The only exit from the wood was the path which led to the road, for the roughness of the ground and the closeness of the trees and bushes made it impossible for horses to proceed in any other direction. If Martin and his companions abandoned their steeds, and hid themselves in the brushwood, they would be very soon discovered; if they tried to go on foot across the plain, they could easily be overtaken by the Sal-

vadores, who were mounted on swift horses.   What course
should then be adopted?   This question was asked him by
the robbers, when the band of the Salvadores, only about
forty paces distant from them, was advancing in their direction as quickly as the nature of the ground permitted.

"Companions," said Martin, placing himself at their head,
"no other resource remains for us but to break through them,
sword in hand, and endeavour to reach the plain, whether we
are killed or not."

"Yes, yes, forward!" they all cried out, knowing that Martin
had indicated the only means of escape left for them, and they
put spurs to their horses.   As that of Martin was the best, the
least fatigued, and the lightest, the young man preceded his
comrades by a short distance, and rushing, with sword in hand,
into the midst of the Salvadores, he unhorsed one of them
with almost each stroke, and the others followed him, and broke
through their opponents, not less boldly and promptly.   At
last they succeeded in gaining the main road, from whence they
heard the death-cries of those whom they had left in the wood,
struck down by the swords of the Salvadores; they then fled
across the plain in the direction of the mountains of Oca.

Martin had received several wounds, although none of them
were serious, and was losing much blood.   After some time
they arrived at a small hill, surrounded by trees on all sides,
and from which the surrounding country could be seen for a
considerable distance.

"Brother, let us dismount here, that we may examine your
wounds," said his companions to Martin.

They at once dismounted, and all the bandits embraced
Martin, calling him their deliverer.

"You shall be our captain," said one of them, "for you are
worth more than a hundred like Raposo."

"Yes, yes, you shall be our captain, brother.   Long live our
captain!" they all cried out unanimously and with enthusiasm.

"I thank you, comrades," replied Martin; "and I swear by
those dogs of Salvadores whom my good sword has sent to the
other world, that I shall prove myself worthy of the honour
you confer on me.   You have heard the cries of agony of our
companions, who have been cowardly butchered by those
fellows?"

"Yes, yes, we have heard them!   Poor Captain Raposo!"

"Well, then, it is for us to avenge them.   You do not yet
know the name of your new captain.   I call myself the

Vengador,[1] brothers. Let the band, then, of the Vengador be as much feared as was that of the Raposo; war to the death against the grandees who urged on the king to institute the brotherhood of the Salvadores. At present we are weak, but in a short time we shall be strong; we are persecuted to-day, to-morrow we shall be protected everywhere, if you will only obey my orders and be guided by my advice."

"We shall be your slaves, brother captain. You are skilful and brave, we owe you our safety, and we trust in you to avenge our comrades."

"Now listen, brothers," continued Martin; "I wish to explain to you what our conduct is to be from this day."

"But, captain," interrupted one of the band, "let us first bandage your wounds, for you will lose much blood if we don't do so."

"No, by Beelzebub! My blood must run till the venom, which the cowardly conduct of those vile Salvadores has put into it, has all left it."

This answer of their bold captain captivated more and more the hearts of the bandits, to whose eyes tears came—tears which they would not have shed on hearing the pitiful wailings of poor peasants from whom they had stolen the small store with which they had hoped to support their families; of unhappy parents whose daughter was about to be their victim; of the sad wife whom their swords had condemned to widowhood; of the weak children whom they had made orphans, without means of subsistence.

"Hear me, brothers," continued the Vengador; "from to-day, war to the strong and help to the weak! If we go near the poor, it must be only for the purpose of alleviating their misery with what we shall have taken from the powerful. Have any of you daughters or a wife?"

"Yes," replied one of the robbers; "I have a daughter who is worth more than those of the king, and I love her more than the apple of my eyes."

"I have a wife," answered another, "and, although a peasant, she is of more value than the most noble dame in Castile. For this I love her as well as people say the son of the Grandee of Vivar loves the daughter of De Gormaz."

"Well, then, what would you do if your daughter were torn away from you?"

"Anger of God! If such were done, I would never rest till

____
[1] Avenger.

my dagger was buried in the heart of him who took her from me, even were he hid in the bowels of the earth, even if he fled to the ends of the world! Brother captain, say no more, for God's sake; thinking only of such a thing makes my blood boil."

"And you," he said, turning to the other, "what would you do if your wife were taken from you and dishonoured?"

"If such happened," he exclaimed, placing his hand on his dagger with an instinctive movement, and his eyes flashing fire, "my sword would pierce a hundred hearts and then my own! But for what reason do you ask us such questions, captain?"

"Because I wish to put you on your guard,—you on account of your wife, and you, of your daughter, if they live in this district; for there is in it a ruffianly count, who carries off wives from their husbands, and daughters from their fathers."

"Who, then, is that count?" asked all the bandits, full of indignation.

"The Count of Carrion," replied Martin, repressing with difficulty the joy he felt on seeing how successfully he had disposed his companions to aid him in his projects of vengeance. "The Count of Carrion," he continued, "is the most cruel, the most treacherous, and the worst of men; when you return home to clasp your daughters or your wives to your hearts, perchance you will find that he has stolen them from you."

"May the earth open and may we sink into hell, if we suffer such a wretch to live any longer!" exclaimed the robbers; and Martin continued, more warmly and solemnly—

"Yes, yes, comrades, let the Count of Carrion die, if we ourselves do not desire to die like the Raposo and the greater part of his band. It is that count who has sacrificed our brothers, for to him is due the creation of the brotherhood of the Salvadores."

"Let us attack his castle!" all exclaimed; "let us bury our swords in the breast of that traitor count!"

"But Don Suero, for such is his name, will be able to say to us, that if he carries off young girls and married women, we also do the same; that if he attacks and wounds poor people, and deprives them of their means of subsistence, we also do the same."

"But from this day forward we shall not do such things.

Let us all now swear that we will plunge our daggers in the breast of any comrade who dares to commit such crimes." Thus spoke the bandit who had a daughter.

Without the slightest hesitation, they all then took a solemn oath, that in future they would not ill-treat women, or injure and rob the poor and helpless.

Martin now began to feel weak on account of the quantity of blood he had lost, and considered that he should not delay any longer the binding of his wounds.

One of the bandits gathered some herbs that were abundant in that country, and applied them to the wounds of his captain, having first washed them in water brought in a helmet from an adjacent spring. They were bound up with bandages, made from a handkerchief which was torn up for that purpose.

The much reduced band of the Vengador rested under the trees of the thick wood, where the horses found abundant pasture; and when the vesper bells began to ring in the surrounding villages, the bandits mounted their horses and, according to the orders of their captain, continued their way towards the Sierra de Oca.

CHAPTER XI

HOW THE DE VIVAR FAMILY RECEIVED LETTERS FROM THE KING, DON FERNANDO

A few days after the events which we have related in preceding chapters, Diego Lainez and his family, including Rodrigo, were seated at table in the castle of Vivar. All were in good spirits, all were eating with excellent appetites, except the last-mentioned, who in vain endeavoured to take part in the general joyousness; but the smile departed suddenly from his lips, as if there came to drive it away some sad memories, which the most trivial phrases of those present seemed to awake in his soul.

Teresa, who was observing her son, saw his inquietude and sadness, and from that moment she shared them with him; for the feelings of a son reflect themselves in a mother, especially when she is as good as the mother of Rodrigo was.

"My son," she said to the youth, who was then buried in thought, "why are you so sad when we all have such reason to be joyous, especially you, who have washed off the blot that stained our honour?   What is the cause of your sadness?"

"Mother," replied Rodrigo, "have you not heard that Casilda, the solitary of the lake of San Vicente, shares her home with a noble maiden who also has gone to bury herself in that solitary place?"

"Yes."

"That maiden is Ximena Gome."

"Let her then, my son, weep in solitude over the perfidy of her father, let her consecrate some of her days to God, and to the care of the poor invalids who resort to the lake to seek their health, for grief finds its first consolations in God and in those who suffer.   If she loves you still, of which I have no doubt, her grief will pass away, and her love will remain; for true love is eternal, and grief, no matter how deep, is transitory."

"Do you believe, my mother, that Ximena can love the slayer of her father?"

"Yes, my son, for in killing her father you gave another proof of your noble character, and Ximena herself would have abhorred you if she saw you regard with indifference the stain which her father had cast on the honour of yours."

"Do you not know that, before she quitted the court, she demanded vengeance against me from the king, supposing that I had wrongfully killed her father?"

"Yes," interposed Diego Lainez, who until then did not wish to interrupt the conversation between his wife and son; "and such is the duty of every daughter.   The king, however, is too wise and just to believe such a thing, and to punish one who not only committed no offence, but rather added fresh lustre to his honour."

"Notwithstanding, my father, I fear that the king is much displeased with us, for the question regarding Calahorra is now the foremost one, and he has not asked your advice, as he always was in the habit of doing in similar cases."

Just as Rodrigo said this, a servant entered, announcing the arrival of a messenger from the king, from whom he brought letters for Diego Lainez and Rodrigo.

A perceptible uneasiness came upon the countenance of Diego, as well as on those of his wife and son. A moment afterwards the old man was reading a sheet of parchment, upon which was the royal seal, and the young man was reading a similar one.   This is what the first contained :—

"Much honoured Diego Lainez, the King of Leon and Castile salutes you, whom he loves the most of all his subjects.   Know that we await you impatiently in our Alcazar, for it is our wish that you should devote your wisdom and prudence to the education of the princes, our sons, as we informed you but a short time ago, in the presence of the cavaliers of our court.   Pay attention to your health till it is quite restored from the injury which the wounds made on your honour must have caused it, and as those have been healed, receive the congratulations which, on that account, we offer you.—THE KING."

The second letter, directed to Rodrigo, was conceived in the following terms :—

"To you, Rodrigo Diaz, a good son as well as a good knight, the king sends his greetings ; be it known to you that the King of Aragon disputes with us the possession of Calahorra, alleging injustice on the part of the king our father, who made it over to us of his own good will, when God was pleased to call him to Himself.   And as we have agreed to confide the decision of the dispute to the valour of two cavaliers, one to be named by us, and the other by the King of Aragon, it is our will that you shall be he who is to defend our rights, combating with Martin Gonzalez, who has been appointed to defend those which Don Ramiro claims to possess. You have given proof of being an honourable and valiant knight, by slaying De Gormaz to avenge the insult offered to your father's and to your honour, and we doubt not but that the enterprise, which we confide to you, shall come to a successful issue.—THE KING."

"Martin Gonzalez," exclaimed Rodrigo, trembling with joy, "is then the champion of Aragon ! Father, Calahorra shall remain to Don Fernando, and I shall have another claim on Ximena for her love. Let God put me front to front with Martin Gonzalez, in order that my sword may cause to bite the dust the only man I hate in this world, now that De Gormaz is dead—a man whom Ximena also abhors."

"Yes, my son," replied Diego, participating in the delight of his son, both on account of the honours which both of them had received from the king, and the enterprise which had been entrusted to Rodrigo, in which he was likely to gain still further glory. "Yes, you shall fight for your king and for your love, and you shall conquer ; do not doubt of it, Rodrigo. To-morrow we shall return to the court, where happier days await us than those which we recently experienced in it."

Thus speaking, both parents embraced their son, for Teresa also shared in the satisfaction of her husband and Rodrigo.

The latter, indeed, was about to engage in a fight in which one of the combatants was almost certain to lose his life, but Teresa trusted in the valour of her son, and at that period the sentiment of honour was superior to all affections, to all fears, to all interests. Then the mother who most loved her son was the very one who most ardently desired to see him engaged in some honourable and hazardous enterprise, even though the chances of gaining honour were less than those of losing life.

The reader, who doubtless remembers the interview between Ximena and Rodrigo in the halls of the Alcazar, will also remember the fears which both of them entertained, that Don Gome might bestow the hand of his daughter on another man. Let us see if such fears were well founded.

Before the battle of Atapuerca, and when enmity was commencing between Diego Lainez and Don Gome, the latter was sent to the court of Aragon, in reality as the ambassador of Don Fernando, but he imagined that it was a kind of exile, brought about by the artifices of De Vivar. Martin Gonzalez, who was one of the most powerful grandees of Aragon, gave him hospitality in his mansion, and entertained him magnificently, apparently for no reason but to return the marks of friendship which he had received from the count, some time before, at Gormaz, where he had been at the celebration of a tournament, in which were engaged both Castilian and Aragonian knights. Martin then saw Ximena, and was charmed with her beauty and prudence; but he did not demand her hand, believing that it would not be accorded to him, as he was aware that it had been promised to Rodrigo. However, whilst Don Gome was enjoying his hospitality, Martin Gonzalez discovered the recent bitter feelings which he entertained towards De Vivar, and he believed that the time had arrived for winning what he so ardently desired. He fanned the flames of discord between Diego Lainez and Don Gome, strengthening by means of calumny the belief which the latter entertained, that he owed his disfavour at the court to the artifices of De Vivar. Then, when he had sufficiently worked on the mind of Don Gome, he asked him for the hand of Ximena, which was granted, on condition, however, that she should be in no way forced to grant it against her will, for, with all his faults, De Gormaz, as we have said before, loved his daughter, and, although he had then resolved that she should not marry Rodrigo, he did not intend that she should become the wife of another, except with her own free consent. These infamous schemes, which were the principal causes of the division between the two families, were known to Ximena and to Rodrigo, and that is why they both entertained a deep hatred towards Martin Gonzalez, and certainly that hatred was legitimate and just.

We do not wish to leave the castle of Vivar without knowing the condition of affairs between the squire and his two sweethearts, for which reason we shall enter a chamber, which must be that of Fernan, for he is in it, and a lance and other instruments belonging to his profession are suspended on its walls.

The valiant squire must be in very low spirits, for when he is not so he talks, when in company, as much as four, or if alone, sings ballads of love or chivalry ; but now he is silent, with his head bent down, as if buried in deep and disagreeable thought. Another servitor, however, enters the apartment, and from his words we shall perchance learn something of that which we desire to know.

"On my soul," said the page, for such he was, "you are now just as much what you used to be as I am a bishop. What are you doing with your head sunk on your breast, and so miserable, when such glad news has come to our lords and masters ? "

"Tell me, then, Alvar, what news have come ? "

" I will tell you willingly as much as I know. I swear that the tidings must be good — and so good that my masters gave the messengers who brought them presents so valuable, that if they are not worth at least more than a hundred ounces of good silver, may the saints forsake me at the hour of my death ! "

"But will you not tell me, accursed chatterer that you are, what the news is which the messenger has brought ? "

"Yes, Fernan, I will, and I am just coming to it. But what good has it done you to visit so often the witch of the torrent, if you have not yet learned to know things beforehand, an art in which people say she excels ? "

"I vow by Judas Iscariot that I'll throw you out of the window if you don't cease talking such nonsense, and get out of this at once."

Alvar stepped backwards on seeing the threatening gesture of the impatient squire, for he knew that it was the habit of Fernan to accompany his words with acts, to which his ribs, almost broken more than once by the squire, could testify. As the reader has already perceived, the page was one of those young men who are so fond of circumlocutions that they go to the grain, as sparrows, through the straw. We have corresponding types in our own times, as may be often seen in meetings of Parliament, in which is often heard the cry, "To the grain, to the grain!" or "Question, question," which is the same thing.

Thanks, then, to the threats of Fernan, the page related, without any more roundabout expressions, what had brought the messenger of Don Fernando; adding, as we already know, that both Diego and Rodrigo had decided to set out for the court on the following day.

"I am much pleased to hear that," said Fernan, "for my life at Vivar is but a lingering death, since that ungrateful Mayorica repays my love with scratches and insults, and that vixen of an Aldonza shuts the door in my face."

"Then you love them, Fernan?" said the page, much surprised.

"And I must love them, I fear, in spite of the fact that they treat me worse than a captive Moor."

"By the soul of my grandfather, he who goes on in that way deserves a hundred lashes. Oh, how vain are the intentions of lovers! Why don't you swear, you unfortunate man, that as long as you live you'll have nothing more to do with women?"

"What do you desire, Alvar? Man proposes and woman disposes. I was born with such weaknesses, and I fear that I shall die with them."

"Conquer these inclinations of yours, Fernan."

"It's not easy to do that. However, I swear to you, friend Alvar, that my eyes are opened with regard to the fair sex, and I'll do my best to be done with them from this time forward."

"If you don't do so soon, I tell you again, as I have already said, that you will deserve a hundred good lashes."

"It is easily seen, Alvar, that you have no heart. You never knew, and don't know now, what love is."

"Alas!" said the page, heaving a deep sigh; "I know it but too well, friend Fernan. If we carried our hearts on our foreheads, you would see mine, and it would move you to compassion."

"By Judas Iscariot! what do you tell me, friend Alvar? You in love?"

"Don't be surprised, Fernan, for one should be made of

stone not to fall in love with the tyrannical and gentle maiden for whom I sigh."

"Tell me, who is this sovereign beauty?"

"Yes, I will tell you, Fernan. You and your master brought her to Vivar"—

"Explain quickly what you mean!" exclaimed the squire, becoming suddenly very angry again.

"I tell you," hastened to answer Alvar, fearing the look of Fernan, "that Beatrice, the maiden whom you and Don Rodrigo rescued at the inn, has me almost dead with love."

"You will soon be dead by my hands!" cried the squire, rushing at the page and furiously seizing him by the throat. "What is that you dare to say, ill-born lout? You in love with Beatrice! you dare to place your eyes where I have fixed mine!"

"Fernan, Fernan, let me loose! you are choking me with your hands of iron! If I had known that you were in love with her, I should have had no more thought of loving her than of turning Moor."

Fernan let go the page, feeling convinced that he had set his eyes on Beatrice, not knowing that doing so would offend him.

"Yes, I love her," said the squire; "and, except my master, no one has any right to interfere with me, for my lance made the fellows that were carrying her off bite the dust. Although up to the present she has showed herself insensible to my prayers, she shall learn how worthy I am of serving her, and will yield to me, so that I may requite myself for the cruelty of Mayorica."

The page found it hard to give up the conquest of the maiden who had been rescued from Don Suero, but he found the hands of Fernan harder; for that reason he promised him solemnly that he would not expose himself again to his anger by paying attentions to Beatrice. The thrice enamoured squire was satisfied with this, and both continued to converse amiably, when they heard some persons exclaim in an adjacent room—

"Father!"

"Daughter of my soul!"

To these exclamations followed sobs and repeated kisses.

The page and the squire proceeded thither, and found Beatrice in the arms of a peasant, advanced in years.

It was the father of the maiden, who had been informed

that she was in the castle of Vivar, and who had not come sooner to clasp her in his arms for the reason which his own words will explain.

"My daughter, how were you rescued from that accursed Don Suero? How is it that I find you here?" asked the elderly man ; and she began immediately to inform him of what had happened since she had been torn from his side.

The poor farmer shed tears of gratitude on learning the protection that had been given to his child by Rodrigo and the other inmates of the castle.

"Ah," he exclaimed, "God will bless those who have restored a daughter to her father; God will protect the good cavalier who drew his sword in defence of the oppressed, and for the punishment of a wicked tyrant."

But as Beatrice was impatient to learn what had happened to those who were her companions when returning from the pilgrimage, and what had taken place afterwards at Carrion, her father hastened to relieve her uneasiness and anxiety.

"The father of Martin," he said, "was killed by a stab which he received in the horrible fight from one of the retainers of Don Suero.   Martin embraced his dead body and cried out, weeping—

" ' Father, father ! your son will avenge you ! '

"He then turned to your mother and to me, and added, ' Your daughter shall also be avenged ; I swear it by the love I always had for her, and by the salvation of my father's soul.' He then disappeared, and no one since then has learned where he is."

"But was he wounded ? " asked Beatrice anxiously.

"No, my daughter," replied her father.

And the girl murmured in a low tone—

"I thank thee, O my God! I am still worthy of him— I trust in his love."

These words were a dagger-blow to Fernan, who doubtless believed that the lover of Beatrice had fallen in the combat, and that the maiden had already forgotten him. It was little less for Alvar, who, although he had promised the squire to renounce his pretensions to the love of Beatrice, still nursed the idea of following them on, acting prudently behind the back of the squire. Thus it was that they looked at each other gloomily, and, with a certain kind of despair, Fernan said to the page—

"It appears to me, friend Alvar, that we fail in courtesy

and good manners, listening to conversations which do not concern us."

"Certainly," replied Alvar.

And although Beatrice and her father told them that they did not inconvenience them in the slightest, each one retired in a different direction, Fernan muttering—

"Ungrateful, ungrateful women! The more one loves them the worse is he treated. But I, curse me! am myself the cause of the misfortunes which have come upon me, for I have enraged Mayorica, looking out for too much love. There are certainly more than two women in Spain for each man, and I swear by the soul of Beelzebub that I am right in my calculation ; but as women are so stupid that they won't listen to reason, why should I not resign myself to their foolishness, and enjoy the love of one of them. Well, then, from this day forward I shall devote myself heart and soul to Mayorica, and let the others see what a treasure of love they have lost in me. Mayorica is fierce when I annoy her, but kind and affectionate when I please her. Oh, Mayorica of my eyes! you shall not have to complain again of your lover, for if you guard your honour for him, he will do the same for you."

And Alvar—

"What a fool I was to fall in love, when I saw how things were going with Fernan. It is a sad thing to find the position occupied, when for the first time a man bestows his affections on a woman. They seem to be born provided with lovers, just as they are with arms and legs. O Lord, what a blessing it would be to men if you had created them without hearts!"

The old man continued—

"We arrived at Carrion, and on the following day your mother was stricken down with an illness which nearly cost her her life. She called out for you in her delirium, and she could not be consoled. Then the news of your safety arrived, and her health improved so much that I was able to leave her to come to you."

"Let us set out at once, father, for I must return to my mother. No danger threatens me at Carrion, for the sword of my deliverer deprived the count of life."

"It deprived him of his prey, my daughter, but not of his life, for Don Suero returned to his castle the next day, and has recovered from his wounds, which he says he received fighting with a band of robbers."

"Then what shall we do, father?" exclaimed Beatrice; "what shall we do to protect you and my mother from his anger, for having thwarted his criminal intentions, and to protect me from a fresh attempt on his part? But, ah! do not be uneasy, father, go and bring hither my mother; let us fly from the estates of the count. I am certain that the generous and noble family, to whom we owe our safety, will give us a small piece of ground to farm, a humble refuge, in which we shall be able to enjoy a tranquil life, and show our gratitude to, and bless our benefactors every day."

Beatrice was not wrong in trusting to the generosity of the lord and lady of Vivar. A few days after, she and her parents were installed, content and happy, in a small farmhouse, situated at a short distance from the castle, surrounded by fields which Pero Lopez, for such was the name of the girl's father, was ploughing with a pair of mules which, a short time before, had been feeding in the stables of Diego Lainez.

CHAPTER XII

THE COMBAT BETWEEN RODRIGO AND MARTIN GONZALEZ

THE cocks were crowing in Vivar, when Diego Lainez and Rodrigo, accompanied by squires and pages, amongst whom were Fernan and Alvar, started for Calahorra. All the roads were alive with people, who were making their way towards that town, desirous of being present at the combat between Martin Gonzalez and the knight of Castile and Leon; for the champion of the King of Aragon enjoyed the reputation of being a doughty cavalier, and it was believed, not without good reason, that, to confront him, Don Fernando would select the bravest of his cavaliers. The morning was beautiful, the road had been recently put into good condition by order of the king, who had proceeded to Calahorra, and everything contributed to make the journey pleasant, the district then being as full of animation and life as it was dull and gloomy during the greater part of the year. This conduced to the fact that Diego and Rodrigo arrived at Calahorra, preserving the pleasant feelings which the letters of the king had brought with them.   More than once the brave youth heard the good wishes which the passers-by expressed for the success of the champion of Don Fernando, although they did not know who he was; and, far from feeling any fear as to the result of the contest, he became more and more confident, and felt sure that he would be the victor, notwithstanding the fact that the wounds which he had received from Don Gome were not yet quite healed.

Diego and his son proceeded, immediately on their arrival in Calahorra, to the temporary residence of the king.   Don Fernando received both of them most warmly, and Diego could not forbear feeling, with great pleasure, how much brighter his honour then shone than when he was last at the court.

"Sire," said Rodrigo, as much moved as his father, "you have conferred on me an honour which I do not deserve, and which the best cavalier in the world might well envy.   If I had done anything to merit it, you would now only be paying me a debt; but, not having done such, I owe you one, and I am longing for the moment when I can repay it."

"That moment, Rodrigo, is very near: this very day the place for the combat shall be arranged and the conditions settled, so that the fight may begin at sunrise, as you are so anxious for it.

"Would to God, Rodrigo," continued Don Fernando, throwing his arms round the neck of the young man, "that I had a son like you!   I would give my crown to have one as brave and good as the son of Diego Lainez."

Diego raised his rugged and noble brow, with a movement caused by paternal pride, and at that moment he would not have exchanged his happiness for a king's throne.

"You have such a son, sire," replied Rodrigo, with much modesty.   "Don Sancho will be a brave cavalier and a prince worthy to succeed his father on the throne of Castile and Leon. Sire, ask the few Moors and Christians that were left alive at Atapuerca, who the valiant cavalier was that struck terror into the army of the King of Navarre, and they will tell you that he was a beardless youth, as cool as he was daring, as fearless as he was skilful in the use of his sword ; they will also tell you that he was Don Sancho, your son.   The laws of the duel authorise the champion to select a second according to his pleasure, and I, using that right, select as my second the Infante Don Sancho if such a choice does not displease you and your family."

"The Infante will feel honoured by your selection, which I

6

as his father, approve of.   Go and take some repose, Rodrigo, and prepare yourself for to-morrow's combat.   And you, honoured Diego, from this day forward shall reside in my Alcazar, for I desire to have you near me, so that you may assist me with your advice, and also to have you near my sons, that, from your experience and loyalty, they may become endowed with all the good qualities which are so conspicuous in your son."

"Sire," said Diego, "permit me to kiss your hand."

" I give you, not alone my hand, but also my heart ; " and he embraced the old man affectionately.

The following day dawned, peaceful and beautiful as the one which had preceded it, and an unusual animation could be noticed in the town.   Ladies and cavaliers, citizens and rustics, all, indeed, were proceeding to a place at the junction of the rivers Cidacos and Ebro, where, in a beautiful meadow, had been erected the enclosure in which the combat was to take place between Rodrigo Diaz and Martin Gonzalez.   The circumstances connected with the two champions, and the grave question which was about to be decided, raised to the highest degree the public curiosity : it was not a private affair, but a matter that concerned two kings, and in which two powerful kingdoms were interested.   As to the knights selected to settle it, Martin Gonzalez was one of the most valiant warriors of the period ; and the killing of Don Gome de Gormaz had given to Rodrigo Diaz extraordinary celebrity, for the count had been considered invincible, and he who conquered him had a just right to be looked on as also invincible.   The love affairs of Rodrigo and Ximena had already become public property, and also the pretensions of Martin Gonzalez to the hand of the orphan ; therefore it was believed that the Castilian champion was about to fight, at the same time, against the sustainer of the rights of the King of Aragon, and also against him who had endeavoured to snatch from him the love of Ximena—the love which was his glory, his hope, and his life.

In the following manner was arranged the place for the combat : a quadrilateral enclosure had been formed by means of stakes driven into the ground, and bound together by an interlacing of branches, the verdure of which gave it the appearance of a natural hedge.   At both sides were placed, on platforms erected for the purpose, long seats, or thrones ; that on the one side for the royal family, and that on the other for the umpires of the combat ; canvas tents had also been set up at the extreme ends of the enclosed ground, one for each champion and his second and squires.

The sun had just risen in the east; the high and luxuriant trees, which on that side hung over the arena, shaded it from his rays, which were then very strong, as it was the warmest season of the year. Multitudes of people pressed round the enclosure, and spread out for a considerable distance into the surrounding fields, like a sea, the waves of which were incessantly agitated. The king occupied the throne arranged for him, having at his side the queen, Doña Sancha, and his son, Prince Alonzo; the umpires also occupied the place allotted to them. They numbered four; two named by Don Fernando, and two by Don Ramiro. The former were Peransurez and Arias Gonzalo; and as to the others, history only says that they were "two very noble and very accomplished Aragonian cavaliers." On the platform beside them stood two heralds, with trumpets suspended from their girdles. A prolonged murmur was heard throughout the multitudes: this arose when the champions were making their way to the field of battle. Rodrigo was mounted on a splendid sorrel charger, with flowing mane and of noble appearance, which had been presented to him, the day before, by Don Fernando; the Infante, Don Sancho, accompanied him as his second, and Fernan and Alvar preceded him, the first as his squire and the second as his lance-page. If Ximena could have seen him at that moment, poor maiden, how sad would have been the contest in her heart between love and the memory of her father! How brave and haughty stood the son of Diego Lainez, clad in his strong and brilliant armour! How many fair ladies, who had felt pity for the orphan, envied also the lot of her who was loved by Rodrigo!

The horse mounted by Martin Gonzalez was black, and more fiery even than that of Rodrigo, although not quite as strongly built: the second of the Aragonian champion was Don Suero, who, being a friend and relation, had repaired to the court for that purpose, although he had not yet quite recovered from the wounds, which, as it was spread abroad, he had received whilst fighting with a band of robbers. Martin Gonzalez was also accompanied by a squire and lance-page, and his armour was white.

The heralds sounded their trumpets, and that loud murmur which, by its increasing volume, showed that the numerous spectators were at the height of their arguments regarding the combat about to commence, became silent, as if it were the trumpet of the last judgment that was heard. Then a proclamation was read, commanding all present to remain silent and motionless until the termination of the combat, under penalty of "*losing their goods and the eyes from their faces*," whether men or women, young men or old men, nobles or peasants. When the reading of the proclamation had ended, the two champions advanced until they nearly met, and Martin Gonzalez called out three times—

"Calahorra for Don Ramiro!"

To which cry Rodrigo replied, also calling out three times—

"Calahorra for Don Fernando!"

Having thus spoken, Martin Gonzalez threw a glove on the ground, which Rodrigo took up, and then threw down another, which, in his turn, his adversary hastened to pick up. The two champions, with their squires and pages, then retired to their respective tents, and the seconds only remained in the enclosure, where they were sworn before the umpires to loyally do their duty. This oath having been taken, Don Sancho and the Count of Carrion proceeded successively to the tents of Rodrigo and of Martin, in order to examine the arms of the combatants, and to ratify the conditions of the duel. When these matters were adjusted, the champions again made their appearance on the arena, and they were asked by the oldest of the umpires—

"Do ye swear to fight according to the laws of cavaliers, using no foul play or witchcraft, either in blows or in arms?"

"We swear it!" answered at the same time both Rodrigo Diaz and Martin Gonzalez.

"If ye thus act, may God and His saints aid ye; if not, be ye accursed as evil-doers and traitors, as ye would then be, and descend to hell, where Judas the traitor is!"

When this had been spoken, the champions, who had advanced to the middle of the arena, retired to the extreme ends of it, and took their shields and lances, which their respective squires and pages handed to them, placing themselves in position to rush to the encounter, whilst the judges were marking the ground.

"The *Ave Maria*, the *Ave Maria!*" cried out the heralds.

And all the spectators uncovered their heads, and recited

the *Ave Maria.* When it was finished, the blast of a trumpet was heard, and the champions rushed onward.

The first assault was terrible. Both lances struck simultaneously the shields of strong steel, and the violent impact caused both horses and riders to reel, notwithstanding their strength. Scarcely giving themselves time to recover from this first shock, the combatants again rushed against each other, and the lance of Rodrigo struck harmlessly the shield of Martin, whilst that of the latter, glancing off from the shield, broke the armour on his left arm, and wounded the youth above the elbow. The Castilian champion had very considerable advantage over the Aragonese in agility and dexterity, but was much inferior to him in strength. The blood of Rodrigo stained the accoutrements of his horse, and dolorous cries, mingled with others of joy, were heard amid the crowds that were spectators of the combat. The knight of Vivar, however, far from being discouraged by this mischance, became more and more excited with anger, and endeavoured to have satisfaction by again rushing on Martin, who, however, warded off the blow with his shield, for Rodrigo had not only against him his own inferior strength, but also that of his steed, which swerved to one side through the impetus and force of the blow. The same tactics were repeated several times, without any advantage to either combatant; but it was evident that the contest could not last very much longer, for both cavaliers were fighting rashly and recklessly. They took their positions for another charge, which all the spectators believed must be the final one, and, burying their spurs in the sides of their horses, they rode on at full speed, and the encounter was so violent that both lances were broken into fragments, and the steed of Rodrigo was thrown on his haunches. Then Martin Gonzalez drew his sword and raised it above the head of his unarmed rival. Another cry of horror arose amid the crowds around, notwithstanding the severe penalties that had been proclaimed against such manifestations, and all eyes turned, with pitying glances, towards Diego Lainez, who, with other cavaliers, occupied one of the platforms erected inside the palisade, in order that noble dames and cavaliers might be able to witness the combat. No one could accuse the champion of Aragon of foul play or treachery for acting thus, for he was only taking advantage of a favourable opportunity to strike his opponent, and in such circumstances this was permitted.

All, however, trembled, not so much for losing Calahorra as for losing Rodrigo, who promised to be one of the bravest cavaliers of Castile and Leon.

When Rodrigo saw the sword of Martin above his head, he sprung to his feet with incredible rapidity, and avoiding thus the stroke of his adversary, which wounded the horse, as if chance thus punished it for its weakness, he quickly drew his sword and plunged it into the breast of the charger of Martin Gonzalez. He was then in a similar position to that in which Rodrigo had been; but the youth, far from imitating him, stopped and said—

"Arise, and let us fight on our feet, for our swords must now do what our lances have not been able to accomplish."

Thunders of applause were the recompense which the spectators bestowed on Rodrigo for his generous conduct. Both knights put themselves on their guard, and then attacked each other with desperate fury. In vain did Martin endeavour to render unavailing the defence which his shield afforded to Rodrigo by trying to get at his sides; but the champion of Don Fernando avoided all his strokes by his dexterity and agility, in the same way that his opponent was taking advantage, in every way in his power, of his superior strength. Rodrigo took his sword in both his hands, notwithstanding the embarrassment caused by his shield, and was about to bring it down on the helmet of Martin Gonzalez, when he held up his shield almost horizontally. The helmet remained uninjured, but the shield was broken to pieces, and Martin consequently remained without any protection except the coat of mail with which he, as well as his opponent, was covered.

Martin Gonzalez believed himself lost, and all his friends shared in this fear; Rodrigo, however, gave another proof that the noblest blood of Castile ran in his veins.

"Let us fight with uncovered breasts!" he exclaimed; and he threw his shield far from him.

If the face of the Aragonese knight had not been hidden by his visor, the spectators of that sanguinary scene could have seen it covered with the blush of shame.

The combat continued, ever more obstinate, more bloody, more ferocious. Anger blinded Rodrigo, and gave advantage to his adversary, who remained much cooler. Martin observed this, and endeavoured to win the victory by enraging more and more the young cavalier; and, according to the "Chronicle of the Cid," he said to him—

"It was an evil day for you when you entered into this contest with me, for you shall never marry Doña Ximena Gome, whom you love so much. You shall not return to Castile alive."

To which Rodrigo answered, according to the same chronicle—

"Don Martin Gonzalez, you know, as a knight should, that such words are not for an occasion like this; we are here to fight with our swords and not with idle words."

"Then let us finish quickly," said Martin in a low voice, "for Ximena awaits me with open arms."

These words were scarcely uttered when the sword of Rodrigo was darted at his visage, and, breaking the front part of the helmet, it entered his mouth with such force that the point came out through the back of his neck.

A providential chastisement. The calumniator, Martin Gonzalez, was punished where he had most sinned.

Enthusiastic cries resounded on all sides.

"Calahorra for Don Fernando!" cried out the heralds three times; and no one came forward to maintain the contrary.

The umpires then declared the result of the combat, and adjudged to Don Fernando the disputed town.

The king descended at once to the arena, embraced Rodrigo, took off his armour with his own hands, and led him off.

A short time after, the brave youth entered the town, amid the enthusiastic cheers of the multitude, and his father and the king were seen to shed tears of joy.

CHAPTER XIII

OF AN UNEXPECTED VISIT WHICH XIMENA RECEIVED IN HER RETREAT

For some time the king, Don Fernando, had been thinking of changing his court to Burgos, partly in order to be nearer to the frontiers which the Moors of Aragon were continually devastating, and thus be able to keep them in check; and partly in order that the Castilians might not think that he gave undue preference to the kingdom of Leon.   He determined to carry out this project as soon as the question regarding Calahorra was decided by the single combat between Rodrigo Diaz and Martin Gonzalez.   The desire to extinguish at its very commencement the enmity between the partisans of the houses of Gormaz and Vivar, which he believed was about to spring up in Castile, also induced him to hasten this change. Don Fernando considered that the best way to cut short the existence of those two bodies of partisans was to unite Ximena with Rodrigo, but this presented serious difficulties on the side of the maiden; he, however, proposed to himself to overcome them, not alone actuated by the desire of seeing his states in a condition of tranquillity, but also by that of making Rodrigo happy, for he knew he could never be so without Ximena.

We shall leave that wise and prudent monarch on his way to Castile, and learn something concerning the solitaries of the lake of San Vicente.

Ximena had believed that in solitude, in prayer, in penitence, and in the service of her afflicted fellow-creatures, she could forget Rodrigo, and find tranquillity and resignation, of which she was so much in need; she had, however, completely deceived herself, for when love has struck deep roots in a heart, it resists all violence, it resists all waves, it resists all storms.   Can such a love die, unless those who experience it also die?—a love which had its birth in the cradles of two children, which grew up with their growth in their paternal homes, amid the flowers and the butterflies of the meadows, beneath the trees which shaded the avenues of their native place, and under the eyes of devoted mothers? How could this paradise, which loving souls dream of, be renounced?

In vain had Ximena striven against her love for Rodrigo; in vain had she invoked the terrible memory of her father in order to give it the place in her soul which the remembrance of Rodrigo occupied; in vain had she asked their assistance from the holy maiden and from the affectionate and faithful old woman who had accompanied her into that solitude, in order to tear from her heart that enduring, deep, immense love.   On all sides she found incentives to that love, everything seemed to conspire to strengthen in her the remembrance of it.   One day there arrived on the shores of the lake a young invalid, accompanied by a youth who called her by the sweet name of wife, who lavished loving cares on her, who became sad when he saw her sad, and joyful when she was joyful ; who surrounded her with an atmosphere of affection, emanating from his words, from his looks, from his every action, and Ximena remembered that such was the love she had dreamed of, that such a husband she had seen in Rodrigo. Ah ! then she could realise how miserable is a woman who has no husband to protect her weakness or to sustain her when she is cast down by physical or mental pain ! Another day she was wandering through the shady groves that bordered the lake, and this brought to her mind the time when she and Rodrigo wandered through the woods which surrounded the castle of Gormaz ; and every fountain, brook, or flower-covered meadow which she saw, reminded her of some other fountain, brook, or meadow, with which were connected memories of Rodrigo.

In this struggle between love and the blood-stained shade of her father, the former was gaining the mastery more and more as time went on. But if Rodrigo still loved her, as once he did, how could he refrain from seeing her? how was it that, in order to do so, he did not travel the short distance which separated Vivar from the lake of San Vicente, as in former days he had journeyed the long distance between Vivar and San Estéban of Gormaz? All the projects of hatred, of revenge, of oblivion ; all the endeavours of Ximena to forget him who had slain her father, had resulted in the girl becoming wearied by her struggles against love. After a night during which she was tortured by horrible dreams and nightmares, she arose from her humble bed,—the bed in which she had shed so many tears and abandoned herself to so many sad reflections,—and knelt down before an image of the Virgin of the Dolours, to address to heaven her morning prayer, as the birds were doing, that sang in the trees which, with their aged trunks and leafy boughs, protected the rustic hermitage.

" Mother of the unfortunate, consolation of afflicted souls ! " she cried, raising to the holy image her hands and her eyes wet with tears, " console and sustain me, that I may not succumb to the weight of my tribulations ! Have pity on my tortures, apply the balsam of thy grace to the wounds of my heart ! Pray to thy Son to have mercy on me ! "

Ximena had scarcely finished her short prayer when Lambra —who had gone to the door of the hermitage to see if Casilda, who had set out at daybreak to console and succour the family of a poor and infirm shepherd, was returning—came hastily to her mistress, and said to her—

"Look, my lady, see those cavaliers who are coming in this direction."

Ximena allowed herself to be led mechanically by Lambra, who took her hand and conducted her to the door of their dwelling-place. As she had said, about twenty well-accoutred cavaliers were riding along the shore of the lake, on a path that led to the hermitage, which was erected on the summit of a hill and overlooked the country for some distance.

These cavaliers were not accompanying a lady. Who were they, then? Why were they coming to the hermitage? Ximena asked herself those questions, and her heart beat quickly, although she did not know what caused it to do so. The cavaliers were advancing nearer and nearer, and, with unspeakable surprise, she recognised the king, Don Fernando, who rode in front. He appeared astonished, in his turn, on recognising Ximena, when he arrived at the hermitage.

"Ximena!" he exclaimed; "you here?"

And he hastened to dismount.

"You here?" he repeated; "when I believed that you were in your castle at Gormaz."

"Sire," said the young girl, "I came here, desirous of finding the tranquillity which was denied me at the court. Shall I offend you by asking to what circumstance I owe the happiness of seeing you in these solitudes."

"To my desire of seeing Casilda, for you already know, Ximena, that since she lost the affection of her father in order to merit the love of God, she has no protection amongst men but mine. I bless the moment in which I thought of undertaking this journey, for at the end of it, instead of meeting one, I meet two persons whom I love very much."

Those who accompanied the king, as well as Lambra, had moved away respectfully to some distance from the speakers.

"How is it that I do not find Casilda with you?" asked Don Fernando.

"You will soon see her, sire," replied the maiden, "for she has gone to exercise her mission of mercy not far from here."

"I am not alone delighted to see you on account of the pleasure which your presence always causes me, but also for the reason that I bring news which I feel sure will be agreeable to you," said the king, fixing his eyes on her at the same time, in order to see the effect which his words might produce. "You remember that you demanded justice from me on him who killed your father?"

"I have not forgotten it, sire."

"I have done justice already, Ximena!"

"O my God!" exclaimed the young girl, full of anxiety and fear. "Sire, explain."

"Rodrigo has been punished as he deserved."

A deadly pallor overspread the face of Ximena, and she would have fallen on the ground if the king had not supported her and made her sit down on a rustic bench which stood near them.

"I engaged him in a single combat with Martin Gonzalez, certain that it would be one to the death, and I was not mistaken. The sword of Martin Gonzalez was stained with the blood of him who shed that of your father."

Ximena uttered a cry of agony, and fell back senseless against the wall which served as a support for the bench.

"Dueña, dueña!" cried Don Fernando, "bring water quickly. Your mistress has fainted on being reminded of her father."

"O my God! may the Mother of Dolours and all the saints aid me!" cried Lambra, running to fetch what the king had asked for. "He might have spoken of the living instead of the dead, when he ought to have seen that it is only a chance whether she is going to the angels or not."

The dueña brought, in great haste, a vessel of water from a spring which was very near the hermitage, and bathed the face of Ximena, who was slowly regaining her senses, whilst Lambra was saying to the king—

"By the glorious Saint Isidore, sire, you should be cautious as to what you say to my mistress, for in one of those faints she might fly from our hands like a bird. Do you not know, sire, what ravages the death of her father has made in her health? and at night she dreams of nothing else, and never ceases calling out the name of that mad Rodrigo who killed him."

"Retire, honoured dueña, for she has returned to herself," said Don Fernando to Lambra, and she hastened to obey him.

"He is dead! Rodrigo is dead!" murmured Ximena, before opening her eyes and becoming aware that the king stood at her side.

"Ximena," said Don Fernando, "Rodrigo is not dead. It

was he who killed Martin Gonzalez with the point of his sword."

Ximena could not repress a sudden rush of joy, and did not even try to conceal her feelings from the king.

"Sire, have compassion on me!" she cried. "Tell me the truth? Is it certain that Rodrigo is alive, or is it that you fear to tell me again that he is dead, lest I might fall into another swoon, such as that which your former words caused?"

"Ximena, I swear to you that Rodrigo lives, to love you ever. Are you not glad that he is alive? Are you not glad that he loves you?"

"Sire, lay the blame of being an unnatural, ungrateful daughter on me, of being a woman unworthy of the noble blood that flows in my veins; but I cannot help it. His life is my life, and without his love I am without hope in this world. I demanded justice of you against Rodrigo, and I was not deceiving you, for then it appeared to me that in obtaining it my entire happiness consisted; but I soon knew that I was only deceiving myself, that his punishment, which I asked from you, would be the cause of the deepest misery to me. My father demanded vengeance from the depths of his sepulchre, but my love for Rodrigo asked pardon for him from the bottom of my heart. Ah, sire! God alone and myself know the terrible combat I have had to sustain, and the anguish I have had to suffer."

"Well, then, Ximena, that combat and that agony must now cease. Rodrigo killed your father, but your father had tarnished the honour of his; Rodrigo desired to fight loyally and honourably with the Count of Gormaz, but the count insulted him; then Rodrigo did not kill your father in any unfair way, but whilst fighting with him, arm to arm and face to face, as a good knight. This should be sufficient, Ximena, to remove your scruples and quiet your conscience, so that you may be the bride of Rodrigo."

"It is impossible, sire, for ordinary people do not reason thus; and it would be always said that I married the murderer of my father."

"Ximena, to the eyes of the world you will be the victim of a tyrannical order—you will have given your hand to Rodrigo in obedience to my command; and only you, Rodrigo, and I shall know that you gave it to him in accordance with the impulses of your heart."

"Ah, sire! how shall he and I be ever able to pay you for the happiness that we shall owe to you?"

"By choosing the queen and me as bride's-lady and groom's-man at your wedding," replied Don Fernando, with a pleasant smile.

Ximena knew not how to express her gratitude to the king; she threw herself on her knees before him and exclaimed—

"Sire, let me kiss your feet! let me even kiss the ground where you have stood!"

"Arise, Ximena, for she who, like you, is worthy of Rodrigo, should kneel only before God."

Just as the king was raising Ximena affectionately from the ground, Casilda approached, coming from beneath the trees which grew nearest to the hermitage. Don Fernando, who loved her as a daughter, and whose kindly feelings were then much aroused, hastened forward to meet her. Casilda uttered a cry of joy on seeing him.

"Casilda," said Don Fernando to her, when both he and the holy maiden had remained silent a short time, as those who love and respect each other often do, when they meet after a long absence, "Casilda, I bring you tidings of your father."

"Of my father?" exclaimed the girl in a joyful tone; and at the same time a few tears trickled down from her beautiful and calm eyes.

"Yes; your father has confided to me the hidden feelings of his heart, in order that I may make them known to you. Read this, and his words will tell you more than mine."

"To you, who have children, whom you love as I do mine," wrote Almenon, having prefaced his letter with the usual ceremonious phrases and salutations, "to you an unhappy father appeals, certain that you will understand his feelings and carry out his wishes. I have been informed that my daughter did not embrace the religion of the Christians for the purpose of enjoying the luxury and magnificence of your court, but in order to live in solitude and poverty, and to consecrate her life to the service of the poor and afflicted. If I formerly cursed her, I now bless her from the bottom of my heart; if I hated her before, I now love her: tell her this, and tell her, moreover, not to abhor her father, believing that he is cruel towards the poor captives, for he only is so because the creed of the nation over which he reigns, and the desire to preserve a crown for his son, compel him to act thus. A maiden reared in the shadow of a throne must suffer much and run grave risks in a desert in a foreign land, amid pain and poverty.   Act as a father to Casilda, protect and watch over her, and I swear that I shall act in a similar way to your children, should fate bring them some day into the dominions of—ALMENON."

Sobs almost smothered Casilda when she finished the reading of the letter; but her heart rejoiced because her father still loved her, still blessed her, and no longer wept on her account.

"Casilda," said Don Fernando to her, "it is not in vain that your father appeals to my heart to satisfy the desires of his. From this day forward you shall have a father in me; and as it is your ambition to possess means wherewith to aid misfortune, my treasury is open to you—avail yourself of it, and let no one, who is really in want, apply in vain at your door."

Some days after the visit of the king to the solitaries of the lake, Ximena entered Burgos, accompanied by a brilliant escort of cavaliers, belonging to the court of Don Fernando, who had himself come to meet her, riding a considerable distance on the road of Briviesca.

Some peasants, who were journeying at the same time to the city, stopped to gaze on the young girl and her richly-dressed companions, and as they were ignorant of the news of the court, on account of the distance they lived from it, and did not know Ximena, one of them went up to a workman who was standing at the door of a house, and asked him—

"Do you know who that splendid girl is? On my soul, she looks like a queen."

"What? you don't know her? She is Doña Ximena, daughter of the Count of Gormaz, who is going to be married to the son of the grandee of Vivar," replied the man who had been questioned.

"Nonsense! Is it not said that the youth killed the count?"

"Certainly."

"And he is going to be married to the daughter of the dead man! Well, queer things happen now-a-days. One must be badly off for a husband."

"Be silent, you bumpkin, and don't speak badly of a lady who is more honourable than you and your whole clan."

"Keep quiet yourself, you Burgos ruffian, for I swear I have fists, and won't listen to insults,"

"And do you imagine, you clown, that I haven't got fists also? I swear I'll break every bone in your body."

Saying this, the workman rushed on the peasant; the spectators, however, got between them, and the man of Burgos had to return to his post when only a few blows had been exchanged.

"Do the rustics imagine that the townspeople are made of sugar paste?" he said.

"And why do the townspeople insult us?"

"Why do you judge of things without understanding them?"

"Explain them, and I'll understand them."

"Then know that Doña Ximena, instead of being found fault with, should be pitied, for they are marrying her to Don Rodrigo much against her wish. She certainly was in love with him one time, but she took a dislike to him when he killed her father, and if she now marries him, it is in obedience to the command of the king, who so arranges matters, for he considers that the union of the houses of Vivar and of Gormaz will prevent the formation of bodies of partisans who would flood the kingdom with blood, and he says that public good must be thought more of than private sentiment."

"And the king is right."

"Of course he is; and the more so, because Don Rodrigo did not kill the father of Doña Ximena unfairly. Yes! Don Fernando knows well what he is about, and does not fear being accused of doing wrong. I hold, for my part, that there's not a better king in the world."

"Do you know that the maiden is worth half Castile?"

"And the young cavalier knows it, too, and he is certainly worthy of her."

CHAPTER XIV

HOW RODRIGO AND XIMENA WERE MARRIED, AND HOW THE DEVIL TERRIFIED THE PEOPLE OF BURGOS

THE month of September was commencing, and it was the early morning of a Sunday, calm and mild as a day in spring, for the burning heats of summer had ceased, and were replaced by the cool breezes which autumn brings with it, especially in the country about Burgos.　There might have been noticed in that city an unusual animation, and a multitude of people were flocking towards it from the districts all around ; but where that throng and bustle was most perceptible was in the immediate neighbourhood of the church of Santa Gadea.

The reader will already have surmised what the circumstance was which in this manner was disturbing the habitual tranquillity of the capital of Castile and its suburbs ; on that day were to be celebrated the nuptials of Rodrigo Diaz and Ximena Gome, and the king and queen were to give away the bridegroom and the bride.　In the streets which led from the Alcazar to the church, all the balconies and windows were magnificently adorned with flowers and rich hangings ; the ground was strewn with flowers and sweet-smelling herbs, and at intervals beautiful arches, covered with foliage, had been erected.　These nuptials were the cause of great satisfaction, not alone to the relations and friends of the bride and bridegroom, but also to the good people of Castile, who now felt sure that there would no longer be any danger of feuds and bloodshed.　For these reasons the citizens had done their utmost to adorn and make gay the streets through which the bridal procession was to pass.

The sun had not long risen, when the crowds which peopled the streets began to move and direct their eyes towards the Alcazar, for the chiming of the bells of Santa Gadea was announcing that the wedding party had issued from its gate ; for, it may be mentioned, Don Fernando, desirous of doing honour to Rodrigo and Ximena in every possible way, had lodged them in his palace.　A few moments afterwards the brilliant cortège was in full view of the expectant multitude.

How beautiful　was　Ximena, and　how　high-spirited Rodrigo !　They walked between the king and queen, and near them were Diego Lainez and Teresa Nuña, on whose countenances beamed joy and parental pride.　There accompanied them also many of their relations, and the most distinguished dames and cavaliers of the court.　The crowds pressed on to gaze at them, and the king's guards found some difficulty in keeping the way clear for the procession.　At last they arrived at the church, where the bishop, Don Ximeno, awaited them, and then the multitudes began again by rough shoving and pushing to endeavour to secure the best positions for seeing them when they returned after the sacred ceremony.

The agitation and disorder which for a considerable time had reigned in the crowd, packed tightly together opposite the church of Santa Gadea, gradually ceased, and all were peacefully expressing their opinions on the richness of the dresses, on the beauty of the bride, on the brave appearance of the bride-groom, and on the circumstances which had preceded these famous nuptials.

" As God lives, that Ximena is of more value than all her estates, and they are so large that the Moors could make four kingdoms out of them, each of the size of those which they rule over," said a youth who seemed to be a page by his dress, and who, with two companions, was mounted on the railings which protected the porch of Santa Gadea.

" Rodrigo and his estates at Vivar are worth just as much," replied another of the youths.

" And I tell you," added the third, "that Rodrigo Diaz will soon be the ruler of an empire.　Have you not heard of the gifts which Don Fernando has given to the bride and bride-groom ? "

" I know nothing of them, for my lord and master, the Count of Carrion, hates the family of Vivar so much, that nobody dares to mention their names in his castle."

" Then you must know that he has given to them, and to their heirs for ever, the seigniories of Valduerna, of Belorado, and of Saldaña."

" By the saints, how generous Don Fernando must be ! "

" The king knows right well what he is doing, for he should be generous to him who won Calahorra for him, which he had lost if the knight of Vivar were not as valiant as he is.　And for my part, I believe that Don Rodrigo will win for Castile, from the Moors, more castles than there are houses on the estates which Don Fernando has given to him."

" And it is certain that Don Rodrigo is valiant.　My master could tell a good deal about that, and the son of my mother also, if the people round us were not making such a noise."

" I'd like to hear all about it, Guillen."

" And I also."

" Then you'll have to be satisfied with the desire of hearing it, for this is not the place to relate adventures in which my lord came off very badly."

This refusal of Guillen, as may be supposed, whetted the curiosity of his companions, who, one on each side of him, edged themselves on, along the bar on which they sat, until they were in contact with him.

"Relate the adventure to us, Guillen, for I bet it is worth hearing," said one of his friends.

"I shall tell it, just to please you; but if Don Suero, my master, knew that I related this adventure, I should soon be in a condition to relate no more of them, but like my companions, the other servants of the count, who remained at the Inn of the Moor with holes in their hearts, made by the lance of that terrible squire of Don Rodrigo, named Fernan."

"Cease your nonsense, friend Guillen, and go on with your story."

"I shall do so at once."

And Guillen related to his friends the carrying off of Beatrice, almost exactly as the reader already knows it.

"And is it possible that the Count of Carrion commits such outrages?" asked one of the listeners.

"Very little surprises you, my friend," replied Guillen, still in a low voice, and looking about cautiously to see if he could be overheard by any of those who were standing about, waiting to see the wedding party come forth from the church. "Your astonishment would be greater," he continued, "if you only knew the circumstances of the carrying off of another girl by Don Suero, some time before his attempt on Beatrice."

Illan and Garcia, for such were the names of the other pages, squeezed themselves more closely, if such were possible, against Guillen, bending their necks and bringing their ears close to his mouth. Seeing, however, that the servant of Don Suero did not satisfy their curiosity with the promptitude they desired, they abandoned gestures in order to question him with words.

"And how did this other outrage take place?" asked Illan, who was the more curious of the two.

"It happened as you will soon hear, if those who related it to me were not liars, for at that time I was not in the service of Don Suero. There was in the neighbourhood of Carrion a maiden—a peasant girl, indeed, but one of the handsomest that could be found in Castile or Leon. Don Suero thought little of taking her from her father, as he was smitten by her beauty; and, using cunning devices, he succeeded in inducing both father and daughter to go to the castle of Carrion, and there he dishonoured the girl, and deprived the father of his sight, so that he might not be able to find his daughter, or take vengeance on him for what he had done. The girl, who was good and modest, resisted his wooing for a long time, but the count had recourse to violence, and Sancha, for such was the name of his victim, had to yield at last to the brutality of her jailer. Days and months went on, and Don Suero, who was much in love with the peasant girl, redoubled his caresses, hoping to make her love him also. The girl was becoming, by degrees, more yielding as time went on, softened by the tenderness and by the gifts of Don Suero. But behold! an old gipsy woman entered her apartment one day. This old woman was in the habit of telling fortunes, and the count put up with this, and with other queer things which she did. She and the girl, however, disappeared from the castle, some say by witchcraft, for they thought it could not be by any other means, and it was well known that the old gipsy was an expert in the black art, like all the rest of her race. It is easy for you to imagine the despair and the rage of the count when he was informed of the flight of Sancha. It is only necessary to say that, in order to give vent to his anger, he nearly killed all his servants and vassals with beatings, and, hoping to forget the girl, he established in his castle a kind of harem, to which he carries off the handsomest girls of the country, when he gets a chance of doing so."

"And have they never learned the abode of the unfortunate Sancha?"

"No; all the efforts which Don Suero has used to find her out have been in vain."

"And those of her father to discover her?"

"Have been also unavailing."

"What has become of him?"

"He seeks his daughter in every direction; but the unhappy man cannot find her. He goes from town to town, weeping over his loss, and earns something to live on by playing a lute."

"Anger of God! and are you not ashamed to remain in the service of such a wicked master?"

"I am ashamed, in truth, but you must know that I cannot go away from his residence; for if I lived far from the castle of Carrion, I should die of grief."

"By the glorious St. Isidore, I do not understand you!" exclaimed Illan.

"Guillen, you want to bewilder us with your mysteries," added Garcia. "Are there not plenty of masters who would be only too glad to get a respectable page or squire?"

"Leave that wretch of a Don Suero immediately, for my master, the Count of Cabra, wants at present an honourable and brave page like you, and he would engage you at once."

"I tell you that I cannot leave the service of the Count of Carrion."

"If the count were a lady, I should say you were in love with him."

"Then learn that I am in love, and very much in love, my friends."

Illan and Garcia broke into a loud laugh, caused not so much by the words of Guillen, as by the sentimental tone in which he pronounced them.

"By the saints! if you laugh at me, I will spit you on the points of these bars!" exclaimed Guillen, made angry by the laughter of his friends, which had caused the people standing about to fix their attention on them.

Illan and Garcia felt that Guillen had just cause for his annoyance, and ceased laughing.

"Don't be vexed, Guillen," said the former, "but explain yourself to us."

"I tell you that I am in love, and by confiding to you this secret, for no one else must know it, I am proving to both of you the warmth of my friendship."

"But who are you in love with?"

Guillen looked around on all sides, and then replied in a very low voice—

"With Doña Teresa, my mistress."

Illan and Garcia found some difficulty to restrain themselves from again bursting out into laughter. However, they checked themselves when they noticed the angry gesture of Guillen when he saw the fresh symptoms of hilarity.

"With Doña Teresa! with the sister of the count your master!" exclaimed Illan. "Are you mad, Guillen, or are you making fun of us?"

"I am not making fun of you; but I am mad—mad in love, my friends."

"But is it returned?"

"How could it be, when I have never dared to declare my love to her who is the object of it?"

"But don't you know, you fool, that if the noble Doña Teresa, the sister of the Count of Carrion, happened to discover that you were in love with her, she would laugh at you, if indeed she did not get you driven with blows from the castle. Don't you know that if Don Suero learned it, he would get you flayed alive?"

"I know nothing, my friends,—I know nothing but that I love her with all my heart and soul."

"But what right has a poor page to love so great a lady?"

"It is easy to know, my friends that you are as low-minded and ignorant as the bulk of pages. Tell me, however, is not a lady a woman, no matter how rich and noble she may happen to be?"

"Certainly."

"And is not a page a man, no matter how poor and obscure he may be?"

"Certainly, likewise."

"Then, is it extraordinary that a man should love a woman, and a woman a man?"

"No."

"Then, you simpletons, don't be astonished that I, a poor and obscure page, love my lady Doña Teresa, and that she, rich and noble as she is, may love me some day or other."

"You argue, friend Guillen, as well as if you had attended lectures in the School of Palencia; but I am quite certain that neither your lady nor the count would see it in the same light as you."

"If my mistress were like the ordinary run of women, or even like the generality of men, who think only as others think, and not as they themselves should think, my love would be certainly great folly; but I know well that Doña Teresa is guided more by reason than by custom. Besides, who has told you, ignoble as you are, that I may not be rich and noble some day, if Doña Teresa desires that he who is to obtain her hand and heart should be so? I am young, and, 'fore God, I am not wanting in courage. Only let the Moors get up a war on the frontiers, and you will see how I can wield a lance, and perchance return to Carrion as much a cavalier as the count my master. You will see how, once dubbed a knight, I shall collect together a hundred or so brave fellows, enter the country of the Moors, and conquer it. Then I shall become a lord over vassals, for, on my faith, it will not be the first time that such things have happened. You can't imagine, my friend, how my love for Doña Teresa increases when I think over those chances."

"I hope in goodness that your love won't bring you to perdition!" said Garcia in a prophetic tone of voice.

"It is to glory that it shall lead me," replied Guillen enthusiastically. "This love which I feel, impossible as it may seem to you, will exalt the humble page whom you see here. The greater the prize is, for which the wrestler struggles, so much the more bravely does he brace himself up for the contest. Do you imagine that Rodrigo Diaz could have fought so well if, in addition to conquering Martin Gonzalez, he had not hoped for the embraces of Ximena?"

Illan and Garcia could not but feel that amid the wild fancies of Guillen there might be well founded hopes. For that reason they thought it best to leave him in the paradise of his illusions. Just as in our times he who believes in nothing, he who considers but vain words the faith of his ancestors, the love of country, the love for a woman, is the man who most probably will raise himself over others, so, in the times when Guillen lived, that man had the best chance of elevating himself who believed in all those things, and, exalted by such sentiments, acted in accordance with his beliefs. Oh for that age, when, in order to be honoured, the cavalier had to consecrate his heart to God, to a king, and to a woman,— three sovereigns, who had their thrones respectively in heaven, on earth, and at the domestic hearth, and all of them in the soul of a man. If amongst those who at the present day bear the name of cavalier, there are any who do not wish to bear it in vain, they must be cautious with regard to acknowledging that they adore God, that they would die for the anointed of the Lord, or that they love or are faithful to a woman; for they would be laughed at and looked on as madmen, and in vain would they argue that the idols are false and loathsome which have usurped the altars on which these three divinities were formerly enthroned.

Our three youths had arrived at that point in their conversation at which we left them, in order to heave a sigh over lost beliefs, which it would be very difficult to replace. The bells of Santa Gadea announced, with a loud peal, that religion had sanctified the union of the noble scions of the trees of Vivar and of Gormaz. The crowds began to move, to crush, to squeeze, if we may so express ourselves, and with the sounds of the bells were mingled cries of pain, angry exclamations, threats, supplications, weeping, curses,—all that Babel of sounds which is usually heard amongst a great multitude, when it is compressed into a space which cannot well contain much more than half its numbers.

"The women ought to be at home spinning!"

"The men should be killing the Moors!"

"Your eyes are killing Christians, Moorish women!"

"Hi, hi, hi! Don't be tickling me, dueña!" ·

"Is my face rosy, you bumpkin?"

"It smells of roses, by my faith!"

"Who is the jade that's crushing me?"

"I swear it's an old witch; has she come here to cast the evil eye on the bride and bridegroom?"

"You brute, you are crushing in my breast with your elbows."

"A thousand legions of demons! my pocket-handkerchief has been stolen."

"Oh, my silk petticoat is falling off!"

"Confound those court festivals."

"And also that Don Rodrigo and Doña Ximena."

"I swear I'll cut out your tongue if you say a word against them."

"Ay, ay, ay!"

"May the devil take the women!"

"*I am coming for them, I am coming for them!*"

This whirlwind of exclamations, which are only faint samples of the hundred thousand which were heard every minute, changed its character, when the one which we have emphasised was heard.

"I am coming for them, I am coming for them!" repeated a rough and terror-striking voice, which seemed to issue from a dilapidated house, just beside the church of Santa Gadea, and which, even before it had begun to fall into ruins, was uninhabited for a long time; for it was said that whenever the devil came to carry off an inhabitant of Burgos, he took lodgings in it, for two reasons: firstly, that he might not have to pass the night in the open air, as Burgos is rather cool and the devil is accustomed to a warm climate; and secondly, to terrify, with the infernal glitter of his eyes, the pious people who were accustomed to pray at night-time before a holy statue, which stood at the gate of the adjoining church, and which was much venerated.

Loud cries of terror arose from the multitude; the children took refuge under the petticoats of the women, like chickens beneath the wings of a hen, and the women clung to the men, as ivy does to the oak. A minute had scarcely passed, when a terrible-looking figure emerged from the ruined house, a figure

which made even some of the boldest tremble. It was the
devil, without doubt, if appearances could be trusted. It was
clad in a flame-coloured suit ; it had a tail which moved from
side to side|like a whip ; its forehead was furnished with two
enormous horns, and through its large mouth smoke was issuing
as from a chimney.

"I am coming for them, I am coming for them ! " he
roared again, as he came out of his hiding place, and rushed
towards the crowd.

"Jesus, Mary, and Joseph ! " was exclaimed in all directions.
Not seeing, however, that the devil was stopped by the holy
invocation, everybody took to flight in the wildest disorder.
The children came forth from their hiding-places under the
petticoats, and in a few moments all the streets around the
church of Santa Gadea were empty, for even the men did
not wait for the devil, although he had declared that he only
came for the women.

We have said that no one remained in the immediate
neighbourhood of the church, but we have not been strictly
accurate. Illan and Garcia jumped down from the railing
as soon as the devil appeared, and fled like all the rest ; but
Guillen thought that he who was not afraid of the Count of
Carrion need not be afraid of the devil, and he awaited him
without moving from his position.

"Sir Devil," he said to him, seeing that he came in his
direction, "leave me in peace if you desire to have a good
friend in Carrion, should you ever go there."

The devil looked round in all directions, and, seeing that
no person observed them, he pulled off his horns and his tail,
which he had been able to set in motion by a simple contriv-
ance, and took off a mask, under which was burning tow, from
which proceeded the smoke that had issued from the mouth.

"Pelayo ! " exclaimed Guillen, on seeing the face of the
supposed devil ; "what foolishness has put such a ridiculous
notion into your head ? "

"On my soul," replied Pelayo, "I see no foolishness in
clearing the road for the king and the wedding procession.
If I had not done so, twenty heads at least would be broken
during its return by the maces of the royal guards, to judge
by what I saw at its going. And look," he continued, pointing to the vestibule of the church, "the cortège is just coming
out ; you will see how quietly and comfortably it will get to
the Alcazar."

The bride and bridegroom, with their companions, were indeed just issuing from the church. They proceeded along the road to the Alcazar, the mace-bearers not having to clear a way for them, as the spectators had ascended to the windows and balconies, and even to the roofs of the houses, leaving the streets almost empty.

On their arrival at the Alcazar, everyone inquired what was the cause of this unusual condition of things, and, as can be proved with certainty, Don Fernando called aside Pelayo, who was one of his servants, and, according to tradition, gave him sixteen maravedis, on account of his strange enterprise, which was much spoken of and laughed over during the banquet which the king gave in honour of the newly-married couple.

CHAPTER XV

HOW RODRIGO BECAME THE POSSESSOR OF BABIECA, AND WHAT HAPPENED WHILST HE WAS RIDING HIM

THERE is a place in Burgos known by the name of the "Solar [1] del Cid," and an inscription placed on it by the municipality of the city shows that the famous cavalier, Rodrigo Diaz de Vivar, was born there.

One of the ancestors of Diego Lainez, appointed governor of the district of Castile, and obliged to fix his residence in its chief city, had erected an unpretentious house in Burgos, and his descendants preserved it and resided in it when their duties at the Court obliged them to leave their ancestral home at Vivar. Diego Lainez and his wife Teresa were residing in it when Rodrigo came into the world, and quitted it shortly afterwards, in order to make Vivar their permanent abode. Now, however, as Don Fernando had changed the court to Burgos, and as Diego was charged with the duty of watching over the education of the princes, that old house, deserted for so many years, was again inhabited by its noble owners. They had entered it only a few days before the wedding of Rodrigo.

Here are reunited all those whom we have seen in the castle

---

[1] The place on which stands the original mansion of a noble family.

of Vivar, and even some more. Here are Rodrigo, Ximena, Diego, Teresa, the good Lambra, Mayor, Fernan, and Alvar; all contented, all happy, contemplating the felicity of the two first mentioned. Already were being realised the beautiful dreams of Rodrigo and Ximena; already were being brought to their fulfilment those golden hopes, so often combated and opposed, so often dead and brought to life again! What will Rodrigo now do? Will he consecrate his life exclusively to love, to Ximena, to the pleasures of the domestic hearth, and to the luxuries which his wealth can procure for him? No, a hundred times no! Noble souls, generous hearts, are never without honourable aspirations. Rodrigo, the noble descendant of the Judges of Castile, of so many excellent men, who had consecrated their lives to the glory of their God and of their country, will not wear away his life devoted to the effeminate pleasures of love and wealth. He feels that man has come into the world for something more than to pass through it like a shadow which leaves no trace behind it; he knows well that the most just and most honourable nation and the holiest religion have implacable enemies, and require generous souls and brave hearts to come to their defence; he knows that in Spain, as in all other places, there are weak who require the aid of the strong, that there are oppressors and oppressed. The contest which he had fought with his heart being ended, he is about to sustain with his arm another, not less difficult and arduous, certain that victory would crown it, as it did the former. The sons of Mahomet raise their impious standard at the frontiers of Castile and Leon, and frequently invade the dominions of the king, Don Fernando. To fight against them and conquer them is now the ambition of Rodrigo. What strength will not the thought of his Ximena lend to his arm, feeling that the aureole of his triumphs will also shine around her head; certain that on his return to Burgos she will receive him with open arms, and with love in her heart, in her eyes, and on her lips,—that beautiful woman of whom he had dreamed during so many years, with whom he had shared the joys and sports of childhood, and the hopes and illusions of youth! What joy will it not be for him to pass from the arms of his wife to those of his old and honoured father, and then to those of his beloved mother! What recompense will it not be for his prowess when he will see his parents and wife weep with joy, tremble with pride; and hear them bless him, and bless God for having rewarded their love and their sufferings by giving so good a son, so good a husband! Mean and vulgar souls consider as worthless such triumphs, such joys, such raptures, rich with holiness and with poetry; but souls like those of Rodrigo know their full value. Happy art thou, Ximena, having such a husband. How many maidens are there in this fair Castile who look on thy triumph with envy, who look angrily on thee for having taken from them the youth of their dreams, the youth with the honourable soul, the loving and ardent heart, the handsome and valiant mien, of whom they had dreamed a thousand times, whilst the guardian angel of maidens watched beside their beds under the appearance of a mother.

It was an autumn morning, beautiful, peaceful, mild; the sky was blue, and the birds were singing, as if mistaking the season for springtime. Rodrigo impressed a sweet kiss on the lips of Ximena, received a sweeter one from her in return, and went forth from his paradise, accompanied by his good squire Fernan. They issued from Burgos on foot, and, walking along the bank of the Arlanzon, they proceeded in the up-stream direction, not as master and servant, but as two good friends. The meadows which they passed were very beautiful, but they had never before appeared so fair to Rodrigo, for love and happiness are prisms, which make all things appear as if clothed in brilliant hues. Whither were Rodrigo and his squire going on foot, and at so early an hour? Let us listen to them.

"Sir," says Fernan, "for a journey on foot we are going rather far from Burgos, and my lady Ximena will be very uneasy before we return, as we shall have to spend half a day in a walk which she thinks will only take an hour. Besides, sir, as you are not used to walking, you will be very much fatigued."

The reader will remember what we said on another occasion, namely, that the slyness of the squire caused him to attribute to others his own weaknesses. These traces of hypocrisy must, however, be forgiven him, on account of the sincerity which, in other respects, characterised him. The fact of the matter is, that, having made his peace with Mayorica, in honour of the marriage of his master, as farther on we shall learn in more detail, it was the maid of Doña Teresa who likely would be uneasy, for he had told her that he would be back within an hour, as, going on foot, he believed they were only about to take a short walk, not far beyond the fortifications of the city.   For that reason Fernan had also postponed his breakfast until his return.   With regard to fatigue, he was likewise thinking of himself, as he also was not much accustomed to walking, and, being rather stout, would feel it much more than his master.

"Indeed," replied Rodrigo, with joyous familiarity, "the beauty of the fields and thoughts on our approaching adventures amongst the Moors have occupied my mind so much, that I forgot to tell you where we are going.   You know already that, amongst the wedding gifts, my godfather Don Peyre presented me with two horses, and he left it to myself to take from his stables, which contain many, those which might please me most.   Well, then, we are now going to select them—one for me and the other for you."

"But, sir, you have been so generous to me at your marriage"—

"I wish you to have this souvenir of it also.   The steed on which I was mounted when I fought against Martin Gonzalez was handsome and high-spirited, but I would never ride again, if I could avoid it, so weak an animal.   I shall never again trust to a horse by his appearance, as you shall see when we are in the stables of Don Peyre."

Master and squire continued conversing on this and other subjects until they arrived near a village, in which arose a tower with ramparts, and near it a low building, which, from its appearance, must be the stable of which they were in search.

Rodrigo and Fernan entered the tower, the occupant of which was Don Peyre Pringos, and in a short time they came forth again with him and proceeded towards the stables, much against the will of Fernan, who, in order to accompany them, had to leave an excellent breakfast, which on a slight hint from him had been served up in the kitchen of Don Peyre.

The stables were divided into two compartments, one fitted up for the horses and the other as a harness-room.

"Godson," said Don Peyre, "stand near the stable door, and, according as the horses are driven out, select those which most please you."

"Fernan," said in his turn Rodrigo, "place yourself at the other side of the door, and choose whichever horse you like best."

"I shall do so with very great pleasure," replied Fernan,

who was exceedingly well contented, notwithstanding the slight annoyance he felt at having to leave the succulent breakfast that had been prepared for him; for he saw in the stables sufficient horses from which to choose not alone two, but even two dozen.

The stable-boy then began to drive the animals out, and they came on through the harness-room. Fernan placed his hand on a white-and-red spotted horse, very high and of handsome appearance, and said—

"If you don't take him for yourself, sir, this one shall be mine."

"'Fore God," exclaimed Don Peyre, "the squire is not a fool!"

"Some day you will know, as Agrajes said,"[1] replied Rodrigo, "that such horses are good for riding on festive occasions, but for war I desire another kind, as you shall now see;" and as a horse, black, slender, not very tall, and almost as gentle-looking as an ass, came forth, he touched him with his hand and said, according to the "Chronicle of the Cid"—

"This one do I like."

"*Babieca*,[2] you have badly chosen," said Don Peyre.

"This shall be my horse," replied Rodrigo, "and his name shall be Babieca. Have you not called me *babieca*? My horse must be so called also, in order that both you and I may remember this difference of opinion. I feel quite sure, godfather Don Peyre, that it is you who shall have to change your mind regarding battlehorses, and not I, should I be in a fight with him."

"I say to you, godson, as you remarked recently to your squire, 'you will know some day, as Agrajes said,'" replied Don Peyre. He then ordered the stablemen to caparison the two horses with handsome accoutrements.

Shortly after, Rodrigo and Fernan started on their return to Burgos; the latter was particularly well pleased with the fine-looking speckled horse which he bestrode, and which attracted much attention on the part of those they met on the road.

Having entered the city, and as they were passing the mansion of the Count of Carrion, they saw at its door a number of squires, pages, and other servitors of the count, who were holding harnessed horses by the bridles, and were apparently ready to set out at once. Guillen, who has already been introduced to the reader, was amongst them. Certainly

<hr>

[1] An old Spanish expression. [2] Stupid fellow.

the steed of Rodrigo, which in future we shall call by the name of Babieca, as such had been given to him by his master, might be fairly considered a subject for the jokes of the wits and loiterers in the streets. However, Rodrigo was so respected and feared in Burgos, that no person had the temerity to laugh at his steed, until he arrived at the place where the house of Don Suero stood. When he and Fernan had got thus far, the servants of the count began to make observations to each other, and to laugh loudly, to which at first the newly-arrived paid no attention; but soon they were obliged to notice their insolence.

"Honoured squire," said one of them, addressing Fernan, "could you tell us whether the steed of this cavalier, your master, belongs to the horse or to the ass species?"

"It is a horse," replied Fernan, with difficulty restraining his anger, "for if it were an ass, you certainly would recognise your brother?"

"Then, brother, I thank you for your courtesy."

"By the soul of Beelzebub, I shall mark the face of Don Bellaco!"[1] exclaimed Fernan, directing his horse towards the insolent fellow, and striking him across the face with the reins.

All the servants of Don Suero uttered a cry of indignation, and were making ready to rush on the unarmed squire of Rodrigo, although Guillen did his best to pacify them, trying to prove to them that it was they who were in the wrong. When Rodrigo, who had proceeded some distance onwards, heard the uproar, he turned round, and, seeing what was taking place, he turned back and hastened, with dagger in hand, to defend his squire.

"Remain where you are, sir," cried Fernan, "for I am well able by myself to chastise these fellows, who have dared to make fun of your horse.

It almost seemed as if Babieca understood what Fernan said, that is, that they had been speaking disrespectfully of him, for, without his master having to touch him with the spurs, he rushed upon the servants of the count, whom Rodrigo dispersed in a moment, although, not having any weapon but his dagger, he inflicted no wounds on them.

On hearing the noise of the quarrel, Don Suero came to a window and cried out—

"Who is the coward that is trampling down my servants?"

"A cavalier who will forfeit the name of such if he does not

<hr>

[1] Rogue, Villain.

prove to you this very day that it is you who are the coward," retorted Rodrigo, turning angrily towards Don Suero.

The count trembled on seeing that he whom he had insulted was Rodrigo, the brave youth whose sword had left indelible marks on his throat at the Inn of the Moor; but as he was out of reach of his dagger, and in the presence of his servants, he made a great effort to overcome his fear, and replied—

"My sword, as God lives, shall prove to you that you are an ill-born clown!"

"Then give me but time to fetch my sword, treacherous count, and prepare yourself for the combat in the meantime, which shall take place on this very spot, where you can await me, as I shall be back immediately."

Thus speaking, Rodrigo set spurs to Babieca, and rode on to his residence, followed by Fernan. Having arrived there, he put on his coat of mail, girt on his sword, and took his lance and shield. The squire also got his heavy lance, and both of them, again mounting their horses, returned to the mansion of the count. The door and the street before it were now, however, deserted; Rodrigo approached the former and gave a heavy knock on it with the butt-end of his lance, but as no one answered, he cried out, in a loud and angry voice—

"Come forward, calumnious and insolent count, and abductor of women!"

"Sir knight," called out a woman from an upper window of an adjacent house, "according to the description you give, it must be the Count of Carrion you are seeking."

"The very same, honoured dueña," replied Rodrigo.

"Ah, sir knight, would to God I had never set foot in Burgos, and my eyes would not be now two rivers of tears! Hi, hi, hi!"

"Can you not tell me, woman, if"—

"Pardon me, sir knight, I am just going to do so; but you must know that I had a daughter, more beautiful than a May morning—Hi, hi, hi!— Daughter of my heart!"

"Anger of God, stop your weeping!" exclaimed Rodrigo, impatient to procure information regarding the count.

"Why should I not weep, sir?" continued the old woman, with a calmness sufficient to deprive Job himself of patience. "Why should I not weep, when that accursed count has stolen my daughter! Hi, hi, hi! Woe is me, I must now die of hunger, when I have no one to earn anything to keep me alive."

Rodrigo had let his impatience and annoyance give way to compassion, and was about to alleviate the affliction of the old woman. Fernan, however, whose heart was not so susceptible to the misfortunes of others, now interfered, exclaiming angrily—

"By Judas Iscariot! if I were up there, I'd soon make that old chatterbox hold her tongue."

Her weeping and the excitement of her mind prevented her, doubtless, from noticing that it was the squire who had spoken, for she continued, as if it were Rodrigo himself who had addressed her so roughly—

"Ah, sir knight, I am a respectable dueña, as you first named me, and now you call me a chatterbox! Hi, hi, hi! That is too bad, when I have lost my daughter, who was the best girl in the world! Ah, woe is me! What will become of me without my Aldonza!"

"Aldonza!" exclaimed Fernan, giving such a start that he nearly fell from his saddle, and then added, turning to his master—

"By the soul of Beelzebub, sir, this old procuress is making fun of us to her heart's content! The jade that she says has been stolen from her by the count, is not a bit better than herself."

Rodrigo, whose patience had been almost exhausted by the talkativeness and lamentations of the old woman, lost it entirely when he heard what his squire said, and cried out—

"Let there be an end of this nonsense, whether you are respectable or not! Where is the count?"

"Oh, if it's that, sir knight— A short time before you knocked at the door, he and all his attendants rode off very rapidly."

"Confound both him and you, old witch, who have delayed us here for half an hour!" cried Rodrigo, driving the spurs into the flanks of poor Babieca. "Let us follow him, even should it be as far as Carrion!"

Babieca and Overo, the speckled horse, started as quick as lightning on the road that led to Carrion.

"I promise that I will prove to him that he is a coward," said Rodrigo; "and even should he hide himself in his castle, my lance shall there find his breast. Fly, fly, my good Babieca, for thou also art interested in my vengeance!"

But at a short distance from Burgos, Rodrigo and his squire

distinguished, in a south-easterly direction, a dense column of smoke ascending towards the sky, and in succession farther on they saw another in the same direction.

They were the smoke signals which were lit on the watch-towers, in order to give warning whenever the Moors crossed the frontiers.

" The Moors have crossed the Moncayo ! " exclaimed Rod-rigo. " Before avenging injuries done to myself, I must avenge those against God, the king, and my country. Fernan, let us return to Burgos."

" Yes, let us return," replied Fernan, "and make preparations for an expedition against the Moorish power. As God lives, my heart is almost bursting my breast with joy. It is a long time now, my beloved lance, since thy temper was restored by the blood of those Moslem dogs. Ah, and what splendid thrusts thou wilt give ! And you, sir, will have splendid spoils to lay at the feet of my lady Doña Ximena ! "

" Fernan," cried Rodrigo, with enthusiasm, "I must have a throne, that Ximena may sit on it ! I must have Moorish queens to wait on her ! "

And, guiding Babieca close to his squire's horse, he held forth his hand to Fernan, and said warmly—

"Fernan, this hand which clasps yours, and the heart which I feel beating in my breast, shall win a throne and subjugate Moorish queens ! "

Fernan, on hearing the words of his master, and on receiving the pressure of his hand, felt a tear trickle down his rough and sunburned cheek.

CHAPTER XVI

HOW RODRIGO ROUSED UP THE COUNTRY, AND DEFEATED THE MOORS IN THE MOUNTAINS OF OCA

" Up, up, cavaliers of Castile ! cover yourselves with your steel coats of mail, buckle on the golden spurs, bind on the sword, grasp the lance and the shield, and mount your fiery chargers, which neigh and paw in their stables, impatient to career over the wide plains. Fly over them, and close with the Moors, until your battlehorses trample down the Moslem standard, and the impious Crescent is made a pedestal for the Cross !

" Up, up, cavaliers of Castile ! Five Moorish kings have crossed the Moncayo, and overrun with a large army the dominions of Don Fernando : they now lay waste the fields; burn the towns ; steal and carry off property from palaces as well as from huts ; destroy churches ; bear off women, both single and married ; and take prisoners and kill old people and children, women and men !

" Up, up, knights and squires, those who pay taxes, and those who do not ! Hurry to Burgos, where the honoured cavalier Rodrigo Diaz of Vivar has raised his green standard, —the son of Diego Lainez, he who was born in a propitious hour, he of the strong lance, he who fought at Atapuerca, he who slew the Count of Gormaz, he who conquered Martin Gonzalez of Aragon in single combat."

Such was the war-cry that resounded throughout Castile, almost immediately after its invasion by the Moors, on the day when we have seen Rodrigo abandoning his pursuit of the Count Don Suero, in order to return to Burgos with the intention of raising an army to march against the Moorish power. And that cry did not resound in vain ; from all sides armed men hastened to Burgos, and already the cavalier of Vivar had collected together a number sufficient to instil terror into the invaders, who, like a wild torrent, which in its rapid and devastating course tears up everything that lies in its way, had rushed on from the right bank of the Duero to San Estéban of Gormaz, then to the mountain chain of Oca, and by the Sierra de Urbiad to Bureva, which it desolated, without finding any resistance worth speaking of.

Rodrigo was burning with impatience to proceed to the camp ; but, as his prudence was equal to his valour, he did not wish to give any advantage to the Moslems by leaving their audacity unpunished, and disappointing the country by march-ing against them an army incapable, by its numbers, of con-quering the terrible hostile forces. More than two hundred cavaliers, related to him by blood, had hastened to obey his summons, and even his nephews, the sons of his natural brother, Don Fernando, were preparing to set out, notwith-standing that they were all younger than Rodrigo.

The army was complete, and the hour of departure was approaching. Rodrigo asked for the blessing of his parents, who gave it to him both with their hearts and their lips, and, embracing Ximena warmly, he mounted Babieca, at the same time that Fernan went out to mount his steed, grumbling at the cowardice and faint-heartedness of woman, for Mayorica had not been able to restrain a flood of tears on seeing him set out for the wars, for the young woman loved him more than ever from the time that he had made peace with her.

The signal was given, and the brilliant army of the knight of Vivar set out from Burgos in the direction of Bureva, towards which the Moors were then advancing.

It was a beautiful morning, and as it had not rained for some time, the road was in good condition. Thanks to this, thanks to the desire that all had to attack the Moors, and thanks, above all, to the fact that they had sallied forth from Burgos before the sun had risen in the east, the troops arrived at the mountains of Oca before midday, having been joined on the way by additional large bodies of armed men. The territory at the other side of the mountains had not yet come in sight, when the scouts, whom Rodrigo had sent forward to explore the country, returned to meet him, and informed him that the Moors were beginning to ascend the opposite slopes with great cheering, and other demonstrations of satisfaction, doubtless on account of the booty they had seized on in Najera, in Santo Domingo, and other districts of Rioja. On learning that the enemy was approaching, all those who composed the army uttered shouts of joy, and Rodrigo, Fernan, and the sons of Fernando Diaz distinguished themselves not the least in this show of enthusiasm and valour.

Rodrigo advanced the first, and on arriving on the highest point of the mountain, he distinguished the vanguard of the enemy, scarcely more distant than three shots of a crossbow. As he had already given orders to his captains, as to the manner in which the attack was to be commenced, he cried out, putting his lance at rest and his shield in position —

"St. James. St. James!"

"St. James! onward, Spain!" was the cry which responded to his,—a cry so resounding and so universal, that not alone did the Moors hear it, but it even reached the level country.

Scarce was it given, than they rushed on the Moors, who were broken up and thrown into disorder in a few minutes; such being the terror that this unexpected and vigorous attack caused them, that even the bravest warriors amongst them thought at first of seeking safety in flight. However,

Abengalvon, the King of Molina, who was one of the five who commanded the Moors, raised his voice, loud as thunder, and was the first to face the Christians; his example encouraged his squadrons. The conflict then became bloody and obstinate; but the Castilian hosts, although inferior in numbers, were superior in valour, and were fighting for their God, for their country, and for their brethren kept in irons and ill-treated in the Moorish dungeons. Their enemies were therefore in a short time defeated and routed on all sides, and the field of battle was covered with Moorish corpses.

The victory was complete : not a Moor had been able to escape from the onslaught of the Christians, as a very large number were killed in the battle, and the remainder were taken prisoners. Everything was in the power of the cavalier of Vivar,—the Moors who had not fallen under the blows of the Castilian steel, the captives whom they had taken, and the flocks and herds which they had seized on during their devastating march. The cries of joy of the rescued prisoners, and the agonised cries of the dying, were mingled together in one great volume of sound.

Rodrigo, followed by his nephews and by Fernan, all covered with the blood of the enemy, were riding over the fields of battle, when the fight was almost terminated. Some wailings, which seemed to be those of a child or of a woman, came to their ears. Rodrigo hastily went in the direction from whence they proceeded, and the sight which presented itself to him moved his heart, which until then had been of stone, notwithstanding the carnage that had taken place all around him. An old Moor was breathing his last, and a boy, a Moor also, and very young, was embracing him, uttering cries of despair, as if he thought he could preserve the vital heat which was leaving the dying man, by the pressure against him of his small body. Rodrigo believed that the old man was already dead, and made a sign with his hand to the boy to approach him; but the dying man opened his dim eyes, and, seeing that the young Christian warrior was showing signs of compassion for the disconsolate child, he made a last effort, and murmured with his failing voice—

" You, Christian captain, who are brave, and must therefore be generous and good, will protect this unfortunate little creature,—the only flower of the garden of my love. Oh, Christian, have pity on my son, aid the helpless orphan ! "

" He need never call himself by that name," answered

Rodrigo, filled with emotion, "for if he loses a father in you, he shall find one in me."

"May Allah send a protector to your sons, if they should ever be in need of one, and may the Prophet open to you the gates of his holy paradise!" exclaimed the old man, and tears of gratitude mingled in his eyes with those of death, which oozed from them, as he fell back a corpse.

Rodrigo removed the unhappy child from the dead body of his father, and ordered that he should be led to his tent, lavishing on him all the consolations and endearments which his condition required.

Some hours afterwards, the victorious army set out on its return to Burgos, bringing with it the rich spoils which it had taken from the enemy. The inhabitants of all the towns and villages on the way crowded out to salute the conqueror, and in many places there had been erected, as if by enchantment, handsome triumphal arches of foliage, and the road had been strewn with flowers, which perfumed the air. Enthusiastic cheers arose as Rodrigo passed along, and the sounds of drums and other instruments enlivened the country, mingling with the fervent acclamations of the good Castilians.

What a happy day was that for Castile, for Rodrigo, for all who loved him, and for all good people!

Before the squadrons rode the youthful commander, surrounded by his relations and his captains; joy shone in his countenance, and warlike enthusiasm sounded in his words. Babieca moved on swiftly, but Rodrigo was wishing that he had the wings of Pegasus, that he might arrive in Burgos with the speed of lightning, for of what value were to the son of Diego Lainez that victory, those triumphal arches, those acclamations, those ovations of an enthusiastic and grateful populace, compared with the triumph, with the glory, with the love which awaited him in Burgos, beneath the paternal roof? The happiness which filled his soul made Rodrigo love all about him, and thus it was that Babieca presented himself to his eyes from a point of view different to that from which he might have seen him on any other occasion.

"Yes," cried Rodrigo, "this is not alone a day of triumph for us men; but my good Babieca has gained glory also, and I feel quite sure that his former master, my godfather Don Peyre, will hold him in more esteem from this day forward. With what intelligence he let himself be guided by my hand in the combat! With what ardour and vigour he rushed on the enemy!"

And he added, giving the noble animal a slap on the neck with his hand, which raised his head as if he understood the praises which his master was so freely giving him, and was filled with pride by them—

"Babieca, if you have taken part in the efforts we have made to win the victory, you also shall have a share in the spoils of it; I promise to give you the handsomest trappings that we have captured. Many another day, like this, you shall have to fight against the Moorish forces, and mingle your sweat with infidel blood. You shall be my companion in camps and in cities, on the roads and in combats; and if you ever want food and shelter, it will be only for the reason that my lance has not been able to procure them for you."

If Rodrigo was well satisfied with the conduct of his steed in the battle which he had just won, it was not so with Fernan with regard to his.

"I vow by Judas Iscariot," said Fernan to some squires, on hearing Rodrigo praise Babieca, "that my master must have taken lessons from Beelzebub himself, to judge by the knowledge he has of everything. It seemed to me that it was an ass and not a horse that he selected in the stables of Don Peyre; but he took it into his head that he was a good one, and, as it has turned out, knight or squire never bestrode a better. Now look at mine, which looks as if he were fit for an emperor, and with all that he nearly left me in the clutches of four Moors, as big as four Goliaths."

"Tell us all about it," said one of the squires, "for I have an idea myself of what would likely happen you when you followed into the ravine those who fled from the main body of the army."

"I shall do so in a few words. I spurred on my horse after four Moors, as tall as towers, and I continued the pursuit for a considerable distance; I was nearly touching them with my lance, when, just about jumping over a wide ditch, my horse stopped; I spurred him violently, and he sprang forward, but not far enough, and he went down into the ditch. The Moors saw my mishap, and turned on me, crying out, 'You shall die there, Christian dog!' They had already raised their powerful scimitars over my head, when Overo,[1] ashamed, I suppose of his conduct, made an effort, raised himself, and

---

[1] Speckled red and white.

got out of the ditch. 'It is ye that shall die,' I cried in my turn; 'I vow it by the bones of Mahomet!' And closing with the Moors, will ye, nill ye, two of them were transfixed by my lance, and the others fled, without waiting to help their companions."

"And you complain of your horse?"

"I find fault with him for good cause; and I would have thrown him over a precipice, only that in the end he retrieved his character; but if he ever acts in that way again, I swear by the soul of Beelzebub that he shall not do so a third time. I am always unfortunate with regard to horses."

"But you are very fortunate with regard to women, though it is not quite the same thing," said Alvar; and he added with a malicious smile, "If I only had such a sweetheart as Mayorica, I would be satisfied with a bad ass."

Fernan heaved a deep sigh, drawn from him by the remembrance of Mayorica, and also perhaps by that of Beatrice and that of Aldonza.

"It is some time now since I saw scratches on your face, Fernan," said a squire. "I suppose you have been faithful to Mayorica?"

"I have been always so," replied Fernan, with much seriousness, which caused his comrades to laugh maliciously.

"Aldonza would be able to testify to it; is not that so?" retorted the inquisitive squire.

"And Beatrice also," added Alvar.

"I vow by Judas Iscariot, that you, Alvar, are the most confounded chatterer that ever was known. Had the son of my mother ever love-affairs with Beatrice?"

"But it was not your fault that he had not."

"By Beelzebub, I'll break every bone in your body as soon as we dismount."

Alvar, who knew well the danger of offending the vanity of Fernan, thought it best to retract what he had said; by that he pacified the squire of Rodrigo.

Another, however, of the order of squires, named Lope, a serious man, advanced in years, who had a wife and children, and who some time before had been scandalised by hearing of the liking of Fernan for plurality in love-affairs, profited by the occasion to throw his weakness in his face and to endeavour to convert the amorous squire.

"Brother," he said to him, "in vain will you try to persuade us that you have been discreet in your love affairs; your weaknesses have been notorious in Vivar, in Burgos, in Leon, and in all places where you have resided even a few days. That an inexperienced youth should have as little sense as you have might be tolerated, but such cannot be excused in a man of your age. This Mayorica, to whom you pay your homage, and whom I scarcely know,—if she is not worthy of your affection, well, then, leave her, and do not continue to look on her with carnal eyes; she will soon find another that suits her, and you also one who may please you better. On the other hand, if she is worthy of your affection, then, brother, serve her with your soul and with your life; but do not serve more than her, for to be in love with two women at the same time will neither be pleasing to God nor to the women. If not, tell me on your honour what you would do if Mayorica shared her love with you and with another man."

"What I would do?" replied Fernan angrily. "I would kill both Mayorica and the fellow that dared to look on her!"

"Well, then, brother, God has said, 'Do unto others as you would that others should do unto you.' Love Mayorica faithfully, if she is deserving of your love, and marry her if your means permit it; for a woman without means to support herself and the children that God may give her, is miserable in her house."

"I shall do so, as soon as I am a little better off, and I trust that will be in a very short time; for you must know, comrades, that since the marriage of my lord and master, Don Rodrigo, I am most desirous of getting married also; and if I can't marry two, I must be satisfied with one. Besides, do you think I would cease to love Mayorica if I took a fancy to twenty or a hundred others? Your great simplicity astonishes me, brothers. Does she who loves the child of her neighbour love her own less? Certainly, since I fell in love with Mayorica, I have also been in love with Leonora, Brianda, Sol, Alfonsa, Ivana, Aldonza, Beatrice, and twenty more; but I only loved them with my eyes, whilst I loved Mayorica with my heart, and that is the only real love. Apart from that, I have got a certain idea into my head, and all the preachers in the world could not get it out of it, and that is: a man can safely be in love with two women at the same time—provided that they do not know of it."

"On my conscience, comrade, you are either very simple or very depraved. Did that old witch, Mari-Perez, whom you used to visit near the torrent, teach you that? According to you, if to-morrow you marry Mayor, and your wife, whilst you are away on a campaign, should be seduced by another man, it would be no harm as long as you did not know of it. What answer have you to that?"

Fernan bowed his head and remained silent in face of this argument of Lope. The conviction, which he said all the preachers in the land could not overcome, had just been pulverised by that rough squire.

"Lope," he said at last, "you have convinced me. I confess to you that until to-day I have been blind, and have understood love-affairs no better than my horse. I swear to all of you, that even if Beelzebub himself should come to tempt me in the shape of the best-looking girl in the world, I would not let myself fall into temptation."

"I hope in goodness," Alvar ventured to say, "that the witch, Mari-Perez, who has her power from Satan, will not make you fall into temptation by presenting the devil to you under the form of Aldonza."

"Have no fear of that, Alvar, for if such a devil should appear before my eyes, I would drive him away, not with holy water, but with the reins of my horse. I'd like to confess one thing, now that we're speaking of Aldonza. You know, comrades, that I was in love with her once; but I think only through the witchcraft of her mother. Well, then, I took a turn against her on account of a certain kind of caresses which she lavished on me one morning, and I swore I'd never look on her as long as I lived. But as time went on, I began to think of her again, also, I believe, by reason of the incantations of her mother; and I was almost tempted to hunt her up once more, when I learned yesterday that Don Suero had brought her off to his castle at Carrion; stolen, according to what Mari-Perez says, but, as I believe, of her own free will. My soul was fired by this act of Don Suero, whom I look on as an enemy since the time when my master and I fought with him and his followers in order to rescue Beatrice, whom they were forcibly carrying off; and I thought of seeking out the Count of Carrion, in order to take the girl away from him; but I now swear that I shall do no such thing, and that from this day forward I shall have nothing to do with any woman except Mayorica."

"I trust in God it may be so," said Lope; "but he who has bad habits "—

The worthy squire was interrupted by the exclamations of

some of his companions, who, on seeing at the door of a house near the road three or four maidens, as bright-looking as May roses, commenced to address tender words to them, at which they laughed and seemed much pleased.

"I vow by Judas Iscariot, that girls like these are enough to make even a saint go wrong. What eyes, what complexions, what figures, what sprightliness!"

And, thus speaking, Fernon stopped his horse to gaze on the young girls, and seemed even inclined to ride towards them. However, as his comrades, far from imitating him, continued their onward course, laughing at him, he rode on to overtake them, muttering rather angrily, and looking up towards heaven—

"O Lord, you have created angels like those who stand at the door of that house, only that fools like my companions may pass them by without being thankful for such wonders. What faint hearts the majority of men have!"

CHAPTER XVII

HOW THE ARMY OF RODRIGO MARCHED BACK TO BURGOS WITHOUT BEING WEARIED, AS THE READER MAY BE

THE conversation of the squires and pages was resumed when Fernan overtook them.

"We were talking of the girls you were in love with," said Alvar, "but did you ever seek out Beatrice, to pay your attentions to her again?"

"I have sought to soften her, but in vain," replied Fernan. "Every time I go to the castle of Vivar, I have to pass near the farmhouse of Pero, and the devil sometimes tempts me to go in; and I cannot look on Beatrice without burning myself with her eyes. But she, the ungrateful hussy, always puts on a most scornful look. But I am certainly astonished at such constancy in a woman, who has not seen her betrothed since she was near being carried off to Carrion, and which same gentleman seems to have forgotten her, as he takes no trouble to see her again."

"But he has seen her, my friend," replied Alvar, who, as

the reader will remember, had been also in love with Beatrice, and therefore had managed to keep an eye on her, and had endeavoured to gain her affections with greater zeal even than Fernan ; taking good care, however, that the latter should know nothing about it."

"What do you say, friend Alvar?" exclaimed Fernan, full of curiosity, and also somewhat angrily.

"I tell you, brother, that Martin has been at Vivar, and in the house of Pero. Mine own eyes have seen him, and mine own ears have heard Beatrice speaking to him. Know, however, comrade, that the young man is not a rustic, as people think, but a cavalier armed at all points."

"Alvar, you were always a simpleton, and imagined you saw visions. When did you see and hear that? I suppose it was after drinking too much wine in some inn."

"The night I saw and heard it there was not a drop of wine in my body.

"What night was it?"

"I will tell you how it was. I am very fond of walking at night through the fields; for when it is fine weather, and the moon shines bright, and the day has been hot "—

"I swear by Judas Iscariot! Have done with your roundabouts!" exclaimed Fernan, beginning to get impatient with the circumlocutions of which Alvar was so fond.

"I wish to say," he repeated, "that when the weather is fine, and the moon shines, and the day has been hot "—

"I swear," cried Fernan, again interrupting him, "that if you don't get quickly from the straw to the grain, you shall feel the flat of my sword. Was there ever such a stupid bore as this fellow is?"

"Pardon, friend Fernan, I shall not again abuse your patience. Well, then, you must know that, wandering one night over the fields which Pero cultivates, I heard the steps of a horse on the road that leads from Carrion. I approached it, and concealed myself behind a fence. Then I saw a horseman, well armed, approaching, and, by my faith, his steed was fit for a king—what fire, what a step! I'd swear he was of the breed of Don Suero's celebrated mare. One must be blind and stupid not to know the horses of the Grandee of Carrion."

"'Fore God! I'll break your bones if you don't get on quickly to the main point."

"Then I shall, Fernan. The cavalier dismounted at the door of Pero's house and entered "—

" And then ? " asked Fernan, with impatient curiosity.

" Nothing more.   How could I hear what they were saying inside ? "

" I swear that the story of this fool is rather interesting," remarked Fernan.

" I could not hear what they were saying in the house, but I remained concealed behind the fence fully an hour, to see if the cavalier would come out, and if I could discover who he was by what he might say before his departure.   At last I heard the door opening.   Beatrice was holding a candle in the porch, and, thanks to its light, I was enabled to see what took place there.   Pero and his wife embraced the cavalier, Beatrice was weeping, and I distinctly heard the name of Martin pronounced.   The stranger crossed the threshold at last and mounted his horse.   The young girl gave the candle to her mother, followed him a short distance from the house, and said to him, 'Martin, since you are resolved not to abandon this vengeance, do not forget that if you die in carrying it out, I also shall die of grief.'   'Trust to my love, Beatrice, and it will bring you happiness,' replied the cavalier, and he disappeared like a flash of lightning.".

" And how long is it since that happened ? " asked Fernan.

" I remember it as if it only happened yesterday, for I have a good memory.   Memory is a valuable "—

" Alvar ! make use of your memory to remember how I punish stupidities.   Is it long since that happened ? "

" I don't remember the exact time ; but I know it was at the period when the band of the Vengador was proceeding to Burgos."

" And now that you mention the band of the Vengador," said one of the squires, " do you know the news that is going about concerning it ? "

On hearing these words, all tried to get their horses as near as possible to him who pronounced them.   This general anxiety to learn something of the band of the Vengador, showed that it had acquired such importance that public attention in Castile was fixed on it.

" What news of it have you ? " was asked with lively curiosity.

" You must know, as has been related to me by men-at-arms coming from the neighbourhood of Carrion, that the Vengador has now got together more than three hundred bandits, and with them he not only laughs at the Salvadores, but faces them, and has even defeated them in two skirmishes, so that the Count of Carrion, seeing his district and even his castle threatened, proceeded to it with the greatest speed, having left Burgos, where he had recently fixed his residence."

" Perhaps," observed Fernan, " the bandits caused the count to leave Burgos ; but the reason he went off with such rapidity was because he was afraid that the lance of my master might reach him. However, leaving that aside, for it does not much matter, can't you tell me who this Vengador is, who has gained so much fame in so short a time, and who has got together so numerous a following ? "

" As to the Vengador, nobody knows who he is, as he always conceals his face when he is in the presence of persons who are not members of his band."

" I am of opinion," said Alvar, " that, as he conceals himself in that way, he must be a grandee of Leon or Castile, who has become a brigand in order to revenge himself on his enemies."

" It is more probable that he is a civilian, for it is said that he has a mortal hatred for all who call themselves noble, and that he protects the peasantry, and even shares with them what he takes from the grandees."

" But how did he manage to get together such a numerous band, when the Raposo, who is now in hell as he deserves, was never able to get more than twenty to join him."

" Well, then, the reason is—the Raposo was hated by the country people, whilst the Vengador is loved by them."

" May the devil take me if I understand you, comrade. How is it possible that a captain of bandits can be loved by either peasants or nobles ? "

" It is possible, and that is proved by the fact that the Vengador has succeeded in it. The Raposo carried off women ; murdered children and old people, from the peasant to the count, from the curate to the bishop ; he pillaged the cabin of the labourer and the hut of the shepherd, as well as churches and palaces. Therefore all hated him, and did their utmost to deliver him up to the Salvadores, and plotted his destruction in every way they could. Who, that had any respect for his skin, would enlist under such a chief, for he who did so was also abhorred and cursed by all, and ran continual risk of his life? The Vengador acts in quite a different way ; his dagger is never stained by human blood, except in self-defence, or fighting in the cause of the helpless, unjustly oppressed by the strong; the poor man can leave the door of his cottage open; the muleteer can travel safely along the loneliest roads, as there is no danger of the band of the Vengador depriving him of his humble possessions. Inquire how many women the band of the Vengador has carried off, how many churches he has pillaged, and you will be told that such outrages are unknown in the districts which it frequents, since the time that the Salvadores destroyed the band of the Raposo."

"Then if the band of the Vengador does not commit robberies," observed Alvar, "I hold to my opinion, that its captain is some rich grandee; how else could he have money to support it?"

"He does commit robberies, brother; but he does not rob poor people. The Vengador attacks the mansions of the rich and takes from them all that he can. With that he maintains his band, and when he has more than he wants for that purpose, he relieves the necessities of the poor people in his vicinity. That is why the peasants love and respect him; and his band can encamp wherever he likes, without any risk of falling into the hands of the Salvadores. And for the same reasons the number of his followers increases from day to day."

They were still speaking of the band of the Vengador when Alvar, who was fond of saying what he considered witty things, but which were generally very foolish, took it into his head to say something which he believed would create a sensation amongst his companions.

"My friends," he remarked to them, with much mystery, "I desire to impart a piece of news which I believe won't be such for some of you."

All the squires and pages stopped at once their sprightly conversations, in order to listen to what Alvar had to reveal to them.

"My mistress, the Señora Ximena, bears the reputation of being an irreproachable lady throughout all Castile; is not that so?"

"Certainly, and with good reason," was the universal answer; and Fernan added—

"And if any calumniator were to cast a doubt on the honour of my lady, I have a lance here to convince him of it."

"It is not me who would calumniate her," continued Alvar

in the same mysterious manner; "but I must tell you that my master, Don Rodrigo, although he has only just got married, and never had any sweetheart but Doña Ximena, has a son, a fine little chap."

"I vow by Judas Iscariot!" exclaimed Fernan, seizing his lance, fire flashing from his eyes. "What is that you dare to say, you villain, you traitor? Does your scorpion tongue dare to calumniate your mistress, the most honoured lady, not alone of Spain, but of the entire world? For this ingratitude to those who supply you with the bread you eat, you shall die, traitor that you are!"

Saying this, he made a thrust of his lance at Alvar, forcible enough to pierce a wall; but his anger blinded the squire, and caused him to miss his aim; to this also contributed a rapid movement of the page, who threw himself back on his saddle-bow just as Fernan was giving the thrust.

All those who saw what had occurred hastened to pacify the enraged squire, some with words and others by seizing his arms from behind.

"Let me go, let me go!" cried Fernan, struggling to get free, so that he might attack Alvar again, who hardly had breath to excuse himself. At last they quieted him down a little, and he said in threatening accents to the page—

"Speak, you rascally traitor, and retract the calumnies that you have dared to utter against the most honoured of women. If you don't do so at once, I'll spit you on my lance like a sucking pig."

"Calm your anger, Fernan," murmured the page at last. "It was not in my mind to stain the characters of my lord and lady, but to praise the compassionate and kind heart of Don Rodrigo."

"Confound you for a stupid chatterer: have I not told you a hundred times that your roundabout way of stating the most simple facts would certainly get you into trouble some day or other?" said Fernan, understanding at last what the page had intended to convey in his would-be witty style. "Speak out, you fool, and tell us what son it is that our master has."

"The little Moor that he picked up after the battle, when you left us to run after the four big Moors to the ditch into which your horse fell. That is what I was going to speak about, and I was only having a little joke with you, in order to excite your curiosity."

"I swear to you, Alvar," said Fernan, brandishing his lance, "that such jokes may cost you dear, if you persist in them. A respectable page or squire can be pleasant without defaming the honour of anyone, and least of all that of ladies, for even the purest cannot escape calumny."

"And I swear to you," replied Alvar, "that from this day forward I will cut out my tongue rather than say, even in jest, a word against either my mistress or master. My discretion with regard to speaking about people will increase, but my affection for those we both serve can never be greater than it is. But, returning to the little Moor, whom my master has adopted, what has become of him, that we do not see him?"

"He is coming along amongst the captives," answered Fernan; "and, by my faith, neither he, nor the Moorish kings who have been taken prisoners, can complain, for they are carried in litters, as if they were going to the court as conquerors."

"God save us!" exclaimed Alvar; "my master does things, and I am a Moor if I understand them. Some of the Christians are jogging along on horseback, with sore bones, and others are blistering their feet on these roads, hard as those of purgatory, and the Moors are quite comfortable in soft litters."

"You fool, and a hundred times more than a fool, who has given you authority to find fault with what our master does?" interrupted Fernan. "He is so good a subject that he respects even Moors when they bear the name of king,—even though they may be greater Moors than Mahomet himself."

"However, if they were kings before they were conquered, they are now no longer such."

"Good cavaliers, like our master, have more respect for a conquered enemy than for one whom they have still to conquer. No doubt those kings entered our territories pillaging and slaying, but they believed that they were right in doing so, just as we would think the same if we invaded their kingdoms. As to the Moorish child, would you yourself like to see him painfully toiling on amid the legs of our horses. The heart of our master is as tender towards the weak as it is stern towards the strong, and he has thought and acted in a different manner. That poor boy, who has seen his father die before his eyes, and who is being brought into a foreign country at the mercy of strangers, is very unfortunate. On account of his grief and despair, Don Rodrigo ordered that he should be carried in the litter of one of the kings, as the company of one of his own race would naturally be more pleasing to him than that of a stranger. You will see how our mistresses, Doña Teresa and Doña Ximena, will console him when he arrives at Burgos, with those blessed words which they have always ready, to give joy to the sad and consolation to the wretched."

With conversations such as these the squires and pages were proceeding onward, when Rodrigo and those who accompanied him stopped on an extensive plain, at a short distance from Burgos, from which several roads branched off in various directions. According as the different bodies of warriors arrived, they halted in that place, and, when they were all reunited, Rodrigo summoned together the leaders, in order to proceed to the division of the spoils, according to the rules which were observed on such occasions.

As the spoils were numerous and valuable, everyone got a good share, which, with the fact that the division was fair and equitable, contributed much to the satisfaction and pleasure of all who participated in them.

After this the army broke up, each captain marching off his men to his own district. All of them, when departing, bade farewell to Rodrigo with loud and prolonged cheers.

It is almost unnecessary to add that, if the captains of the various bands received such valuable shares of the spoils, that portion which their general, Rodrigo, received was very rich indeed. He then proceeded to Burgos with all that had been allotted to him, bringing on amongst the captives the five Moorish kings, who, according to the "Chronicle," on arriving at Burgos, knelt with great respect before Teresa and Ximena, who were very pleased and contented therewith, and praised the Lord God, weeping with joy on account of the brave deeds which Rodrigo had performed.

CHAPTER XVIII

HOW THE VENGADOR AND RUI-VENABLOS, ALTHOUGH ONLY
BANDITS, THOUGHT AS CAVALIERS

SOME days had passed and the district of Carrion had not experienced any fresh outrages from bandits, when its honest and peaceful inhabitants heard the news of the destruction of the band of the Raposo by the brotherhood of the Salvadores. There was no doubt that the terrible band had been totally exterminated, since its chief, who had often escaped even when all his comrades perished, had been killed in the attack made on them, which has already been described. It is easy, then, to imagine the joy which all the inhabitants of that part of the country experienced, and also that of all those who had to travel through it.

But, when it was least expected, a rumour began to be circulated from mouth to mouth that a portion of the criminals had reorganised themselves in the Sierra de Oca, and had already made forays into the level country. This new band was at first composed of scarcely a dozen men, but on that account it did not inspire the country people with less terror. The band of the Raposo was not much larger, and, nevertheless, it had spread mourning and desolation all over the district. But it happened that the terror of the peasantry, instead of increasing, began to diminish, as the bandits confined their raids to the populous towns and most frequented roads; and for that reason the fear of the wealthy classes increased in proportion. It is not necessary to explain the reason of this, as it has already been done in the remarks of one of the pages in the army of Rodrigo, which have been given in the preceding chapter. What he had told his companions was quite accurate. The band of the Vengador had indeed increased rapidly; it had faced the Salvadores, and even defeated them in different encounters, provoked, as it was said, by the bandits themselves, with the object of avenging the death of the Raposo and the greater part of his followers, who had been killed by them on the hill near the Leon road. The Vengador, protecting, instead of doing injury to the country people, carrying off the herds and crops of the grandees, and even assaulting, sacking, and burning their mansions, was by degrees getting to be loved by the former and detested by the latter. Thus it happened that the band, respected and protected by the poor, and attacking with impunity wherever its leader thought fit, was joined, day after day, by discontented people, adventurers, criminals, and idlers; very many of whom hastened to enlist in it.

Don Suero had received notice of the outrages it had committed in the country about Carrion, and had also learned that the terrible band had just stolen the famous mare of which he was the owner. All this urged him to leave Burgos and hasten on to defend his property, as his castle was situated in the centre of the district, that is in the town which gave it its name. It was now threatened by the bandits, and already other castles less strong than his had been attacked, sacked, and burned by the band.

The fears of the count were not unfounded, as we shall soon see. On the day on which Don Suero hastened his departure from Burgos, fearful also, as Fernan said, of the lance of Rodrigo, the band of the Vengador was assembled in a wood, a day's journey distant from Carrion. That body did not appear to be a band of bandits; judging by its numbers, its arms, and by the orderly way in which it was marshalled, it seemed rather a regiment of a regular army, such a one as the best captain might wish to have under his command in a campaign against the Moors. The bandits were provided with excellent arms, both offensive and defensive, had good horses, and obeyed the orders of their chief like the best disciplined soldiers. He, the Vengador, or, if the reader prefers it, Martin, had retained to himself the chief command of the band, and had appointed to inferior positions in it those amongst his followers whom he considered most suited to fill them; to these he gave the title of captain, calling himself the chief. Two had been appointed captains, both having had considerable experience in military matters, as they had served during several years, as men-at-arms, in the pay of various masters; sometimes in the campaigns against the Moors, and on other occasions in the civil strifes which at that period were unfortunately but too frequent amongst the grandees of Castile and Leon. The name of one of these was Bellido Dolfos, that of the other Rui-Venablos; the first was formidable on account of his vindictive and cunning disposition, the second for his colossal strength, his bravery, and his calmness in the greatest dangers.

The place in which the band was assembled had all the appearance of a regular camp, as tents were set up here and there, over which were fixed military trophies. The Vengador had summoned the two captains to his tent, and was there conversing with them in a very animated manner.

"I have summoned you," he said, "as I desire to have your advice. Do you think our forces are sufficient to attack the Castle of Carrion?"

"Yes," replied Rui-Venablos, "I answer for the success

of the enterprise. What avail the fifty crossbow-men whom the count retains for the defence of his castle, compared with the three hundred brave fellows who compose our band? I am rejoiced to see that you have decided to attack that traitor count, for you must know that our men are beginning to get dissatisfied with you, as you first stirred up their hatred against him, and then prevented them from reducing his castle to ashes."

"I have waited for an opportune moment to undertake that enterprise, so that my vengeance may be complete. The count has not been at his castle since he went to Calahorra, on the occasion of the combat between the cavalier of Vivar and Martin Gonzalez, as he went direct from it to Burgos with the Court. We should have found in the castle two children, eight or ten years of age, and a lady, who is as good as her brother is bad. The band of the Vengador does not wreak vengeance on such weak beings. What advantage could we then have gained by attacking the castle? Plunder it and burn it? That would be but a small punishment in comparison with that which Don Suero deserves. If he were one of those poor grandees, whom the burning of his castle would leave without a home, as he could not build another, the blow would be a heavy one; but the Count of Carrion is one of the wealthiest grandees in Spain. For something more than the frightening of a lady and two children, the plundering of a well-appointed mansion, and warming oneself with the flames of a burning castle, have the men of the band of the Vengador to risk their skins."

"May the devil take us if we understand you!" said Bellido and Rui-Venablos. "If that appears a small revenge to you," added the latter, "of what kind is that which you desire to have?"

"The vengeance which I ardently desire, that which our people are resolved on, and which is demanded by the wickedness of the count, and by the slaughter of the band of the Raposo by the Salvadores, chiefly founded by Don Suero, is his death."

"Certainly, certainly, that is the vengeance we should take," said Rui-Venablos. "But how will it be if the count is in Burgos?"

"The count," replied Martin, "is now in Carrion, and that is why I believe that the opportune time has arrived to attack the castle."

"Let us lose no time, then," exclaimed Rui-Venablos, much excited; "let us hasten to the den of that accursed count; let us break open its gates with our hatchets; and let us plunge our swords into the heart of that murderer of peasants and carrier-off of women."

"We must have revenge on the Count of Carrion, but not in the way you think," said Bellido, who until then had remained silent, and as if thinking over some important project. "The Castle of Carrion is strongly fortified and has brave men-at-arms to defend it. Do you consider it prudent to expose our unprotected breasts to arrows and other projectiles, whilst those who hurl them against us are protected by the turrets and ramparts of the castle? To act so would be excusable if there were not another plan more certain and less dangerous."

"And what is the plan you are thinking of?" asked, at the same time, the Vengador and Rui-Venablos.

"It is this," replied Bellido. "The count fears, no doubt, that some day, when he is least expecting it, we shall make a sudden attack on his castle, and for that reason he will lose no opportunity of reinforcing its garrison. Well then, I will present myself to Don Suero as a soldier who desires to enter his service, and I am sure I shall be well received. Once having gained entrance into the castle, our band shall approach it during the night, and with all possible caution. On a signal, arranged beforehand, I shall open the postern-gate, the band will enter by it, we will surprise the garrison and its inhabitants, and, without any risk, will make ourselves masters of the fortress in a very short time, together with all it contains, including the count."

If Bellido had carefully observed the faces of the Vengador and Rui-Venablos, he could have easily guessed the reception which his proposition would receive. Indignation and contempt were stamped on the countenances both of the chief and of the captain, when Bellido Dolfos concluded the description of his project.

"Brother," Martin replied to him, with an ironical smile, "do you propose this seriously to us, or do you only wish to find out if we are as great cowards as the count whom we intend to attack, for we should be even more cowardly and treacherous than Don Suero himself were we to do what you propose?"

"Yes," said Rui-Venablos, "explain yourself; for if we

have cowards and traitors here it is not necessary to go to seek them at Carrion."

Bellido could not conceal his vexation on hearing these words, although he was a skilled master in the art of dissimulation, when such was necessary for the accomplishment of his ends.

"May hell take me if I do not punish your insults!" he exclaimed, putting his hand on his dagger.

The Vengador and Rui-Venablos quickly unsheathed theirs, and held them directed towards his breast.

"Traitor!" said the former, "if you move foot or hand, you are dead."

Bellido recovered very quickly the command which he almost always exercised over himself, and said, smiling, in an apparently frank and natural manner—

"I knew well that you would not approve of my proposal, for you are loyal and brave, as I like men to be. Comrades, do not condemn me without hearing me. If I said that I made such a proposition in order to test your valour, I should only lie, which I have never been in the habit of doing. I acted in full seriousness, not because it would be pleasing to me to make the attack unfairly, even if those whom we are about to assail are traitors, but because I fear that our forces will be of no avail against the strong walls of the Castle of Carrion, and because I love so much the brave fellows, who trust in our prudence, that I would prefer to shed all my blood, rather than that a drop of theirs should be lost. You might well consider me a coward if I proposed an enterprise to you in which I myself would have little trouble or risk ; but tell me, whose will be greatest in carrying out the project which I described? Do you not think that I shall run more danger than any other member of the band, of being hung on the battlements of the Castle of Carrion ?"

The excuses of Bellido were not of much weight, to speak the truth ; his reasonings were those of one who does not know what to say, and only says something because he must do so ; however, they sufficed to pacify the Vengador and Rui-Venablos, as they, although exercising the by no means honourable profession of bandits, were endowed with a certain amount of good faith, and besides, they knew that it was not a convenient time to do anything that might cause division in the band. Martin therefore answered—

"Brother, let us forget this matter ; I do not doubt your

good intentions. But do not be astonished at our having been filled with indignation and anger on hearing such a proposal made to us, one unworthy of men who have hearts and arms, and which would make us appear to the eyes of the whole country cowards and traitors as vile as the Count of Carrion. There are some who may say, 'Set a traitor to punish a traitor'; but I say, and also all those whose hearts are not cowardly and base would say, that it is an honourable man who should punish a traitor. If you fear to expose your breast to the bolts which will be shot down on us from the crossbows of Don Suero, you are at full liberty to leave the band before it enters on this enterprise; but if not, prepare your arms, inform your men, as we shall also do, that to-morrow at nightfall they are to march upon Carrion; that the count must die, and that his castle must be destroyed; or that we ourselves must lose our lives in the attempt."

"Anger of God!" exclaimed Bellido. "If another had thrown any doubt on my courage, he should e'er this have felt the point of my dagger. With you, comrades, I desire to conquer or to die."

"Right, brother, right!" said Martin and Rui-Venablos, and they held out their hands to Bellido Dolfos, who pressed them, with force perhaps, but we will not say with sincerity, for Bellido was as treacherous as Judas, and sooner or later he was sure to avenge himself, in some cowardly way, on anyone from whom he believed he had received an insult.

A short time after he had left them, he was walking in a solitary place, not far from the encampment, now and then striking his forehead with his clenched hand and muttering a blasphemy, as if vexed by his want of imagination; he suddenly stopped, however, meditated for a moment, more deeply than before, and then pleasure beamed in his eyes and a smile came on his lips, whilst he exclaimed—

"Excellent thought, not one of them shall escape! Oh, my cleverness is well worth the two hundred gold marks! Night is now coming on; I must try to get, on some pretence, to Carrion."

He then proceeded to the tent of the Vengador, and said to him—

"On the Burgos road lives a girl that I am in love with. I should like to see her, in case I may be killed during to-morrow's attack."

"You can go if you so desire, comrade," replied Martin.

"Then I shall depart at once, as you give me permission," said Bellido.

He then went to his tent, as joyful and contented as Rodrigo Diaz could have been when he was returning to Burgos after the battle in the mountains of Oca.

When the night was well advanced he mounted his horse and started for Carrion, although, when leaving the camp, he rode in an opposite direction.

CHAPTER XIX

HOW THE SINGLE PAINT THE LIFE OF THE MARRIED

SOME hours after the events which happened in the encampment of the bandits, as we have just described, the scenes which we are about to relate took place in the Castle of Carrion.

Ten years before the period in which this history commenced, Don Gonzalo, Count of Carrion, died, leaving two sons, the elder named Gonzalo and the younger Suero, and also a daughter named Teresa. Gonzalo inherited the title of count, but also died in a short time, Suero succeeding him, to whom Teresa should be heiress, and after her two boys, both very young, Diego and Fernando, whom Gonzalo, the younger, had left behind when he died.

The heirs presumptive, within a certain degree of relationship, bore the name of *Infantes*, and that is the reason that Teresa and her nephews, Diego and Fernando, appear with that title in the "Chronicle."

Teresa was scarcely eighteen years of age at the time of which we are writing. God had endowed her soul with all the perfections and virtues that an angel might desire, if he left heaven in order to seek a mortal woman as his companion for eternity, just as all those perfections had been denied to her countenance, which are the only charms sought for by men, when they look on a woman as a material being. Teresa, then, was the reverse of her brother, both physically and morally; her soul was all compassion, all love, all sadness. Her face was as white and delicate as her soul, sad as her heart; and her entire physique was languid and infirm, by which the graces she had received from nature were concealed. That sweet and candid dove appeared always desirous of spreading her wings to mount again to heaven. If God had placed a lyre in the hands of Teresa, her soul would have exhaled itself in holy and immortal harmonies. But, alas! the sweet dove lived for ever trembling, threatened by the cruel falcon, and her angelic spirit was suffocating within the gloomy walls of the Castle of Carrion.

There was a narrow window in it, from which could be seen an extensive tract of country, covered with hamlets, the situation of each of which could be at once recognised by its belfry. Teresa delighted in sitting at that window, in order to gaze on the azure of the sky and the verdure of the fields; and to breathe the air sweetened by the perfumes of the flowers. But those were not the sole enticements which attracted her to that window: there were in addition happy souvenirs of her childhood. In the distance, on the slope of a hill, Teresa could see a smiling village; when gazing on it she was reminded of her mother, and tears trickled from her blue eyes; but to this remembrance of the loss of her mother was also joined that of the happiness which she had enjoyed by her side. She recalled to mind the delicious spring and autumn evenings, when her mother and she left the castle alone and went to wander through the fields, for then the affection of their vassals was to the lord and lady of Carrion as the wing of the guardian angel which protects the forehead of the righteous, just as, from the time that Suero inherited the title, the hatred of his retainers was as the sword of the archangel which constantly threatened the head of Luzbel. Teresa and her mother went in those times as far as that village, which could be seen from the castle window; visited, on their way, the cottages of their vassals, one by one, in order to console the sad and succour the needy; and when the sun was near setting behind the hill, they left the village crowned with blessings, and their hearts refreshed by tears of joy and gratitude, in order to return to the castle where the peace and tranquillity of the good, and a father and husband, as loving as he was honoured, were awaiting them. Some of the villagers accompanied them, in order to act as their protectors, till they were near the castle, and there, on the summit of a hill, crowned with evergreen oaks and sown with sweet-smelling herbs, from whence the eye could embrace an extensive view, the mother and daughter seated themselves, to gaze on the plain, illumined by the first rays of the moon, to listen to the songs of the shepherds who led their flocks to the sheepfolds, or those of the villager who was leaving the fields with his bullocks and plough, and proceeding to his home where his wife was impatiently awaiting him, or, if a youth, the loving maiden, who, pretending to her mother that she was going to the fountain, had left her house to meet him in the grove, through which ran the brook that served as a mirror to the country damsels. There also they could hear the toll of the vesper bell from all the church towers which were visible from the castle, and could lend an attentive ear to those numerous mysterious and confused sounds, which arise through the fields even when men and birds are silent.

At that window Teresa was standing, absorbed in her memories of former times, when she heard behind her the pitiful whining of a dog, which was running towards her, as if imploring her aid, and also the laughter of two boys, eight and ten years old, who were following it with much noisy hilarity.

"Poor Leal, what is the matter with you?" said Teresa, going up to the dog, which continued its sad whine. On caressing the poor animal, she hastily drew back her hand, feeling a painful sensation.

At the same time the boys came up.

"Aunt," said one of them, "give us some pins to stick in Leal's other ear."

Teresa knew then why the dog was whining, and understood the reason of the pain which she had felt in her hand when stroking it. The boys had stuck pins in its ear.

"You cruel boys," she said to them, "what has Leal done to you, that you should torture him so?"

"It's to make him sing," replied the elder brother.

"Aunt," said Fernando, the other boy, "give us pins to stick them in his other ear, and you will hear him singing and see him dancing."

Teresa heaved a sigh on seeing such cruelty on the part of the boys, and hastened to extract the pins from the ear of the dog, which ceased its whining and showed its gratitude by caressing her and licking the hand from which blood still trickled, caused by punctures of the pins.

At the same time the bell of the town church tolled for evening prayer. The children continued, with much noise, to make fun of what they had done to the dog.

"Be silent!" said Teresa to them, in a severe tone of voice; "kneel down and pray for your mother."

"What's the good when we won't be heard?" replied Diego. "Our uncle says that when one dies it is just the same as when a dog dies."

"Yes, aunt," added Fernando; "our uncle says that, and you know that he never says prayers."

"Alas!" exclaimed Teresa, filled with grief, "cruel and impious at the same time." She then added, raising her eyes towards heaven, "O my God! have pity on the house of Carrion!"

She then knelt down, and directing her gaze on the blue and star-covered firmament, which could be seen through the window, she prayed fervently, moistening the floor with her tears.

"Alas!" she murmured, shortly afterwards, again standing at the window; "my heart is very sad! I fear and desire, without knowing what! How sad and long the nights are, O my God! Where can Guillen be? He has not come this evening, as usual, to make more bearable, with his pleasant conversation, this solitude which surrounds me. He is the only one who feels compassion for me; he is the sole person here who understands me, for his is the only generous and good heart in the castle. What lofty feeling he has! With what enthusiasm he speaks of everything that is good and noble! The ambition which animates him is worthy of a cavalier. Son of a poor commoner, he has a soul as noble as those of the best grandees of Castile. Happy would be the maiden who could gain his love!"

Teresa interrupted her meditations, as a soft and respectful voice just then asked permission to appear in her presence. The maiden willingly conceded it, and Guillen entered the chamber.

"I thought you would not have come this evening, Guillen, as it is now so late," remarked Teresa in a tone of sweet reproach.

"Pardon me, lady," replied the page, with great sweetness; "your brother, my master, has kept me occupied till now"—

"Well, then," interrupted the sad maiden, with one of her melancholy smiles, "as a punishment for your delay, I desire that you sit down in that chair, and here, near the window, and by the light of the moon, converse with me for a short time, and relate to me the news of Burgos, for you have not yet told it to me."

"Ah!" exclaimed Guillen, moved by the kindness of Teresa, "how generous and indulgent you are towards me, my lady!"

He then seated himself opposite the young lady, near the embrasure of the window; looking, however, at the face of Teresa, he saw a tear still on her pale cheek, a tear which sparkled in the rays of the moon, as the drop of dew suspended on the leaf of a flower shines in the light of the rising sun. Guillen was troubled, and said—

"Lady, have you been weeping? Who has offended you? Tell me, tell me, as I, though a humble page, son of a poor man, have an arm and a heart to chastise anyone who dares to offend my mistress "—

And Guillen stopped, fearing that the sentiments of his heart might tempt him to say something which his position would not warrant.

"No one has offended me, Guillen," replied Teresa, much moved; "I thank you, however, for the interest you take in me, for you are generous and good. I was thinking of my mother, and that is why you have seen my cheek moist with tears."

These words tranquillised the page.

"Will you tell me the news from Burgos?" continued the maiden. "Since the Court moved thither, many things must have happened worthy of being related. I have been told that splendid festivities were celebrated in that city, on the occasion of the marriage of the son of Diego Lainez and the daughter of the Count of Gormaz."

"That, my lady, was the most notable event during our stay in Burgos," answered Guillen in a low voice; "but I cannot venture to speak of it, for you know that your brother, my master, has commanded that the name of any of the family of Vivar should not be mentioned in his castle."

"I know it," said Teresa; "but do not fear, for the count cannot hear you in this chamber. Has the marriage been one of love, or only by order of the king, as some say, in order to prevent feuds which might have arisen between the two families? Do not be surprised at my curiosity, Guillen, for, knowing that the daughter of Don Gome and the son of Diego Lainez are honourable and good, their happiness interests me."

"Oh, they are completely happy, my lady," exclaimed the page. "You must know that Don Rodrigo and Doña Ximena have loved each other since they were children, so you can easily imagine how great their joy must be now that they are united for ever! A garland of sweet flowers must be the bonds of that marriage which joins those whose hearts were already united by love."

An involuntary sigh escaped from the breast of Teresa on hearing Guillen utter these words. She had contemplated in her parents the happiness which the page described in such enthusiastic words, and even without an example like that, her own heart revealed such felicity to her. But, alas! the only thing that Teresa had to expect was that some day her brother would say to her, "I wish you to marry such or such a nobleman; the interests of our family demand it; prepare to go to the altar." And, miserable and resigned victim, she would have to ascend the altar of sacrifice, to which fraternal tyranny was leading her. And even if she had sufficient courage to open her lips and say to her brother, "That which you demand of me is the most barbarous of sacrifices; I do not even know the man with whom you are about to unite me with eternal bonds; the chains which are to bind me from to-day are those of interest, are those of vanity, are those of mean ambition, the tyranny of which may cause my soul to rebel, and look with horror on her most sacred duties. The nuptial blessing should only be the sanction of an agreement arranged beforehand between two hearts. Permit that mine may be united with another which throbs in unison with it, and then I shall be a good wife, and a good mother, and will bless the brother who left open for me the gates of Paradise." Yes, it would be indeed useless to say this to her brother, for that man without God, without law, without pity, would put a gag in her mouth before she had even finished her entreaties, and drag her, mute and helpless, to the altar of the inhuman sacrifice. How could Don Suero understand the yearnings of a soul, tender, loving, and compassionate, as was that of his sister? How could he understand it, who himself did not comprehend what love and compassion were—he who found in violence the only means of triumphing over women?

All these bitter reflections crowded into the mind of Teresa when the page had spoken that beautiful panegyric of a marriage contracted through love. The two young people remained silent for some moments: the thoughts of Guillen were not less sad than those of Teresa : first he thought of the happiness that would be his if Teresa loved him, and if they could be united, and this dream lulled him for a moment ; he then awoke from it, and thought how difficult, if not impossible, the realisation of it would be.   Who was he, to aspire to be the husband of the noble sister of the Count of Carrion, of the Infanta Doña Teresa, whose hand would honour the most noble of the Castilian lords ?   And if Teresa, the goodness of whose soul was of far greater worth than her birth, should ever love him, was she mistress of her own hand ? Would the count, full of ambition, of pride, of hatred for common people, permit his sister to bestow her hand on a poor page, the son of a humble man ?   Then, however, a ray of hope shone upon his mind, for hope and gilded illusions are the inheritance of hearts which are enthusiastic and in love, generous and good.   He repeated to himself what he said to his friends in Burgos on the day of the wedding of Rodrigo and Ximena : "I am young, and not wanting in courage ; I will take a lance and fight against the Moors ; I shall be armed a knight, and then a hundred brave men will follow me ; I shall enter the Moorish territories, shall conquer them, and shall be a lord over vassals, and then Don Suero will not refuse me the hand of his sister."   These foolish hopes, these vain illusions, again strengthened his heart.

"The idea which you have conceived of those bonds is very beautiful, Guillen !" said Teresa, abandoning her gloomy reflections.

"Lady, is it not the same idea which you yourself have formed ?" replied the page.

"You will please me exceedingly if you explain yours to me more fully, so that I may see if it corresponds with mine," said Teresa. "The watches in the castle are so long and gloomy that it is necessary to endeavour to pass them some way or other."

"I shall do so, my lady, if it pleases you," replied Guillen with delight ; for Teresa had afforded him an opportunity of unburdening his soul, of telling her indirectly how he would love her, and what the happiness of both of them would be if a day should ever arrive when they could become husband and wife.

"Lady," continued the page, "what great happiness it would be if the soul could be shown on the palm of one's hand, like a material object !   If it were so, I would say to you, 'Gaze on my thoughts, gaze on my soul, examine its deepest secrets.

And you would read it with one look, you would know it such as it is, you would comprehend the idea which you ask me to explain to you with my lips. In the lives of two married persons, united by love, joy and sadness, pleasures and pains, happiness and grief, are mingled together and become common to both; all sentiments, all feelings are dual, for each thinks and feels for both. The maiden and the youth who have desired for a long time to belong to each other, body and soul, considering such a union as the supreme felicity of this world, and one to which they have been looking forward from day to day, from year to year, and reflecting over its future, from the happy day on which they will be united by the priest, to that on which death must separate them. Both would thus say, 'In the early days of our marriage we shall enjoy all the illusions and joys of both lovers and spouses, and our hopes will be even sweeter than now, for we shall have more confidence in their realisation; new bonds will soon come to unite us closer and closer, and those bonds will be beautiful little creatures, whom we will love as parts of ourselves, and by whom we shall be loved, not alone for the life which we have given them, but also for the ceaseless care and affection which we have lavished on them. We will not feel that our lives proceed on towards the grave, for the plants which the sun of our love has caused to spring up will remain beautiful and luxuriant, above the tomb which shall cover our ashes, as the reproductions of our beings.' Will not the maiden and the youth who have had such ambitions, who have so reflected and have so spoken, consider themselves happy? will they not believe that they shall find that supreme felicity on the day when their hopes begin to be realised, the day on which they become each other's for ever? That, lady, is the way in which I look on the happiness of those who are united to each other by love. I do not even imagine them rich and surrounded by all kinds of comforts and luxuries, although in that case the picture would be still more enchanting, for misery and hard work irritate the soul. I suppose them to be only poor labourers, who by instinct alone preserve their souls pure and open to good and elevated sentiments, for education and intelligence have not perfected and developed their feelings. They live in a rustic hut; the gardens which surround them have been formed by nature, and it is nature that takes care of them. In them grow the carnation, the mignonette, the thyme, the sage, and a thousand other flowers and plants, the perfumes of which rival those of the gardens created and cared for by the hands of man.   There are no trees there planted in rows to form beautiful and shady walks, no fountains of water to sparkle in the sunshine ; but there grow there, scattered and without order, trees bearing cherries, pears, figs, apples, nuts, and other fruits, which exhale rich perfumes, delight the eye, and supply food for the frugal rustics ; and near that poor dwelling is a spring which bubbles from the rocks, and which fertilises the fields and quenches the thirst of those simple people.   The sounds of music and the incessant noise of cities do not awake those peasants, but the crow of the cock, and, later on, the warbling of the birds, which salute the dawn from the leafy trees, amid which the humble dwelling appears like a white dove, half concealed in foliage.   Then the labourer leaves his bed, in which he has enjoyed sound sleep, caused by a good conscience, wakes up his wife with a loving kiss, and impresses another on the smiling cheek of his child, who still sleeps on, and dreams, sometimes imagining he is with his mother, and sometimes that he is with the angels, who, as he has been told, come down every night to watch over him. The father then proceeds to the adjoining field, just as the east is beginning to be tinged with gold and purple, announcing the rising of the sun.   Whilst he is working he hears, coming from his cottage, songs which rejoice his heart.   His wife is singing whilst she performs her household duties, and her songs sound to the ears of her husband as pleasing as the most perfect music, for they are the same which she sang for him in her maiden days, when they lovingly wandered through the woods and fields.   The sun shines fiercely and the work is hard, but the labourer is not discouraged, for hopes encourage him.   In that field which he moistens with his sweat will grow up golden corn which will enrich his granary.   Evening comes on, and then he realises another of the sweet hopes which animate him ; he quits the field and returns to his cottage, where he is welcomed with tenderness and delight by his wife, who has looked forward to that moment as a rich reward for the labours of the day.   What a beautiful picture is then presented by that family, reunited around their hearth !   Lady, my words are too poor to describe it ; your own heart can imagine it."

Oh yes ! the heart of Teresa pictured to itself that which the page could not find words to describe, and understood the scenes which Guillen had so imperfectly sketched.

"Guillen," said Teresa, feeling her heart throb rapidly, "you were right when you said that the idea you had conceived of nuptial bonds sanctified by mutual love was the same as that which I had formed of them. Alas! why were not my parents poor peasants?"

"Why were not mine nobles?" exclaimed the page; and as if frightened by his words, and fearful of revealing to that noble maiden the love which burned in his heart for her, he stood up from his seat, and said—

"Allow me to retire, my lady, for I am sure the count is expecting me, and you know what punctuality he requires from his attendants."

Teresa made no objection, and the page departed.

Was that indifference?

But when Guillen left her side she felt sad and unhappy, in her heart was a great void.

Was that love?

CHAPTER XX

HOW THE COUNT OF CARRION GAINED NOTHING BY BULLYING

JUST at the time when Guillen was describing to Doña Teresa the idea which he had formed of marriage accompanied by love, a very different scene was being performed in the lower portion of the castle, in the room which had been occupied, and was now occupied again, by Sancha, the peasant girl, whose father Don Suero had deprived of his sight. The reader will have suspected who the girl was that the count had carried off from Burgos; it was she who had assumed the name of Aldonza at the time of her flight with Mari-Perez.

The girl was standing at a barred window which looked out on the open country, for the Castle of Carrion consisted of a square turreted tower, without exterior fortifications. At her side stood Don Suero, addressing to her bitter reproaches, to which she was listening with apparent disdain, gazing indifferently on the fields lit up by a very bright moon.

"Ungrateful one," the count was saying, "did the love which I felt for you deserve that you should fly from my side as you did? Were you not the only woman to whom the Count of Carrion ever humbled himself? What was ever wanting to you in my castle?"

"I wanted liberty, and I fled away to seek it; I wanted a father, of whom you, cruel man, deprived me, and whom I have not succeeded in finding."

"And were not those privations easy to be borne, being compensated by the comforts and luxuries which you enjoyed in my castle, and more than all, by the love of the noble Count of Carrion?"

The girl laughed, and replied disdainfully—

"More pleasant to me than the comforts and luxuries of your castle have been the coarse apparel, the poor food, and the wretched habitation of Mari-Perez, for they reminded me of what I had in my childhood; and as to the love of the noble Count of Carrion, that of a poor squire of the grandee of Vivar was much more agreeable to me."

"May you be confounded!" exclaimed Don Suero, scarcely able to speak with rage, for that was the first time that a woman dared to scoff at him, and that jealousy tortured his perfidious heart. "With tears of blood you shall weep over your ingratitude; you shall never again see your father, nor rejoice in that liberty which you sigh for so ardently, nor enjoy any other love but mine."

The girl answered the threats of the count with another loud burst of laughter, which caused his anger to rise to its highest point. Don Suero then placed his hand on his dagger, but the girl threw herself on his neck, changing suddenly her sarcastic words and her disdainful smiles into the sweetest and most caressing smiles and words that a woman can assume, in order to disarm the anger of a man.

"Thus do I like to see you, my love," exclaimed Sancha, —"thus do I like to see you, for you appear to me the handsomest of men when anger animates your countenance."

These words and the caresses of Sancha changed all at once the tiger into a gentle lamb; that woman was beautiful, but she was endowed with an animal and savage beauty, if we may so express ourselves; for that reason did she exercise such a powerful influence over the soul of the count, who set no value on those quiet kinds of loveliness which are the delight of cultivated and pure minds. Between the souls of Don Suero and Sancha there was a marvellous affinity, just as there was one, of a vastly different description, between the souls of Guillen and Teresa.

"Sancha, Sancha!" murmured Don Suero, intoxicated with pleasure, and returning the caresses of the wily peasant girl. "What pleasure can you take in showing alternatively to me hell and heaven?"

"In order that heaven may appear fairer to you, having looked into hell," responded Sancha, redoubling her caresses. "Oh, my love, what happiness awaits us in the Castle of Carrion, if you do not force me to fly from it!"

"Fly from it?" cried the count, almost terrified; "no, no, if you should do so again, this dagger will pierce my heart."

"Let your heart be entirely mine, and then I will love you more than myself and never leave you. You have called me ungrateful just now. How unjust you are, my love! Learn, then, that I did not fly from you to seek freedom, nor even to search for my father: I fled because you bestowed on others the love which I thought should be mine alone. Do you swear to amend your faults, and never again to set eyes on any woman but me?"

"Yes, Sancha, I swear it to you."

"If you keep that promise, my sweet darling, how I shall love you! But if not—I shall eternally hate you, and ever despise you."

A few minutes after Don Suero left the chamber of Sancha, and he might be heard to murmur, "This, this is heaven. They are fools who seek it beyond this life."

Just at this time a voice was heard, calling out, "Hallo! ye of the castle!"

The count heard it, and, as he recognised it, hastened to order that the stranger should be admitted, impatience and uncertainty exhibiting themselves on his visage and in his words. The new-comer was at once introduced into his presence, in one of the most private rooms of the castle.

"You are welcome," Don Suero said to him; "I was expecting you with impatience. What tidings do you bring?"

"Bad," answered Bellido, for he was the man.

"May the wrath of God confound the bandits!" exclaimed the count. "How is it that they can thus go on, mocking the laws, with impunity? Why cannot some means be found to exterminate them?"

"Calm your impatience, my lord, for you must not yet abandon the hope, which my anxious desire to serve you has caused you to conceive. I have proposed to them what we arranged, and they would not accept my plan; on the contrary, they almost threatened my life for having believed them capable of committing an act of treachery, for they look upon the gaining entrance into the castle without fighting as such."

Don Suero broke into loud laughter.

"Since when," he cried, "have bandits become so very honourable? Perchance they have also converted you, Bellido? So much the worse for you, however; for your honour will cost you two hundred gold pieces, which I promised you if you brought the Vengador and his band into an ambush, in which they all might perish."

"Who has told you," replied Bellido, "that I have given up the idea of earning the two hundred gold marks? Do you imagine that Bellido Dolfos, when he undertakes an enterprise, abandons it at the first check? Is it a small matter to have enlisted in the band of the bandits; to have borne hunger, cold, and fatigue; to have been at the very head of the band whilst attacking the castles of twenty other grandees—all to gain the confidence of the Vengador? After all that, do you think I would renounce the fruit of my labours because our plans have met with a slight check? You know me but badly, count."

"Pardon me, Bellido," said Don Suero, recovering the hope which he had almost completely lost. "I am so unlucky that I thought there was no further expedient."

"We have still hopes."

"Tell me, then, what they are."

"I shall do so, if you listen to me without getting impatient."

"Speak, then, for I am very desirous of hearing you."

"The Vengador indeed spurned my proposal, but there is another way to ensure the destruction of the band. We have arranged that the castle shall be assaulted to-morrow night. The plan adopted is to force the postern, to seize on the men-at-arms who guard the castle; all this would be an easy matter, as the Vengador has three hundred bandits, and the garrison of the castle consists of only fifty crossbow-men. Well, then, I have thought out a very simple plan to dispose of the band: arrange the postern in such a way that there will be but little difficulty in forcing it open; loosen the stones of the arch which covers the first chamber inside that gate, so that, on letting a heavy stone fall violently on the upper part of the arch, it may give way at the opportune moment; and finally, secure well the door between the first and second chambers. As soon as the brigands get in through the postern, they will rush to the next door, and whilst they are occupied in forcing it open, the arch will crush down upon them, and they will almost all be annihilated beneath the heavy stones, to the weight of which will be added that of those which will cause the arches to give way."

"Bellido," exclaimed the count, filled with enthusiasm, and extending his hand to the traitor, "I congratulate you, and I am in thorough accord with your plan, which appears to me to be an excellent one. What a joyous day it will be for me when I succeed in exterminating that infernal band, which is a perpetual nightmare to me! It is not two hundred golden pieces that I will give you, but three hundred, as soon as your scheme succeeds as well as we both hope it shall."

"I can rely upon you to carry out exactly the instructions which I have given you. You will not forget that the attack is to take place on tomorrow night?"

"I shall not forget it, Bellido; nor shall I forget either to have the three hundred gold pieces ready counted for you. Take care not to enter the postern at the head of the band, for it would be very ungrateful of me to wish you ill, when you are serving me so well."

"You may be quite sure I shall not do so; I shall remain outside, and if the door has not been closed after the bandits enter, I shall take care to shut it and also to bolt it outside, so that none of them may get out when the arched ceiling is about to fall."

A short time after, Bellido Dolfos returned to the camp of the bandits.

As soon as he had sent the traitor away, and when almost all were asleep in the castle, Don Suero summoned one of his servants, who acted as architect whenever repairs had to be carried out in the castle, and gave him instructions as to what was necessary to be done to the arched ceiling of the chamber which was to serve as the sepulchre of the bandits. During what remained of the night heavy hammering could be heard in the direction of the postern, and before morning everything was arranged as Bellido had ordered; the key-stones of the arch had been loosened, two enormous stones had been suspended over it, by means of pulleys fastened to the roof, and the postern had also been manipulated so that it could be pushed open without much force, and afterwards bolted outside.

Notwithstanding the certainty which the count felt of destroying the bandits by the ingenious plan which Bellido had devised, he was very uneasy, when he reflected on the insult which he had offered to Rodrigo Diaz by calling him a coward, and he doubted not but that De Vivar would endeavour to take revenge on him. All this weighed heavily on the mind of the count, as he feared the serious consequences which it might bring upon him.

He was thinking on this, when he was informed that four cavaliers had arrived at the castle from Burgos, and that they were the bearers of a message for him. The greatest fear seized on Don Suero when he received that announcement, and, as he did not at once reply to the servant who was awaiting an answer, the latter ventured to say to him—

"My lord, what reply shall I bring to the messengers?"

"May hell swallow me!" exclaimed Don Suero, violently stamping on the floor. "I should like to have the entire human race in my power, to destroy it with my hands!"

Thus speaking, he sought for a dagger in his girdle, and not finding it, he took up a stout piece of wood, which lay amongst those beside the fireplace, and gave several blows to the unlucky servant, who bore them resignedly, persuaded that submission was best when the count was in a passion.

When he had treated his servant in this unjust manner, he sat down beside the fireplace and remained for some instants buried in thought; he then suddenly exclaimed—

"No, I shall not fight with him; Martin Gonzalez was stronger and more skilful than I. . . . . Lucifer protects De Vivar."

Having said this, he raised his head, and seeing the servant, who was still patiently awaiting his orders, he added—

"Are you still there, fellow?"

And he was about to take up again the piece of wood with which he had belaboured his shoulders; suddenly, however, abandoning his threatening attitude, he said—

"Pardon me, Gonzalo; I have beaten you, not knowing what I was doing; introduce to my presence those cavaliers, or whatever they are."

The servant obeyed, and a minute after Antolin Antolinez,

Alvar Fañez Minaya, and two other cavaliers, also of Burgos, stood in the presence of Don Suero.

"To you, Don Suero Gonzalez, Count of Carrion," said Antolin, "Don Rodrigo Diaz de Vivar sends us,—he whom you insulted in Burgos, by calling him coward and low-born "—

Don Suero interrupted Antolin Antolinez, saying humbly—

"Certainly, I called him coward, not knowing that it was he; for my anger, at seeing my servitors ill-treated, blinded me."

"Don Suero, you must give this apology to the offended on the field of battle, and not here," replied Antolinez.

"For two cavaliers to engage in deadly strife," answered the count, still humbly, "it is necessary that they should hate each other, and I have no rancour towards De Vivar, nor do I consider him a coward or low-born ; on the contrary I acknowledge him to be one of the bravest and most honourable cavaliers of Castile."

"If, then, you believe that," said Antolin Antolinez, "publish it, and make it known in all parts. Thus only, except by fighting face to face, can you satisfy the offended. The honour of De Vivar is of such value that its master will defend it with the greatest ardour."

"Do you believe that the humiliation, which you propose to me, should be inflicted on a good cavalier, such as I am ? "

"And do you believe that a good cavalier, such as Don Rodrigo is, should be called a coward with impunity? No, no, as God lives ! If Rodrigo Diaz is not himself able to avenge the insult which you have cast on him, there are a thousand cavaliers in Castile ready to unsheath their swords in defence of his honour. Listen, mean and calumnious count ! Don Rodrigo Diaz de Vivar challenges you to single combat, and tells you that, if you do not accept the challenge, he will put up notices all through Castile and Leon, denouncing your villainy and cowardice to the execration of the public."

"Be silent, be silent ! and do not force me to add fresh insults to those which I addressed to De Vivar in Burgos," exclaimed Don Suero, abandoning the submissive tone which he had hitherto used.

"In fine, what is your reply to him who has sent us ? "

Don Suero stood up with haughty demeanour, and answered, with supreme disdain—

"Tell De Vivar,—tell him that he may do what suits him

best; tell him that the Count of Carrion does not choose to fight with so base a cavalier."

"We have delivered the message of Don Rodrigo, and we shall carry back your reply to him," answered Antolin Antolinez; and he and his companions immediately set out on their return journey to Burgos.

They had scarcely left the castle when Don Suero began to meditate on the reply which he had just given; he thought on the stain of cowardice which would be cast on him, broke out into furious imprecations, and maltreated in a barbarous way the first servants who presented themselves to his sight. Very soon, however, his rage changed into discouragement and terror, and he wept like a weak woman. But the hope of destroying the bandits on that very night roused up his spirits, and, full of that subject, he ceased to think on the challenge of Rodrigo.

Two days after, Rodrigo Diaz caused proclamations to be posted up throughout Castile and Leon, publishing the cowardice of Don Suero, and returning, with interest and the greatest justice, the insults which he had received; two days after, the Count of Carrion, who before was well hated by some, was now abhorred by all; two days after, the country people were singing the ballads which the troubadours had composed, setting forth, in the blackest form, against Don Suero, the question between him and De Vivar.

CHAPTER XXI

HOW ONE MOOR REMAINED, AND FIVE WENT AWAY

Two days had passed from the time that Rodrigo entered Burgos with the spoils which he had taken in the mountains of Oca, and Teresa Nuña, Ximena, Lambra, and Mayor were amusing themselves, talking to and caressing the Moorish boy, saved by the kind-hearted Castilian general on the field of battle. The boy was very handsome, and spoke the Romance language with tolerable facility, as he had learned it from the Christian captives who had always been servants in the house of his father.

Those kind women had received him well, as Fernan prophesied, and lavished on him all the caresses which a tender mother has for her children when she sees them sad and disconsolate. The poor little fellow, who, notwithstanding the kind manner in which Rodrigo treated him, had been sad and downcast, now recovered courage and joyousness; and even tears of gratitude and pleasure sprang from his beautiful and expressive eyes. Lambra was almost mad with delight on account of the handsome boy; the honoured and faithful dueña, who had envied a thousand times the happiness of mothers who had children to caress and to be caressed by, saw in anticipation the joy she would experience when her mistress and Rodrigo would be married, a joy which was her golden dream, and which would consist in having children by her side, to whom she could be, in a certain sense, a mother. Even Mayor participated in the contentment of her mistress and of the dueña, for without doubt she saw in that pretty child what she hoped the fruit of her love for Fernan would be.

The tender sympathy which binds children to women certainly moves and consoles the soul, whether those women are mothers or those who have never experienced the pains and delights of maternity. A poor, unprotected child often appeals in vain to the heart of a man, but never to that of a woman. When, covered with rags, shivering with cold, and famished with hunger, it appeals to public charity in the streets, let us count the men and the women who aid it, and we will see that the number of the former is very much less than of the latter. What consoling words often escape in such cases from a woman's lips!

"Have you no mother?"

"Poor little angel!"

"Alas for mothers who have given birth to children, to see them thus!"

Such as these are the words which the lips of women pronounce over the unhappy child.

Let us bring back our memory to the calm days of our childhood, let us bring to mind what sex it was that dried our tears, impressed kisses on our cheeks, lulled us to repose with songs, watched over our sleep, took part in our games, divined our wishes in order to satisfy them, wept when we were in grief, and celebrated with deep contentment our good health and joy. The name of a woman will be always bound up with those recollections, whether it be that of our mother or of some other. God, who foresees everything, who never entirely abandons the weak, has given the child a mother in almost every woman.

Let us wander through the streets, let us go into villages, let us enter the dwellings of the wealthy, and then let us pass on to the cottages of the poor—wherever God has not given a vulgar and stony heart, we shall find the essence of poetry and of sentiment in the multitude of names with which, everywhere, women express their tenderness for children.

"My love!" "My delight!" "My treasure!" "My glory!" they exclaim, kissing with rapture the rosy cheek of an angel. And those names, not studied, but rushing spontaneously from the heart, are they not of more value than all the loving expressions that poets have ever invented?

The sentiments with which children inspire women raise them above vulgar surroundings, and purify their souls with the holy fire of poetry. When we see women filled with such feelings, let us ask them why they love children, and they will reply to us with these words, or similar ones—

"Because, when we seek for angels on earth, we can only find them in these little children."

If for other qualities, for other virtues, for other attractions, women do not merit the love and respect of all generous and good souls, they deserve it for the sympathy which children awaken in their hearts.

Let those be blessed and loved who understand and experience the feeling which moved the lips of the divine Nazarene when He said, "Suffer the little children to come unto Me!"

"Ismael," said Ximena to the Moorish boy, "did you ever know your mother?"

"Yes, kind Christian; she was beautiful and good, and loved me as you do; but Allah took her to Paradise just at the end of the last Ramadan."

"Son of my soul!" exclaimed Teresa Nuña, "and did you love her much?"

"Ah yes," replied the child, "and yet she did not take me with her."

His eyes overflowed with tears, and he continued—

"When holy Allah called her to Paradise, my father and I

wept very much. A short time after the king was enrolling people for the war, and my father asked me, 'Would you wish to go see your mother?' 'Oh yes,' I answered. On that very day he took me up behind him on his horse, and we set out for the frontiers of Castile. 'We are going to the war, my son,' said my father to me, on the road; 'I trust that we may be killed in it, for then we shall fly to Paradise, and never again be separated from your mother, who is there.'"

The boy interrupted his story for a moment, bursting into sobs, and then added—

"My father went to Paradise to see my mother, . . . and he too did not take me with him."

"Poor little fellow!" exclaimed the compassionate women, who surrounded Ismael, caressing him and endeavouring to console him, just as affected as he was.

"Unhappy child!" said Lambra; "what he wishes is to return to his own country."

"Would you like to go back to your native country, my son?" asked Teresa. "Do you wish to return to Molina?"

"My parents are not there now," answered the child in a despairing tone. "I wish to remain with you, who are good and loving like my mother."

"Well, then, remain with us; for we will love you, as your mother did, my son."

"How good the Christians are, how good!" exclaimed the child, not knowing how to show his gratitude to those who were pitying and consoling him.

"And would you like to be a Christian?" asked Teresa Nuña.

"If you are to be my mothers, I will adore the Prophet whom you adore. My mother used to say that children should adore the God that their mother adored; and does not the Nazarene, your Prophet, love children?"

"Yes, my son; children are the principal objects of His love: He delighted, when He was on earth, to converse with them, He was angry with those who ill-treated them and prevented them from going to Him, and He leaves the gates of heaven always open for them."

"Oh, how good your Prophet is! I wish to adore the Nazarene," exclaimed the child enthusiastically.

Teresa Nuña and Ximena then left him for a short time, feeling sure that Lambra and Mayor would take good care of him while they were away.

Soon after Fernan came in, whilst the two women were

questioning the child respecting his country and parents, and the boy was replying to them with visible emotion.

'By the soul of Beelzebub," exclaimed the squire, "they are simply fools to torment this poor little chap by reminding him of the good things he has lost, which is the saddest of remembrances. That's the way women always understand tenderness; they kiss just as cruelly as they bite. I will ask my mistresses, Doña Teresa and Doña Ximena, to entrust the training of this little Moor to me; he is worth all the Moors in the world. They will soon see how I shall make him a perfect horseman, and also able to give lance thrusts, which will be worth a king's treasure."

The tone of Fernan was rough enough, and his words severe; but the face and manners of the squire were stamped with such frankness and goodness of heart, that Ismael, far from being frightened, ran to meet him, and clasped his legs affectionately with his little arms.

"May I turn Moor," said the soft-hearted squire, "if this young chap isn't worth all the spoils we took in the Oca mountains! Every time I think of it, I feel more inclined to give that fool of an Alvar a good cudgelling for finding fault with Don Rodrigo because he put this splendid little fellow into a litter."

And Fernan took up Ismael in his herculean arms, and kissed him with enthusiasm, saying—

"I would give you a thousand kisses, only that I am afraid of rasping your rosy cheeks with my beard; but I will shave, and then I can kiss you as much as I like. Are you fond of arms and horses, my boy?"

"Oh yes!" cried the child, jumping with joy. "Have you arms and a horse?"

"Of course I have," answered the squire. "To-morrow morning we will go to the stables, and there I will teach you to ride, and to use a lance and sword. I swear by Beelzebub, that when you grow up, you must come to the wars with Don Rodrigo and me, and fight like Bernardo at Roncesvalles."

"Bring me to the stables now," said the child, "and show me your horse and arms."

"You are very impatient, little chap. But I suppose I must humour you; and your vivacity pleases me."

And thus speaking, Fernan took the little Moor by the hand, who was jumping with pleasure and impatience to get to the stables.

"Don't take the child away, Fernan," said Mayor, "for if my mistresses ask for him, they will be annoyed with Lambra and me for not having kept him with us."

And she went to take Ismael by the hand which was free, in order to remove him from Fernan; the squire, however, pushed her away, and disappeared with the boy, saying—

"He will go wherever I please, and all the women in the world shall not take him from me. By the soul of Beelzebub, that is a nice way to train up children—keeping them always tied to women's petticoats! That's the way hens bring up their chickens—and they become hens."

When the squire and the boy arrived at the stables, Fernan showed the horses to Ismael, who was insisting on being put on the backs of all of them. At last, to satisfy the child, Fernan mounted him on Overo, which he saddled, and the animal, with a patience comparable to that of his master, yielded to all the caprices of the child; sometimes quickening his pace, sometimes going slowly, now turning to the right, now to the left. They then went to the harness - room, and Fernan prepared to give Ismael his first lesson in the use of the lance. He made him mount, in a saddle placed on an arm-stand, put into his hand, to serve as a lance, a stick a few feet long, made a mark on a post in front, and fastened a strong piece of cord to the front of the arm-stand; he then gave him, as a shield, the cover of a tin vessel used for carrying water to the horses, through the handle of which he put his arm; when he had thus accoutred him, he lectured him on the proper way of holding both offensive and defensive arms. Then the good Fernan ordered him to prepare to charge, and to keep his feet well in, so that they might not be hurt; the boy did this, and the squire, taking hold of the cord, dragged on, by means of it, the arm-stand and him who was mounted on it, very quickly. The boy made his thrust too soon, and did not strike the mark.

"I vow to Judas Iscariot," exclaimed Fernan, "that he will spoil his best strokes by his impetuosity."

"My horse did not gallop fast enough," replied the child.

"Well, then," said Fernan, "get ready for a second charge, and take care not to miss your aim."

"You will see, you will see how I shall hit the mark this time."

The little Moor got ready again, and Fernan pulled the cord more rapidly than before; Ismael, however, made the thrust too soon, and went even farther from the mark than on the first occasion.

"By the soul of Beelzebub," cried the squire, stamping fiercely on the ground, "that would put holy Job himself out of patience. He thinks, I suppose, that he will do better by making his thrusts too soon."

"I won't charge any more now," said the boy, more vexed by his own want of dexterity than by the annoyance of Fernan. Then throwing away the tin cover and the stick, he began to run back to the place from which the squire had taken him.

"Come back, my son, come back," cried Fernan; but it was in vain, for Ismael was already with Lambra and Mayor.

"Curses on my impatience!" exclaimed Fernan, giving himself a cuff on the side of his head. "What else could the poor little fellow do but run away from me, when I treated him worse than a slave?"

He then went off in search of the little Moor, and shortly afterwards they were playing together as if both were children.

Whilst Fernan was thus amusing himself with Ismael, another scene, not less interesting, was being performed in a large apartment, in which the De Vivar family usually assembled. Rodrigo was relating to his parents and to his wife the innumerable brave deeds of his soldiers at the battle of Oca, remaining silent as to his own, for the noble cavalier was as modest as he was valiant. He spoke also of the bravery of the enemy, for he was so just and honourable that he could not refrain from praising merit wherever it might be found.

"The hostile army," he said, "was numerous; but there were very many who fought for no other cause but that of pillage, and it was those who first turned their backs on our swords and lances. The Castilian troops fought with great bravery; but the victory could not have been won so soon if the enemy had had a few hundred men as brave as their leaders. Those Moorish kings, whom I brought here as prisoners, in order that they might do homage to my parents and to my Ximena, for you are all worthy of it—those kings, I say, and especially Abengalvon of Molina, fought as valiantly as the most perfect cavaliers in the world."

"Oh, how unfortunate they are, and how worthy of being well treated!" exclaimed at the same time both Teresa and Ximena, whose souls were always inclined to compassion.

" For that reason," said Rodrigo, " I have treated them not as wretched captives, who are generally loaded with chains, but as kings, to whom those who receive them in their houses allot the best apartments, believing themselves honoured by having them under their roof; for that reason I intend to restore them to liberty this very day, if you, my parents, and you, Ximena, approve of my resolve."

" Yes, Rodrigo, yes," exclaimed all, with pleased accents. " Sad captives !" added Teresa. " In their own land they have, most likely, wives, children, or parents who weep over their absence, believing them dead or lost to them for ever."

" My son," said old Diego, giving his trembling hand to Rodrigo, and visibly affected, " your heart is worthy of a cavalier; not in vain was I the author of your being, not in vain does my blood run in your veins, not in vain are you descended from the noblest race of Castile. Oh, if Lain Calvo, your grandfather, could raise his noble head from the sepulchre ! During my long life I have constantly laboured for the cause of Castile—to make it greater and better—for the honour of our house, and for the triumph of the faith ; and God has amply recompensed me by giving me a son as good as you are. My strength is failing, my breathing is becoming difficult, my term of life is but short; but what is death to a cavalier when he dies honoured, as I am, and when he leaves a successor as good as you are? Restore to freedom at once those royal captives ; in the eyes of your father, and in the eyes of all that are good, such an act of generosity will be one of your best triumphs."

Yes, Diego was right ; on that day Rodrigo achieved one of his noblest triumphs, for to him, the most affectionate of sons and the most loving of husbands, the greatest glory was the words which he heard from his parents and from his wife, and the pleasure which they experienced by his act.

" Dear parents and dear Ximena," he said, as moved as they were, " let us go now to set the captives free. If they wish to acknowledge themselves our vassals, let them do so, but if not, they shall be equally free."

Rodrigo and his family then proceeded to the prison of the Moorish kings. We have said to the prison, but the apartments of Abengalvon and his companions did not deserve such a name. They were situated in the ground floor of the building, having an entrance into beautiful gardens, and were certainly in every respect suitable for kings. Rodrigo and his family descended to them by a wide staircase, which placed in communication the two habitable floors of which the building consisted, and then requested permission of the Moors to be permitted to present themselves to them. The royal captives came forth to meet them with signs of respect and apprehension, and were about to prostrate themselves before Rodrigo; but he prevented them, with kind words, which filled the hearts of the Moslems with confidence and gratitude.

"The chances of war," he said to them, "placed your destinies in my hands, and for that reason it is my right to dispose of you as I may wish. Do you acknowledge that right?"

"We are your slaves," humbly answered Abengalvon, who was more conversant than the others with the Castilian language, and who was also the youngest of the five Moorish kings, as he was only about five-and-twenty years of age.

"Well, then," continued Rodrigo, "you were my enemies when I conquered you on the field of battle, but you fought with valour, and you bear the title of kings; for these reasons I treated you all, not as slaves, but as friends."

"Who would not be ambitious to be considered as such?" exclaimed Abengalvon.

"My desire is to be your friend," said Rodrigo. "Know," he continued, "that I consider myself so good a subject, that I love and revere all who bear the name of king, and I should consider myself dishonoured if I retained kings as prisoners, even though they are Moors, enemies of my faith and of my country. Return, then, to your kingdoms, and be, according as your hearts may dictate, my friends or my enemies. I comply with what my heart, and the hearts of my parents and wife, whom you see here, dictate to us."

"Oh, blessed Allah!" exclaimed the Moors, raising their eyes, moist with tears, to heaven. "The prayers of our children and wives have reached you and caused you to feel compassion for love and misfortune. We shall sound the praises, in the midst of our families, of the noble Christian who to-day teaches us to be generous and good."

And Abengalvon continued, addressing Rodrigo—

"No, we shall not be your enemies; we desire to become your vassals, as such to respect you and to pay you tribute, and also to become your friends, in order to love you. Let us kiss your hand."

"Come to my arms, if you believe me worthy of yours!" exclaimed Rodrigo, as much moved as the Moors were.

They embraced him, weeping with joy, as did also the honoured old Diego Lainez, Teresa, and Ximena, who were looking on the scene with much emotion, and whose hands the Moors then kissed, manifesting that they felt honoured by being allowed to do so.

"Mother!—Ximena!" said Rodrigo a moment after, "open the gates of their prison for those who have been our captives, but who, from this day, shall be our friends."

Teresa and Ximena then went to a door which gave egress to the street, and pulled open the two wings of which it was composed.

"The gate of your prison is open to you," said Rodrigo to the Moors. "Return to your homes, bring consolation to your wives and to your children, and may God be with you, my friends! Outside you will find good steeds to carry you, and squires who will accompany you as far as the frontier, bearing my green standard, so that neither nobles nor peasants shall dare to molest you."

"We are your vassals, and every year you shall receive tribute from us," said Abengalvon.

He and his companions then left the palace of De Vivar, their eyes dimmed with tears, and blessing Rodrigo, Diego, Teresa, and Ximena with all the fervour of which their souls were capable.

CHAPTER XXII

HOW THE BAND OF THE VENGADOR ATTACKED THE CASTLE OF CARRION

THE band was advancing towards Carrion just at nightfall, in order to make the attack on it at the hour arranged by the leaders, of which attempt Don Suero had received notice, thanks to the treachery of Bellido.

The Castle of Carrion was built on an eminence near the town, beside a road, named at that period the Atalaya Road of Villasirga. Before arriving at it there was found a very thick wood. The night was dark, and for that reason the band could reach that wood without being seen by the sentinels. Martin and his captains, Bellido and Rui-Venablos, ordered a halt to be made in it, with the object of preparing for the attack without being perceived, even though the clouds might clear away and the moon shine forth.

The bandits, all on foot, were provided with steel hatchets, iron-shod clubs, and pikes, with which they might force an entrance into the castle.   Martin had given orders to all not to strike down the count, Don Suero, as he wished to reserve to himself the consummation of the vengeance which he so ardently longed for; he wished to bury his dagger in the heart of the murderer of his father.   The band was divided into two well-ordered companies; one was to rush on in order to force open the postern of the castle, and whilst this operation was being carried out, the other was to protect the attacking body, discharging their arrows against the loopholes and battlements of the fortress, in order that the crossbow-men who guarded them might be wounded, or, not seeing their opponents, might shoot at random.   Rui-Venablos, who always considered the most dangerous position the best, asked permission to lead the attacking body, and Martin went with him. Bellido, therefore, commanded the other company.

Thus arranged, the bandits issued forth from the wood, and immediately the cry of alarm was given in the castle, and the defenders hastened to the combat.

Some of the bandits fell to the ground, pierced by the first arrows discharged from the fortress, and this circumstance increased the courage of the band.   As the obscurity was very great, and as the ground behind the castle—that is, where the postern was situated—was covered with bushes, Bellido succeeded in separating himself from the men whom he was commanding, and in hiding behind some shrubs, where he remained until his companions all passed forward, discharging a cloud of arrows against the castle.   Rui-Venablos, Martin, and their company at last succeeded in reaching the postern. This was strengthened outside with iron plates, on which the bandits began to deal terrible blows with their iron-covered clubs.   It was not necessary to continue to do this long, as the door soon gave way, the bolts which kept it shut having, seemingly, been broken.   Then the entire band rushed in, uttering fierce cries of fury and wild joy.   It was, however, found necessary to force another door in order to get from the place where they were into the interior of the castle, and that door was even stronger than the outer one. Martin was furious when he met this new obstacle, just as he believed the moment had come to avenge himself on the count.

"Break it, burst open the door quickly!" he roared to those who were provided with clubs.

Those then began to discharge furious blows on the door, which did not yield in the least, for it was also well strengthened with iron outside, and securely fastened inside with thick bolts of the same metal. Impatience became a torture to the heart of the Vengador, and, taking a club from the hands of one of his men, he began to wield it with the strength of a giant against the door. At that moment a fearful blow was heard above the arched ceiling of the apartment in which they were, a blow which made the entire edifice tremble, a blow so terrible that it almost seemed as if the whole castle had crumbled down above their heads. All the bandits uttered a cry of terror, except Martin, who continued his assault on the door, for he only heard the voice of vengeance, which was commanding him to execute his on Don Suero, so terrible that he might expiate by it the innumerable crimes which he had committed.

"Out, out! the arch is falling!" cried all the bandits, precipitating themselves, in fearful disorder, towards the outer gate, for indeed the roof was yielding, the stones, as we know, having been loosened under the blow of the enormous weight which had fallen on them. At the same moment some person outside fastened strongly the postern-gate; but just then the second door yielded to the blows of Martin, and he, with Rui-Venablos, and about fifty of their men, rushed into the interior of the castle. The others tried to imitate them when they found that the postern-gate was closed against them, but they had not time, for the arched ceiling came down with a fearful noise, crushing the unfortunate bandits beneath its ruins. A satanic burst of laughter resounded then in the upper part of the castle, and a countenance, on which was depicted savage content, appeared, to gloat over that horrible butchery, at the hole which had been made in the upper floor, in order to suspend through it the heavy blocks of stone which were to fall on the top of the arch beneath.

The laughter had issued from the mouth of Don Suero, and his was the hellish countenance.

The count and the traitor, who had aided him in his work of extermination, did not know that several of the bandits had escaped without injury, and that the second door had yielded and given entrance to them. Soon, however, was this fact made known to Don Suero by the cries and the tumult which he heard in the principal apartments; cries and tumult which seemed to approach the chamber in which he was. Indeed, the Vengador, Rui-Venablos, and their followers, and almost all the armed men who guarded the castle, were fighting furiously in the corridors which led to the rooms usually occupied by Don Suero. Then the most abject terror took possession of the count, for he was as cowardly as he was tyrannical, cruel, and heartless; and running to a secret staircase, he descended into the vaults of the castle, and escaped from them, by a private door, into the open country.

The fight between the bandits and the defenders of the castle was bloody and obstinate. The latter, collected in one of the corridors which led to the apartments in which the De Carrion family resided, resisted the attack with valour equal to that of the bandits. The Vengador and Rui-Venablos, however, filled with fury on account of the destruction of their comrades, and of the resistance offered to them, resolved to make a final attempt, for they must either fight their way onward or die. They rushed, therefore, on their opponents, striking down all who barred the way, and their companions followed their example. Many remained dead or wounded in this bold attack; the others broke through the living wall which their enemies opposed to them, and dashed on, like hungry lions, to the apartments in which they expected to meet their prey. As they did not find him there, they uttered furious maledictions, which terrified even the soldiers who were defending the castle; they, wounded and discouraged, had dropped their weapons, and only hoped to find safety in flight. The bandits, having examined the apartments of the count, left them, believing that he had sought refuge in some other room, and they soon found one with the door locked. This was the chamber of Teresa. They tried to open it, but as it did not yield, the Vengador dealt it a terrible blow with his club, which caused it to fall in fragments on the floor. A young lady, the Infanta Doña Teresa, was standing in a corner, almost dead with terror, and before her stood Guillen, sword in hand, ready to defend the maiden.

"Stop!" cried the page to the bandits. "Hold back, for you shall only get near this lady when some of you have felt the edge of my sword, and when there will be no other shield to defend my mistress but my dead body."

Martin and Rui-Venablos halted; their companions, however, were about to rush on Guillen, but the Vengador prevented them, saying—

"Whichever of you advances a step to injure this young man or this maiden will fall dead at my feet; we do not desire to wreak our vengeance on a weak woman, or on him who defends her."

At the same time a great outcry was heard from the direction of the town. The Vengador looked through the window, which we have already described, and by the light of the moon, from which the clouds that had covered it had just passed away, he saw a numerous body of men approaching the castle. At the same time he heard the voice of Don Suero, who, seeing light in the window, was crying out—

"Defend yourselves, my crossbow-men; succour is coming."

The count had gone to seek reinforcement in the town, and his vassals hastened to give it, for he told them that Doña Teresa's life was in danger. More than two hundred men, of all ages, were advancing with him, armed with the weapons that first came to hand. The bandits were worn out with fatigue, and their number was reduced to little more than twenty. The Vengador knew that the death of all was certain if they did not at once leave the castle. If he had avenged his father he would have thought little of dying, but as he had not yet done so, life was precious to him.

"Let us escape," he cried, "or the count will succeed in killing all of us, and our comrades shall never be avenged. Do you hear those cries? Don Suero has managed to get out of the castle, and he is now returning with such force that his triumph is certain. Many of our comrades, who lie wounded in the passages through which we have come, must remain in his power, for we have not time to succour them and bring them off with us. They will be sacrificed by the barbarous count if we do not take hostages. We have this maiden in our power, and Don Suero will respect the lives of our comrades, in order that we may spare that of his sister."

"The sister of the Count of Carrion," said Guillen, continuing in his threatening attitude, "shall not remain exposed to your outrages whilst I am alive."

"I swear to you that she shall be respected," replied the Vengador, "but I must take measures to save the lives of my comrades. Sheath your sword, and come with her and with us, for if you seek to defend your mistress here you must die, and she will have no one by her side to see that the promise I make you will be kept."

Guillen felt that it was best to follow the advice of the leader of the bandits; he felt that it was necessary that Teresa should have someone by her to assist her if her strength failed, to console her when she wept, to guard her whilst she slept, to protect her if her honour was threatened. He therefore sheathed the sword which he had drawn to defend her, and, sustaining the feeble footsteps of his mistress, he went off with the bandits.

They all left the castle and penetrated into the adjacent wood, just as Don Suero and his vassals entered the fortress, which had been the theatre of such sanguinary scenes. They walked on for some hours by rough and deserted paths, for the bandits, now too few in number to face the Salvadores, feared to meet them. At last they halted in the thicket, which but a few hours before the band had left, full of strength, hope, and valour. During that fatiguing journey the strength of the unhappy Teresa had failed entirely several times, and Guillen was obliged to carry her for considerable distances in his arms, his love giving him force to bear that precious burden, in truth not so heavy as would have been almost any other woman, for Teresa was worn away by sadness and grief.

There still remained there the tents and the other things, which had been left to the care of a few of the bandits who had not been able to go with the others. The Vengador allotted one of those tents to the sole use of Teresa and the brave youth who accompanied her, and he and his comrades lay down in the others, half-dead with fatigue and discouragement, first having placed sentinels in the best positions for such, as they feared that Don Suero's men might have followed their tracks.

All the bandits were soon in a heavy sleep, except Martin and Rui-Venablos, on whom fatigue and grief seemed to have had an effect quite different from that which they exercised on their companions.

"Ah, poor Bellido!" said the former, "he must have found his tomb in the Castle of Carrion. We were fools not to have followed his example; we desired to act as cavaliers, forgetting that we were only bandits, and that we had to do with one of the most depraved and pitiless wretches that was ever born of woman. It is we who should have found our deaths in the castle, and not our loyal and brave comrades who have been the innocent victims of our stupidity. What have we to do now? Only to lament over our error, and the mishap of our companions."

"Anger of God!" exclaimed Rui-Venablos, irritated at the discouragement of Martin. "Does the Vengador become faint-hearted, and does he shed cowardly tears just when the moment has arrived to work with more firmness, with more bravery, and with less pity than ever? Can you avenge our comrades with tears, which suit women well enough, but which are quite out of place in a man; by killing the count I have to avenge our comrades, and something more "—

"I have to avenge our comrades, and something more also, by reducing to ashes the Castle of Carrion and plunging my dagger into the heart of the count," said Martin, excited by the words of Rui-Venablos.

"Thus do I like to see my chief!" exclaimed Rui, filled with savage joy.

"Do not call me by that name," said Martin, clasping the hand of his companion. "Call me brother, for from this day we shall begin to reorganise the band, and it shall have two chiefs. To prove to you how burning is the vengeance which consumes me, and how great is my friendship for you, I will confide a secret to you. Know, then, that I did not join the band of the Raposo in order to exercise the calling of a bandit, and that I did not continue such a life or take the name of the Vengador in order to avenge those who were slaughtered with the Raposo, but to avenge my father, who was vilely assassinated by the count."

Martin then related to Rui-Venablos all that had happened as they were returning from the pilgrimage, when Beatrice was carried off, adding—

"I have kept this secret from our comrades, in order that they might not mistrust me, knowing that I was working for an object different from theirs, and that I was only desirous of avenging an offence solely connected with myself."

"For the same reason," said Rui-Venablos joyously, "I have concealed the true cause of my rancour against Don Suero. You must know, brother, that I also did not embrace the life of a bandit through affection for it, for I always held a more honourable position. I have been a soldier since the down was on my lip, and I have always fought in defence of the faith, of my native land, and of the oppressed; and have never entered into the pay of any but honourable gentle-men. Being in the service of Don Ordoño de Lara, an unfortunate old man, quite blind, came to me one day and said, ' For a long time I have sought a man of kindly heart and with a strong arm, who might feel compassion for and avenge a wretched father, whom the Count of Carrion has deprived of his sight and of his honour.' He then related to me, with tears capable of softening stones, how Don Suero had carried off from him a daughter, who was his sole happi-ness in this world, depriving him at the same time of his eye-sight, in order that he might not be able to find her or avenge so horrible a crime.

" ' I have been told,' he added, ' that your aid has never been asked for in vain by those oppressed by the powerful, and therefore I come to you full of confidence.'

" His words moved me ; I pitied his grief and his misfor-tunes ; I was indignant at the baseness and cruelty of the count, whom I already regarded as an enemy, on account of other acts of a similar kind which had been related to me, and I swore solemnly to the poor blind man to avenge his wrongs. He then departed, full of satisfaction and of hope, to seek his daily sustenance through the country by singing to the accompaniment of his lute. When he had gone, I thought over the best means of keeping my promise to him ; I knew that it would avail nothing to challenge Don Suero, as he would treat such a proceeding with contempt, the challenger being a poor and obscure soldier, and he one of the most powerful grandees of Castile and Leon. Should I seek to encounter him unexpectedly in some lonely place and force him to fight with me ? That also would be unavailing, as Don Suero is always accompanied by armed men to defend him, and my death would have been but a useless sacrifice. Allies were necessary to me in order to attack the Castle of Carrion, and put the count to death, and as, just then, I heard your band talked of, it seemed to me that it would be the best instrument for the revenge I longed for ; I therefore went to seek you, and I succeeded in gaining your confidence."

" Brother," said Martin, rejoiced at being able to call by such a name a man who was actuated by feelings identical with his own, and who would not have embraced the life of a bandit merely to live by plunder, "similar sentiments animate us; the goal for which we are striving is the same; our strength and courage are equal, wherewith to confront the difficulties which we may find in our way. Perhaps Bellido would have brought the same ambition to the band if he had been inspired by some noble sentiment."

"Comrade," said Rui-Venablos, "you are exceedingly simple, and by no means a good observer, if you imagine that any kind of noble sentiments are to be found in Bellido. He is dead, and it is just as well that he is. I do not like to speak badly of the dead, but nevertheless I say that he was very far from being an honourable man. Did you never observe his cruelty whenever we made an assault on a castle? Our attacks were always directed against tyrannical and evil-living grandees; was there not a vast difference between the way in which you and I treated the conquered, and the way in which Bellido treated them?"

"You are right, brother," replied Martin; "Bellido is dead, and there is another person, who is in great grief here near us, who is much more deserving of our compassion. I speak to you of Doña Teresa, of that unfortunate young lady, whom we have taken with us as a hostage. Her brother and she have always occupied the reversed positions of St. Michael and the devil: the devil held the angel beneath his feet. Yes, the angel, for she is as good and pure as the angels in heaven. That brave and faithful youth, who would not abandon her, will watch over her; but we also must guard her; yes, we must take good care of the innocent dove which has been snatched from the talons of the hawk, and who, nevertheless, weeps because she has been saved from them. Many of our comrades are lying in Carrion, covered with wounds, and it was but just that we should endeavour to save their lives, for the facts of their having been wounded and having shared our dangers are sufficient to make us pity them. We have threatened the count that we will take the life of his sister if he does not spare our comrades and give them their liberty, but if he is barbarous enough to sacrifice them—even in that case Doña Teresa shall return uninjured to Carrion."

"That is the very advice I intended to give you," said Rui-Venablos. "If all men were as generous and good as you are, the world would not be as it is. In what way, indeed, can that poor girl be responsible for the crimes of her brother? In the world, and especially in war, the just have often to suffer on account of sinners, but we must not be guided by so cruel a law.   Certainly, the bandit, when he requires food, must take the bread of his neighbour, but there are plenty of neighbours who well deserve to die of hunger.   We shall take the bread from them and leave it with good people."

"Yes," answered Martin, "and in that way, even though we are called by the name of bandits, our consciences will give us another name ; our consciences will tell us that, when we were forced to choose between two bad roads, we took the better one."

"Do you think, brother, that it is prudent to remain here ? We are too near Carrion, and Don Suero will endeavour to take advantage of our weakness."

"We must only keep on the alert, and not change our encampment for a safer one until those return who remained alive in the castle."

The day was begining to dawn.   Martin and Rui-Venablos knew that it was necessary to recruit their strength, worn out by fatigue and the emotions of that sanguinary night; they therefore stretched themselves on the ground, taking care that their weapons were within reach.   A few minutes after they were sleeping soundly, and the silence which reigned in the ' camp of the bandits was only interrupted by a few words, mingled with sobs, which were heard from time to time in the tent occupied by Teresa and Guillen.

CHAPTER XXIII

IN WHICH IT IS PROVED THAT COLD AND LOVE ARE NOT INCOMPATIBLE

THE following night had arrived, and was somewhat advanced when the bandits retired to sleep.   The much diminished band of the Vengador remained in the same encampment, and Teresa and the page in the same tent.

The night was dark and cold, for it had rained during the evening, and to the rain had succeeded a thick fog, with which the day had ended.   Teresa and Guillen were sitting near some badly-burning pieces of wood, the heat of which could not warm the page, for it was deadened by the dampness of the ground, and by the fog, which penetrated the canvas of the tent, almost like an icy fluid.

Teresa was shivering with cold, and a deadly pallor overspread her face; but a pink circle extended around her sweet eyes, a sign that the unhappy girl had been weeping. Tears also had come to the eyes of the youth, although he had done his best to keep them in. Who would formerly have said that the page, so manly, so brave, so joyous, would one day mingle his tears with those of a weak girl? What an affecting sight was that of the poor maiden, with a body so frail and delicate, accustomed to all the comforts of a castle, almost dying of cold and mental prostration, seated on an icy stone, with her feet resting on the wet earth, her clothes saturated with moisture, and with scarce strength enough to approach her hands to the partially extinguished fire; and then that kind-hearted youth, with the robust body, with the brave soul, accustomed to arms, and to manly exercises, trying to cheer her with his words, and cover her with his clothes, timidly warming the hands of the maiden between his own, reviving the fire which was going out, and, after all, his eyes filled with tears, feeling that all his tenderness, all his love, all his efforts, were unavailing to bring comfort to that delicate girl.

"You are very cold, is it not so?" asked Guillen, with all the tenderness, anxiety, and love with which a father could question a dying daughter. "Oh! to see you dying of cold— I who would wish to see you seated on a throne! Are you very cold?"

"Yes, Guillen," answered the girl, shivering, "I am very cold."

The page, who had already covered Teresa with his mantle, took off a kind of jacket which he wore, and was about to put it also on her.

"No, no!" exclaimed Teresa, "I will not take your jacket; you will die of cold."

"Have no fear for me," said the page, endeavouring to smile pleasantly, "for I am strong, and accustomed to hardships. If I should feel cold, I will put it on again as soon as it has warmed you a little."

Teresa let him cover her with the jacket.

Guillen then considered how he could best keep up the fire. But how could he do it? He did not know what was to be done, but he felt that something must be done, one way or another, for the life of Teresa depended on the fire being kept burning, and his own life also, for he neither hoped nor desired to live if his lady died.

"I am going in search of wood; wait but a few moments," he said to her, and he went out of the tent, walking with difficulty, for the cold was paralysing his limbs. He had advanced a few steps, not knowing in what direction he was going, when his foot struck against a solid body, not hard enough to be either a stone or a block of wood. He examined it with his fingers, and found that it was a saddle; with it he returned, exceedingly rejoiced, to the tent.

"Cheer up, lady," he said on entering; "for I have brought something with me that will make a fire warm enough to put heat into a dead man."

"Oh, how kind you are, Guillen! You always come in time to save me," exclaimed Teresa, with a weak and rather startled voice,—the page, however, did not notice the latter.

He then broke the saddle in pieces; the leather with which it was covered had prevented the rain from reaching the straw and the wood of the framework. Thanks to the former, Guillen was able to light a good fire, even though he had to be economical with the fuel, for it was not plentiful, and the night would be long.

The heat of the fire soon warmed Teresa, and a slight smile began to appear on her lips, which Guillen looked on as the return of life. If the joy that shone in the dark, full eyes of the page could have been seen, one would have believed that these moments were the happiest of his life.

"Ah!" said Teresa, trying to smile, "if you but knew the terror I was in, during the few minutes you were away from the tent in search of wood."

"In terror—of whom, lady?"

"When you went this evening to the tent of the Vengador a bandit approached ours, gazed on me with much attention, and then went away, uttering some words, the meaning of which I did not catch. Then, a moment before your return with the fuel, I thought I saw again the face of the same man over there, at the entrance of the tent; I was about to cry out, but I heard your footsteps, and the face of the bandit disappeared."

"Have no fear, lady," said the page in a pleasant voice, "for the Vengador promised me that he would hang up on a tree the first who tried to injure us, and besides, I have a sword with which I would strike dead anyone who dared to attempt such a thing. Be tranquil, lean against— But there is nothing here on which you can rest your head," exclaimed Guillen in a sad tone; and then he added, timid and stammering, "Pardon me, lady—if you like—lean your head on my shoulder."

"Thanks, Guillen," replied Teresa in a pleased tone of voice; "I do not feel sleepy as yet, but when I do, I will rest myself in the way you propose."

The page raised his hand to his eyes to brush away a tear, and was near throwing himself on his knees before the young lady to thank her for the happiness she promised him.

At the same moment a rough hand quickly raised the piece of canvas which covered the entrance of the tent, and a bandit, with a ferocious countenance and brutal manner, entered. Teresa uttered a cry of terror, for she recognised the face, which she had seen twice before. Guillen seized the sword which lay unsheathed by his side, and asked the bandit threateningly :—

"What do you seek here?"

"Do you know, my gentle youth, that you are by no means courteous to those who try to serve you?" answered the bandit very calmly, and with an ironical smile.

"Go out of this tent at once," said the page to him.

"I have come to spend in it the remainder of the night."

"God's anger! Speak, for what are you come?"

"To relieve guard," replied the bandit, with his sinister smile.

"I do not understand you."

"It is a very simple matter, my gentle youth; as you have acted the sentinel so long a time to this maiden, or whatever she is, I thought that you must be fatigued, and I have come to relieve you for an hour or so."

"Be off, ruffian! be off at once, if you wish to leave the tent alive!" exclaimed Guillen, preparing to make use of his sword; but the bandit replied, still in the same calm tone—

"I shall not do so, my gentle youth, for it pleases me to act as guard over ladies, even though they may be thin and pale, like her who is listening to us. You will see how the colour will have returned to her face by the time you return."

"Treacherous ruffian!" cried Guillen, and he made a thrust of his sword at the bandit, not being able to restrain his indignation; but the fellow stepped rapidly back, and avoided the stroke, then drawing his dagger, he continued, with agile leaps, to avoid the sword strokes which Guillen aimed at him, until, taking advantage of a false move which [Guillen made, caused by the dampness of the ground, he rushed on the page, and succeeded in wounding him in the hand which held the sword. Teresa uttered a piercing and dolorous cry on seeing Guillen wounded by the bandit; but the page, far from losing his courage on feeling the point of the dagger in his hand, rushed violently on his opponent, and reached him twice with his sword, wounding him slightly. A furious fight was just commencing, when the Vengador and Rui-Venablos suddenly entered the tent; the former seized the bandit by the neck with the strength of a giant, and threw 'him out of the tent, saying—

"Traitor, you shall atone for your villainy with your life. Do you imagine that this youth alone guarded the lady?"

The page then approached the young girl.

"You are wounded, Guillen!" she exclaimed, as soon as her terror allowed her to open her lips.

"It is nothing, lady," replied the page, trying to conceal his hand; "it is but a slight scratch, which I scarcely feel."

"No, no, Guillen; you must let me bind it with my handkerchief. Oh, my life would be but a small thing with which to repay your sacrifices for me!"

Then Teresa took hold of his arm and forced him to let her bind the hand, which she did with her handkerchief, which was wet with her tears.

The page blessed, in the depths of his heart, the dagger of the bandit, which was the cause of his receiving such care from Teresa, whose eyes were shedding tears for him, for the humble servitor, whose blood no other mistress but Teresa would have considered of any value.

"Guillen, Guillen, for how many sacrifices am I not your debtor! how good, how generous you are!" exclaimed the noble girl, raising her mild, moist eyes to the youth, with such an expression of gratitude and love, that the page was overcome with joy, and, not without much difficulty, he murmured—

"You owe me nothing, lady; my life is worth less than the least of the kindnesses which you have shown me."

"See, Guillen," interrupted Teresa, with an affectionate, almost childlike tone of voice, "you must not call me lady, for—I know not why—but I do not wish you to call me by that name. How am I to be your lady, when you are my sole protector, my saviour, my angel guardian? I cannot explain it, Guillen, but I feel an immense void in my heart whenever you call me by that name. For a long time I have recognised in you, not a servant, but a loyal and loving friend, and now even the name of friend seems to me cold and ungracious. If the word 'brother' did not make me tremble, if it were not so odious to me, I would call you by that name, Guillen, for it would express the feelings which your affection, your unselfishness, and your protection inspire in me. Ah, Guillen! do not call me your lady, call me simply Teresa."

The page knelt down before her, overcome by gratitude, by joy, and by love.

"Well, then," he said, "I will call you Teresa, I will call you the holiest and the kindest of women! I also find it necessary to call you by a name which expresses the feelings of a heart full of gratitude, of happiness, and of"—

The page stopped suddenly, for the word "love" was about to escape his lips, and who was he, to make a declaration of love to her, the noble heiress of the countship of Carrion? A poor page had little claims on the love of one of the noblest ladies of Castile and Leon, simply for having amused her a short time, now and then, with his conversation in the Castle of Carrion; for having accompanied her to the camp of the bandits, when she was carried off by them; for having spent four-and-twenty hours in that tent near her, without even having had the consolation of being able to protect her from the rain and the cold; and for having shed a few drops of blood in her defence. If such services deserved a recompense, were they not amply rewarded by the kindness of Teresa, who had carried that so far as to permit the humble page, the son of a poor peasant, to treat her as her equal?

These considerations sealed the lips of Guillen, in order that he might not reveal the intense love which burned in his heart.

"Teresa," he said, after a moment of silence, desirous of changing the subject of their conversation in order to conceal his feelings, "it is now late, and you have need of sleep, even for an hour or so; who knows but that we shall have to pass all to-morrow in travelling to the mountains of Oca?"

"You are right, Guillen," she replied; "but you think only of me, and not at all of yourself. Have you not also need of rest?"

"I shall sleep at the same time as you, for we need now

have no anxiety; you know that the leaders of the bandits watch over us," said the page, sitting down beside the girl, so that she might rest her head on his shoulder, as had been arranged between them.

Teresa understood the intention of the page, and leant her head on his shoulder.

What Guillen felt at that moment may be understood, but it is difficult to explain it; it is not necessary, however, to do so. We can comprehend it if we identify ourselves with him, in his love and in his situation; we can comprehend it if we have not souls of ice and hearts of stone; we can understand it, best of all, if we have kept concealed for a long time in our breasts a love, as pure as it was ardent, equally distant from triumph and from despair.

Almost at once a deep and calm sleep fell upon Teresa, for pure consciences and innocent souls find in the peace of their night's sleep compensation for the cares and troubles of the day.

Whilst Teresa slept, leaning her head on his shoulder, the page would not have exchanged his happiness for that of the most powerful of the Castilian counts; for that of Rodrigo Diaz; for the crown of Don Fernando. To feel on his shoulder the head of the maiden, to breathe her breath, to be able to put his lips timidly on her hair, to feel the beatings of her heart! Oh! the empire of the world would have been but a small happiness for Guillen, compared with that which he experienced during that short space of time.

The fire had nearly gone out, as the page had not been able to feed it, fearful of awakening Teresa by making the slightest movement. The chill of the morning, which was approaching, at last aroused her. She, believing that Guillen was asleep, removed her head very gently from his shoulder, but, seeing that he was awake, said—

"O, Guillen, how peacefully I slept resting on you! I dreamed that this tent was the cabin of the labourer, which you pictured to me a few evenings ago, and that I was not the Infanta of Carrion, but a poor and simple country girl."

"Ah! would to God that you were!" cried Guillen, full of enthusiasm and scarce knowing what he said.

"But I remember that it is only a very short time since you said you would like to see me on a throne," responded Teresa, with an affectionate and pleasant smile.

"Oh, pardon me, lady—pardon me, Teresa, if my natural

rudeness has made me say a stupid thing," said Guillen. "I only meant, that perchance you would be more happy if that dream were a reality,—and I also would be more happy if such were the case," he timidly added.

The love of the page was so great that his heart was scarcely large enough to contain it. The life which Teresa had reminded him of, that life, rich with peace and with love, which he himself had sketched—sketched only, for although he conceived it in all its beauty, he had not skill enough to paint it in its completeness; that life, we repeat, presented itself to his eyes, and the enamoured youth had not the power to conceal his love any longer.

"And why, Guillen," asked Teresa, "why would you be more happy if I were a poor peasant girl?"

"Because then I could always call you Teresa, and would be at liberty to love you as no man ever loved, in the world," replied the page enthusiastically.

"Guillen!" said the Infanta in a voice trembling with joy and emotion, whilst a glow of colour overspread her pale cheeks, and her blue eyes shone with unusual brilliancy, "Guillen! I have already told you, that for you I shall be only Teresa."

"My God!" exclaimed the page, falling on his knees before her, and raising his eyes, moist with tears. "I am the happiest of men!"

He then added, looking up to her—

"Well, then, I will love Teresa now, whilst I am but a poor peasant, and the Infanta of Carrion, when I shall be worthy of her."

"And why should you not love her now, Guillen? Is it a crime for a man of humble birth to love the daughter of a count?"

"It is not so in the sight of God, but it is so in the eyes of men, Teresa," he answered.

"Well, then, let us do what God does not find fault with, and let us treat with contempt the injustice and the false laws of men. I, weak and cowardly until now, shall be strong and courageous enough to resist all the efforts of him who should be my protector, but who is my executioner."

"Oh, what happiness can be compared with mine!" exclaimed Guillen, wild, mad, with joy. "I also, weak, and timid, and humble until to-day, consider myself strong and daring, and almost touching the clouds with my brow. Teresa, you are my good angel; you fill my soul with noble ambitions, you urge me on to all that is good and exalting."

"Guillen, I am no longer an unhappy woman; when I despaired of meeting noble hearts in the world, I found one in you, and loved it as the captive loves the hand that breaks his chains."

The light of day was penetrating into the tent, the morning was very cold, and the fire all but extinguished for want of fuel. Guillen went forth from the tent, almost weeping with gladness, and walked towards some trees which were near it. When he got to them he raised his eyes to the branches of an oak, and saw hanging from one of them the corpse of the bandit who, a few hours before, had wounded his hand.

CHAPTER XXIV

HOW TWO WOMEN DISCUSSED THE MAKING OF THEIR FORTUNES—HOW TWO CHILDREN DIVERTED THEMSELVES —AND HOW TWO MEN PLOTTED TREASON

IT would be difficult to describe the feelings of Don Suero, and his rage, when he learned, on entering the castle with reinforcements, which he considered quite sufficient to destroy the bandits,—as he believed that but few were left alive after the falling of the arched roof,—that they had fled, carrying Teresa away with them. When he received this news regarding his sister, he at once thought of Sancha, and anxiously asked what had become of her. His retainers were not able to give him this information, as the confusion and terror, which reigned in the castle when the bandits abandoned it, had not permitted them to see whether they had carried off any others with the Infanta. He ran at once, filled with fear and uneasiness, to the chamber which Sancha occupied in the lower floor of the castle. The door was locked. Don Suero threw himself violently against it, and as it did not yield, he cried out—

"Sancha, Sancha! open the door; the bandits have fled."

Don Suero heard bolts drawn and articles of furniture pulled away, which evidently had been placed there to strengthen the door. It was then partially opened. Sancha stood there, trembling, and pale as a corpse. The count uttered a cry of joy on seeing her, and the girl threw herself into his arms, murmuring with difficulty—

"O my lord, can I believe my eyes? Is it indeed true that your life has not been taken by the daggers of the robbers; that a life more precious to me than my own has been preserved for me? During the fierce combat which has just taken place, I put my ear to the keyhole to try to hear your voice. I heard it at first, but then it ceased. I believed you were dead, and I searched for a knife or some other weapon with which to pierce my heart and breathe my last at the same time as you; but I could find nothing; I had no means of ending my life. The cries of 'Fire! the castle is on fire!' came at that moment to my ears, and I felt quite sure that the Castle of Carrion was about being reduced to ashes. I then bolted this door and heaped up the furniture against it, in order that no one could enter to save me from the flames, so that my ashes might be mingled with yours."

Sancha had in reality fastened and barricaded her door in order to protect herself against the fury of the bandits, and terror had changed her appearance; but she had learned to take advantage of all the different chances of life, and as an excellent opportunity presented itself of adorning herself with a fresh claim to the love of Don Suero, she profited by it. She felt fully persuaded that the count loved her, and as, from the first day she entered the Castle of Carrion, she had had numerous opportunities of studying lovers' ways, she knew that they are credulous in proportion to the love that dominates and blinds them.

"The count," she had said to herself, "will believe me madly in love with him, if I let him see that, without him, I look upon life as of no value."

And Sancha had not deceived herself, for Don Suero interrupted her, clasping her to his breast, and exclaiming in passionate accents—

"Sancha! my own Sancha! How stupid I have often been, doubting of your love! I will be your slave as long as I live, and if death should snatch you from my side—then Sancha, I shall cease to live also."

The girl abandoned the respectful tone and manners with which she had received the count, hanging from his neck and making use of her most winning caresses.

"O my love, my sweet charmer, my deity, my all! Should

a day come when you would thrust me from your arms, cast me from your heart,—then plunge your dagger in my breast, and my death will not be so full of anguish."

"Throw you from my arms? Cast you from my heart? Never, Sancha, never! Bonds unite us which not even death can break."

"Ah!" exclaimed the young woman in a sad tone of voice, and as if suddenly all strength had left the arms which had clasped the neck of Don Suero, she let them fall down, as if she were overcome with fear. "The bonds of love unite us, it is true, and they are the only ones which establish the union between man and woman in private life; but can one always live shut up in a castle, or in a miserable cabin? What men and women are there who do not sometimes appear in public? To the eyes of the vulgar it is only permitted to them to present themselves in it with one name—with that of husband and wife. There will be tournaments and other festivals to which you must go; you will have to be present at the Court and assist at its entertainments. Will you have me then at your side, and will I be able to satisfy that desire, that imperious necessity, of hearing constantly your voice, and of warming myself in the fire of your eyes?"

Don Suero was fascinated by his love and by the words of that cunning and ambitious peasant girl; not so much, however, as to suddenly abandon his aristocratic feelings and his pride of birth. For Don Suero, although one of the vilest of men, believed himself to be one of the noblest cavaliers of Spain, not considering that nobility of birth is valueless when nobleness of heart is absent. Who was Sancha, that the Count of Carrion could bestow his hand on her? The count asked himself that question before replying to that of Sancha, and thus, doubtless, he answered it: "She is an obscure peasant girl; she is the daughter of a labourer, who has been well cudgelled more than once by not only grandees like me, but by miserable, beggarly hidalgos; she is the pupil of Mari-Perez; she is a woman whom I love only for her beauty." Yes, in that way the count must have answered himself, for he replied to Sancha, with marked disdain—

"You hold the love of the noble Count of Carrion of so little value that you ambition still more? Do you not consider yourself sufficiently honoured and happy with him as you are? Sancha, if you desire that my love should not change into hatred, if you desire to be the mistress of my riches and of my heart, if you desire, as you say, never to leave my side, be content to remain as you now are."

"My ambition is satisfied with being as I am," answered the girl ; and she added, again throwing her arms round the neck of the count, "Pardon me, my sweet love, for my affection caused me to forget for the moment my humble extraction and the honour which I owe to you. I asked of public opinion what bonds were those which guaranteed to a woman the fidelity of a man, and I was told that they were those of marriage. My mind was confused by the joy of seeing you uninjured at my side, and I was guided by the views of ordinary people."

The count was calmed down by this apology. Sancha had learned much at the side of Mari-Perez, and felt that she could not then persist in urging her ambitious longings. The first step had been taken ; there was time enough to continue the journey, and she would await an opportune time to do so. Cunning and perseverance were necessary, for she was playing for a very valuable stake—that of becoming Countess of Carrion.

The next day an old woman in ragged garments approached the castle. Her face was bandaged, as if it were wounded, and she leaned on a staff, asking charity from the passers-by. "That old woman," narrates the "Chronicle," "stopped under the window of the girl's room, and, weeping bitterly, asked for alms in the names of God and of the Holy Virgin ; and when the girl heard her she went to the window, and they spoke for some time in secret." We, however, are more fully informed than the writer of these lines, and know what they were talking about.

The girl, indeed, went to the window, as soon as she heard the voice of the old woman, and said to her in a low voice—

"The count is mad in love with me."

"That is all right, my daughter," replied the old woman joyfully ; "if he loves you, and if you profit by my lessons, we shall succeed in what we desire, and shall not have to live by amusing hidalgos, who must be flattered and made much of for their good looks. O my daughter, I was very uneasy respecting what took place last night in the castle, until I was informed in the town that the bandits only carried off the Infanta."

"Go away, mother Mari-Perez, for if the count should

recognise you and see you speaking to me, we might, perchance, lose all we gained up to the present."

"I will do so, daughter," said Mari-Perez, for we now know that it was she. "Please God, when I see you again you will be the wife of Don Suero."

"I hope so, mother."

And the old woman walked off from the castle, commending to God and all the saints the lady, from whom people thought she had received bounteous alms.

Let us now return to Don Suero. The reader can calculate how enamoured he was of Sancha, having seen him occupied with her for some minutes, just at a time that was the least suitable for love affairs. It is not easy to guess how long he would have remained by the side of the peasant girl, if his nephews, Diego and Fernando, had not arrived on the scene.

The two boys were looking for him in the vicinity of Sancha's chamber, calling out his name in loud voices. Don Suero heard them, and went out at once to meet them.

"O uncle," cried out Diego, on seeing him, "what a lot of dead men there are down below and in the passages! If you only knew how afraid we were when we heard the awful uproar throughout the castle! Fernando and I were in bed, and when some men came into our room we pretended to be asleep. Tell us, is it true that they have taken off our aunt?"

"Yes, my children," answered Don Suero, as he liked the boys very much, chiefly because he had noticed their evil dispositions.

"I am glad of it," said Fernando, "for she was always scolding us because we did not say our prayers, and because we stuck pins in the dogs and cats, and cut off the hens' feet, to see how they would walk lame."

Don Suero almost repented of his work, that is to say, of the bad education which he had given to his nephews, when he heard them speak in such a way of his sister, for he loved Teresa, although his affection was of that barbarous and tyrannical nature which tortures while it caresses.

"Be silent, and do not speak badly of your aunt," said the count; "go back to your beds."

"We want to see first the dead and the wounded men," replied Diego. "If you were only to see all the blood that is coming from their wounds, and the gestures they are making."

"And I want to see them too," said Fernando.

Don Suero did not hear these cruel words of the children, for he had hurriedly walked off towards the corridors where the fight had been the hottest.

His vassals, the peasants who had come with him, were busy in aiding the wounded of both sides.

"God's anger! what are you doing, fellows?" exclaimed the count, seeing that his vassals were attending to the wounded bandits. "Kill all those that belonged to that cursed band; let that be your first care."

"My lord, do you know what you order?" was said to him from all sides. "The Vengador has sent to tell us that the Infanta Doña Teresa is held as a hostage for the lives and liberty of all those of his band who are here, and that Guillen, who would not leave your sister, will also answer for them with his life."

"Oh!" exclaimed Don Suero, almost howling with rage, and stamping on the ground, "why does not the ground open and swallow up the castle and all in it? The bandits shall die, even though my sister dies also! My sister—poor Teresa! No, no, care for them and bind their wounds, let none of them die, for those ruffians—may God confound them!—would kill my sister without pity."

The count then took precautions for the proper guarding of the entrances into the castle, and sent off his vassals, except a few whom he retained to keep watch on the ramparts with the few crossbow-men who were still alive and uninjured after the fight.

When the townspeople left the castle, Bellido Dolfos entered it, and proceeded to the apartment of the count, who was preparing to take some rest. He was covered with blood, which was dropping from a wound in the front part of his head; his face was pallid and disfigured, his voice was feeble, and his legs bent under him at every step.

Bellido considered that he had a just right to treat Don Suero with familiarity, considering the services he had rendered him, and the pitiful condition in which he now was on account of those services; he therefore entered the chamber without any previous intimation, and before he was perceived he threw himself down on an arm-chair. It creaked with the weight of Bellido, and Don Suero then turned round, and seeing a wounded man whom he did not recognise, doubtless by reason of the blood which covered his countenance, he stepped backwards and exclaimed—

"May Lucifer confound anyone who dares to enter my chamber! Get out of this at once, fellow, whether you belong to my men, or to the band of the accursed Vengador! It was enough for me to give orders that the wounded should be cared for, without having to attend to them myself."

"Don't you know me, count?" said Bellido in a weak voice. "Don't you recognise your faithful servant, Bellido Dolfos?"

"Bellido!" exclaimed Don Suero, approaching the traitor quickly. "You are wounded, you are losing your blood. How did you get into such a state, tell me,—but no, it is necessary first to staunch your wounds."

The count summoned his domestics, and at once sent for one of the townsmen who practised the art of surgery, and who then happened to be in the castle, lending his aid to the wounded. A moment afterwards he arrived and bound up the wounds.

Bellido, whose wounds were not dangerous, according to the opinion of him who had attended to them, felt himself much relieved, and he and the count remained alone in the room.

"I was very uneasy regarding you, as I knew nothing as to what happened to you," said Don Suero. "I feared that some misfortune had come upon you."

"What troubles me most," replied Bellido, "is that the Vengador and Rui-Venablos have escaped from the trap we set for them, and even got away, carrying prisoners with them."

"Now, leaving that for the present, tell me how you received those wounds, and where you were from the time the attack commenced until you came here."

"I shall tell you all in a few words, for my head is not in a condition for much talking. I swear to you that I will go out of my mind altogether, or else exterminate the Vengador and his band. However, learn now how I received this cursed wound. The entire band entered by the postern, and I remained outside, having taken advantage of the darkness, of the tumult, and of the bushes which surround that part of the castle. When all were within, I approached the door, shut it, and fastened it as well as I could, taking advantage of the nails with large protruding heads, which are on its exterior, for the purpose of resisting blows from outside. When the arch began to bulge down just before falling, many of the bandits made a rush to the door, trying to escape through it; I did my utmost to keep it shut, using all my strength, but, notwithstanding, the bandits pushed it forward against me; suddenly the arch fell in, and doubtless the block of stone, which had occasioned its fall, rolled towards the postern, and, striking violently against it, dashed it outwards, and I received such a blow on my head that I was thrown several feet away on the ground, deprived of my senses ; and know not how the nails did not split my head open. When I regained consciousness, I found myself covered with blood and in very great pain ; I tried to rise, but I fell again on the ground, and remained there for a long time, until, making a fresh effort, I was able to come here, having heard the bandits depart, and the townsmen return to their homes, talking together as they went."

"You shall be well rewarded for all you have suffered in serving me," said Don Suero, holding out his hand to Bellido. "I promised you three hundred gold marks if the Vengador and his band were destroyed, and I shall pay you the full amount. If they were not all killed by the falling of the arched roof, it was my fault, and not yours. But, as you know more of the constitution of the band than I do, think you that the Vengador will be able to get together again a band such as that which he has now lost?"

"I swear to you that he will not be able to do so, nor even keep with him the men that he now has," answered Bellido, in so confident a tone of voice that the count was agreeably surprised.

"And who will conquer him, when the brotherhood of the Salvadores, in whom all the grandees of the country have such confidence, has not succeeded, and probably will never succeed, in suppressing the bandits?"

"I alone."

"You?"

"Yes. Do you think that Bellido Dolfos will be discouraged because he stumbles at the beginning of a journey? Do you believe that it is the gold from your coffers that urges him to make short work of the Vengador and his band? If you so think, and so believe, you know me but little, count. In souls like mine there is no place for discouragement, nor for the forgetting of insults. The Vengador and Rui-Venablos dared to call me traitor and to point their daggers at my breast. I would lose a hundred lives rather than relinquish the chastisement of such audacity."

"You are wounded and weak from loss of blood. It will be some time before you can attack the Vengador ; meanwhile, he will have time to reorganise his band."

"The wound which I have received will favour my projects."

"I do not understand you, Bellido."

"It is easy to understand me, my lord count. As soon as I can travel, which will be in a few days, I shall set out to rejoin the Vengador. The bandits will believe that I received the wound when the arch fell in, and I will tell them that I had a miraculous escape. I will relate to them a long story of the sufferings which I went through before I could get back to them, and if formerly they simply looked on me as a member of the band, they will in the future not alone consider me as such, but also as one who became a victim through my devotion to it, and through the cruelty of the Count of Carrion. At this moment I cannot tell you exactly to what plans I must resort in order to win the full confidence of the Vengador and his men, because my head is not capable of thinking them out, but you shall know them soon, and your desires and mine shall be fulfilled."

"Bellido, you are my best friend," said the count, again extending his hand to the traitor. "All the gold in the world would not be too much to reward your skill and the services which you are rendering me."

He then opened a strong chest and took money from it, which he handed to Bellido, saying—

"Here are the three hundred marks, which you have so well earned."

The eyes of Bellido shone as brightly as the gold which the count had placed in his hand.

"Look there," added Don Suero, pointing to the interior of the chest, which certainly contained a treasure; "see how much gold I have, wherewith to reward your services, should we succeed in exterminating the bandits."

The eyes of Bellido shone like burning coals, and seemed as if they wished to attract the gold, which they devoured, as the magnet attracts iron.

"You will return to the camp of the bandits," said Don Suero, "as soon as you are able, and—count on my gratitude. My sister is there, and I fear that they will take base advantage of her weakness. Watch over her, Bellido, for the noble family of the lords of Carrion must not have a fresh crime committed by the band of the Vengador to lament over."

"Trust in me," replied Bellido. "Permit me now to retire and seek some repose amid the wounded bandits, so that I may be still thought one of them, and then watch them, should you intend to set them free to rejoin their companions when they are strong enough to do so.".

"Such is my intention," said Don Suero, "and the sooner the better, for the Vengador will not give freedom to my sister until every man of his who is alive returns to him."

"You will often hear me protest against your bad treatment of the wounded, and even threaten you with the vengeance of the band. Pretend that what I do angers you, but bear with me, for all will turn out to your advantage."

"I shall do as you desire, Bellido."

Don Suero and Bellido Dolfos then separated, both content; the former with fresh hopes of destroying the bandits, and the latter confident of revenging himself and, at the same time, of making the count more and more his debtor.

CHAPTER XXV

WHAT HAPPENED TO RODRIGO ON THE ROAD TO COMPOSTELA

THERE could be seen in the palace of the lords of Vivar, at Burgos, great commotion amongst knights, squires, and pages, as if preparations were being made for a journey which was to immediately commence. At the gate of the palace stood several horses fully caparisoned, the number of which was increasing every moment, according as fresh cavaliers arrived, dismounted, and proceeded into the apartments occupied by the noble family. Amongst the squires, who held the horses by their bridles, were Fernan and Alvar, who was trying to keep Babieca quiet, as his prancing and neighing were throwing the other horses into confusion. That noble animal seemed quite excited by the preparations for a campaign which were going on around him. He was no longer the poor-looking hack which Rodrigo had selected in the stables of Don Peyre, and which excited the laughter of the passers-by. His body had filled up, his coat had changed and acquired gloss, he carried his head well and bravely, and his entire appearance and movements were noble and free.

"By the soul of Beelzebub," Fernan was saying, "this

Babieca thinks that he will be soon in close quarters with the Moors, and he can't contain his delight. My lord and master is fortunate in everything. If the son of my mother had a horse like that, he would not exchange it for the steed of a king. And," he added, passing his hand over the sides of the intelligent animal, "my good Babieca, what you eat puts a shine on you. If you were mine it is not oats you would get, but the best bread."

Overo, which was also there, brilliantly caparisoned, approached his head to Fernan, rubbing it against him, as if jealous of the praises which were being lavished on Babieca. The squire turned towards him, stroking him also with his hand, and said—

"Hola, Overo! are you jealous, my son? If you were as brave as Babieca, I would caress and reward you in fine style. But do not let my praises of Babieca trouble you, for your well-filled sides witness that I treat you well. You are not very spirited, indeed; but everyone is as God made him, and it is not just to punish failings which come to one from his mother. Here are our masters, who treat Alvar as the very best of their servants, and for all that he has not even as much spunk in him as you have, Overo."

'By my soul, Fernan!" cried Alvar in a passion, "you must give up comparisons of that kind."

"If you only were braver, I would compare you to Babieca."

"It is my misfortune that this knave of a squire is always making fun of me!" muttered Alvar, still very angry, but fearing to irritate Fernan. "I wonder why you show such enmity towards me for some time back," he added, turning towards him. "Have I offended you in any way, Fernan?"

"And you dare ask me such a question, when the reins of Overo answered a similar one on your ribs yesterday? I swear to you, Alvar, by the soul of Beelzebub, that I will break every bone in your body if you don't treat the Moorish boy like the son of a prince."

"I certainly do scold him sometimes, but it is because his pranks, which you laugh at and applaud, irritate me."

"I applaud them because sprightliness in children should be applauded. Ismael, or rather Gil, for our masters have given him that name, is a little turbulent; but for that very reason I believe that he will grow up to be a brave youth, and a skilful and daring warrior. I have given him only about a dozen lessons in horsemanship and the use of arms, and he is now, as God hears me, almost as expert in such things as I am myself."

The squire and the page had got thus far in their conversation when they had to interrupt it, as they heard the cavaliers coming.

Rodrigo Diaz was indeed about to undertake a long journey, and his cousins and several knights of Burgos, who considered it a great honour to be permitted to do so, were to accompany him. He was going to Compostela, to visit the shrine of the apostle St. James, for the purpose of returning thanks to him for the victory of the mountains of Oca, and also to comply with the custom, which every good knight practised at least once in his life, of prostrating himself before the holy patron of Spain, on whose aid he counted in all his warlike deeds. At the same time Rodrigo desired to pay a visit to the king, Don Fernando, who at that time was personally superintending the reconstruction of Zamora, from whence he had sent him letters, congratulating him on the victory of Oca, and expressing an earnest desire to see him. Zamora the Beautiful, as our romance-writers call it, had been destroyed by the Moors in the time of Don Bermudo III., the last King of Leon, whom Don Fernando had defeated in a battle fought on the banks of the river Carrion, in which Don Bermudo lost his life; after this the King of Castile had joined the two crowns. Don Fernando had the intention of leaving it to his daughter Urraca as a legacy, and for that reason he was assisting in person at its reconstruction, endeavouring with much trouble to make the jewel, which he was preparing for his daughter, worthy of her who was to be the possessor of it.

Rodrigo Diaz, with the cavaliers, squires, and pages of his escort, mounted their steeds at the gate of the palace, and waving adieu to those who came to the windows to bid them farewell, they quitted Burgos and took the road to Zamora, all in excellent spirits, although Rodrigo felt that he was almost leaving his soul behind when he parted from Ximena and his parents. Fernan also felt rather sad on leaving Mayor, whom he had sworn would henceforth be his only love, even if there were wars, in which so many men should be killed, that there would be fully four women left for each of those who survived.

The name of Rodrigo Diaz resounded through all parts of the country; the son of the grandee of Vivar was an object of love and admiration to both Castilians and Leonese, for his brave deeds had reached the ears of all.   For this reason, wherever he passed, the people crowded out to welcome him; and in the plains, where he halted to spend the night, there was warm rivalry as to who should have the honour of entertaining him in his house.   This was naturally very pleasing to Rodrigo, but, in order to give offence to none, he arranged that he, and those who accompanied, should lodge in the public hostelries which were not wanting on that route.

The night was somewhat advanced when they came near to Medina de Riosico; it had rained so heavily during the day that the roads were almost impassable; it was, moreover, very cold, and the darkness was complete.   Our cavaliers were crossing an extensive morass, when they thought they heard very doleful moans issuing from a thicket, which lay at the side of the road, and when they stopped their horses, in order to hear better, a weak voice became audible, which said—

"Help me, travellers, whoever you are; if not, I shall die in this thicket!   Alas! I have lost my sight, and I cannot save myself with my feet and hands."

"Be not uneasy," replied Rodrigo in a loud voice; "you shall be succoured without delay."   He then continued, addressing his companions: "It must be some unfortunate mendicant who has lost his way in the darkness and amongst the thick bushes which grow hereabout.   Let us seek him out and bring him with us to Medina, which is near here, and where we are to halt for the night."

He then guided Babieca towards the spot from whence the groans proceeded, but the ground was so cut up, and the thicket so dense, that the horses were scarcely able to advance a dozen paces.   Rodrigo therefore dismounted, and, giving the reins of Babieca to Fernan, advanced so rapidly into the thicket, that none of his companions were able to follow him. Guided by the voice of him who had lost his way, he came to where he was, and found an old man stretched on the ground, covered with mud, soaked with water, and his limbs paralysed by the cold, as well as by some nervous affection he had in them.   He raised him from the ground, filled with compassion, and endeavoured to encourage and console him. When he asked him how he got into such a place, the old man replied—

"I lost my way in the evening, and tried for a long time to find it again, but without success, for the more I moved about in this thicket, the more did I become perplexed, until, my strength having become exhausted, and my body benumbed with cold, I fell in the place where you found me. In vain did I call out for aid to those who passed by, but they either did not hear me, or did not want to give themselves trouble. I had then resigned myself to die, and become the food of the wild animals which frequent this thicket, when I heard you, and summoned up sufficient strength to call out. God will protect him who raised up the weak, and guided the blind!"

Rodrigo endeavoured to get the unfortunate man to walk out of the morass, but he was soon convinced that he could not move a step, and then, finding more strength in his kindly heart than even in his shoulders, he took him up on them, and, although he met with many obstacles, got back to the road, which he had left, in a very short time. The old man wept with gratitude and joy. Fernan wished to put him on his horse, and walk by its side to Medina, for he did not consider Overo strong enough to carry a double burden, especially as the road was so very bad. Rodrigo, however, did not wish to share the credit of saving the unfortunate old man.

"Babieca," he said, "is well able to carry two men, not alone to Medina, but even the entire distance to Zamora. You will see how easily and bravely he will continue his journey."

Thus speaking, Rodrigo mounted Babieca, and, with the assistance of Fernan, got up the old man on the saddle behind him. They all proceeded then towards Medina, where they arrived half an hour afterwards.

The table was ready laid, and knights and squires prepared for their supper. Rodrigo made the old man sit down beside him, to eat with them, notwithstanding that this determination displeased the other cavaliers, whom the dirt and the wounds of the mendicant disgusted. The supper, however, began, and as the hands of the old man were palsied, he let fall the food when carrying it to his mouth, which only moved Rodrigo to compassion for him. The other cavaliers could scarcely eat their meal on account of the repugnance which the old man caused them, and at last arose from the table, saying that they could not bear the sight any longer. Rodrigo rebuked them sharply, and obliged the mendicant to remain at the table in order to finish his supper, although he was desirous of leaving the room, so as not to trouble the companions of his generous benefactor.

When the supper was ended; when the blind man had somewhat recovered his strength; when the heat of the hearth

had taken the numbness from his limbs ; when his heart, in
fine, had been consoled by the kindness of Rodrigo, the
young cavalier began to talk familiarly to that unfortunate
man, and by degrees the other cavaliers, who had gone to sup
in another apartment, returned, desirous of hearing the stories
which doubtless the blind man would relate.

"Ah, sir knight," he then said to Rodrigo, "how much would I
rejoice to be able to repay your kindness !   But what remains
to me in this world ?   Nothing but a sad heart to express its
gratitude,—and this instrument, with which I earn a poor
subsistence," he added, pointing to his lute.

One of the nephews of Rodrigo—the youngest and most
cheerful of them—said, on hearing these words—

"If it will be pleasing to you, my uncle and lord, and to
himself also, this old man can amuse us for a while by singing
to the accompaniment of his lute some of the ballads which
he doubtless knows."

"I shall do so with very great pleasure," answered the blind
man.

And as he felt that Rodrigo was not opposed to the proposal, he took up his lute and began to touch its strings with
considerable skill and lightness, notwithstanding the palsy
with which he was afflicted. He then suddenly stopped and
said—

"Listen, cavaliers and squires, listen to the true story of a
peasant from whom a traitor count stole his daughter, in order
to dishonour her, and whose eyes he put out in order that he
might not be able to avenge himself."

He then sang, with the accompaniment of his lute—

> " Cavaliers of Leon,
>   Castilian cavaliers !
>   Haughty with the strong,
>   But gentle with the weak !
>   Through Leon and Castilian lands,
>   Wanders a poor old man,
>   A count's foul crimes denouncing—
>   For a vile wretch is that count.
>   He cannot take revenge himself,
>   For age his body bends,
>   And his eyes now only serve
>   To weep o'er his sad fate.
>   Come to the aid of that old man,
>   In his most wretched plight,—
>   Cavaliers of Leon,
>   Castilian cavaliers !

> That vile count stole his daughter,—
> She was fair as a May rose,—
> And put him in a prison dark,
> Where the tyrant then did blind
> That sad, ill-fated, wretched man.
> Who will dry his constant tears?
> Who will give him back his child?
> Cavaliers, if such ye are,
> Punish that accursed count,—
> Him who bears off maidens fair,
> Him who vilely blinds old men.
> Such is the duty of the good,
> Such is the mission of the great
> Cavaliers of Leon,
> Castilian cavaliers!"

The old man ceased his song, for he became almost suffocated with sobs and tears. Those who had been listening to him were also much moved, and their indignation was so great against the count, who had been alluded to, although they did not know who he was, that if he appeared in their presence at that moment, they would have rushed at him with their naked swords.

"Do you tell us that your story is true?" asked Rodrigo.

"Yes, it is true, sir knight, unfortunately for me," he replied.

"Unfortunately for you? As I hope to be saved," exclaimed Rodrigo, remembering the adventure which Beatrice had related to him and to Fernan, "that count is the Count of Carrion, and you are the old man whose daughter was stolen!"

"You are quite right, sir knight."

"I vow by Judas Iscariot, that I would willingly give ten years of my life to be able to put ten inches of my sword into the breast of that felon count!" exclaimed Fernan, giving vent to his indignation, which he could not restrain, although he knew it was contrary to his duty to interrupt the conversation of his master.

"And you know nothing of your daughter?" asked Rodrigo of the blind man.

"I do not know, sir knight, what has become of her, but I suppose the count keeps her shut up in his castle, for, if not, she would have endeavoured to find her unfortunate father, whom she loved so much, and loves still if she is alive."

The poor old man, as we see, was far from suspecting how different his daughter had become since the count had deprived her of her robe of innocence.

"And have you found no cavalier to take upon himself the carrying out of the revenge which you desire?" asked Rodrigo.

"I have found," replied the old man, "a soldier, as brave as he is kind-hearted ; but up to the present he has not been able to do anything."

"Then we will assist him in his task, and, as God lives, it shall not avail the count to shut himself up in his castle and lend a deaf ear to every challenge, as is his custom," said Rodrigo.

"Yes, yes !" exclaimed all present ; "we must punish that accursed count, who is a disgrace to the nobility of Leon and Castile."

"Oh," cried the unfortunate old man, filled with joy, "God will assist you in your noble enterprise. My journey to Medina has not been in vain, for if I have not met the valiant and noble cavalier whom I was in search of, I have found another, not less kind-hearted and compassionate."

"Who was the cavalier whom you were seeking?" asked Rodrigo.

"Don Rodrigo Diaz de Vivar, he who was expected to lodge here to-night," he replied.

"Then you find here him you were in search of."

"My God !" exclaimed the old man, scarcely able to speak, such was his surprise, kissing the hand which Rodrigo held out to him. "Can it be possible that he who carried me on his shoulders, and seated me at his table, is Don Rodrigo Diaz de Vivar, the conqueror in the mountains of Oca, the son of Diego Lainez, the descendant of the Judges of Castile, the most noble, honoured, powerful, and brave cavalier of Spain ?"

"Rodrigo Diaz is he who took you on his shoulders, seated you at his table, and intends to share his bed with you," replied the son of Diego Lainez.

. "Oh, my lord," cried the old man, not knowing how to express his gratitude, "your kindness to me has been too great ; but to share your bed with me, a beggar, full of misery and dirt ! No, no, that cannot be, my lord."

"You say that I am noble, honoured, and powerful. Who but the powerful, the honoured, and the noble should console and protect the afflicted, the sad, and the defenceless? Let us go to rest, for we all stand much in need of it, and particularly you, a feeble old man."

Rodrigo, his companions, and the blind man then retired,

and in reality the former did share his bed with the mendicant. Divine rays of charity which would have adorned the noble brow of the cavalier with the aureole of the saints, if his brave deeds had not adorned it with the laurel crown of the hero; for charity modestly hides herself, whilst warlike heroism cannot do so.

It is impossible to describe the gratitude of the unhappy old man when, the following morning, he parted from the compassionate cavalier. It is impossible also to describe the inspired accents in which, shedding abundant tears, he said to Rodrigo—

"My lord, I feel confident that God has sent me to you to bring you glad tidings. You are loved by Him; you will conquer in all your battles; your honours and your prosperity will increase; you will be feared by the bad and loved by the good, and you will die happy, blessed by God and by men."

Rodrigo looked on these words as a divine prophecy. The accents in which they were pronounced made him believe that it was such.

At the rising of the sun, that bright and beautiful sun which follows a storm, Rodrigo and his companions departed from Medina de Rioseco, with the intention of reaching Zamora on that day; which they succeeded in doing.

Here, where but a short time before could be seen heaps of rubbish, between which nettles and brambles grew and reptiles hissed, where it might have been said, "Here was Zamora," using the expression applied in old times to the city of Æneas —here, we repeat, were springing up magnificent temples with high turrets, superb palaces, and strong fortifications; and bustle and animation had succeeded to the silence and solitude which had but recently reigned there.

The king, Don Fernando, was just going to dinner when he was informed that Rodrigo had arrived in the city. The joy of the wise and good monarch was very great; Don Fernando did not look upon the cavalier, whom he was about to see, as a vassal, but as the most beloved of his friends—even more than that, as one of his sons. Even the circumstance of being separated from his family, which had remained in Burgos and was so dear to him, had caused him to desire with greater eagerness the arrival of Rodrigo, for he had now passed a considerable time without being able to expand his heart in the calm pleasures of family life. He therefore longed to have at his side one, with whom he could feel himself joined by closer and softer bonds than those which usually unite the lord to his vassal, in order that he might satisfy the most imperious necessity of his soul, that of living in the bosom of friendship. He had scarcely learned that Rodrigo had crossed the threshold of the palace when he went to meet him, like a father who goes out to meet a son after a long absence from the paternal dwelling. The brave and noble cavalier was about to prostrate himself at the feet of the king, like a good vassal as he was, but Don Fernando did not allow him to do so, for he opened his arms and pressed him in them, with an effusion of affection and esteem almost paternal, saying to him, "You are very welcome, Rodrigo, glory of Castile and strongest pillar of my throne."

"Oh, sire," exclaimed Rodrigo, much moved by so flattering a reception, "the strongest pillars of your throne are your own wisdom, your goodness, and the affection which your subjects feel for you. I am one of them, and I would not change my condition for yours, for the honours you confer on me are of more value in my eyes than a throne."

"I love you, Rodrigo, as the best of my vassals, and I repay but poorly all your services to me. I do not alone admire and respect you as the descendant of Lain Calvo, as the son of Diego Lainez, as the valiant youth who knew how to avenge the insult inflicted on his honour, as he who conquered the bravest of the Aragonian knights, and finally, as the hero who gained one of the most glorious triumphs over the Moorish power; but as the magnanimous and generous cavalier who restored to freedom Abengalvon and his companions in misfortune. How great loyalty must not the King of Castile and Leon expect from him who, having conquered them, respected even the enemies of his God and his country, because they bore the name of king."

All the cavaliers who were with Don Fernando were also much rejoiced at the arrival of Rodrigo, and felicitated him on his victory at Oca. Rodrigo was soon seated at the king's table, which honour he enjoyed during the few days he was obliged to spend in Zamora, for Don Fernando was unwilling that he should depart, and only consented at last on account of the sacred object of his journey.

The day at last arrived on which he had to resume it. Everything was ready for his departure, when a great commotion was noticed amongst the townspeople who were thronging towards the avenue which led to the royal Alcazar.

The king, Rodrigo, and the courtiers went out on a balcony, and were much surprised at the strange spectacle which they saw. A large number of Moors, richly clad, were leading more than a hundred horses gorgeously caparisoned, and in addition several mules all heavily loaded.

When the Moors arrived at the gates of the Alcazar, they sent to ask Rodrigo's permission to appear in his presence. He conceded it, having obtained the assent of the king, and they entered the apartment in which the noble cavalier awaited them, seated beside the king, who thus honoured him in order that the Moslims might see in what estimation he was held.

"*Cid*," said to Rodrigo he who seemed to be the leader of the ambassadors, "Abengalvon, king of Molina, Mahomad, king of Huesca, Ali, king of Zaragoza, Osmin, king of Teruel, and Hamet, king of Calatayud, whom you took prisoners in the mountains of Oca, and to whom you generously restored their freedom, send you their tributes and pay you homage, as vassals who are pleased to do so. In addition, they send you, as marks of friendship and gratitude, thirty sorrel horses, thirty black horses, twenty white, and twenty dapple-grey, besides valuable ornaments and precious stones for your spouse, and rich cloths and good arms for yourself and your knights."

"You are mistaken in your errand," replied Rodrigo modestly and humbly; "you have called me *Cid*, which in your language signifies 'a lord over vassals,' and I am not a lord where my king is, but only the least of his vassals. Here you see my king, and to him you must pay homage, and to him you must offer the tributes and the marks of friendship which Abengalvon and his friends have confided to your charge."

"Say to your masters," interrupted the king, exceedingly pleased by his humility, and addressing the Moors, "that although their lord is not a king himself, he is seated beside the King of Castile and Leon; tell them also that to him I owe a large portion of the territories which I possess, and that I consider it a greater glory to have him as my vassal than to be a king myself. As you have called him 'Cid,' it is my will that from this day he shall bear that name."

Rodrigo then received the tributes and gifts which the Moorish kings had sent to him, and wrote to each of them a letter, expressing his thanks, and promising to return their loyalty and friendship.

The ambassadors received from the hand of Rodrigo valuable presents, and departed, repeating the name of 'Cid,' which the son of Diego Lainez was henceforth to bear, and to which was soon added *Campeador*,[1] which both Moors and Christians conferred on him, on account of his constant and glorious triumphs on the fields of battle.

A few hours after he had received this honourable embassy, Rodrigo left Zamora, with the friends and servants who accompanied him on his journey; all were in good spirits and desirous of arriving at Compostela, in order to fulfil the duties of Christian cavaliers before the altar of the holy apostle, and afterwards practise other duties in the districts which were frequently invaded by the Moors.

CHAPTER XXVI

HOW THE VENGADOR AND RUI-VENABLOS CHANGED THEIR OPINION REGARDING BELLIDO

THREE days after the disastrous attack of the bandits on the Castle of Carrion, those that remained of them were still encamped in the place where we left them in the twenty-third chapter.

It was near nightfall, and the weather, which had been cold and rainy on the preceding day, had become mild and calm.   The Vengador and Rui-Venablos were conversing together, walking through the camp, in which were four tents, one for the chiefs, one for the Infanta of Carrion, who was still their prisoner, one for the wounded who had been brought from Carrion, and one for the other members of the band.

Near the encampment was a hill, from the summit of which could be seen all the approaches, principally the road from Carrion, for a considerable distance.   The bandits kept watch on it, and had been given strict orders to give notice when they saw anyone approaching the camp, which proved that the Vengador had lost the blind confidence which he had before placed in his strength and in his good fortune; for when he

[1] "Warrior," in old Spanish.

had but a dozen followers, and had as his enemies not alone the brotherhood of the Salvadores, but all the inhabitants of the country, he did not take such precautions. With all their valour, the Vengador and Rui-Venablos could not but feel discouraged by the terrible blow which they had just received. Grief and despair had at first given them courage and confidence, but when reflection came, the thought of those who had remained entombed under the arched roof of the castle, and the contrast between what the band had been and what it now was, changed their energy and confidence into discouragement.

" The life we are leading here is a miserable one," said Rui-Venablos. " Inaction not only causes discontent in our men, but leaves us open to a sudden attack by our enemies ; it deprives us, besides, of precious time, which should be employed in filling up the wide gaps which have been left in our ranks."

"We should indeed move away from here and shake off this inaction which, in more ways than one, is weakening us," replied the Vengador ; "but how can we do so until all our companions who remained at Carrion have returned, and thus place us in a position to give the Infanta her liberty ? If we departed hence, God only knows where we should have to go ; our companions would arrive with the hope of finding us, and having made a long journey, which in their condition would be very painful, they would be disappointed, and have to proceed in search of us through the whole country, and many of them would probably succumb before they could find us."

Martin bent down his head and continued—

" You, Rui-Venablos, and I, only bandits in appearance, and our comrades being so in reality, should, it might be supposed, have no compassion for them, and need not be loyal to them ; but we act as it is but right for us to do : every honourable man should be loyal and compassionate towards those who share their good or evil fortunes, whether those men happen to be honourable or not. In truth, our comrades are as honourable as we are, for if we examine into the depths of their hearts and of their conduct, we must place them, not in the category of bandits, but in that of men whom hunger and oppression have forced to exercise a shameful profession, and who, nevertheless, exercise it as honourably as they can ; for you know already, Rui, that if there are in the band many men inclined to pillage and assassination, more by inclination than by necessity, we have curbed the instincts of several of them,—sometimes by persuasion, at other times by punishment,—and got rid of the others. Perhaps those who appear least worthy of compassion are the very men who most deserve it. What are you and I in the eyes of the public but bandit chiefs, deserving of being hung and quartered, and exposed to public obloquy on the highroads? Nevertheless, we dare shame and death for one of the noblest causes,—one which even cavaliers have fought for. Oh, how far are people from imagining that Rui-Venablos and the Vengador, redoubtable bandits, who attacked, pillaged, and consigned to the flames the mansions of grandees, have no ambition but to avenge the murder of one father, the tortures inflicted on another, the dishonour of a girl, and the oppressions and crimes which noblemen, wrongly so named, practise on the weak and unfortunate."

" That is quite certain, brother," replied Rui-Venablos. " And Bellido himself, of whom both of us, I the first, had suspicions, is a proof of this. Who can say but that he enlisted in the band with an object just as honourable as ours? I have changed my opinion regarding him so much, that if the count should retain him in his castle, as God lives! Rui-Venablos would risk a hundred lives to restore him to liberty. Who does not love him, and desire that he should return to us, having heard all that the wounded, who have come back to us, relate of him? Certainly a man deserves praise and love who, severely wounded in his head, forgets his own sufferings, dedicates himself to serve and console those who most likely suffer less than he does, protests with a brave heart against the inhumanity of the count, whom he rebukes, risking his anger, and will not leave the castle until the very last of his companions has quitted it, saying, that as he is one of their leaders, it is his duty to die rather than abandon his comrades ! Besides this, the circumstance of Bellido having been the only one who escaped of all those on whom the ruins of the arch fell, is another reason to consider him worthy of our affection."

" Yes," said Martin ; " from this day Bellido shall be our equal. Amongst us there shall be no first or second ; all three shall be but as one, all three shall command the band, all three shall have the same power. And, indeed, Bellido forecast things better than either of us, and you see how events have justified his opinion that half the band would perish in the assault on the Castle of Carrion. We were indignant at the plan he proposed to us, in order to carry out our enterprise; but although we never could have approved of it, perhaps our words would have been less severe if we could have foreseen the dangers which he foreshadowed. Now that we know how much Bellido is afflicted by the misfortunes of his comrades, we must not feel surprised that, in order to save us from an almost certain death, he should have ventured a proposal which made him appear to us dishonourable and disloyal."

Their conversation had proceeded thus far when the sentry signalled that people were coming from the direction of Carrion. The chiefs of the band joined him in order to see who they were; and what was their surprise and delight when they found that those who were approaching were Bellido and the last of the bandits who had remained wounded in the power of Don Suero.

Martin and Rui-Venablos hurried to meet them, and embraced Bellido warmly, whose face, pale and emaciated, gave expression to his satisfaction.

"Welcome, brother!" exclaimed both; "welcome, all of you!"

"We were awaiting you with very great anxiety," said Martin.

"It was not greater than the longing I felt to return to you," replied Bellido.

"Brother," said Rui-Venablos, "we have learned how loyal your conduct has been in Carrion with regard to our companions, and we, together with the entire band, shall consider you in the future as its best and most faithful member."

"Oh, you confer an honour on me which I do not deserve," replied Bellido, with feigned modesty and emotion. "All our comrades are so kind and grateful that those who arrived first must have spoken too well of me, exaggerating the trifling services I rendered them."

"What a terrible blow it was to us, Bellido! You prophesied only too truly when you said that half the band would be destroyed if we assaulted the castle by force," said Martin.

"Let us speak no more of that," replied Bellido, as if his modesty resented any allusion to his foresight. "Let us forget all that is past, and let us only endeavour to recover lost ground. Let us work together with earnestness, with zeal superior to all adverses, until we regain our lost strength, and have again sufficient to ensure victory. Let us then return to

Carrion, to avenge our unfortunate companions who were butchered by the count in so barbarous a manner; for you must know that the arched roof, which fell down on us, had been previously prepared so as to kill all of us; and deaths caused by such dastardly artifices can only be called vile murders."

"And how were you able to save yourself from that slaughter?"

"Only by a miracle."

"Relate to us then, brother, all that happened to you at Carrion," said Martin, just as they reached the tents.

The wounded bandits entered that which the chiefs of the band had arranged in the best possible manner, and the Vengador, with his two companions, entered his tent. Martin and Rui-Venablos could not do too much for Bellido, with the view of ensuring his comfort and ease. They prepared, with the utmost solicitude, a place where he could seat himself. They saw that a meal was prepared for him, and they examined the condition of his wound. Their care might be compared to that which a father or mother would have lavished on a sick and debilitated son.

"Do not trouble yourself, brothers, in preparing comforts for me, for when with you, I feel well however I may be placed. I assure you that this cursed wound which, during the entire journey, made me suffer all the pains of hell, has ceased to trouble me since I have seen you again. One would say that you have the hand of a saint," added Bellido, with a pleasant smile, "for you scarce touched me when I felt myself completely cured. However, learn now what I suffered in Carrion."

Martin and Rui-Venablos then seated themselves by his side, ready to listen attentively to him.

"When that terrible blow was heard above the arched roof, I foresaw the danger which threatened us, and I rushed to the postern, to endeavour to facilitate the exit of my comrades by opening the door, which had suddenly closed through the impulse of the violent shock which made the entire building quiver; however, the door, when closing, must have dragged on with it some of the fragments which fell from the roof, and wedged them in the door frame, for all the strength which I exerted to open it was useless. Nevertheless, it was just yielding when the arch crashed down, and I received so violent a blow on the head that I instantly lost consciousness.

I am ignorant of the length of time I remained buried amid the ruins and the dead bodies. When I regained my senses, the moonlight was penetrating through the postern, which was partly open, just as it was at the moment the catastrophe took place. The spectacle which then presented itself to my view was terrible; rivulets of blood were flowing from the ruins, and on every side were protruding corpses, horribly disfigured and mutilated; but not a voice, not a groan, not a sigh was to be heard around me, which proved that I was the only one in whom any life remained, of all those who were in the place when the arched roof fell in. I turned my eyes away from that horrible sight, and reflected as well as I could, for the loss of blood, which continued to run from my head, had weakened my faculties. I knew then that if I could not procure assistance, I should soon lose my consciousness a second time, and the count would find one corpse more under the ruins of the roof. I managed to get out into the fields; bathed my wound in the river which flows near the walls of the castle, bandaged it as well as I could, and was thus able to arrest the flow of the blood. I advanced a few steps on the road which leads hither, but I stopped, hearing some people approach, and concealed myself amongst the bushes. I was thus able to overhear the conversation of some peasants who were coming out of the castle and proceeding towards the town, talking on their way of what had occurred. I thus learned that there were in the castle several of my wounded companions, in danger of being sacrificed to the anger of the accursed count, and I considered that it would be a cowardly act not to share their fate. I then entered the castle, taking advantage of the confusion which still reigned there, and in a few minutes I was with my comrades again. You know the rest; and I have only to add that the count is not taking any precautions to protect the castle against a fresh attack, for he considers us too much weakened to attempt one again. For that reason we should endeavour to recruit our forces as quickly as possible, and strike another blow, which will certainly have better results, as Don Suero will be unprepared."

"We shall do so, brother," exclaimed in one breath Martin and Rui, clasping one after the other the hand of Bellido.

The three men continued to converse in a friendly way for a short time, principally regarding the best means that could be adopted in order to restore the band to its former strength; and an hour later there was no other sound to be heard in the camp but the footsteps of two or three sentries, stationed on the paths leading to it, and who continued walking to drive away the cold, which, if they had not done so, would almost have frozen the blood in their veins. Nevertheless, all who were in the tents had not gone to rest: Teresa and Guillen were awake, seated beside a lamp, in the same place where we have seen them but a few days previously. The Infanta was no longer the same young girl, worn out by grief, for whom the few kindly souls who saw her in the Castle of Carrion felt so great compassion: a sweet and pleasant smile now played constantly on her lips; her cheeks, a short time before pale as those of a corpse, were commencing to be tinged with the colour of the rose; and her soft eyes, formerly dim and sad, shone with joy and animation. Teresa was born to love, and love was the only element in which she could really live; from the time, therefore, that her soul had commenced to satisfy that imperious necessity, it might be said that she had returned again to life, for the contentment of the soul is a fountain of health for the body. How rapidly time sped on for Teresa and Guillen in that poor tent, into which penetrated from all sides the wet and the cold, in which there was not even a rustic bench to use as a seat; where it was necessary to lie on the ground, moist and rugged; where they had not sufficient coverings to keep themselves warm; where food was scanty and of the very coarsest kind; and where, finally, they were in the power of a band of bandits. How true is it that love adorns everything, and makes all things easily borne and even sweet! All those privations were little thought of by them, for they were sufficiently compensated by the pleasure of constantly seeing each other, of caring for each other, and of building beautiful castles in the air.

"Teresa," said Guillen, with a loving smile, "we have been painting the future with rosy tints, we have forgotten the real world in order to make ourselves happy in an imaginary one; would it not be well now to reflect for a few moments on the obstacles against which our love must contend from the time that we return to the castle? It is sad to have to awake from so delicious a dream as ours has been, only to find ourselves in a reality as bitter as that which awaits us."

"Let us think over that reality," replied Teresa, also trying to smile, but in truth becoming very sad at the discomforting prospect which Guillen had conjured up before her.

"We must consider," said the page, "as to the kind of life we shall have to lead when we arrive in Carrion; we must see each other as little as possible, and in the presence of your brother you must address me coldly and haughtily, in order that he may not suspect our love."

"And do you believe, Guillen, that I could live without often seeing you, or that I could speak coldly to you?"

"It will be also very painful to me to spend even an hour without seeing you, but we must accept such a bitter sacrifice, for what would be our fate if your brother found out that there were any other relations between us but those of a mistress and her servant?"

"Guillen, I repeat to you that I, formerly a weak and timid woman, now feel myself strong and courageous; so much so, that I would not hesitate to confess to my brother—ay, to the whole world—that I love you."

"Confess it to your brother, Teresa! Ah no! for the count would kill you, as he would look upon the love of the Infanta of Carrion for an obscure page as a crime deserving of being punished with death; for he considers that such as I should kiss the ground on which their masters place their feet. Let us conceal our love until the day arrives when you need not be ashamed, in the eyes of the world, of loving me."

"Ashamed of loving you, Guillen! No, I shall never be ashamed of that, for what armorial bearings could be found more noble than the good and chivalrous soul which animates you?"

"I know, Teresa, that for you such armorial bearings are sufficient, but not for your brother, not for the world. Let us conceal, I repeat, the love which we have for one another whilst I remain in Carrion, for it will be only till the day that the infidels make the first of their frequent raids into Castile and Leon. I shall then join the first body of soldiers which sets out to oppose the enemy, and the first fight in which I take part shall win for me the first of the titles that will enable me to demand your hand from your brother."

"Ah, Guillen, what bitter trials await our love, if they were only those of the long separation which we must endure!" exclaimed Teresa, thinking how illusory the hopes of the page were, and on what a weak foundation his dreams of happiness rested.

"Teresa," said the page, smiling in order to encourage her, "do we not feel ourselves strong and courageous? Well, then, let us trust in God and in our love, for after a short period of tempest we shall enjoy years of calm."

Whilst the lovers were thus conversing,—without thinking of who might hear them, without even lowering their voices, as if fearful of being heard and ridiculed by the bandits, who would have found in the love of the Infanta and the page only a subject for jests and noisy mirth,—a man issued from the tent of the chiefs and approached, as noiselessly as possible, that of Teresa. The man applied his ear carefully to the canvas of the tent, greedy to hear the conversation of the lovers, and when it had ceased, or at least had changed its character, he returned to the tent from whence he had come. If the darkness had not been so great, he might have been seen to smile with satisfaction.

That man was Bellido Dolfos, who, surprising the love-making of Doña Teresa and the page, had made up his mind to gain some gold marks in exchange for—who knows but for the lives of two good and innocent fellow-creatures !

All ages have had their traitors, but none of them more vile, more despicable, more wicked than Bellido.

CHAPTER XXVII

HOW TERESA AND GUILLEN BELIEVED THAT GOD HAD TOUCHED THE HEART OF DON SUERO

On the following day, just as the sun was beginning to lessen the intense cold of the morning, Teresa and Guillen departed from the encampment of the bandits, with their consent, which had been obtained on the previous evening, when the last of the wounded, who had been in the power of Don Suero, returned with Bellido. As the journey was long and the roads were bad, even worse than usual on account of the heavy rain which had fallen, the Vengador had taken compassion on the weak state of the Infanta, and had given her a very strong horse, which was able to carry both her and the page. They both, therefore, mounted it, extremely grateful for the generosity of the bandits, and, above all, for the kindness of their chief, who had afforded them protection and cared for them as well as he possibly could in that solitary place.

The two young people were journeying thus towards Carrion, conversing lovingly, when about half-way they met a servant of Don Suero, who, on perceiving them, stopped, full of joy on seeing his mistress at liberty, for all the inhabitants of the castle, and of the surrounding district, loved and respected her.

Teresa and Guillen were informed by him of all that had occurred in the castle during their absence, and when they were about to continue their journey, the Infanta asked Gonzalo, for that was the name of the servant, whither he was going.

"My lady," he replied, "Don Suero sends me with a letter to the Count of Cabra."

"Is he sending to his friend the count for aid, fearing that some other band may attack the castle?" asked Teresa.

"My lady, I can only tell you that my master received tidings yesterday from Zamora, which caused him great annoyance, so great that he beat me with a stick, shut himself up in his apartment, and spoke to no person until this morning, when he summoned me in order to give me a letter, which he said I should bring to the Count of Cabra as quickly as possible."

"Ah, you do not know, my good Gonzalo, what fear the bandits inspire me with, now that I know how far their audacity may go," said the Infanta, in order that the servant might not suspect that she had any other object in having thus questioned him. "Proceed on your way now, my good Gonzalo, proceed whither your master sends you, for we shall soon arrive at the castle, and relieve the anxiety which my brother feels respecting us."

Gonzalo then continued his way to Burgos, and Teresa and Guillen proceeded towards Carrion.

"Guillen," said Teresa, "that letter which my brother is sending to the Count of Cabra causes me to foresee events which may effect the peace of my family. The Count of Cabra is the instrument which some of the grandees of Leon and Castile have made use of, for many years, to plot treasons and to carry out their mean revenges; for Don Garcia is a skilled master in the art of conspiring, in everything that is cowardly and cunning. To be in relations with him is the same as being engaged in some treacherous action. Since he fled from his estates, although he had sufficient armed retainers to resist the Moors, and came to Castile, he lives by what those who have need of his assistance in carrying out their plots, pay him."

"And I would stake a hundred to one that your brother is plotting some treachery against the knight of Vivar, for he considers him his greatest enemy, especially since Don Rodrigo challenged him, and, on his refusing to fight with him, got notices posted up throughout Castile and Leon, denouncing his cowardice, calling him a bad, disloyal, and treacherous cavalier, together with other disagreeable names of a like nature, which your brother has not forgotten. Besides, the great success of the cavalier of Vivar has made him jealous, and he would be only too glad to clip the wings which in so short a time have soared so high."

"I trust in God that we all shall not have to weep tears of blood on account of the ambition, the injustice, and the wild and ungovernable character of my brother. The house of Carrion, formerly loved and respected by all, is now surrounded by enemies. Who now treats it with respect? Who would draw a sword in its defence, on the day when all its enemies will rise in open hostility against it? It is indeed powerful, and its vassals are numerous enough to form an army, before which even the King of Castile and Leon might well tremble; but how weak is power when it has not love for its cement!"　.

Whilst engaged in this and other such conversations, the Castle of Carrion appeared to their view. Teresa remembered the joy with which in other times she had seen again those grey walls, when returning with her parents from the frequent excursions which they were in the habit of making, and when they were always received with ovations by their vassals, amongst whom the lords of Carrion were looked on as a second providence. She remembered what she had suffered within those walls from the time she had lost her parents, and thought of what she might still have to suffer; and the comparison of those two periods, so different from each other, filled her heart with sadness. The Infanta almost felt grief at having to return to the castle in which she had been born; she was almost sorry for having left the camp of the bandits, for in it, although she was the captive of the Vengador, she had Guillen continually by her side, she could enjoy freely the sweet and ardent ove which dominated her soul, and

God alone knew what awaited her in the castle, God alone knew if there she should ever see Guillen near her.

At length they arrived at the castle gate. Don Suero came out to meet them, and, almost the first time in his life, he embraced Teresa, and held out his hand to Guillen.

"You are heartily welcome, my sister," he said to the Infanta. "If the natural roughness of my character, which contrasts with the sweetness of yours, has ever caused you to doubt of my affection, that want of confidence in me must henceforth cease. Think, Teresa, how much I must love you when, in order not to draw upon you the vengeance of the bandits, I renounced the exercise of mine on those accursed wretches, when they were in my power. You, who know how undeserving of pity those bandits are, who committed so many outrages in the district of Carrion, who attacked so treacherously my castle; you, who know the terrible chastisements which I am in the habit of inflicting on those who offend me; you, my sister, can now understand the great sacrifice I have made to ensure your safety. If you had not been in the power of the bandits, my men-at-arms would have followed the track of the miserable remnant of the band of the Vengador, would have overtaken them, and could have completely exterminated them; but how could I pursue them when you were amongst them, for, at the shooting of the first arrow by my men, those pitiless wretches would have plunged their daggers in your heart."

"Oh, thanks, thanks, brother!" replied Teresa, much moved, and forgetting the brutal tyranny which the count had practised on her during so long a time; for the heart of Teresa was always open to gratitude and affection; and to the poor girl, who had always seen frowns and severity on the face of her brother, a kindly smile from him was of inestimable value.

"To you I return my best thanks, my good Guillen," said Don Suero to the page, "for having so loyally accompanied and guarded your mistress. I have always looked on you differently than on my other attendants, and from to-day you shall be the friend rather than the servant of the Count of Carrion, for I know that you will become more and more worthy of my esteem."

"My lord," replied Guillen in a stammering voice, "your goodness is greater than my deserts. Was it not my simple duty to protect and defend my mistress in every way in my power?"

The honourable page accused himself at that moment of disloyalty to his master; his conscience was so upright, his soul was so noble and delicate, that he could not help thinking to himself—

"I am vilely deceiving my master: Teresa is the most valuable thing he has in his castle, and I have stolen it from him, like an unfaithful servant; my lips speak one thing and my heart feels another." Such were the thoughts that were disturbing the page and bringing a colour to his cheeks.

If the words which her brother had addressed to her were sweet to Teresa, those which he had spoken to Guillen were far sweeter to her. Oh, how delicious did the name of "friend," which Don Suero had given to the page, sound in her ears!

The Infanta entered her chamber filled with gladness, consolation, and the hope of having happy days there instead of the sad ones she had before spent in it; all this was not founded so much on the favourable state of mind in which she had found her brother, as on the certainty she felt that henceforth there would be one in the castle who loved her tenderly and disinterestedly.

"I shall see Guillen every day," she thought to herself, "for my brother will be grateful to him for the sacrifices he has made for me, the cares he has lavished on me, his grief at seeing me deprived of almost the necessaries of life; and thus he will attribute to my gratitude alone the preference I will show him, my affection for him, and my desire to see him constantly near me."

These thoughts, these hopes filled Teresa with happiness. That apartment already seemed to her less lonely, less sad, less gloomy; she no longer looked on herself as alone in the world; she breathed with freedom; she saw the horizon of her life smiling and bright. She went to that narrow window, at which she had so often shed tears, and directed her gaze on the wide stretch of country which was visible from it. The sun had just disappeared behind a hill, and in the fields could be heard the songs of the shepherds and labourers, and the summons to prayer which was sounding from all the belfries that arose on the extensive plain. This sight, which had so often formerly saddened her heart, which had filled her with an invincible and deep melancholy, now caused in her an entirely different feeling; the songs of the country people, the chimes of the bells, seemed to her as if they were celebrating her happiness and announcing it to her.

She stood for a long time motionless at the window, buried in the contemplation of her newly awakened hopes, blessing God who had sweetened the bitterness of her life, and giving thanks to her mother, to whose prayers she believed that she owed a great part of her happiness; for that mother who, in other times, loved her, pitied her, and consoled her, must have implored the mercy of God in her favour, in favour of the sad orphan, isolated in the world and persecuted by her own brother, by him who, when her mother died, should have loved, pitied, and consoled her.

When Teresa was most absorbed in those sweet reflections, she heard some person entering her chamber, and almost at the same moment the voice of her brother, who thus affectionately addressed her :—

"Teresa, my sister, I could not retire to rest without first embracing you, without seeing that you have everything necessary for your comfort, without beseeching you to forget for ever my harshness towards you, for, from this day, I shall not be a tyrant to you, as I have hitherto been, but a brother to my good and gentle Teresa!"

Saying this, Don Suero opened his arms and clasped the Infanta to his breast, with a seeming tenderness, which filled the sweet girl with pleasure.

She endeavoured to speak, but could not, for the excitement of joy smothered her voice. If at that moment Guillen had come to the door of the chamber, he would have blessed God for having granted to him the felicity of being loved by that angel, whose heart was overflowing with affection and tenderness. For, when the noble maiden exhibited such affection for her executioner, what would it not be for the kind-hearted youth who loved, who adored her with the purest affection and the most reverent adoration that a man can offer to a human creature.

Teresa was not able to express to her brother by means of words the gratitude, the tenderness, and the joy which filled her heart, but a kiss, which her lips imprinted on the cheek of Don Suero, spoke for her.

"My sister," continued the count, still in an affectionate tone of voice, "until I saw you in danger, until you were absent from me, I did not really know how much I loved you. Until one loses a thing, he often does not recognise its value;

whilst your sweet voice, your tenderness, and your cares for me, soothed my troubles, and made life more tolerable—a life constantly tortured, I know not how, whether by a fatal destiny that thwarts all my plans, that constantly opposes my will, and makes me hateful even in the eyes of those most disposed to indulgence and affection; whilst I enjoyed this blessing, I did not know how to appreciate it; but as soon as I was deprived of it, I understood its value, and constantly lamented its loss. You cannot know, my sister, how much I felt your absence, how I longed for your return, what anxiety on your account drove my sleep away, whilst you were in the power of the bandits. Every moment I feared either that a dagger might be plunged in your breast, or that some villain might treacherously stain the purity of the angel, whose custody the most tender and holy of women confided to me when she went to heaven."

"Oh, may God bless you, brother!" exclaimed Teresa, at last recovering her speech, as if God had come to her aid when she wished to praise her mother; "God bless you, brother, for speaking thus of her who gave us our being, and for so reverencing her memory! What will not be her pleasure in looking down from heaven on the love you manifest for me! Do you remember her last words, brother, do you remember them? 'Love each other,' she said'; 'let you, my son,' she added, looking towards you, 'watch over your sister; be her guide, her shield; for she is weak, and has no one in the world but you to protect her!' We both then knelt down by the bedside, and the last words she heard was the solemn promise we made to follow her counsels and fulfil her wishes."

"Yes, my sister, I remember the last words of our mother; perhaps I have forgotten them for a long time; but I repent of that forgetfulness, and wish to expiate my fault, and give back to you that affection which I have denied you; loving you henceforth, and, if necessary, sacrificing my life for your happiness."

"Oh, my brother," exclaimed the Infanta, "how can I ever repay you for those dear promises?"

"With your love, Teresa, with your love, and with the cancelling from your memory of any cruelty with which I may have hitherto treated you. From this day you shall be absolute mistress of this castle, and even I will submit with pleasure to your commands. Mention to me the dueñas and the maidens you wish to attend on you, the servants you desire to have at your orders, and from this very night they shall be ready to obey you."

"Those who have hitherto waited on me, my brother, will be sufficient."

Teresa believed that the occasion had presented itself to speak of Guillen, to justify in the eyes of her brother the preference she intended to show him, and to heighten the good opinion which Don Suero already had of him. Her cheeks, however, became covered with blushes, for the maiden had never concealed her real feelings, but now she felt herself obliged to do so, and was fearful lest her words might reveal them to her brother; she ventured to say, nevertheless, endeavouring to conceal her agitation—

"The good Elvira is sufficient to attend to me; but as years have deprived her, to a great extent, of her hearing, I cannot pass, conversing with her, the long winter evenings, and I would wish that Guillen might sometimes keep me company; you know how pleasant his conversation usually is, always brightened with narratives which his natural cleverness has enabled him to treasure up, and which he knows how to make very entertaining."

"Well, then, sister, although Guillen is very useful to me, you can have him with you as often as you desire, for indeed that youth is not only the most discreet of our servants, but also the most loyal and noble-hearted."

"Oh, if you only knew, my brother, the proofs of devotion and loyalty which he gave me during our sojourn with the bandits! If you only knew the cares he lavished on me, with what assiduity he guarded me whilst I slept, with what solicitude he endeavoured to lessen the privations I had to endure, and above all, with what self-forgetfulness, with what bravery, in short, he shed his blood to defend me from one of the bandits! Oh, my brother, Guillen is the son of an humble man, but the heart of a cavalier beats in his breast."

Teresa stopped, fearing that if she continued to praise the page thus, she might go farther than it was prudent to do.

"Do you say, Teresa, that Guillen shed his blood for you?" asked Don Suero, much astonished.

"Yes; one night we were watching together in a dilapidated tent, which the bandits had allotted to us, when one of those men entered it, and commanded Guillen to leave him alone with me; but the faithful page answered, that rather than do so, he would lose his life by my side. A terrible fight then took place between Guillen and the bandit, and I was saved, but the dagger of our persecutor wounded the hand which was defending me."

"Oh, thanks, thanks, my good page, my good friend, for that is the name I shall give him henceforth!" exclaimed Don Suero, with a seeming tenderness and enthusiasm which increased very much the happiness of Teresa.

"My sister," added the count, "both of us have need of repose, for it is near midnight. You have not slept well for a long time, and I may almost say the same of myself, for the thoughts of the dangers that menaced you drove slumber from me."

The count then quitted the chamber of Teresa, having embraced her affectionately. He proceeded to the place where Guillen was awaiting his orders, and extending his hand to him, he said—

"Guillen, my friend, thanks for your loyalty. My sister has just related to me all that you did for her, and I shall know how to recompense you. From to-day it is my desire that you should always be at the orders of the Infanta. Go to her apartments before retiring to rest, and see if she has any commands for you."

The page felt himself almost wild with joy. He could not find words to reply to his master, for all appeared too poor to express his gratitude, but went off at once to her apartments, his head almost turned with the delight he felt.

Had it not been for the habit he had acquired of respectfully calling out the name of the Infanta on approaching her rooms, he would have allowed himself to be borne away by the gladness which was intoxicating him, by that species of madness with which he was possessed; he would have approached Teresa, pouring forth the most affectionately familiar names that the vocabulary of love contains. As he approached the chamber, in very high spirits, he was evidently on the point of doing so, but he checked himself, and only said, on entering the chamber—

"My lady, the count has sent me to receive your orders."

However, Teresa made him a familiar sign to come near her; then Guillen abandoned his gravity, at once approached the maiden, and said to her—

"Oh, how happy I am, Teresa—how happy! To be always by your side, to see you at all hours!"

"Yes, Guillen, yes," interrupted the Infanta. "The finger of

God has touched the heart of my brother. How happy we are, Guillen!" And she added, with the smile of a child who amuses itself with other children, " Let us now be content with the happiness that we have already experienced, for there will be time enough to enjoy that which smiles on us from all sides."

"Yes, Teresa, yes, my angel," murmured the page in a low voice, "let us retire to rest, for when the heart is full of love there is happiness in sleep. Go to your rest, my love, lulled to sleep by the happiness which will lull me to sleep also."

And the happy lovers parted from each other.

Teresa did not send for Elvira to undress her, as she was in the habit of doing, for she desired to be alone, entirely alone, in order to give herself up unreservedly to her happy thoughts. She knelt down and prayed, thanking God for the joy which she experienced, with as much fervour and earnestness as a saint could have shown if the gates of heaven, in a divine vision, had been opened before him.

She then retired to her bed, and in a very short time was in a deep sleep.

The count was also sleeping—but let us not approach his couch, for the angel of purity does not repose in it, for it is profaned by unholy love. Let us approach that of Guillen or that of Teresa—let us only approach that of the latter, for the chaste love which sleeps in the one also sleeps in the other.

Teresa was dreaming of Guillen.

Guillen was dreaming of Teresa.

There is scarcely anyone in the world who has not dreamed, some time or other, that the bonds of love united him to a being who until then had been indifferent to him, and on awaking, and for some time after, had thought with delight on that being, and where formerly he had seen only an ordinary individual who awoke no feelings in his soul, now sees a being surrounded with enchantment and poetry. How many constant, ardent loves, fruitful of joys and sorrows, have had their birth in a dream !

Well, then, if the being who has been always indifferent to us, and to whom we do not owe sacrifices of love, appears in dreams surrounded with enchantment, ideality, and poesy, how must not that being appear to us whom we have long loved, and who loves us sincerely, who has exposed his life to save us ; who is our only hope in this world ; who physically and morally has so many claims on our love, and appears to our eyes surrounded with so many charms? Such was the case of Teresa in regard to Guillen.

How beautiful, how sweet, how celestial, if it is right to employ that word to express complete earthly happiness, was the dream which presented itself to the Infanta of Carrion immediately on her falling asleep, picturing to her the last loving words of Guillen! She dreamt that she was in an enchanted land, in a paradise; light, flowers, perfumes, harmonies, palaces of gold and diamonds surrounded her; there men and women had the bodies of angels, and also the souls of angels; there were neither masters nor servants in that beautiful place, neither oppressed nor oppressors, for the will of one was the will of all; there was a common soul-feeling amongst them, as there is a common atmosphere for all living beings; there the sky was ever blue and calm, and the sun was never clouded; there the verdure of the fields, and the colour, and the freshness, and the perfume of the flowers were eternal; there the birds always sang, but their music was ever sweet and in delicious harmony, like the harps of the seraphim; there no serpent hissed, and no wild animal lurked in the thickets; there the feet of the wayfarers were not wounded by thorns or brambles; there storms did not rage, the sun did not parch the ground, and the frost, snow, and biting blasts of winter did not benumb; there the trees were ever laden with scented blossoms and delicious fruits; and there, in the midst of that land of enchantment, of that heaven, she and he lived, the two beloved of each other, Guillen and Teresa, and their love was so great, and their happiness so immense, that they almost feared to excite the envy of the inhabitants of that paradise, all happy, all lovers, all intoxicated with boundless and endless delights. And that sweet dream, marvellously like to one which had presented itself also to Guillen at the same time, bound Teresa in calm sleep, until she was aroused from it by the songs of the birds and the bright morning light, entering through the window, which in her happiness she had forgotten to close.

———

CHAPTER XXVIII

HOW THE COUNT OF CABRA SANG A BALLAD FOR THE COUNT OF CARRION

VERY few conspiracies were worked out in Castile and Leon without Don Garcia, Count of Cabra, having taken part in them as the chief plotter, for, in order to obtain employment on such occasions, he had versed himself thoroughly in such matters.

Don Garcia had formerly possessed a rich seigniory in Andalusia, as its name indicated. As this district of Cabra was very much coveted by the Moors, and as their territories lay adjacent to it, their attacks consequently were very much to be dreaded; as the count was a coward and powerful at the same time, his possessions were defended by strong fortresses and numerous men-at-arms. These circumstances had prevented the Moors from attacking them, even after Don Garcia had become their owner through the death of his father, who, with a handful of soldiers and fortifications by no means strong, had repulsed on repeated occasions the expeditions which they had organised against him. They, believing that the son had inherited the valour of his father, and seeing that he had better means of defence than the late count, thought it useless to renew their attacks; however, the effeminate kind of life which Don Garcia led and the circumstance of his never being seen in combats, as all other Christian cavaliers were, soon made them understand that Don Garcia was only heir to his father's name and estates; they therefore got together a large body of men and entered the territory of Cabra.

The vassals of the count and the soldiers, who garrisoned the fortifications on the frontiers, defended themselves bravely; but, as Don Garcia did not send them aid,—having kept the main body of his men in the town, the most important place in his seigniory, fearful for his personal safety,—they yielded chiefly on account of the desperation and anger which the conduct of the count caused them, and the Moors advanced as far as the town of Cabra.

That town was surrounded by good walls, had a strong castle, and fortifications capable of sustaining a long siege; nevertheless, Don Garcia abandoned it precipitately, with his family, without even an arrow having been discharged.

He went to Castile, and established his residence in Burgos, where he had some property; accustomed, however, to ostentation and extravagant living, it was not long before he had sold all he possessed, and soon found himself, if not in a state of misery, at least surrounded by privations such as he had never before experienced, and which were insupportable to him. Another cavalier, with more courage than the count, would have collected together a sufficient number of adventurous soldiers, who were abundant at that epoch; would have proceeded to one of the provinces in the power of the Moors; would have fought against them, and perhaps regained his patrimony. Don Garcia, however, would have preferred to die in misery rather than fight, face to face, and arm to arm, against either Moors or Christians.

He had hopes of getting his son, Nuño Garciez, married to some rich maiden of Castile or Leon, and until such hope could be realised, he subsisted on the payments he received from many grandees, who had great confidence in his cleverness and in the cunning which he knew well how to employ in the planning and carrying out of their schemes and conspiracies. This, then, had become the almost constant occupation of Don Garcia.

His son Nuño was still very young at the period of which our story treats, and his heart was just as effeminate and cowardly as that of his father. The latter, however, possessed a genius for intrigue, which quality was wanting in Nuño; he was stupid, he was but a puppet whom his father used for his own purposes, he had no will of his own, and he was looked on with contempt by his equals in rank.

Don Garcia had solicited for his son the hand of the Infanta of Carrion, but Don Suero hád refused it, not on account of the personal disadvantages of Nuño, for in his eyes such things were of little moment, but because avarice was a passion which dominated him,—why should he consent to the marriage of his sister with the son of the Count of Cabra, who was not the owner of a square foot of ground?

Don Suero had often thought of having recourse to Don Garcia, in order that he might obtain his aid in a conspiracy against his enemies, and especially against Rodrigo Diaz; but he had always hesitated to do so, feeling that the return for his services, which the Count of Cabra would demand, would be the hand of Teresa for his son.

The fame of the cavalier of Vivar was increasing rapidly

and in the same proportion were the hostile feelings between him and Don Suero becoming more bitter; the latter considered, therefore, that the time had arrived when he should take some decisive step, in order to clip the wings of one who was soaring so high, as Guillen had said; for, if he did not do so, he felt that his own ruin was not very far remote.

Four-and-twenty hours after the departure from Carrion of Gonzalo, the messenger of the count, with a letter for Don Garcia, the latter arrived at the gates of the castle, accompanied by the same Gonzalo and some well-armed attendants, whom he always kept about him, and whom he paid handsomely for acting as his guards, as he knew well that such protection was necessary for him.

Don Suero was in the company of Teresa, with whom he was chatting affectionately, when the arrival of Don Garcia was announced to him. The joy of the count was as great as the dismay of Teresa. She was ignorant of the fact that he had solicited her hand for Nuño, but, nevertheless, the presence of the Count of Cabra in the castle filled her with forebodings and fear; for, as the reader already knows, she had learned much concerning him, and knew that his visit to her brother could not be for any good purpose.

Don Suero hastened to receive Don Garcia, so much the more pleased as he had feared that the refusal of Teresa's hand to his son might have prevented his coming. A short time after he had left his sister's chamber, he and his guest were together in a private apartment, where they could not be overheard by anyone.

" I thank you, Don Garcia, for having come so promptly to honour my house by your presence," said Don Suero, intending to secure the goodwill of the Count of Cabra by the friendliness and softness of his accents.

" It is I who am honoured," answered Don Garcia, "and you will not doubt how honoured I feel at being with you, if you remember how much I desired that we might be united, not alone by the bonds of friendship, but also by those of relationship."

Don Suero knew that the count had not abandoned his old pretensions; however, as he only intended to accede to them when he could accomplish his ends by no other means, he thought it better to pretend not to hear the allusion of Don Garcia, and said—

" What news has been received from Zamora ? "

"Very satisfactory tidings for the friends of the cavalier of Vivar have come to Burgos; not only has Don Fernando conferred great honours on him, but also rich tributes have been sent to him by Abengalvon and the four other Moorish kings who were taken prisoners by him in the battle of the Oca Mountains. I assure you that this news has pained me not a little, as, De Vivar being your enemy, his great success must be exceedingly disagreeable to you : as your friend I cannot but deplore the triumphs of your enemy."

"I am thankful to you, Don Garcia, for your devotion and friendship; but do you only deplore the rise of Rodrigo because it militates against me? Have you no other motives for hating him?"

"What other motives could I have?"

"It is strange, my lord count, that in this matter you have so little foresight when in all others you forecast events so well. Do you not belong to the most illustrious nobility of Castile?"

"Yes, and that confers such honour on me that I can never forget the fact."

"Well, then, in a very short time the most noble and powerful grandees of Castile and Leon will be at the side of De Vivar, as your squire is at yours ; in a short time De Vivar will regard only as vassals those who to-day are greater than he is ; soon the king, Don Fernando himself, will be ruled by that audacious and haughty soldier, to whom he now dispenses so many favours, never thinking that he is cherishing the raven which will pick out his eyes. And do you not think, Don Garcia, that it is your duty to curb this wild steed, which threatens to trample down you, as well as so many others? Do you believe that De Vivar, to whom even the king is inferior in pride and ambition, will not consider himself greater than you, and consequently will humiliate you under his feet?"

"De Vivar, if he is not my friend, is also not my enemy," replied Don Garcia, the words of Don Suero not having changed in the least his habitual calmness; and he added, with a smile, slightly sarcastic : "Does it appear to you that it is fitting for one good cavalier, as I consider myself to be, to envy the good fortune of another cavalier, much less to injure one who has never done me a wrong? Let that be for you, good count, let you thwart the plans of De Vivar, as you are his mortal enemy, on account of insults which one who prides himself on being a noble and a cavalier should never forget. I, far from disapproving of the enmity you bear to Don Rodrigo, and your intention to endeavour to prevent his rise, sincerely applaud it. If I were in your position, I would wage a war, without truce, against De Vivar; I would sacrifice my repose, my property, even my life, to the avenging of my honour,—for it must be confessed that you have been cruelly outraged by Rodrigo Diaz. Who in Castile and Leon does not remember the proclamations he caused to be posted about, branding you as a coward and a felon? Go through the country places and the towns of Castile, and you will hear the people singing gentle ballads, in which those proclamations of De Vivar are amplified and improved on "—

"Cease, Don Garcia, be silent, for the fire of hell is burning in my breast!" exclaimed Don Suero, stamping so violently on the floor that it vibrated.

"Pardon me," continued Don Garcia, "but as your friend, knowing that you do not often go far from your castle, and therefore are ignorant of what is said of you, I thought it well to inform you, so that you might take steps to punish the offenders. If you had travelled hither with me from Burgos you could have heard the rustics chanting the ballads I have mentioned. Just listen, in order that you may have some idea of the malice of the Castilian peasants; listen to what I heard sung shortly after I left Burgos."

And the count repeated, in that monotonous and melancholy chant with which the women of Castile lull their infants to sleep—

> "In Carrion, in its Castle,
> At his dinner seated,
> Was its owner, Don Suero,
> That disloyal count.
> Pages, elegant and young,
> Served to him his cup,
> And in the polished cup
> Was wine to make him drunk.
> The count is fond of wine,
> But dreads to shed his blood."

"Earth, earth! Open and bury me in your depths!" roared Don Suero, writhing as if he were suffering the torments of the damned. "Be silent, Don Garcia! I would throw myself from this window, or plunge a dagger into my heart, if it were not necessary to live in order to bury it in the breasts of those who thus calumniate me and scoff at me."

"I like to see you thus, enraged when insulted," said the Count of Cabra, clasping the hand of Don Suero, whose veins had swelled to such an extent that they appeared as if they were about to burst; whose eyes were injected with blood, and from whose mouth foam was oozing, as from that of an infuriated wild beast,—"thus do I like to see you, enraged and not resigned."

And Don Garcia continued—

> " Envoys, sent by Don Rodrigo,
> Castile's bravest cavalier,—
> Born in a lucky hour,
> Fearing no one in the world,—
> Then announced to him their message,
> And these words to him they spake:
> ' Don Suero, brave Rodrigo,
> The good cavalier of Vivar,
> Calls you forth, for having libelled
> Him ; for having called him coward.
> If you don't accept his challenge,
> Cavalier no more are you.
> Buckle on the spur no longer,
> Never mount again a charger,
> Eat no white bread at your table,
> Ne'er divert yourself with ladies.'
>
> ' Now depart from this, ye envoys,
> Bear the message to your master,
> That he may do as he pleases ;
> On the field I shall not meet him.'
> Thus then spake Count Don Suero,
> That disloyal cavalier ;
> And he turned to his pages,
> To receive his sparkling cup ;
> For the count is fond of wine,
> But he is not fond of blood."

"Ah ! they say that I am not fond of blood ! I shall make that of those rustics flow in torrents," cried the Count of Carrion, infuriated, mad with anger. Tell me, who are those that dare to insult me with such accursed ballads ? "

"All the peasants of Castile are constantly singing that which you have just heard. Judge how often I must have listened to it, when my memory retains it, and I have not, indeed, a good memory for such things. But it is not the rustics alone who revile and mock you ; it would be as unjust and difficult to chastise them as the echo which repeats the words of a calumniator. Return insult for insult to De Vivar, humiliate him as he has humiliated you, and you will see how those very same rustics will call you in a short time—

> " ' The bravest cavalier,
>   Born in a lucky hour,
>   Fearing no one in the world.' "

"Yes, yes, you are right; my vengeance must fall on De Vivar, for he is my real enemy, my persecutor, my fate, my evil genius. But how shall I be able to conquer him? How can I humble him? How can I throw back in his teeth the ignominy which he has heaped on me?"

"Why? can you not bind on your sword; does not the heart of a knight beat in your breast? Fight with him as the bandits have fought with those who, at the Inn of the Moor, were bearing a maiden off from them; fight with him as Don Gome de Gormaz, as Martin Gonzalez, the Aragonian, fought with him "—

Don Suero trembled at this recalling to his mind of the valour of Rodrigo, which Don Garcia saw with much satisfaction, and replied, interrupting the Count of Cabra—

"I would do so, if God had given to my arm as much strength as He has given to my heart; but the bad health, which constantly darkened my youth, and which still afflicts me, has not permitted me to perfect myself in the use of arms, so as to be a match for De Vivar, who, thanks not to his heart, but to his strength and skill, is able to unhorse an adversary with a stroke of his lance."

The Count of Cabra smiled, not so much at the puerile excuse of Don Suero, as with satisfaction at seeing that the road was being made easy which would lead him to the accomplishment of his desires.

"Certainly," he replied, "De Vivar, fighting against you in the lists, would have that advantage; but there is another kind of contest, more safe, and allowable to a cavalier whose natural incapacity to avenge his honour with sword and lance has been taken advantage of in order to insult him. Where the sword cannot reach, cunning can, my good count."

"I understand you, Don Garcia, I understand you, and I am resolved to follow your advice; but do you think that I would be victorious in such a fight?"

"If you carry it out dexterously, I have no doubt of it."

"But how can I plot cleverly, when that kind of thing is

new to me? I am wanting in friends to assist me, and De Vivar has many such."

"You say that you are wanting in friends?"

"The only person to whom I can give that name is you, Don Garcia, and you have refused me your aid several times when I asked you to help me in such a struggle as you now advise."

"I never refused you my aid, Don Suero; the only thing I did was to ask from you a hostage, so that I could depend on your silence in case our plans might fail; and if you now desire my assistance you must give me that hostage."

"Don Garcia, my family would be much honoured by being united to yours, for you are as noble as a king, although you have been unfortunate; but my sister is still but a child, both on account of her age and of her natural fragility. And besides, to marry her would be but to kill her, for she desires either to live and die by my side or to go into a convent. If you only knew, Don Garcia, how I love her, how sad my life would be without her, you would praise me for not wishing to force her will. I was still a beardless youth when both of us were left orphans, and from that time she has been my only comfort, and I hers."

"When the Infanta is the wife of my son, you will both cease to be orphans, for in me and in my wife, Doña Elvira, she and you will find parents as affectionate as those whom you have lost."

"I appreciate, as I should, the desire which animates you; however, respect the feelings of that poor girl, very unhappy on account of her sad disposition and her delicate constitution."

"Measure by the love that you have for your sister that which I feel for my son, and you need not be surprised that I desire to procure for Nuño the peace of mind that he has lost since the time he first saw Doña Teresa, and heard both cavaliers and peasants speaking so highly of her virtues and good sense."

"I cannot do less than extol the feelings which move you to ask for your son the hand of my sister," said Don Suero, though now almost certain that he would never be able to obtain the assistance of the Count of Cabra, except at the price of the hand of Teresa, "but it is impossible to comply with your wishes."

"And it is also impossible for me to make known to you an excellent plan for freeing yourself from De Vivar."

"Tell me, Don Garcia, what that plan is, and in exchange demand from me my treasures, demand from me "—

"The hand of your sister. I desire nothing more; I want nothing more."

"Oh, this miserable fate of mine! Can I not advance a step without losing a portion of my heart? Let De Vivar come, let all my enemies come, and tear life from me; for then the torments I suffer will cease."

"Yes, De Vivar will come, your enemies will come, but they will leave you your life, that you may spend it dishonoured, a fugitive, without a spot of land on which to place your feet, without a hut to shelter you, with scarcely a piece of bread to put into your mouth. And then your sister, that delicate girl whom you love so much, will die of grief, of exposure, of hunger, or will marry some peasant, in order to secure an existence for herself. Do you perchance consider yourself powerful enough to continue despising De Vivar? Powerful and rich and haughty were the Count of Gormaz and Martin Gonzalez, and notwithstanding they died at his feet,—and that when Rodrigo was neither as skilful nor as strong as he now is; he had not then kings as his vassals."

"Well, then, Don Garcia," interrupted at this point Don Suero, "my sister shall be the wife of your son if Rodrigo Diaz ceases to live, or, at the least, if he is banished from Castile and Leon."

"He shall die, he shall die; have no doubts of that, Don Suero," exclaimed the Count of Cabra, embracing De Carrion, full of joy; and he added, "Are you quite sure, however, that your sister will consent to a marriage with my son?"

" My sister," replied Don Suero, " shall do my will; and if not, let her beware."

And whilst poor Teresa, the gentle, loving girl, was in her apartment with Guillen, dreaming of a paradise of love, those two cowards, with souls of chaff and hearts of flint, were plotting her slavery, and also a vile plan for the assassination of Rodrigo, the most perfect cavalier of Castile, the good knight, the conqueror, he who was born in a lucky hour, he who in a fortunate hour girt on his knightly sword.

———

CHAPTER XXIX

HOW THE KING AND RODRIGO, HAVING SAID GOOD PRAYERS, GAVE GOOD SWORD STROKES

THE king, Don Fernando, having left the works for the re-building of Zamora in a forward state, was preparing to return to Burgos, where he intended to devote himself exclusively to the improvement of the laws, of agriculture, and of the arts, taking advantage of the tranquillity that reigned in his kingdoms, and desirous of ameliorating many grievances in them, as such had been rather increasing for some time back.

Before returning to Burgos, he desired to go to Compostela, with the object of visiting the shrine of the holy Apostle James. When Rodrigo, just as he was about to leave that last-named city, learned the king's intention, having finished his devotions, he determined to await the king there, in order to accompany him on his journey to Burgos.

Don Fernando arrived in due course at Compostela, and for some days devoted himself with much fervour to pious exercises, for he was as good a Christian as he was a brave warrior. He was solacing himself with the hope of soon being in the bosom of his family, when the Moors of Portugal unexpectedly broke the peace which they had arranged with Don Fernando, crossing the frontiers of the Christian districts, and committing various kinds of outrages.

Don Fernando felt that he must sacrifice his personal tranquillity to the protection of his subjects, and to the punishment of the infidels, who, if he did not arrest their progress, would become more daring, and extend their depredations farther. He asked advice from Don Rodrigo and other cavaliers, and all, especially the latter, counselled war.

That, therefore, was decided on. The king and Rodrigo Diaz collected together in a few days an army sufficiently large, and set out for Portugal, with the determination of attacking the first Moorish castle which they might find on their route ; for this purpose they had provided themselves with good materials of war.

Near Monzao they overtook a large body of infidels who were hastening back to Portugal with the rich booty that they had seized in the district of Tuy, and routed them completely, taking back from them all the plunder which they had possessed themselves of. Don Fernando divided it amongst his troops, and this inspirited the Christian army to such an extent, that it followed the track of the comparatively few Moors who had escaped from the battle, and who, under the command of the Alcaide [1] of Cea, had succeeded in taking refuge in the castle in that town.

The Castle of Cea was very strong, was well garrisoned, and provided with provisions sufficient to bear a long siege; for these reasons Don Fernando believed that an attempt to take it would result in a loss both of time and men. However, as such obstacles were only incentives to the courage of the Cid, for by that name Rodrigo was now known, he believed that the Christian army should not pass on farther without giving a fresh proof of its power by destroying that first bulwark of the Moslems.

"Sire," said Rodrigo to the king, "I am about to ask a favour of you, which I trust you will grant."

"Speak, Rodrigo," replied Don Fernando, "for you already know how desirous I am to gratify you."

"The favour I ask of you is, that you will permit me, this very day, to plant the Christian standard with my own hands on the walls of the Castle of Cea."

"O good Cid, who is there but must love you as the best cavalier in the world!" exclaimed Don Fernando, clasping him to his breast. "With a hundred knights like you, I would undertake to drive the Moors, not alone from Portugal, but from all Spain. It is not idle talk when the people say that you were born in a lucky hour! I applaud your valour, Rodrigo; my heart swells and rejoices when I hear you thus speak; but you know that the enterprise which you desire to undertake is very difficult."

"Sire, it is in difficult and useful enterprises that glory is to be found. In this castle have taken refuge those who have pillaged and laid waste a considerable portion of your states, and they must not remain unpunished. Pardon me if I speak with more heat than is seemly before my lord and king, but Rodrigo Diaz would rather break his sword into fragments than be within a few bow-shots of the Moors and not come to close quarters with them. Let them but see that we do not take into consideration whether their walls are strong or weak, and the terror that will seize on them shall serve us better than our weapons. The same feeling is widespread amongst

[1] Governor of a castle or fort.

those under my command, who desire to be the first to prove to the infidels that there are no Moors capable of resisting Castilian arms."

"Well, then, Rodrigo, let us attack and conquer this fortress," replied Don Fernando, full of hope and joy. "Then let us hasten on to Viseo and other strongholds, and let us not return to Castile till we have freed Portugal completely from the Moslem domination."

Preparations were then immediately made for the siege of the castle. In a few hours it was attacked and defended with extreme obstinacy. The Moors discharged clouds of projectiles from the walls, causing terrible carnage amongst the besiegers. The battering-rams, which the latter worked unweariedly, did not move a stone, for the walls of Cea were extremely solid. The Cid, and those under his command, who fought in the most advanced position, were burning with impatience, seeing that the time for dashing at the fortress was delayed so long.

"To the assault! To the assault!" cried the Cid, full of ardour and courage.

"To the assault!" cried all who were fighting by his side.

But just as they were preparing to put ladders against the walls, a large portion of one of them crashed down, dislodged by a terrible blow from a more powerful battering-ram, which had been constructed when it was found that those which they had been using were inefficient.

"St. James of Compostela!" thundered the Cid. "To the walls! To the walls, my good cavaliers!"

And snatching from the hands of its bearer the standard of Castile and Leon, he clambered up the ruins of the wall, it in one hand, and his sword in the other, followed by many cavaliers as brave as himself.

Blood ran in torrents. The Moors fought with desperation, concentrating almost all their forces on that point; but all was in vain, for the Cid pressed onward, trampling Moslem corpses under his feet, and at last gained the highest part of the wall. There he planted the Christian standard, crying out with resounding voice—

"Cea for Don Fernando!"

This triumph, achieved by the company of the Cid, lent new courage to the besiegers, and struck terror into the besieged. In a short time the castle was assaulted at many other places, and the cross was substituted everywhere for the crescent.

The Castle of St. Martin and others were taken by the army of Don Fernando shortly after the conquest of Cea. The name of the Cid resounded in all directions, filling the Moors with terror; and the brave cavalier, becoming every day more daring, every day more desirous of seeing the holy cross where the crescent hitherto dominated, proposed to the king the siege of Viseo, the only place of importance which the Mahometans still held in Portugal.

"Sire," said Rodrigo to Don Fernando, "your health and your age demand quiet and rest after such severe labours. If a vassal may be allowed to give advice to his lord, I would counsel you to retire to Coimbra, which is a populous and rich town, and where you will find, therefore, all the conveniences and comforts which you have been accustomed to enjoy in Leon or in Burgos. I am a young man, and therefore must not let my arm get out of practice. Leave to my charge the siege and assault of Viseo, and, God aiding me, it shall be yours within fifteen days."

"It is certain," said Don Fernando, "that my health is much impaired, and years are coming on me more rapidly than I should wish. If I were younger, you and I together would soon drive the Moorish power beyond the Strait into Africa. My heart, however, beats and grows young again when I see you fighting. We shall first subjugate Viseo, and then we shall go together to take some repose in Coimbra, which place I am desirous to see, as I am fond of it, if it were only because it cost me a seven-months' siege to subdue it."

"That which pleases you also pleases me, sire," replied Rodrigo, seeing with joy, and being much moved by, the warlike ardour which animated the king.

Two days after, the town of Viseo was surrounded.

In vain did the battering-rams exert all their force against the walls, for they were extremely solid; in vain were ladders brought up in order to take the castle by assault, for the battlements were crowded with crossbow-men who rained down their arrows on all who approached the walls. Three times had the Cid taken up the standard of Castile and Leon, as at the escalade of Cea, and had endeavoured to mount the wall; but each time he had to fall back, seeing those about him killed, and himself preserved almost miraculously.

It was past midnight. Don Fernando had ordered the assault to be suspended, in order that he might deliberate with his captains, and particularly with the Cid, as to the precautions that should be taken in order to prevent the sacrifice of so many men-at-arms, and as to the best means for bringing the enterprise to a successful issue. They had demanded from its defenders the surrender of the stronghold, threatening that all would be put to the sword if they did not deliver themselves up by a certain day. That day had arrived, and the besieged still continued to defend it.

A Moor who was one of the sentinels on the battlements let himself down on the outer side of the wall, and, making his way to the royal tent of Don Fernando, asked to be brought into his presence. He was carefully examined, lest he might have concealed weapons, wherewith to commit some act of treachery, and, none having been found, he was brought before the king.

"Sire," he said to Don Fernando, "I believe it is your intention to take this place by storm and put all the inhabitants to the sword; I have a wife and children, whom I love, and in order to save them I have become a traitor to my faith and to my brothers-in-arms. Many years ago an arrow was shot from these very walls, which killed Don Alfonso, King of Leon, and the father of your queen; he who shot that arrow is now in Viseo. If you give me your word to spare my wife, my children, and myself, I will tell you who "—

"Glorious St. Isadore!" exclaimed Don Fernando, "what do I hear? Can it be possible that the murderer of the good Don Alfonso—for whom Queen Sancha still weeps—yet lives? Tell me who the traitor is, tell me his name, and I promise you, not only to spare yourself and your family, but also to load you with riches."

"Sire," hastened to answer the Moor, filled with joy, "he is named Ben-Amet, and is now charged with the defence of the wall of the Mosque; for, as it is it, above all, that should not fall into your hands, they have confided its defence to him."

"You are now at liberty either to remain here or to return into the town," said Don Fernando. "To-morrow we shall enter Viseo; whether you now go or remain with us, describe the position of your house accurately, and both it and its occupants shall be respected."

"Opposite the great Mosque there is a detached building with a handsome frontage; that is my house, sire, and my wife and children are in it."

The Moor retired to a tent, near that of the king, for he did not dare to return to the town. Shortly afterwards, Don

Fernando summoned his captains and related to them what he had heard.

"We must," said the Cid, "make the assault at daybreak on the wall which that traitor defends, and all of us shall either take it or die in the attempt."

Don Fernando held out his hand to Rodrigo Diaz, rejoiced to know that he had anticipated his own wish.

"Rodrigo," he said, "you always divine what my heart feels. Yes, the traitor Ben-Amet must expiate with his blood that of Don Alfonso; but we must economise as much as possible our own. We have already lost very many brave cavaliers in the assaults which we have attempted, and we must now endeavour to think of some plan to shelter ourselves to some extent from the arrows of our enemies."

"Our shields," said the Cid, "are not large enough to protect our bodies from the arrows of the besieged; it seems to me that it would be a good plan to enlarge them by attaching to them wooden boards; I heard my father say that such a thing has been done at times."

"Yes, yes," said the king, "we shall do that."

And as Martin Antolinez, Alvar Minaya, and the other cavaliers who were present approved, as well as the king, of the plan of the Cid, whose men were the first that offered to scale the wall of the Mosque, they began at once to get the shields enlarged in the manner indicated.

At the dawn of day the Cid and his men approached the wall of the Mosque as quietly as possible, provided with scaling ladders and the enlarged shields. At a signal, that had been arranged beforehand, the ladders were placed against the walls; the Moors, however, discovered this, and began to rain down a shower of arrows. The Christian cavaliers, who preceded the other scalers of the walls, also cast a large number of javelins, which caused great slaughter amongst the defenders; however, as the shields protected the bodies of the besiegers, they did not fall back, but mounted the ladders, and were very near its summit, notwithstanding the furious efforts which Ben-Amet and his soldiers used in order to keep them back.

"St. James of Compostela!" cried the Cid, as at the assault of Cea; all who followed him repeated the cry with enthusiasm, and all rushed on to the top of the wall. Then followed a sanguinary fight; horrible, ferocious, body to body, arm to arm; dead bodies fell in all directions, blood ran in torrents; those who were guarding other portions of the walls rushed to the defence, but at last the Christian army pressed forward into the citadel, through the opening made by the Cid and those under his command, and Ben-Amet was in the power of Don Fernando.

"Sire," then cried out Rodrigo Diaz, "I ask a favour of you; enough of blood has already been shed in Viseo, pardon the vanquished, let not our swords be used against the defenceless inhabitants of the town."

"I grant your request, good Cid," responded Don Fernando. "They shall not be used; let no one dare to kill man or woman."

The soldiers were preparing to put to the sword the inhabitants of the place, but refrained, respecting the command of the king.

And then Rodrigo Diaz planted with his own hand the Christian standard on the walls of Viseo, crying out—

"Viseo for Castile and Leon!   Visco for Don Fernando!"

On that same day the hands of the slayer of Don Alfonso were cut off and his eyes torn out; he then was put to death with arrows on the very wall from whence he had shot the regicidal arrow.

The Moors, fearful that Don Fernando would subject the district over which they still ruled in Portugal, endeavoured to divert his course, and collecting together a numerous army, in the direction of Elvas, they marched on through Estremadura, committing still greater outrages than those which they had practised in Galicia.   Don Fernando learned this, and although he determined to hasten to stem that torrent, he considered that he should not leave unprotected the districts which he had subjected; he resolved, therefore, to divide his army, with the object that half of it should remain in Portugal and that the remainder should go in pursuit of the invaders.

Rodrigo Diaz, to whom inaction was unbearable, for whom the favourite position was that which offered the most dangers and fatigues, and who always anticipated the desires of the king, offered to go in pursuit of the Moors.   Don Fernando accepted his offer, and in a short time the Cid placed himself at the head of a brave body of men and set out for the frontiers of Estremadura.   The king, in the meantime, well satisfied with the results of that campaign, and firmly persuaded that Rodrigo would make the Moors pay dearly for their temerity, made preparations to visit his dominions in Portugal. His objects were to assure himself, by personal observation, of the state of public spirit, of the condition of the fortified places, of the needs of his subjects; and to put in good order the ecclesiastical and civil affairs of that kingdom.

The progress of Don Fernando from district to district presented occasions for the most ardent and sincere ovations that had been offered to him during his long life. The Portuguese, who during very many years had groaned under the heavy Moslem yoke, blessed and honoured with fêtes and rejoicings the monarch who had liberated them, and in doing so they also celebrated the glory of Rodrigo.

CHAPTER XXX

HOW ONE GOOD MAN CAN MAKE A HUNDRED GOOD ALSO

TERESA and Guillen had now been for some days delivered up to their dreams of love and happiness; it may be said that those days had liberally indemnified the Infanta for all she had suffered since the time her mother went to heaven. The joy of her heart was reflected in her countenance, now as bright and smiling as it was formerly pale and sad. Her brother continued to lavish on her assiduous attentions and endearments, and Guillen also experienced the advantages of the extraordinary change that could be perceived in the conduct of the count; a change which, as the reader already knows, was assumed in order to induce Teresa to obey her brother when he would make known to her his wish that she should bestow her hand on the son of the Count of Cabra. Don Suero was far from suspecting the love which united the Infanta and the page; he believed that Teresa had an affection for him, because he was a loyal servant, who amused her with his pleasant conversation, and who had guarded her, with fidelity and self-sacrifice, during her captivity amongst the bandits.

Tidings arrived at Carrion of the victories which the Castilian and Leonese arms had gained in Portugal, and of the fact that very many, both nobles and commoners, were hastening from all quarters to join the army of Don Fernando, some desirous of glory and others of booty. Guillen then began to think of his condition, considered that this was the opportune occasion to endeavour to realise his dreams of glory and advancement, and decided to leave the service of Don Suero, in order to take part in the Portuguese hostilities, however sorrowful the separation between him and the Infanta might be. He therefore made known his resolution to Teresa, and she approved of it, feeling that in it lay the only hope of the realisation of their love. He then went to inform the count of his intention, determined to carry it out, whether he gained the approbation of Don Suero or not.

"My lord," he said to him, "the sacrifice even of my life appears but a small thing to me, if thereby I can repay all the kindnesses which I have received from you whilst I have been in your service, and in my present condition all that I could do to pay that debt would be but trifling. I am nothing at present, but must become something in the world's esteem, in order to be of use to your house. The Christian army is gaining glory and riches in Portugal, and I desire to have a part in its victories; allow me to depart and enlist in it."

The Count of Carrion smiled at what he considered the foolish hopes of the page, and said in a tone of kindly expostulation —

"You must be mad, Guillen! Do you imagine that it is an easy thing for a peasant's son to win the sword and spurs of a knight by means of sword strokes and lance thrusts, in an army where such are given, right and left, in abundance? If such only were necessary, the army of Don Fernando would soon be one consisting of nothing but knights. Rest content to be what you are, as your birth prevents you from being anything higher, and as I am well satisfied with you and desire to have you with me."

"My lord," replied Guillen, "I know that noble blood does not run in my veins, but in my breast beats a heart that feels the ambition of becoming noble. I am still but a youth, and am resolved to struggle boldly to win the nobility which my birth denied to me. If I succeed, my rise will be the greater in proportion to the low condition from which I shall have raised myself; if I die, I shall at least have gained some honour in having sacrificed my life for a worthy and noble ambition."

The enthusiasm and the ardent desire for advancement which the page manifested were noted by Don Suero. He considered that such feelings could indeed make the humble page very brave. He considered also that Guillen was grateful to him; he reflected that he, the Count of Carrion, was in need of friends, for he had not even the friendship of the neighbouring townspeople and rustics; and, finally, he came to the conclusion that the youth might be more useful to him in the army of the Cid than in his own castle.

"Guillen, my good page," he said to him, holding out his hand affectionately, "you are more honourable than many who are of noble birth; there is in you the stuff out of which cavaliers are made; generous sentiments, which I applaud warmly, animate you. Go then to the wars, and I will nourish the hope of treating some day as a cavalier him who had been my servant. I desire that you should bring with you a memento of him whom you have so loyally served; the bandits have left me but few horses, but I wish to bestow on you the best that is in my stables, and also all the arms you require."

"'Thanks, my lord, thanks," murmured the page, forgetting all the evil deeds of the count, and only seeing the generosity which Don Suero exhibited towards him at that moment.

" Rodrigo Diaz feels enmity with regard to me," continued Don Suero, "doubtless because he judges me wrongfully, as I have been calumniated to him; nevertheless, I cannot but acknowledge that he is an honourable cavalier and a very brave soldier. You must enlist in his army, for at his side you will learn all that is necessary for both a soldier and a knight."

The page was astonished to hear Don Suero speak thus of Rodrigo Diaz, whom, up to that time, he had hated, and of whom he had taken every opportunity to speak badly in every respect. He considered, however, that, as the feelings of Don Suero had become so greatly modified regarding the Infanta, they had also changed with regard to the Cid.

" And when do you think of setting out?" asked the count.

" I should wish to do so this very day, my lord," replied the page; "for, as I have now obtained your goodwill, I must arrive in Portugal before the termination of the war against the Moors, and I do not believe it will last long, to judge by the valour which, it is reported, the Christian army is displaying."

"Well, then, Guillen, perhaps Doña Teresa will have some message to confide to you; take leave of her, and depart whenever it suits you."

Guillen went to the apartments of the Infanta, well pleased with the kindness of the count, but sorrowful because the sad moment was approaching when he and Teresa should be separated—perhaps for ever.

Their parting was indeed like that of the nail from the flesh, to use the expressive words of a chronicler of the Cid; and shortly after, Guillen left the Castle of Carrion, mounted on the spirited steed which Don Suero had presented to him, and armed with shield and lance.

Just then Bellido Dolfos arrived at the gate of the castle. Guillen recognised him as one of the captains of the band of the Vengador, for he had seen him in his camp just before he and Teresa had set out on their return journey to Carrion, when the last of the bandits who had been in the power of Don Suero had arrived. Seeing him now enter the castle caused, therefore, much surprise to Guillen.

Guillen pursued his way towards Portugal, thinking of Teresa and building castles in the air. He had been riding on for about four hours, when, on arriving at a wood, almost always deserted, as there was neither village nor inn throughout that district, he thought he heard voices in a thicket. He listened, and caught the following words—

"He must be a cavalier, to judge by his horse and arms, as far as I could take note of them, some way down the road."

"If he were such he would not travel alone through these solitudes."

"Perhaps he has got separated from his followers by accident in this thick wood."

"Whether he is a cavalier or not, go and advise our chiefs. I will remain here and keep a close eye on the road. There may perchance come other men behind him, and 'going for wool we might return shorn.'" [1]

"I shall do it at once, comrade."

Guillen looked carefully into the wood, and though there was no brushwood between the trees he could see nothing. Just, however, as it occurred to him that the speakers might be concealed behind the trunk of a tree, he saw a man coming out from such a position and running towards an adjacent glen; he was

[1] A Spanish proverb.

clad almost exactly like those of the band of the Vengador. Guillen then knew with what kind of people he had to do : the Vengador was evidently encamped in that wood, and had placed sentinels on those high trees. He got into readiness his lance and shield, in case he might be compelled to use them, and continued his way. Scarcely, however, had he advanced twenty paces when four horsemen rode forth from the glen, on a pathway that led from it, and cried out to him—

"Halt, cavalier !"

"I shall do so if you address me more courteously," replied Guillen, without obeying their order.

"Now we shall use courtesy towards a very daring individual."

And the bandits, for those men did really belong to the band of the Vengador, rushed on the ex-page, who received them with the point of his lance.

Guillen defended himself for a considerable time, giving thrusts, each of which was worth four of those of the aggressors; in the end, however, thanks to their numerical superiority, they succeeded in disarming him, and then dragged him off to the glen.

"You need not fear that we will injure you," said one who appeared to be the leader. "You have fought like a brave man, and we, although bandits, are sufficiently honourable to esteem courageous men as they deserve."

And when he who thus spoke saw the face of Guillen, who just then threw back his hood, he added—

"May Beelzebub take me if that face is not known to me ! Confound me ! if we have not taken prisoner no other than the most loyal and attached servitor of the Count of Carrion."

"I have been such, Sir Vengador, or whatever is your name," replied Guillen; "but henceforth I intend to serve Don Rodrigo Diaz, or the Cid, as he is now called. In doing so, I shall also serve Christ and my country, against whose enemies I am going to fight in Portugal."

"And you will fight well, judging by what we have experienced from you," said the Vengador. "I cannot understand how you could have remained so long in the service of De Carrion, for he is such a wretch that you must have been very badly treated by him."

"On the contrary, he has always treated me very well; you see my horse and arms, those are the final proofs of that, for he made me a present of them. Don Suero was indeed a

Don Judas for a long time; but you do not know that of late he has become quite different."

"Such a conversion astonishes me."

"It is indeed astonishing."

"But I would not trust much in it."

"I trust in it. Do you believe that there are no repentant sinners in the world?"

"There are such doubtless; but"—

"You who to-day are bandits, might be to-morrow honourable soldiers."

"Certainly, soldiers and bandits are all fighting men; the business of both one and the other is killing and plundering."

Guillen, who already considered himself a soldier, was not very well pleased with this comparison.

"They adopt, however, different modes of killing and plundering."

"But the certain fact is that they all kill and plunder."

"I am not going to defend, with bandits, the honourable calling of those who are not such."

"Well, then, if that does not please you, let us talk of something else. What has become of your lady, that delicate maiden, whom you took such good care of when in our camp?"

Guillen, who for a moment had forgotten Teresa, changed colour when she was mentioned, believing that the bandits were about to profane her name, mixing it up with some of their coarse jests.

"Do not speak of her," he said, "for only those who are as good as she is should have her name in their mouths."

"Do you think that we do not respect those who are really good? We know that the Infanta is so, and far from saying anything against her, we would cut out the tongue of anyone who dared to speak an ill word of her. And as a proof, do you not remember what we did to a comrade who desired to take your place with her in the tent?"

Guillen remembered what the Vengador referred to; he recalled to mind the way in which the chief of the bandits had acted with regard to Teresa, conduct rather of a good cavalier than of a bandit; and he experienced in his heart a feeling of sympathy with the Vengador.

"Yes, yes, I have not forgotten it; and if you demanded my life, I would give it for you, on account of the noble way you treated my lady."

"Hola! the well-being of the Infanta seems to interest you much! I would swear that it is not for you a sack of straw"—

Guillen coloured up; the Vengador noticed it, and continued—

"May God preserve me! but it would be a good thing if in Portugal, by cutting the heads off Moors, you could make yourself worthy of knighthood and could mount up as easily as a bubble, so that in the end the Infanta might bestow her hand on you, in order to efface, with its gentle rubbing, that cicatrice which was left on yours by the dagger of that fellow whom I have just mentioned."

A peculiar joy shone on the face of the ex-page, as if these words, which were so much in harmony with his hopes, were the prophecy of a saint or of a wizard. The Vengador had gained a new claim on the confidence of Guillen, for with whom does a man more sympathise than with him who most flatters his inclinations? The youth, however, thought that he should not disclose that pure love of his which he concealed in his heart at his departure from Castile.

"Such a ridiculous idea," he said, "has never entered my head. I do love the Infanta, but all love her, because she is good, because she is kind-hearted, because she is the holiest of women; I love her, as brothers love their sisters, and I. cannot find any better way to express to you how I love the Infanta Doña Teresa."

Between a youth and a maiden, not related by the ties of blood, a tender and pure friendship may exist, but it takes very little to change it into real love; or rather, such a friendship, in relation to love, is as the bud to the full-blown rose. The Vengador knew this from personal experience; he knew, and the reader knows, if his memory or understanding is not very weak, and they are almost one and the same thing, a maiden whom he first loved as a sister, and ended by loving as a sweetheart; for this reason the last words of Guillen convinced him more and more that the ex-page was in love with the Infanta, although he would not give the name of love to his feelings regarding her.

And it was the fact that, as Martin and Guillen were both in love, they longed to speak of their love affairs; each was anxious to make a confidant of someone who could understand him. Martin had confided to Rui-Venablos his love for Beatrice, whom he had not seen for a considerable time; but what did Rui-Venablos understand of love, the rough soldier who had spent his life on fields of battle, without feeling affection for anything but his horse and his arms, and whose ears had never been delighted with more amorous accents than those of the trumpets which incited him to close with the Moorish ranks, and to lop off Moorish heads wherewith to adorn Castilian lances?

"But would it not make you happy to marry Doña Teresa?" asked the Vengador.

"It would make me happier than to be King of Castile and Leon," replied the ex-page, scarcely knowing what he was saying.

Of course Martin had not now the slightest doubt of Guillen being in love with the Infanta.

The bandits who accompanied the Vengador, when he dismounted, removed to some distance from the speakers, whilst their horses went to graze on a sloping bank, covered with fresh and abundant herbage.

"Go to the glen," said the chief to them, "and hurry on the meal which we were preparing when we came out to look after this youth; if I want you meanwhile, I shall send notice to you."

The bandits took their horses by the bridles, and obeyed their chief. He and Guillen therefore remained alone, as the sentinels stationed amongst the trees were too far off to hear them.

"Then know, my friend," said Martin, "that I have got to like you since I saw you in the castle of your master on that accursed night in which we assaulted it, and noticed your zeal for the interests of the Infanta, and your courage; your present determination to go to the wars and fight against the infidels has increased my affection for you. Perhaps you will learn some day that if I am a bandit by profession, I am not one by inclination. You love the Infanta; I know it, for it is impossible to conceal it from me. Learn, then, that I also love a maiden, who, if she has not noble blood, has a soul as noble as that of Doña Teresa, and I can make no better comparison. I am dying to speak of my love with someone who can understand it; but I have not met with such a person since I became a member of this band. I know that one of my companions, named Bellido, is in love with a woman whom he has now gone to see; but I also know that his heart is not like that which beats in my breast."

"You say that Bellido loves a woman?" asked Guillen of

Martin, remembering that he had seen the traitor entering the castle.

" Yes, the woman he loves lives on the Burgos road."

" I should rather believe that she lives in the Castle of Carrion, for I saw him enter it just as I was departing."

" May the anger of God strike him ! " exclaimed Martin, enraged. " Bellido Dolfos at Carrion ! The traitor must be engaged in a plot with the count to destroy the band ! My heart told me that he was a Judas. But are you quite certain that it was he ? "

" As certain as that you are the Vengador," replied Guillen, beginning to think that the suspicions of the chief of the bandits were well founded, for he recollected having heard his companions, the servants of the count, saying that they suspected there was some understanding between him and Bellido.

" What a fool I have been ! " said Martin, striking his head with the palm of his hand. " How simple I was not to believe in the perfidy of men ! I always looked on it as a delusion of that good Rui-Venablos, when he often expressed doubts as to the fidelity of Bellido."

" You are a greater fool not to abandon the wretched calling of a bandit," said Guillen, vexed that a young man like the Vengador should not have a better profession. " Is it possible, that in times like these, when infidels fight ceaselessly against the law of Christ, and carry on plunder and murder in your native land, that a brave, generous, and enamoured youth like you can be content to remain leader of a band of highway robbers? I say enamoured, for I cannot understand that, being so, you should not have the same ambitious aspirations in your mind that I have in mine."

" I knew well that you were in love with the Infanta," said Martin, smiling, notwithstanding the vexation and the inquietude which his suspicions of treachery against Bellido were causing him.

" Well, then, I do love her," replied Guillen, letting himself be drawn on by the irresistible confidence which Martin inspired him with. " I love her, and I know that this secret, which I confide to you, will die with you ; I love her, and I must either make myself worthy of her, or die in the effort. What was I before I felt that love, which has raised my thoughts higher than the flight of the eagles, which soar above us, touching with their pinions the azure heights of the

16

heavens?   Listen, Sir Vengador, to what I was then.   I was a man who only looked upon the sky to see if the weather was about to be fair or foul, who only thought of the sun when it was too burning, or when its heat was pleasant; who only envied cavaliers because they were better clad and better mounted than I was; who desired to be rich, because the wealthy regale themselves with dainty fare and dwell in luxurious mansions; who saw supreme happiness in a jar of wine, a loaf of white bread, and a good joint of meat; who in battle saw no pleasure but in personal revenge, no glory but in the booty captured from the enemy; who in women saw nothing but women, confounding the love of a loose wench with that of a girl really good and affectionate; who, on seeing laurel crowns and bouquets of flowers thrown to the soldiers, returning conquerors from the battle, said, 'Why should those cavaliers feel so proud at having those laurel crowns and flowers on their brows, when it is so easy to gather them in the fields of Castile?'   Who often asked himself, 'Why should men trouble themselves about the good or evil which may be spoken of them after they are dead?   What is this world to those who have ceased to exist?   Does not every-thing connected with the world die with a man?'   Thus was I then; my soul was as vulgar as that of the commonest of rustics; but as soon as I began to love the Infanta Doña Teresa, that noble girl lived constantly in my thoughts, by day and by night, when I was awake and when I slept.   I am not the same, Sir Vengador.   It now delights me at all times to gaze on the sky, for it seems to me that there, amongst those white, fleecy clouds floating on its azure transparency, is the world which the Infanta and I dream of every night; the sun of March is as delightful to me as that of July, for the sun is always beautiful, and I adore beauty, wherever it may be found, since I have learned to adore the Infanta; I desire to be noble and rich, that my occupations may be noble, in order to cast no stain on the Infanta with the feelings which cling to those who drag themselves along the ground; vengeance and booty appear to me but trifling pleasures in war; the glory of serving God and Fatherland is that for which I envy the soldier; it is of it that I am going in search on the battlefields of Portugal; I see in women something more than women, I see—I cannot explain it to you, Sir Vengador, but I see amongst them beings who resemble angels, beings who resemble Teresa; love which has not its dwelling-place in the soul is disgusting to me, my heart is all love, all tenderness ; it seems to me that one of those crowns with which I have seen the brows of warriors adorned would make me mad with pleasure ; my reason would almost depart on its touching my forehead ; I would give a hundred lives to win it ; I now envy the happiness of those who, when they die, leave behind them noble memories which shall never die."

"Young man !" exclaimed Martin, who had listened to Guillen with enthusiasm and emotion, "give me your hand, even though that of a man, as honourable as you are, should not clasp that of a bandit."

" My arms, and not my hand, will I give you," said Guillen, pressing the Vengador to his breast. " I do not judge men according as they appear, but according to what they are. I know not why you have embraced the despicable profession of a bandit, but I know that the heart of a cavalier beats in your breast. No, you cannot be a bandit simply for the sake of killing and plundering, in order to enrich yourself ; some desire for revenge has induced you to adopt the life which you are leading."

"Yes, yes, a revenge it was," replied Martin, with emotion ; "a noble, a holy revenge—a revenge which I swore over the dead body of my father, and which I have not yet been able to accomplish. It was it which armed my right hand with the dagger of a bandit ; it was it which changed Martin, a good, peaceful, inoffensive youth, living in Carrion, into the terrible Vengador."

And Martin related his story to Guillen, laid bare his heart to him, just as it was, with the confidence with which one brother relates to another, on his return from a long journey, all that he has gone through, all that he has suffered, all that he has enjoyed, all that he feels ; he then concluded, saying—

"Do you now think that I should abandon the revenge for which I pant, and for which I have hitherto laboured so hard ? "

"If you abandoned it, far from falling in my esteem, I would think vastly more of you ; for, according to my way of seeing things, vengeance is always despicable, is always criminal. However, as custom has sanctified it up to a certain point, persevere in it for the present ; but, in order to succeed in it, make yourself strong by more noble means than those of pillage and homicide. If, when you had three hundred men under your command, you were not able to revenge yourself on your enemy, how can you expect to do it now, when you have only forty? What hopes can you have of increasing your band, when you have got so few to join it, and have suffered such reverses since that which you experienced in the Castle of Carrion? You certainly are right, Martin, in believing that the fear of losing their lives in the band of the Vengador prevents those from enlisting in it who, at other times, by their inclinations, and by misery, would be induced to do so. You know now, moreover, that Bellido is plotting your destruction, for, without doubt, that and nothing else brings him to Carrion."

"And what am I to do, Guillen; what can I do in so critical a situation? Anger of the devil! I, so bold, so daring, so obstinate, only a short while ago; now so irresolute, so faint-hearted, so cowardly. What am I to do, Guillen; what can I do?"

"What are you to do? Does not your heart, perchance, counsel you; that heart so generous, so noble, so deeply in love?"

"Since I have heard your words, my heart tells me that it desires something more than vengeance. The bandit cannot proudly raise his brow without danger of someone spitting in his face, and I feel now that I would risk my life to be able to raise my head like the most honourable men of Castile."

"Well, then, Martin, come with me. Let us go to the Portuguese campaign, in which they are fighting for God and native land; there you will be able to wash off, with Moorish blood, the stain which the world sees on the brow of the bandit; there you will win power to punish the assassin of your father; from thence you will return a hundred times more worthy of being united with that honourable girl whom you love so much."

"Yes, Guillen, yes, let us go to Portugal, for even now my heart beats violently, thinking that the time has come when I can show my courage in more honourable fights than those in which I have been engaged."

"Good, Martin, good! This enthusiasm tells me that you will be a valiant soldier," cried Guillen, embracing the bandit captain.

"Come with me now," said Martin, "as I must inform the members of the band of my resolution, as they will have to follow me to Portugal. They are men to whom my will is law, who, only to free themselves from tyranny and misery, smother in their hearts the voice of honour, and bear the infamy which attaches itself to the life of a bandit. Here, in this glen, is one half of the band, and the other half is with Rui-Venablos, round the turn of that hill which you see there in front of you."

"And do you think that Rui-Venablos will also go with you?"

"Oh, you do not know what he is. Rui-Venablos is more honourable than I am. He joined the band, moved by a disinterested and noble sentiment. He has been a soldier almost all his life, and for him happiness is only to be found on battlefields."

Some hours after, the forty bandits, which now composed the band of the Vengador, were assembled together in the wood, all contented with the resolve of their chief. In reality, those men did not deserve the name of bandits. They had only revolted against the tyranny of certain nobles, and indeed had governed themselves more by the laws of war than by those of vandalism. Admitted, that at the present day they would not have been received as soldiers into any honourable and loyal army, still at that period what was required were soldiers ready to fight against the common enemy, and nobody thought much of inquiring into their antecedents.

Shortly afterwards, Martin and Guillen took the road that led to Burgos, for the former desired to go to Vivar to take leave of Beatrice, whom he had not seen for a considerable time. Rui-Venablos went on towards Portugal, followed by the bandits; a place having been decided on beforehand, where all should meet before their arrival at the frontier.

CHAPTER XXXI

IN WHICH THE PROVERB, "LET THE MIRACLE BE WROUGHT, EVEN THOUGH THE DEVIL DOES IT," IS JUSTIFIED

THE Cid was burning with impatience to overtake the Moors, who were ravaging Estremadura. They were committing more outrages than ever before, for they had not invaded the states of Don Fernando on any former occasion with so much impetuosity and ferocity. Rodrigo saw with the eyes of his soul all their barbarities; he saw the harvests cut down and burned, the flocks stolen, churches and private dwellings sacked, some of the inhabitants inhumanly butchered, and others, even more unfortunate, taken captive and savagely maltreated; he saw those who were still free raising their hands to heaven and imploring God for mercy, beseeching Him to send a warrior who might chastise those savage invaders; an angel who, with his flaming sword, might exterminate those barbarous and impious men, who looked on nothing as sacred. And the brave and noble heart of the Castilian leader bled for the sufferings of those unfortunate people. The Cid crossed the frontier of Estremadura, at the head of his valorous army, filled with joy as if he were entering the Promised Land. On all sides his eyes saw the marks of fire and blood which the infidels had left on their track. Rapidly, however, as the Castilian army marched on, they could not discover the infidels, and Rodrigo and his men were filled with fury, seeing that all their diligence was in vain.

The Moors had learned that the invincible Christian army was advancing on them; to return to Portugal was the same as to go straight to meet them; to proceed towards the kingdom of Toledo was to expose themselves to be driven back from the frontier, for they knew that Almenon would not wish to lose the friendship of Don Fernando by admitting them into his dominions. The only thing that was open to them was to proceed straight on, pass through the centre of Castile and cross the Moncayo, with the object of taking refuge in some one of the many small Moorish states into which Aragon was then divided; they adopted, therefore, that latter course, and continued their march into the interior of Castile, increasing on their way the stores of rich booty which they had taken in Estremadura. As they were, however, a day's march in advance of the Cid, it was not possible for him to overtake them as soon as he desired. Both armies, however, were now in Castile; and Rodrigo, fearing that the Moors might be able to carry out their intention of getting into Aragon before he could overtake them, determined to make a final effort, an almost superhuman one, in order to fall on them and wrench from them the numerous captives whom they were carrying off, and punish their audacity and their cruelties. At last he overtook them, between Atienza and San Esteban de Gormaz, and a battle commenced, furious on both sides.

The army of the Cid, though having the advantage in valour, was less numerous than that of the enemy; however, the circumstance of their being on their native soil, and their courage, which had been increased by their efforts for so long a time to attack the invaders, were elements which were much in their favour. The Moors resolved to defend their booty at all costs, for it was so valuable that they would leave nothing undone in order to retain it. The Castilian squadrons threw themselves several times against the infidels, but were each time repulsed, with heavy loss on both sides. The Cid was always in the very front, spurring on his steed to close with his adversaries, and at his side could be seen Fernan, although to keep up with Babieca, which flew at the slightest touch of the spur, he had almost to flay the sides of Overo.

"On, on! St. James of Compostela!" cried the Cid, burning with anger at seeing the impotence of all his efforts, and preparing for a fresh charge. "We shall all die on those fields of our native land rather than lose the name of Invincibles which Castile has given us, for it is better to die fighting than to live flying. Do you not hear, cavaliers, those lamentations which rise from the enemies' camp? They come from the unhappy Christians whom those infidels drag on with them, loaded with chains and trampled under the hoofs of their chargers. We are their only hope; they trust in us, they call down on our heads the blessing of God, as we have come to fight bravely for them in order to save them from captivity, and they should justly curse us if they saw us turning back like cowards. We conquered in Portugal, shall we be defeated in Castile—in Castile, where the ashes of our brave forefathers repose, where the eyes of a mother, of a wife, or of a beloved maiden look upon our deeds? Onward, cavaliers! follow me, conquer or die with me; for I will conquer, or die as a brave man!"

When he had pronounced those last words the Cid rushed on the enemy, and with him all his cavaliers, shouting enthusiastically, proving the influence which the words and the example of their brave leader exercised on those sturdy warriors.

The hostile army was divided into two bodies, stationed within ten crossbow-shots of each other. At the same time both were attacked by the Christians, whose squadrons got separated when the charge was made; the Cid closing with the Moors to the right, whilst Martin Antolinez, to whom he had confided his standard, attacked those on the left. Both bodies received the Christians with the points of their lances and the keen edges of their cimeters; the division attacked by the Cid was not able to resist the charge, and took to flight in the greatest disorder, followed and cut down by the Castilians.

The Cid and his followers had already disappeared in the distance, pursuing the enemy, blinded by fury and desirous of exterminating them, and as yet Martin Antolinez had not succeeded in breaking the Moorish squadron, which was stationed to the left. The fight was becoming every moment more obstinate and bloody, and its result was becoming more and more doubtful. The soldiers of Antolinez, instead of gaining ground were rather losing it, as the Moors, seeing themselves deprived of all chance of aid, were now fighting with the desperation of those who, having lost all hope of saving themselves, desire to savour death with the pleasure of vengeance. The Christians, rendered more courageous by that strenuous resistance, broke at last into the midst of their enemies, without thinking of the risk of such an undertaking, and then the Moors, availing themselves of a rapid and skilful piece of strategy, surrounded them on all sides, and the conflict became still more furious. The Christians were horribly cut up by the sword strokes, and all their strength was vainly expended against that circle of hostile lances which encircled them, and which was closing round them closer and closer each moment; hope of escape was scarcely left to them, and the green standard of the Cid would soon be in the hands of his foes, although Martin Antolinez, who held it aloft in one hand, whilst he brandished his sword with the other, cutting down an enemy at each stroke, was resolved to save it or to die under its shadow. Fatigue and want of breath was beginning to tell on the Christian cavaliers. Antolinez cast from time to time a rapid glance across the plain to see if assistance of any kind was coming to them; the plain, however, was deserted, and he only could see the line of corpses which the Moors, pursued by the Cid, were leaving behind them, and several captives who had succeeded in escaping from their captors during the battle. Those were wandering about, still manacled and uncertain as to the fate which might befall them.

A multitude of his enemies composed the circle around Antolinez, attacking him with fury, endeavouring to capture the standard. The brave man of Burgos defended himself with the most stubborn courage, but his blood was staining the equipments of his horse; Alvar, Fañez Minaya, and other cavaliers were fighting vainly to free him from his enemies.

"Cowards!" cried out Antolinez to the Moors. "A brave deed, forsooth, is yours—twenty of you to attack one cavalier! Fight with me, not one against one, but four against one, and you will see whether my sword pierce not your hearts, e'er you shall drag from my hand the standard of my Cid!"

Thus speaking, he showered furious blows on his enemies, the number of whom was increasing every moment. At last a cimeter struck the arm which held up the standard, and it fell from his hand notwithstanding all the efforts he made to retain it, for the cut was terrible. The despair of Antolinez then reached its height : the good cavalier, rendered incapable of guiding his steed, spurred it on furiously and dashed into the midst of the enemy, making a bloody opening through them

But behold, when the Castilians were almost completely vanquished, a loud cry was heard in the distance, and about fifty horsemen were seen rushing towards the combat with the fleetness of the wind.

"St. James! St. James!" they shouted, and that cry was full of terror for the Moors, and full of hope for Martin Antolinez and his men.

Who are those who thus come to the aid of the Christians? They cannot be the squadron of the Campeador, for it is pursuing the Moors in the direction opposite to that from which those horsemen appear. Behold them, behold them already at the place of combat : two handsome youths and a man of colossal stature, and evidently of great strength, lead the band.

Justice of God! with what fury they rush into the midst of the Moors, throw them into confusion, and scatter them in all directions! What fierce cuts and thrusts they give! How the dead bodies of the Moslems roll upon the ground!

"Cavaliers, whoever you are, to me, to me! Rescue the standard of the Campeador, which these cowards have torn from my grasp!" cried Martin Antolinez, addressing the leaders of the newly-arrived combatants.

"We will all die or save it," cried Guillen, for it was he, with Martin, Rui-Venablos, and all the bandits who composed the band of the Vengador, that had arrived fortunately before it was too late, to the aid of Martin Antolinez and his soldiers.

And whilst Martin and Rui-Venablos continued to fight like lions in the thick of the hostile force, Guillen rushed like lightning against the Moorish horseman who had succeeded in capturing the green standard of the Cid, and who was holding and defending it tenaciously. His lance caused great slaughter amongst the enemy, who endeavoured to avoid his thrusts, and soon were thrown into disorder : the Moor, however, who had wounded Antolinez and taken the standard from him, would not yield up that inestimable prize, the acquiring of which had been so difficult ; he fought front to front with Guillen, and to judge by the fury of the combat, one or other must soon cease to exist. Blow followed blow with fearful rapidity, and both combatants were wounded more or less severely.

"St. James ! St. James to my aid !" shouted Guillen, grasping his lance with desperate force, and making so furious a thrust at his enemy that he fell from his horse pierced through the breast. The youth dragged from him the standard which, even when falling dead, he still held convulsively clutched in his hand, and, raising it aloft and waving it gallantly above his head, cried—

"Victory ! victory ! St. James !"

When they saw the standard rescued, the Castilian soldiers felt their strength redoubled, and in a few minutes the Moslem squadron was flying before them.

However, as it was numerous, some hundreds of horse soldiers succeeded in escaping from the field of battle, abandoning what remained to them of the rich booty which they had seized on their long march.

The Christians dashed on in their pursuit, guided by the standard of the Cid which Guillen waved in the van, and as the Moors fled they left behind a very large number of their dead, for the Castilians came up with them from time to time and cut them down without mercy.

The soldiers of Martin Antolinez had pursued the Moors for about half an hour, when they perceived in the distance the Cid, who was returning to the assistance of his men, when he had finished with that division of the enemy in pursuit of which he had gone. All the Castilian forces were soon reunited, and the entire army continued the pursuit for more than seven leagues, until the Moorish army was completely destroyed.

Scarcely a Moor escaped the Castilian steel; that formidable Moslem army which, haughty and devastating, had penetrated into Estremadura and overrun all Castile, ceased to exist before they could reach Aragon, and the Cid and his cavaliers made themselves masters of the very rich spoils which they were bearing away with them.

Scarcely had Rodrigo rejoined the division commanded by Martin Antolinez when his attention was called to the band of the Vengador, and especially to the youth who was bearing his standard; but as it was then incumbent on him to continue the pursuit of the Moors, he postponed, till that was ended, the obtaining of information as to what had happened, and as to who those soldiers were who had exhibited such bravery in the fight.

Therefore, as soon as the Castilian army had finished with the Moors and collected the spoils together, he sat down to take the rest of which he was so much in need, and Martin Antolinez and other cavaliers, who were in his company at the commencement of the combat, related to the Cid all that had taken place. Martin Antolinez, who cared only for his wound because it prevented him from using his sword, told his leader that his soldiers were on the point of yielding and abandoning the standard when the unknown band arrived to their aid; he narrated to him the valour and the dexterity with which those men, especially their captains, had fought, and finally the heroic efforts by which that youth, whose name he was ignorant of, had rescued the standard.

Rodrigo advanced towards Guillen, the Vengador, and Rui-Venablos, and opened his arms to them, filled with enthusiasm and gratitude.

"You have saved my standard," he said to the former, "and all the treasures of the world would appear too small a recompense for so great a service."

"My lord," answered Guillen, much moved, and feeling his heart throb with joy, for he was beginning to realise the hopes of glory of which he had dreamed for so long a time, "the service you mention merits no reward, for every soldier should do his duty, and I have done no more than accomplish mine. For good men it is a sufficient recompense to know that they have served God and their native land; but if the rescue from the infidels of your glorious standard merits a greater reward than that which I have mentioned, pay it to me by granting me the honour of being one of your soldiers, to fight in your army and by your side against the Moorish power."

"I shall consider myself much honoured if you and your companions will aid me in this war. You shall be my friends, my brothers-in-arms. In my heart, which the sanguinary scenes of battlefields cannot move, there is a space, by no means small, destined for gratitude and sweet friendship; in that space you will always occupy one of the chief positions."

Guillen, Martin, and Rui-Venablos listened with moist eyes to that noble cavalier, to that valiant leader, who won hearts with a single word, for in that word was manifested the most generous and best soul that could animate a man.

Guillen, Martin, and Rui-Venablos felt it their duty not to conceal their antecedents from Rodrigo Diaz, for he was sufficiently just to do justice to those who had it on their side, sufficiently sensible not to let himself be borne away by vulgar prejudices, and sufficiently clear-sighted to understand the motives by which men were animated. For these reasons it appeared to them a treason, which their consciences could not tolerate, were they to present themselves to that cavalier, so loyal, so kind, and so sincere, otherwise than as they had really been.

A curious observer could not fail to have taken note of an animated discussion which took place on the following day amongst Fernan Cardeña, Alvar, Lope, and other pages and squires, whilst the army of the Cid was marching towards Burgos, in the midst of the noisiest and most enthusiastic ovations of the Castilian people; these were more ardent even than those of which they were the objects on their return from the battle of the mountains of Oca. That discussion was very curious and so connected with the objects we have in view that we think it well to insert it on our pages.

"I say to you, Fernan," said Alvar, "that if I were as old as you are, if I had the prizes you have won in this campaign, and a wife to marry as good and loving as Mayorica is, I vow to God that I would wed her as soon as I got back to Burgos, and give up at once the profession of arms."

"I swear, by the soul of Beelzebub, that you deserve a gag in your mouth, to keep you from talking such nonsense. Give up at once the profession of arms? Is it not an honourable one, perchance?"

"Honourable, I admit, but thankless and severe."

"It may be so for those who possess your mean disposition, but not for those who love glory and advancement."

"And what do you understand by glory, Fernan?"

"I vow by Judas Iscariot that the question of this fool pleases me. What do I understand by glory? I understand by it, sleeping in camps; awaking to the noise of the trumpets and drums which sound the alarm; listening to the neighing of the chargers, impatient to rush on the enemy; giving sword slashes to the Moors; and seeing the heads of foemen fall about, as ripe fruit falls from the trees when a brisk breeze blows. That, and nothing else, is real glory, brother, and the son of my mother would not exchange it for all other kinds of glory in the world, even that of marrying girls as handsome and loving as Mayorica."

"However, comrade," said Lope, the discreet squire, who on another occasion gave two salutary pieces of advice to Fernan on the subject of love, "one could continue to exercise the honourable profession of arms, and still have a wife and children; I have such myself, and nevertheless have not abandoned arms, as you see. Alvar is right in recommending you to marry Mayor, now that you have means enough to support her."

"Whether I marry or don't marry, as long as there remain Moors for my master Don Rodrigo to fight against, I will not give up my lance."

"But don't you love Mayorica?"

"I love her, and will continue to love her with all my soul. Oh, how I long to arrive at Burgos, to see her after so long a separation!"

"Now I see," replied Lope, "that you are begging the question as to whether you will marry her or not."

"I am indeed thinking of marrying, but it is an unfair thing to have to bind oneself before God to love only one woman, considering that there are two or even more for every man."

"Leave aside all that nonsense, comrade, for it sounds badly coming from a man so ripe in years as you are. To think as you think should be only for beardless youths, such as he who yesterday rescued the standard of Don Rodrigo, and I am of opinion that even he would not talk of love with as little sense as you display in the matter."

"Do you know," said Alvar, "that I look on the friendship and honours which Don Rodrigo confers on that youth as signs of mere craziness."

"Craziness?" cried Fernan, whose anger was aroused on hearing the page find fault with his master. "The craziness, which deserves more stripes than you have hairs on your head, is your own, you confounded fool and chatterbox. All that Don Rodrigo does is well done."

"I only meant to say that nobody knows in the least who that young man is; and as to his companions, everybody knows, for they tell it themselves, that they are the band of the Vengador."

"'Let the miracle be wrought, even though the devil does it.' The certain thing is, that only for that youth and those who accompanied him to aid us, the squadron of Martin Antolinez would have been completely routed, and the standard of Don Rodrigo would be now in the hands of the infidels. I swear by Judas Iscariot, that if the Cid, my master, had lost his standard, he would have either died of grief and despair, or else have pursued the infidels to the ends of the world in order to recapture it."

"How much soever they may have extolled to you the valour of that Guillen, whoever he may be, of that Martin, and of that giant who bears the name of Rui-Venablos, and of all their men," said Lope, "it is nothing to what they deserve. I happened to be amongst the soldiers of Martin Antolinez, and thanks to that, I know exactly to what extent those men deserve the recompenses which the Campeador has bestowed on them, and promised to bestow on them."

"Well, tell us, then, what recompenses they have received?" asked Alvar.

"He has given," answered Fernan, "double as much of the spoils to each of them as to the other men in the army; and he has promised Guillen, who is of peasant origin, like Martin and Rui, that he will be knighted in Burgos. You need not imagine, moreover, that Don Rodrigo will allow these men-at-arms to leave his side, for he has taken them into his pay."

"Anger of God!" exclaimed Alvar, "with what a lucky foot this Guillen has walked into the profession of arms!"

"And I have heard that our master, who never makes a mistake, has said that Guillen will be in a short time one of his best captains."

"He will be an emperor if our master goes on thus lavishing favours on him, for some men are born feet foremost and others head foremost, and he must be of the former."

"Oh, you cursed charlatan, how envious you are!" said Fernan. "The good fortune of another man enrages you, no matter how well merited it may be. I suppose you would like to be made a knight? I tell you, Alvar, that if I ever hear you say a word against Guillen, or any of those who have joined the army with him, I'll break your ribs with a cudgel. It is my duty to defend that youth; only for him the son of my mother would be now lying, food for wild beasts, on the field of battle where we defeated the Moors yesterday."

"Relate to us, Fernan, what happened to you," said Alvar; "for I should like to go slow for a while, as my horse is very much fatigued."

"Don't lay the blame of your falling back on your horse, as it is the fault of your own cowardly heart," replied Don Rodrigo's squire. "There is no chance of your scarifying very seriously the flanks of your charger whenever you shall be required to rush on the enemy."

"Comrade, I say of myself what you said of Overo a short time before you sallied forth from Burgos to proceed to Compostela, 'everyone is just as God made him, and faults should not be punished which one brings from the womb of his mother.' But won't you recount to us what happened to you yesterday?"

"I shall do so at once. Don Rodrigo, Guillen, and I were fighting, with more than usual fury, against five Moorish cavaliers, who formed an impenetrable wall before us. At last we succeeded in breaking through them and throwing them into disorder. Don Rodrigo rushed in pursuit of three of them who had fled, and who appeared to be men of rank, whilst Guillen and I remained fighting with the others, who, to give them their due, were much braver than their companions, as they did not seek safety in flight. He who was fighting with me gave so fierce a lance thrust that, striking the pommel of the saddle, the shock threw down Overo, and I found myself on the ground, incapable of defending myself. The Moor was already aiming his lance at me, to fix me to the earth, when Guillen, who saw what was going on, rushed to my aid, overthrew the Moor, my antagonist, with his lance, and returning to him whom he had just left, and who was taking to flight, he pierced him through the breast. Now you see that, were it not for that brave youth, the weakness of my horse would have cost me my life."

"Oh, what triumphs you achieve with that high-spirited

Overo!" said Alvar, laughing, which made Fernan very angry.

"By the soul of Beelzebub, if you laugh at my mishaps, it will cost you dear, Alvar. As to my horse, I swear that if he ever again treats me so, he shall atone for his fault where he commits it, by being left there as the prey of wild beasts."

"You always say that, Fernan; if I were your horse I would laugh at your threats."

"You will see if he laughs the next time he acts in such a manner."

Just as Fernan thus spoke, a bull ran from a herd which was grazing in a field beside the road, and rushed on the pages and squires with a fury such as is seldom seen. All were trying to get out of his way, surprised by such a sudden attack, except Fernan, who, pulling at the reins of Overo, and preparing his lance, exclaimed—

"Cowards! Do you fly from this miserable beast? You will see, I vow to Judas Iscariot, that my lance shall soon bring down his pride."

And thus speaking, he directed his steed in the direction of the bull.

The latter gave a furious bellow, and rushed on him who had thus challenged him. The lance of Fernan struck one of the flanks of the bull, but glanced off it; the animal charged Overo fiercely, and he fell, together with his rider, rolling down a very steep declivity, so that all believed that both of them were killed.

The bull continued to do considerable damage to the squires, none of whom were able to restrain him, although they did their best, having recovered from the confusion which his first charge had caused amongst them.

Rodrigo Diaz, as well as the cavaliers who were conversing with him, noticed the tumult which had just arisen, and, as soon as he learned the cause of it, seized his lance, and turning back, guided Babieca towards the bull. The first victory won by the animal seemed to have increased his ferocity. He rushed madly at the cavalier who was approaching him, but the lance of the Cid buried itself in his head, as deep as its steel head was long.

The bull gave a terrible roar, and fell lifeless on the ground. In the meantime, Fernan and his steed were brought up from the hollow into which they had fallen, without more damage than a few, not very serious, bruises.

"Are you much injured, Fernan?" hastened to ask all his companions.

"No," answered Fernan; "only bruised, but no bones broken. Leave me, by the soul of Beelzebub! leave me, and go see if Overo has a wound on his head."

When he was told that Overo had received no hurt of any consequence, joy appeared on his countenance, and he hastened to mount him again, saying—

"I am always unlucky with that horse. Many, many indeed, Overo, are the mishaps thou hast caused me, but if thou actest so again thou shalt pay for it with thy skin."

CHAPTER XXXII

IN WHICH IT IS PROVED THAT HE WHO SOWS REAPS, AND IN WHICH IT IS SEEN THAT THEY WHO GIVE RECEIVE.

THE sun had not yet risen in the east when Ximena was standing at a window from which could be seen the road, which Rodrigo and his knights had taken when going on their pilgrimage to Compostela. An unusual joy animated her countenance, and her gaze did not wander from that road on which she had seen her noble and beloved husband departing, and by which she hoped to see him returning on that very day.

On that day, indeed, he was expected in Burgos, the city of his ancestors, and Ximena, who, after the receipt of such good news, had not been able to sleep during the night, arose at dawn, and placed herself at the window of her apartment, desirous that her eyes might be the first to see Rodrigo enter Burgos. It is a common opinion that a young woman does not look on a husband with the same eyes as on a lover, that for her has disappeared the golden halo which surrounded him, the inexplicable mystery which had presented him to her as a being distinct from all other beings. Ximena, however, gave a contradiction to that opinion, and every wife who has a soul like hers, who has gone to the altar impelled, not by an artificial love, but by an affection which has been insensibly identifying itself with the soul, becoming part of it, and acquiring its immortal principle. When love is essentially pure, and refined by the various trials which Ximena had passed through ; when it is the thought of one's entire life ; when in it is to be found the sole hope and the sole happiness of this world ; when its object is so worthy of being beloved as Rodrigo was, then love never loses its enchantment, its mystery, its poetry ; it becomes even more beautiful with full possession, more complete in every way. Sermonda, as the Limosin chronicles relate, went one day to her window and saw Raimundo de Castel mounted on a fiery steed, completely covered with white armour, and bearing as his device these words : "*Mi corazon está libre y desea ser cautivo.*"[1]

Sermonda was a maiden of ardent heart, of fantastic imagination, and passionately fond of the love romances of the troubadours and minstrels, especially those of Guillermo de Cabestañ, the sweetest troubadour of Provence. She fell in love with Raimundo de Castel, for in him she saw one of those valiant and enamoured cavaliers whom the good Guillermo described in his lays of love, and married him shortly afterwards. Much time had not elapsed when her love had changed to indifference ; in a short time Raimundo had lost in the eyes of Sermonda the aureole of love and poesy which had surrounded him ; before long she happened to meet the gentle troubadour Guillermo de Cabestañ, and loved him madly. Raimundo found this out, killed the troubadour, caused his heart to be fried and served up to his faithless spouse. When she discovered that she had eaten the heart of her lover, she told her husband that she had never tasted more delicious food, and then threw herself from the window. This is the kind of love which degenerates, which vulgarises itself by intimate and continuous intercourse, a love which has no hold on the soul, for the love of Sermonda was that of the imagination, not that of the heart. The love of Ximena was that love which is almost born with us, which increases in us, which lives with our life ; and that is the love which, instead of becoming weaker, gains strength, preserves always its primitive freshness, mystery, and poesy, and which is as immortal as the soul to which it has clung.

Who is there that has not passed a night feeling somewhat as Ximena did during that which preceded the day of the return of her husband ? Who is there who has not sometimes lost a night's repose for the hope of seeing a beloved being on

---

[1] " My heart is free, but desires to be made a prisoner."

the following day, has not in vain endeavoured to call down sleep on his eyelids, has not counted the hours one by one, and has not several times thought that the light of the moon, feebly penetrating into the room, was the early dawn? And did not that night seem three times as long as usual, on account of her having passed it thinking on him who was expected, seeing him in thought, pondering over the first words that would be heard from his lips, guessing at the costume he would wear, calculating when they would meet each other, and even considering what effect that meeting would have on the countenance of him who was about to return home?

He who has found himself in that position, he who has experienced anything like this, will understand how long that night must have seemed to Ximena; how sweet the singing of the birds must have sounded to her ears on that morning; with what joy she had saluted the day; how excited her heart must have felt, and with what intentness her eyes must have been fixed on the road by which Rodrigo was to arrive. The hope, however, of seeing again her absent husband, her beloved one, the valiant knight, the hero returning with his brows crowned with laurels, was not the only thing which caused Ximena to feel so happy.

She had good news to communicate to Rodrigo; he was about to find in his sweet and loving wife a new title to his love, a new pledge of her affection, for the breast of Ximena enclosed the first-fruit of that love which had filled up almost the entire lives of both of them—she was about to become a mother. What new and exceeding sweet enchantments must she not have experienced from the time she had become aware of that happiness! The wife is then something more than a woman, she has something of the divine, something which separates her from weak humanity; then surrounds her brow a holy aureole, which eyes cannot see, but which the soul distinctly perceives,—a husband must then have a worthless soul and a flinty heart, not to respect her, adore her, bless her! For love has now rendered its work complete, combining matter in the same way as spirit had been combined; for the wife could say to the husband, on feeling the pains of maternity, " Behold, to thee am I indebted for these pains "; for the wife is then a being the most tortured, and the most in need of tender care; for the husband then sees in that woman a mother, a mother such as she who had carried himself in her breast, fed him with her milk, taught him to lisp his first words, to walk his first steps, and who dried his tears with her kisses.

"My husband, a being, a small part of ourselves, moves in my breast."

Should not these words sound very sweet to the ears of the husband who, for the first time, is about to receive the name of father? How sweet must they not sound when they come from the lips of an idolised woman, of a woman whose love he believes to be sufficient to abundantly compensate for all trials, all deceptions, all miseries, all sadnesses, all injustices, all physical pain, all the misfortunes of life! How pleasing, how consoling must not the hopes of paternity be! At first, beautiful children, with complexions like the lily and the rose, with golden hair like that of the angels, who, with smiles on their lips, throw their tender arms around those who have given them their being, as if they were endeavouring to pay the debt of their existence with kisses and innocent caresses; afterwards, gentle youths and maidens, whose ardent hearts are agitated by the generous instincts and noble aspirations of early life, in whom the parents look upon the pictures of themselves, with the same pleasure as the old man looks upon his portrait which, when young, he presented to the maiden of his love, and which she restored to him on the day when they went to live under the same roof. Such, in short, are the hopes which should be awakened in the heart of a husband when his wife tells him that she is about to become a mother.

How sad must be the life of married people whose heads become white, whose limbs become weak, and in whose ears the name of father or mother does not sound! Feel compassion for those spouses who around their hearths see none to whom they can give the title of child; for old people feel the need of children as much as children do of parents; old age requires a staff on which to lean; for death is doubly painful when all goes with ourselves to the churchyard, when no eyes remain to water the flowers placed on our tombs.

Such were the thoughts which passed through the mind of Ximena during that night. She knew that Rodrigo would think in the same way; she knew that the news she was about to impart to her beloved husband would be the sweetest he could listen to; she knew that an additional bond, as firm, as indissoluble, as holy as those which already united them, would soon draw them even more closely together, and her heart leaped with joy, and tears of happiness flowed from her eyes, and she blessed God who had thus increased her felicity, when the being whom she felt in her breast reminded her that Rodrigo, when clasping her in his arms, would embrace two dear ones at the same time.

She, however, was not the only one who had her eyes fixed on that road: those of Teresa and Diego, and also those of Mayor, Lambra, and Gil, were looking in the same direction; besides these, all the inhabitants of Burgos were anxiously expecting the arrival of the victorious leader. Happy are the absent who know that they are expected at the domestic hearth with such great love, impatience, and anxiety!

At last, a dark moving mass was perceived on the white road, which disappeared towards the distant horizon. Numerous cries of joy resounded at the same time from the windows of the house of the lords of Vivar, and shortly afterwards Rodrigo and his escort dismounted at its door. To describe the joy, the caresses, the tears, the embraces, with which his family welcomed the victorious cavalier would be as difficult as to express with words all the joys, enchantments, mutual pleasures, and sweet confidences which the unwritten and undescribable history of domestic life contains.

Rodrigo Diaz, who on the field of battle mowed down Moslem heads as the reaper cuts down the harvest in his fields; who, at the assault of a fortress, rushed against its walls, trampling dead bodies under foot, and covered with blood; the terrible warrior whose name alone filled the ferocious Islamites with terror; that man of iron, who seemed born only to live in combats—that man, we repeat, was at the domestic hearth the personification of mildness, of love, and of simplicity. If he could be seen clasping his parents and his wife to his heart, with tears of happiness in his eyes; if he could be seen, as excited as a child, blessing God and Ximena, when he learned that she bore the first-fruit of their love within her breast; if he could be seen conversing with his servants with the same kindness as if they were his equals; and, finally, caressing Gil, the Moorish child, whom he had taken under his protection, and amusing him with the same playfulness and boyishness as he had displayed at the period when he sported with Ximena at the Castle of Vivar, and imprinted a kiss for the first time on the lips of the innocent little girl; if all this could have been seen, he would have been admired more under the domestic roof than on the fields of battle.

Three days after the return of the Cid to Burgos, on a calm

and beautiful morning, like another which he remembered with joy, for it had been the happiest of his life, that on which he had first called Ximena by the sweet name of wife, a great multitude crowded round the gates of the church of Santa Gadea, and many ladies and cavaliers entered it.

On that morning the order of knighthood was to be conferred on Guillen by the hand of the Cid Campeador, and the noble Ximena was to buckle on the golden spur.

The brave youth had kept vigil over his arms, during the preceding night, before the altar, and was awaiting with impatience the solemn ceremony, when he would receive the sword-stroke on his shoulder, when the golden spur would be buckled on, and when he would be girt with his knightly sword.

And the time at last arrived.

The church was decorated with the Moslem standards, which, from time immemorial, the cavaliers of Burgos had deposited in it, on their return from the wars, as a just and holy homage to the God of battles. Torrents of light spread themselves about in all directions, incense filled the nave of the church, and sacred chants sounded in harmony with the peals of the bells.

"The Lord," sang the priests and the congregation, "has broken the bows, the shields, and the swords of our enemies, and put an end to the war."

"O Lord! Thou hast shed down upon us the rays of Thy goodness, whilst Thou hast filled our enemies with fear."

"Who, O Lord, can resist Thy anger?"

"Seated on Thy heavenly throne, Thou hast decreed the salvation of Thy people, and peace has succeeded to war."

"The universe praises Thee, and blesses Thee, and sings the glory of Thy name."

Many of the people assembled in the church were shedding tears of joy, whilst they accompanied the chants of the priests at the altar, for they were congregated there to thank God for the victories which had been won, as well as to witness the rewarding of him who had fought so valiantly against the enemies of Christ.

The Bishop of Burgos blessed the arms about to be presented to the new knight.

Then Rodrigo Diaz and Guillen, who had both been kneeling, arose and approached the arms, which stood before the altar. They were imitated by the ladies and cavaliers who were assisting at the solemn ceremony.

The young man bent his knee, and Rodrigo said to him—

"The order of knighthood which you are about to receive imposes duties on you in which you must not fail. It commands you to serve God and the king; it binds you to speak the truth always, to be loyal to your friends; to be abstemious, and to seek the companionship of wise men, who can teach you to live well, and of warlike men, who can teach you to fight bravely; it binds you to have good arms and accoutrements, good horses in your stable, and a good sword by your side; it commands that you shall not dare to go to the Court on a mule, but on a horse, nor enter the palaces of the king without a sword; it binds you not to speak flattery, nor to utter jests, nor play any game of chance, nor eat without tablecloths; it binds you not to complain of any wound you may receive, nor to groan during an operation, nor to boast of any deed you may perform; it binds you to have no contention with a young maiden, nor engage in a lawsuit with the wife of a hidalgo; if you should meet a brave and noble dueña in the street, it binds you to dismount and accompany her; if a noble woman or young woman asks a favour of you, and you do not grant it, it ordains that ladies should call you 'a badly ordered and discourteous knight'; it ordains that you must not be at the Court without serving some lady, not to dishonour her, but to make love to her, and, if you are a bachelor, to marry her, and when she goes forth you must accompany her according as she may desire, on foot or on horseback, with your hood removed, and doing reverence with your knee; it binds you, finally, to assist the weak, whatever their position may be, whenever they ask for your help."

When the Cid recited to the youth these statutes, which were, without any doubt, in force two hundred years later, when the statutes of the "Caballeros de la Banda" were compiled, he said to him—

"Do you swear to faithfully comply with all that the law of chivalry commands?"

"I swear," answered Guillen.

"If you so act, may you be accounted a good knight, and may God aid you in all the enterprises that you undertake; if you should do the contrary, cavaliers and peasants will despise you as vile and perjured, and nothing you undertake shall succeed."

He then gave him the kiss of peace on the mouth and the stroke on the shoulder, bound on the sword, which had been blessed, and which a page presented to him on a cushion, and immediately after Ximena buckled on the spur, which another page brought forward in the same way as the sword.

Then the bishop, the clergy, and the people chanted the first verse of a Psalm of David—

"Blessed be the Lord my God, who gave me hands to fight, and taught me the art of war."

And thus terminated the solemn ceremony, the people leaving the church and cheering the newly-made knight, who proceded to the residence of the Cid, accompanied by him, by Ximena, and by the brilliant escort which had been with them in the church of Santa Gadea.

The people of Burgos devoted themselves to merrymaking during the remainder of the day, and even into the late hours of the night, which was calm and beautiful, and lit up by a brilliant moon. Rodrigo had divided amongst the needy a large portion of the spoils which had fallen to his share after the recent victories, and that liberality had increased the public joy, already very great on account of the triumph obtained by the Christian army over the infidels. There was music and dancing in the public places; there were games of various kinds; and the evening terminated with a spectacle, as popular at that period as bull-fights were afterwards. In one of the largest squares of the city a circus was constructed with boards, and in it took place pig-baiting. This singular amusement was carried out in the following manner. Some of those animals were driven into the circus, and men then entered it with stout sticks, having their eyes bandaged, and with iron helmets on their heads. Whoever struck a pig with his stick became the possessor of the animal; however, it happened sometimes that the men cudgelled each other terribly, although it was ordered not to strike violently, and this constituted the principal amusement. During the evening of which we write, there was greater noise and uproar than usual, for the country people had indulged in large potations of wine, in order to celebrate with greater joy the triumph of the army of the Cid, and in dealing their blows in the circus they paid little attention to regulations and prohibitions.

Country people were generally the actors in these games, but when they were celebrated in honour of some very important and propitious event, pages and squires also frequently took part in them. In proof of this we mention the fact that Alvar, the page of Rodrigo Diaz, entered the circus on the day that Guillen was knighted.

The foolish page had, during the day, raised his elbow with marvellous frequency, and was in a humour to fight with something or other—with pigs or rustics, if he could not find a bull as fierce as the one he attacked when returning, a few days before, with the army of his master to Burgos. Thus it happened that, despite the advice of his friends, and especially that of Fernan, who had retired to sleep off his debauch, he insisted on having his eyes bandaged in order to sally forth to the conquest of the pig.

"By the soul of Beelzebub, Alvar," said Fernan to him, when he found that it was impossible to dissuade him from his intention, "you are the greatest fool that eats bread in Castile. You are as full of wine as a grape, and you imagine you will be able to hit the pig."

"May I never drink another drop of it if I don't win as fine a pig as that of St. Antony!" answered Alvar, stretching out his neck so that his eyes might be bound.

"The cudgellings you get from me are not enough, I suppose, and you must needs go off to get more from the rustics?"

"Your preachings are all in vain, brother," replied Alvar. "May I be turned into a pig myself if I leave the circus without one!"

Fernan did not persevere any longer with his counsels. Alvar went into the circus, blindfolded and armed with a stout stick, which he had to use to keep himself on his feet, such was the state of drunkenness in which he was.

The pig which just then happened to be in the circus, finding itself harassed at the opposite side, ran towards the side where Alvar was standing, and rushed violently between his legs.

The animal, finding this obstacle in its path, gave a loud grunt; its pursuers heard it, and made their way, with raised sticks, to the place where they thought the pig was. Alvar was struggling to raise himself, and as the country people, on coming up to him, heard the noise he was making on the ground with his hands and feet, and also his puffing and panting, they thought the pig was before them, and brought down their cudgels with such force on the unlucky page that, but for his cries, they would have made a speedy end of him.

Fernan rushed to the circus, followed by other servitors of the house of Vivar, raised up and carried off Alvar, whose bones were almost broken by the terrible cudgelling which he had received—a cudgelling which, if it moved the pity of some spectators, excited laughter and enthusiastic cheering amongst the great bulk of them.

When Fernan heard this laughter and cheering, which the misfortune of Alvar had caused, he directed his gaze threateningly towards the crowd, and cried out, full of indignation—

"I vow by Judas Iscariot that I would give my soul to the devil for a dozen men to attack with stout cudgels that crowd of rascals, who laugh thus at other people's misfortunes, and beat and bruise them, like pigs as they are."

The good squire then hastened to lead the unfortunate page where he could be attended to; he was as afflicted at the mishap as Alvar himself, for with regard to their relations we may appropriately quote the Castilian proverb, "*Quien bien te quiere te hará llorar.*" [1]

CHAPTER XXXIII

IN WHICH WE CONTINUE TO PROVE THAT THE CID WAS A CID IN EVERY WAY

THE first care of Rodrigo Diaz, having defeated the Moors as the result of his expedition from Portugal, was to send messengers to the king, Don Fernando, to announce to him that victory.

The king was in Coimbra when he received this auspicious news, and he determined to return immediately to Castile, as he wished to see his family again, and also to attend to an important matter which was pending between him and Henry IV., Emperor of Germany, who for a considerable time had been demanding from him vassalage and tribute, which Don Fernando refused, putting forward very valid reasons for preserving the independence of his kingdoms.

When departing from Portugal he had received letters from Rome which caused him deep anxiety, for Pope Alexander II. threatened him with excommunication and a crusade, if he did not comply with the demands of the emperor.

[1] "He who loves thee well will make thee weep."

In whatever portion of the annals of the reign of Don Fernando I. we read, we find incontrovertible proofs of the piety of that great monarch : in his reign were ransomed from the Moors the sacred bodies of St. Isidore, Archbishop of Seville, of Saints Justa, Rufina, Victor, and many other servants of God; in his time were erected magnificent cathedrals and monasteries, amongst which may be mentioned that of Sahagun; in his time ecclesiastical discipline was admirably regulated in Castile; in his time Christian worship, neglected till then, on account of the continual wars with the Moors and internal dissensions, was fully re-established ; and, as a last proof of the piety of Don Fernando the Great, history tells us that he made long and frequent retreats in the monastery of St. John of Sahagun, joining in pious exercises with its monks, and taking part in all the austerities and mortifications which, at that period, accompanied monastic life. We can judge of those which were practised by the monks of Sahagun, when we recall to mind many anecdotes found in history. In one of his frequent visits to that monastery Don Fernando noticed that the monks went about barefooted, a custom which caused many of them to contract deadly diseases; the king felt compassion for them, and supplied the abbot with the money necessary to procure sandals for them. There was in the monastery a glass vessel, which was reserved for the superior and for the king whenever he sought hospitality in that holy house. One day, when Don Fernando went to Sahagun, he found the community in a state of great affliction, and when he inquired the cause of it he was informed that the monastery had lost one of its most precious possessions, the glass cup of the abbot, which had been broken. The king knew that this feeling of the monks was not unfounded, as the loss of that article, in their extreme poverty, was difficult for them to make good, and he ordered a golden goblet to be made, to take the place of the glass one.

A council had been held at Rome, promoted by the Emperor of Germany, at which had assisted the King of France and other sovereigns who supported the pretensions of the emperor, and the letters which we have mentioned were sent to Don Fernando as a consequence of it.

Don Fernando was in a state of perplexity between two courses, either to excite the enmity of the allies of Henry IV., especially that of the Holy See, or to submit his states to a vassalage, hateful to a nation which had worked out its independence with the sword, and which was therefore proud of it and little disposed to submit to a foreign yoke. In this difficult matter he considered that he should not come to any conclusion guided by his own opinion alone, but that he should consult the wisest men of Castile and Leon, particularly the bishops, who might be considered very competent advisers in such a matter.

Whilst the grandees, noblemen, and bishops were assembling from various districts, Don Fernando was taking repose, after his recent fatigues, in the midst of his family, which had come to meet him in Leon. At last the time arrived for the opening of the Cortes, and the dejection of the king was changed into hope and gladness when he saw himself surrounded by so many illustrious men—some famous for their wisdom, others for their nobility. All the great men of the kingdom were arriving in Leon, and, notwithstanding, at the time for commencing the debates, Don Fernando did not see at his side him whom he most desired to be present, Rodrigo Diaz, the brave cavalier, whose advice he thought more of than that of all the other nobles of Castile and Leon. How was it that Rodrigo had not come to the Cortes, to assist the king, when he was so much in need of the counsels of all good men, and when a matter of such vital importance was about to be considered, whether Castile and Leon should or should not be made subject to a foreign yoke?

Don Fernando explained to the nobles the object for which he had summoned them together, and the high importance, in his opinion, of the question which they had to decide.

"Do you believe," he asked of them, "that Castile and Leon should acknowledge vassalage to the Emperor of Germany, whose pretensions are supported by the Pope, or that we should repudiate it?"

"Those who were present," as Mariana relates, "were not unanimous. They who were most religiously disposed advised that submission should be made, in order that the Pope might not be offended, and that disturbances might not be stirred up in Spain, which would necessarily injure the country very much, as in every possible way civil war should be avoided, as the country was divided into many kingdoms, and as so many Moors, enemies of Christianity, were in it. Others, more daring and of greater courage, said, that if they yielded, Spain would be submitted to a very heavy yoke, which it would never be able to shake off; that it would be better to die with arms in their hands than to permit such injury to their country, and such lowering of its dignity."

The views of those last mentioned, who consisted of Arias Gonzalo, Peranzures, and many more, were those which were most in harmony with the opinion of Don Fernando; he, however, considered the opposite one worthy of deep consideration, as it was that of the majority, and especially that of many wise and virtuous prelates, and it was at last virtually decided to yield to the demands of the emperor and his allies.

The debates had already ceased, and those who had been present at them were about to leave the chamber in which the Cortes had been held, when the arrival of Rodrigo Diaz de Vivar was announced. Prolonged expressions of satisfaction on the one part, and of annoyance on the other, arose on all sides, and joy shone in the countenance of the king. The Counts of Carrion and of Cabra bit their lips with fury, and interchanged looks, the significance of which no one knew just then, but which the reader shall learn very soon. The Cid appeared in the council chamber a moment after. Notwithstanding the solemnity of the occasion, Don Fernando arose from his throne, in order to advance to meet Rodrigo, whom he clasped in his arms, not permitting him to prostrate himself at his feet.

All fixed their looks on the Count of Carrion, and all remarked the vexation and rage which were excited in him by those signal proofs of friendship and affection which the king exhibited towards De Vivar.

"Oh!" said Don Fernando, beaming with joy, "my hope was not vain that you would arrive before the question we were considering was finally settled, so that we might have the advantage of your loyal counsels. Why have you delayed so long, when your presence was so necessary? My desire to clasp you in my arms, long before this, was very great."

"Sire," answered Rodrigo, with a certain embarrassment, which the king could not help noticing, "my family detained me rather too long; you, who love yours so much, can easily understand the effect of the tears of a wife, who fears, when her husband is leaving her, that she may not see him again for a very long time. Perhaps I have failed in my duty as a good subject, and in the gratitude which I owe to you, but I assure you, sire, that it was impossible for me to avoid it."

"The proofs of loyalty, which you have always given, suffice abundantly to prove it to me, Rodrigo."

"Sire, dispose of my life and of all that I possess, for they are not sufficient to repay your kindness!" exclaimed Rodrigo, deeply moved.

"Are you well informed, Rodrigo, as to the serious business which has obliged me to summon together all the leading men of my kingdoms?" asked Don Fernando.

"No person in Castile is ignorant of it, sire," replied the Cid. "It is a question of the freedom or of the enslavement of a brave and proud nation, which has won its independence by fighting against foreign foes during four centuries. Has not such a nation some interest in the question which brings us together here?"

The presence of the Cid caused the debates, which were thought to be ended, to commence afresh. Those who were disposed to refuse vassalage to the emperor had now some hopes of seeing their views prevail, as they felt sure that the Cid would support them, and they knew that the influence of De Vivar was very great.

Rodrigo Diaz listened for some time to the arguments of the opposed parties, and then said—

"We have scarcely shaken off the yoke which the Moors held over our humiliated heads, and shall we now allow Christians to make us vassals and enslave us? Our ancestors smashed to pieces the heavy yoke imposed on them by the Romans, and shall we now permit the Germans to bend us down under another? Theirs would then become the power, the authority, the honour, the riches, which our fathers won with their blood. And what would remain to us? Trials, dangers, slavery, and poverty! It is better to die as brave men than lose the liberty which our forefathers left us as a sacred inheritance!"

Almost the entire assembly broke out into exclamations of assent when Rodrigo had pronounced those words. A bishop, however, whose name the "Chronicles" do not mention, arose from his seat and replied to him thus—

"If the vassalage which is demanded of Castile were not supported by the Supreme Pontiff, your reasons would be just and valid, and it would be right to sustain the refusal with the sword; but it is a question of obedience or non-obedience to the Vicar of Christ."

'For the law of Christ Castile has fought for more than

four hundred years," replied the Cid with energy. "For the law of Christ I have fought, and shall always fight, and nevertheless I should consider myself a bad Christian, a bad cavalier, and a bad Castilian, if I were not to oppose to the utmost the demand of the emperor, even though it be supported by the Pope. If Castile is now, when free and rich, only barely able to keep the infidels in check, how can she conquer them when poor and enslaved? The vassalage which the foreigner seeks to impose on us will enervate our strength, will pauperise us, will make us cowards as well as slaves, and then—what will become of the faith of our fathers, what will become of the Cross, which until recently was under the subjection of the Crescent?"

Cries of enthusiasm, which even the presence of the king and the solemnity of the occasion were not able to keep down, answered those words of Rodrigo Diaz. Even those who, with the greatest zeal, had maintained that the demands of the Germans should be acceded to, changed their minds, with the exceptions of the Counts of Carrion and Cabra and a few others, who were envious of the favour and advancement which the Cid enjoyed. The latter turned towards Don Fernando, and continued—

"Sire, you were born in an evil day for Spain, if in your time a people should become enslaved who, until now, have been always free. If you consent to such a terrible humiliation, all is lost—lost is all the honour which God has given you, and all the good He has accomplished for you. Whoever counsels you to accede to the demands of the emperor is not loyal, nor does he love your honour or your sway—he deserves not to be a son of our beloved Castile."

The Count of Carrion and his partisans placed their hands on their swords, unable to restrain their fury; and they would have drawn them if the voice of the king had not been heard above the loud applause which drowned the last words of Rodrigo. Don Fernando cried out—

"Silence, vassals, silence! Who is it that dares to lay his hand on his sword in the presence of his lord and king? A valiant cavalier, a noble, who is as good a Christian as he is a good knight, is he who sustains opinions different to yours. You all have been summoned here to speak freely what you think, and even if I were not present, the gravity and importance of this assembly should restrain you. Speak, De Vivar, for we consider all advice important, whether it be given with the energy which befits a brave soldier, as you are, or with the calm deliberation which characterises ecclesiastics."

Don Suero and his friends became quiet, much against their wills, and the silence and order of the assembly were restored.

"I do not believe," continued Rodrigo, "that the Pontiff will close his ears to our just prayers; let us send those to him who will defend our freedom in his presence, and explain to him how unjust and impolitic are the pretensions of the Germans; but if our reasonings avail nothing, we must then have recourse to the sword. For my part, I am now resolved to defend against the entire world the honour and the liberty which my ancestors have handed down to me, and those who agree in my views I look on as my friends, and as the friends of our country. If the Germans do not recognise our rights, we have good lances in Castile wherewith to prove to them that we have honour and courage. Rouse up the country, sire; get together an invincible host—you can easily do so— and cross the Pyrenees; I shall go in the front with two thousand of my friends, and, in addition, the troops that my Moorish tributaries shall supply me with."

This advice of the Cid satisfied almost all, especially the king, and it was arranged to reply to the Pope with all respect, but at the same time to raise, without delay, an army of ten thousand men, which should be ready to cross the Pyrenees, under the command of the Cid, in case the Germans and their allies should persist in their demands. The assembly then broke up.

Whilst Rodrigo Diaz was thus opposing those who advised the king to yield to the pretensions of Henry IV., Fernan Cardeña, with other squires and pages, was walking about in the large square which fronted the palace which the lords of Gormaz had owned in the city, and which was now the property of Rodrigo, as a result of his marriage with Ximena.

"It appears to me," said a squire to Fernan, "that we could kill time a little in this square by exercising ourselves in arms; if our masters serve Castile in the council chamber, we can serve her here by practising how to give good blows on the battlefields."

"Leave me in peace, comrades," replied Fernan, "for the son of my mother is in more humour to go asleep and rest himself than to exercise himself in arms."

" Are you fatigued, then ? "

" As much as if I had just come from a fierce battle."

" Your journey must have been a very hasty one ? "

" One half of it was."

" Nevertheless, the Campeador arrived very late."

" That was not his fault."

" How was that ? "

" We set out from Burgos in good time, but "—

" You had then some ugly adventure on the road ? "

" It would have been so, in the case of anyone but my master."

" May I turn Moor if I understand you ! "

" Then you need not hope that the son of my mother will explain himself more fully."

" Anger of God ! but you have very little confidence in your friends, Fernan."

" How can I have confidence in anyone at the present time ? No, only believe that people love you, and, when you least expect it, they will get up a plot against your life; and you would lose it, as my master should have done, if he had not been so brave, and if he had not such good cavaliers in his company."

These words excited the curiosity of his hearers.

" Tell us all about it," they cried out; " relate to us the adventure that befell the Cid on his journey from Burgos to Leon."

" I swear that, for a prattler, I deserve to be driven with cudgels from his service by my master ! " cried Fernan, indignant with himself for his indiscretion.

" Relate it to us, comrade, for we shall know from you exactly what took place, and not with the addition of all kinds of embellishments, which the people will invent before long."

Fernan, as it concerned honourable deeds of his master, felt that he should burst if he did not relate them; he seemed satisfied, with regard to his conscience, by the remarks of the last speaker, and said—

" Keep secret what I am about to tell you, for my lord, Don Rodrigo, ordered all who were with him at the time not to speak of it, and he must have had his reasons for doing so, and I should respect them. You must know, then, that we sallied forth from Burgos early yesterday, in order to arrive here in good time. My master had no other cavaliers with him but Martin Antolinez and Guillen of the Standard,

18

as he is now called, because he rescued that of Don Rodrigo; and no other squires but the two who are now asleep in the stable and myself; for that fool Alvar still keeps his bed, as a result of a certain cudgelling he got. Martin Vengador has gone to Vivar to see his sweetheart, and Rui-Venablos could not leave the band, which has entered into the service of my master, and which he commands during the absence of Martin, who is its captain. We were passing through a wood near Carrion, when certain very dolorous wailings attracted our attention; we stopped to listen, when we heard a woman's voice, which cried out—

"'Succour me, succour me, travellers! for my house is on fire, and my children, who are in it, will be burned.'

"We all hastened to the place from which the voice sounded, and, on a small hill, we saw the person who had called out; it was a woman with dishevelled hair, and with all the signs of great despair.

"'Where is your house—in which direction?' we asked, when still at some distance from her.

"'You will find it just round the turn of this hill,' she replied to our question. 'Do you not see the smoke which is rising to the sky? Go thither, good cavaliers, and save my unhappy children, if there is still time; but there will be, if you hasten.' In reality, a column of smoke was rising behind the hill.

"We applied spurs to our horses, and, in less time than I tell it, we turned the small hill, and at a short distance, beside a thick cluster of trees, we saw a house from which cries proceeded, seemingly those of children, and from which dense smoke was arising.

"On arriving at the house we all dismounted, dashed in the door with a few good kicks, and hastily entered."

"And did you save the children?" asked, impatiently, those who were listening to the narration of Fernan.

"The children which we found," he answered, "were ten very big men, who were concealed in one of the rooms of the house, and who rushed, swords in hand, on us, and especially on my master, who was in the front. May Beelzebub take my soul if ever I saw a fiercer fight than that which then took place in the small room. Guilt doubtless caused those ruffians to lose their presence of mind, for they all missed their first strokes and gave time to Don Rodrigo and the two other cavaliers to draw their swords and close with them. The fight lasted only a short time, but it was fierce and bloody. Four of the assassins fell to the ground, pierced by the sword of my master, and the others jumped through a window and escaped through the wood."

"What a terrible picture must have presented that combat in a house which was on fire!" exclaimed one of the squires.

"What was on fire was a lot of straw, heaped up in a yard," replied Fernan; and he then continued: "Guillen thought he recognised one of the assassins, who was weltering in his blood, and when he examined him closely, he uttered a cry of surprise and exclaimed—

"'Illan! you armed with an assassin's dagger! wretched, wretched man! And it was you who expressed surprise that I should be in the service of the Count of Carrion before we separated at the railings of the porch of Santa Gadea.'

"'Pardon, pardon, Guillen!' murmured the man called Illan. "'Avarice — the gold which Don Garcia and Don Suero promised us, if we killed the Cid and you, blinded me. Pardon a dying man, and do not go to Carrion, for Don Suero knows that you love the Infanta '—

"'May God pardon you, as I do,' replied Guillen. And we all left the house, in pursuit of those who had fled through the wood. We spent many hours in search of them, in that hilly country, and at last, despairing of finding them, we continued our journey hither, both ourselves and our horses being much fatigued, as we had to press onward very quickly to make up for lost time."

"And who was the woman that allured you to the ambuscade?"

"Some witch, doubtless, for she became invisible from the time she spoke to us from the top of the hill, and we could find her no more than the others we were seeking."

The squires had come to this part of their conversation when, the Cortes being ended, the nobles who had taken part in it began to issue forth from the Alcazar.

Fernan impressed on his friends the necessity of the strictest secrecy with regard to that which he had related to them, and went off to the residence of his master, whom he saw going towards it, accompanied by Martin Antolinez and Guillen.

———

CHAPTER XXXIV

WHICH TREATS OF CAVALIERS FREE WITH THE HAND AND PEASANTS FREE WITH THE TONGUE

As had been determined at the Cortes held at Leon, the king, Don Fernando, wrote to the allied powers refusing the tribute which the Emperor of Austria had demanded; also giving the reasons on which that refusal was based. Meanwhile the Cid, by his orders, was occupied in getting together an efficient army by means of which Castile would be able to oppose the foreigners, if they appealed to arms to sustain their demands, as they had threatened. Seeing that there was not perfect agreement amongst them, and that, on the contrary, in France and other countries allied to the Germans, warlike preparations were being made, Don Fernando consulted the Cid and other cavaliers as to whether he should cross the Pyrenees or remain in Castile on the defensive. All upheld the former proposition, for they said : " The less we embarrass the foreigners the more time will they have to prepare their armies for a campaign ; and if they see us remain quiet in Castile, they will look upon us as very weak, both in numbers and in courage, as we do not dare to challenge them on their own soil. Let us make a display of valour, and our enemies, seeing that we are neither weak nor faint-hearted, will soon change their opinion."

The Cid then demanded aid from Abengalvon and from the other Moorish kings, his vassals, and as they not only sent it, but also came themselves, leading the regiments which they furnished to the Castilians, the army of Don Fernando soon set out for the French frontiers.

Don Fernando commanded the main army, composed of eight thousand men, and Rodrigo Diaz marched in advance, in order to select good quarters.

When the Cid entered the gates of Aspa he found great disturbance amongst the inhabitants of that district ; so much so that they would not furnish the Castilians with quarters nor sell provisions to them ; moreover, they endeavoured to do as much injury to them as was in their power.

Rodrigo ordered that the crops and houses of the rebels should be burned, but that, on the contrary, all those should be well treated who provided quarters and sold food to them.

On arriving near Tolosa, the Cid learned that large hostile forces were sallying out to meet him, with the object of preventing his advance. Don Ramon, Count of Savoy, was approaching with twenty thousand men, and with full authority from the King of France to engage in hostilities with the Castilians.

"My army numbers two thousand men," said the Cid, "but we must either prove to France, and to the entire world, that two Castilian cavaliers are equal to twenty foreigners, or else die gloriously. Our enemies have decided to attack us before the king's army can arrive ; there are but two things left to us, either to face them as we are, or to turn back in order to reinforce ourselves with the soldiers who are coming on with Don Fernando. Turn back? No, no! Let us rather advance to certain death than turn our backs to the enemy."

Rodrigo now made his warriors ready for the fight, as his enemies appeared at but a short distance from them.

"St. James ! St. James !" he then cried out, and closed with the hostile force.

The combat was fierce, and lasted for an hour. In that time prodigies of valour were performed, not alone by the Castilians but also by the Moorish warriors who accompanied the Cid, at whose side Abengalvon and the other Moorish kings fought, and by Guillen of the Standard, to whom Rodrigo had confided his own, in order to confer a fresh proof of confidence, and to mark the esteem in which he held him.

The army of the Count of Savoy was cut to pieces, and Don Ramon himself was taken prisoner.

This first victory of the Castilians filled the allies of the emperor with terror ; nevertheless, the King of France sent against the invaders a fresh army which he kept in reserve in Gascony.

These forces marched forth to the encounter of the representative of Don Fernando in the same way as those of the Count of Savoy had done, and, like those, they were routed by the Cid and his two thousand cavaliers before the king could arrive to take part in the combat.

The Count of Savoy begged for his liberty, as the fact of his being a prisoner wounded his pride, and because disturbances which had broken out in his own states urgently required his presence there. Don Fernando refused his request, fearing that his object was to organise fresh forces wherewith to avenge the humiliating defeat which he had suffered. Don

Ramon then offered, as a hostage, his daughter, whom he dearly loved, and who was very beautiful and discreet. Don Fernando considered this sufficient, and the count obtained his freedom, leaving his daughter in the power of the King of Castile.

The allied sovereigns sent letters to Don Fernando, praying him not to advance farther, and offering to agree to terms for peace; the King of Castile, as a result, established his headquarters in Toulouse, and sent the Cid, Alvar Fañez Minaya, Arias Gonzalo, Martin Antolinez, and other cavaliers to Rome to inform the Pope that ambassadors should proceed to Spain empowered to treat for peace.

The Pope called together a council, and in it debated as to what steps should be taken. All were of opinion that the demands of Don Fernando should be acceded to, for, they said, "if we should decide to settle this contest by means of arms, no one will dare to oppose this famous Cid, whom all look upon as invincible." In consequence of this decision, the king sent, as his plenipotentiary, the Cardinal of Santa Sabina ; others also were sent, with full powers, by the emperor and the other allied sovereigns, between whom and the King of Castile it was stipulated, in proper form, that vassalage, of any form whatsoever, should never be demanded of Spain.

Six months were spent in these preliminaries and treaties, and at the end of that period the Castilian army recrossed the frontiers, and was received in Castile with the greatest enthusiasm, which the people gave expression to by loud acclamations and splendid festivities.

The people of Castile had loved the Cid very much, and that love now changed almost into adoration after the recent splendid feats of arms of the brave cavalier, and especially on account of the valour and the energy with which he had defended the freedom of the kingdom at the last Cortes in Leon. Nations are extreme in their loves and hatreds. When a public man should be exalted, they raise him to the very clouds; when his humiliation is concerned, they drag him through the mire ; they always exaggerate things, whether it is a question of reward or punishment. The acts of the Cid were really splendid, but in the eyes of the populace they were very much more.

The inhabitants of Burgos were occupied with the feats of Rodrigo, and they explained them and commented on them in their own way. Many of his exploits were pure inventions of popular enthusiasm and credulity; this, however, only strengthens what we have said, that the Cid was the idol of the Castilian people.

Just at the entrance into Burgos, on the northern side, resided a worthy artisan who worked constantly before the door of his house as a farrier. Our readers already know Iñigo, for that was his name, having seen him exchange blows with a rustic on the day that Ximena entered the city to celebrate her nuptials with Rodrigo Diaz. Iñigo was a type of the populace in its most perfect form; he was talkative, irascible, enthusiastic, credulous, fond of news, a grumbler—in a word, all that his class has ever been. A fly scarcely moved in Burgos but Iñigo knew where it flew to: if he had lived in our times he could have made plenty of money as a member of the detective police, or as a supplier of events of the day to some newspaper. If a muleteer entered Burgos on a very hot day, Iñigo would say to him—

"You are welcome, brother. This is a bad time for travelling. What news on the roads? Won't you sit down for a while on this bench, and take a draught of this deliciously cool water which I have here?"

And the muleteer, believing that it would be discourteous if he did not accept the invitation, would stop to satisfy the curiosity of Iñigo.

If a peasant woman came in when the weather was cold, with a basket of eggs or other farm produce on her head, Iñigo would say to her—

"You are welcome, sister. This is a bad time to come to town. Is there any news in your district? Won't you put down your basket, and warm yourself at the good fire I have here?"

And the peasant woman would do just the same as the muleteer.

If there is added to the information he obtained in this way all that he picked up from squires who brought their masters' horses to be shod, from the women and men of the vicinity, who rested themselves, talking meanwhile of their neighbours' affairs, on the bench of the horse-shoer, which was pleasantly shaded from the sun, all the world will agree that Iñigo was exactly suited to fill a position of the nature of those which we have mentioned above.

Two days after the return of the Cid to Burgos, there entered the city the same peasant to whom Iñigo had given so sound a drubbing on a former occasion. The farrier and he had become friends again, to judge by the way they saluted each other.

"You are welcome, Señor Bartolo," cried out the former on seeing the peasant.

"God keep you in His guard, Master Iñigo," was the reply.

"I was just saying to myself, that, considering all the news that is flying about Burgos, it is curious that Señor Bartolo is not coming to hear it."

"Oh, then there is a lot of news, eh? I swear that one might just as well be a captive among the Moors as live in a village."

"What, does news never get to Barbadillo?"

"You may say, none. I tell you we live like beasts in the villages. Whenever I smell any news in the air, I come to the city to see you. And as you are so wise and clever, and all that kind of thing, you polish me up a bit. What is to be learned in a village? That a wolf ate a sheep belonging to Uncle Pellica; that Uncle Colambra got drunk, and gave his wife a beating; that the daughter of Aunt Valeta fell in love with four young fellows; and other things of a similar nature. What wonder is it, then, that one is always bored when living in such a place? I swear I am."

"It is, indeed, Señor Bartolo, great good luck to live in a city."

"And what gets up my blood most is that my wife is constantly wrangling with me because I come now and then to the city to learn the news; she says that I am always neglecting my land and my cattle."

"Your wife must certainly be a great ass, Señor Bartolo."

"And she is not the only one that finds fault with me; all my neighbours are against me. I was formerly stupid and ignorant like themselves, and they don't like to see me getting a little knowledge into my head."

"Certainly, Señor Bartolo, your neighbours must be all great blockheads."

"But I swear I won't stand it any longer; in spite of my wife and neighbours, I'll get rid of the bit of ground I own, and the cottage I have in the village, and come to live in Burgos."

"Certainly, Señor Bartolo, you should come to the city, for it is a great pleasure to know at once all that is passing in the world, and just at present there's good news coming every day."

“What good news, eh ? ”

“Good, Señor Bartolo, very good.”

“And what is it all about, Master Iñigo ? ”

“About the Campeador, as you may well suppose.”

“By San Pedro of Cardeña, the Cid is a splendid cavalier!
But tell me, tell me, Master Iñigo, the latest news of him.”

“I will, Señor Bartolo. You know already what a good
beating he gave the French, don’t you ? ”

“Yes, yes ; you told me all about that already. Anger of
God ! how I should like to have been on the top of the Pyrenees
to see from there how the Cid and his army treated those
French dogs.”

“You know also that the Cid was at Rome, with other good
cavaliers ? ”

“Certainly ; you told me that too.”

“But that which you don’t know is what happened there to
the Cid.”

“What happened to him ? Did he fight a terrible battle
with that Don Vaticano, as they call him ? ”

“Ha, ha, ha ! ”

“Master Iñigo, are you also making game of me ? ”

“I was laughing at your ignorance and simplicity, for you
are mistaking the Pope’s palace for a cavalier ; the Vatican is
a palace, and not a man.”

“Curses on the village ! living in it has made me the ass I
am. May I become a greater Turk than Mahomet if I don’t
leave it at once ! ”

“Learn, then, that the Cid, when he arrived in Rome, went
straight to the church of St. Peter ”—

“It’s something like a church, I’ve heard, and not like the
one in my village.”

“Yes, Señor Bartolo, they tell wonders of it ; they say it is
built of blocks of diamond.”

“San Pedro de Cardeña ! what a great misfortune it is to
live in villages and not in cities, where there are such riches ! ”

“Know, then, that the Cid went to St. Peter’s to see the
throne of the Pope, which is made of solid gold.”

“Anger of God ! It must be a fine thing to be a Pope.”

“All the Christian kings have seats near the Pope’s throne,
and when the Campeador saw that the seat of the King of
France was placed a little higher than that of the King of
Castile, he kicked it down.”

“I swear that it would have been a great misfortune for me

not to know of that act, so worthy of being known. I certainly shall leave Barbadillo."

"As the seat of the King of France was made of marble, it broke into pieces. And what do you think the Cid then did, Señor Bartolo? He took that of the King of Castile and put it in the principal place."

"My God, what a good vassal! May God preserve him!"

"Then out spoke a duke, who is called the Savoyard, and said to the Campeador, 'May you be accursed, Rodrigo, and may the Pope excommunicate you, for having insulted the King of France, the most honoured sovereign in the world.' 'Leave kings aside,' said the Campeador; 'and if you consider yourself aggrieved, let us settle this quarrel between us.'"

"And the Cid and the Savoyard fought? I swear that I am delighted with your story."

"As they were going out of the church, the Campeador went up to the duke and gave him a shove."

"God's anger! And they came to blows, eh? What did the Savoyard do?"

"He remained very quiet, and made no answer to the Campeador."

"By San Pedro of Cardeña, no one dares to oppose the Cid."

"When the Pope heard of it, he excommunicated Don Rodrigo."

"What do you tell me, Master Iñigo? The Cid excommunicated! What a pity! for he will begin to dwindle away, as it is said those do who are excommunicated."

"Such did not happen, for he knelt down with much humility at the feet of the Pope, and said to him, 'Absolve me, holy father, for it won't be prudent of you not to do so.' And the Pope gave him absolution, like a merciful father as he is, saying to him, 'I absolve you, Campeador; but you must be more circumspect in my Court.'"

"Oh, accursed Barbadillo! such fine things are never heard of there! Master Iñigo, I am just going back to dispose of all my belongings, and you shall soon see me here again. You won't see me making an ass of myself any longer."

"You are right, Señor Bartolo; but won't you tell me what is going on in your district?"

"I have told you : nothing whatever, Master Iñigo."

The farrier was about to put fresh questions to the peasant, when he noticed that some muleteers were approaching, who, to judge by their appearance, had come from some very distant locality. He hastened to meet them, saluting them in his customary way, in order to satisfy his curiosity, at the expense of a bench which he kept beside a good fire in winter, and of a draught of cold water which he had ready to attract travellers in summer.

A few moments having passed, the peasant and the artisan were listening with delight to the wonderful bits of news which the muleteers brought with them, but which need not figure in this book, as they were only vulgar gossip.

CHAPTER XXXV

OF THE SORROWS WHICH THE COWARDLY DON SUERO CAUSED HIS SISTER

JUST at the time that Guillen left the Castle of Carrion to proceed to the seat of war in Portugal, Bellido Dolfos entered it. The arrival of the traitor was announced to Don Suero, and satisfaction shone in the eyes of the count, who hastened to receive Bellido, for he doubted not but that he brought him some important intelligence, having returned so soon to the castle.

"What tidings do you bring me? Speak at once," he asked of the new-comer, even without waiting for his salutation.

"I bring you very important news, sir count."

"Speak, speak!"

"Can any person hear us?"

"No one, Bellido."

"Notwithstanding, it is just as well to shut the door."

And Bellido closed the door of the apartment, and then returned and seated himself at the side of the count.

"What have you to tell me of that infernal band?"

"I have but little to tell you of the band."

"Then of whom do you bring me news?"

"Of your sister, and of the page."

"They returned to the castle."

"I know that."

"I do not then understand what the news can be that you bring me of them."

"Calm your impatience, my lord. The attentions of that handsome page were more than a little pleasing to the Infanta."

"And to me also, Bellido; for this very day I rewarded that loyal servant, giving him the best of my horses and arms, in order that he might go to the seat of war. You must have met him near the castle."

"Is he not in the castle now?"

"No."

"I certainly saw a horseman issue forth. Ah, my lord, you have allowed to escape from your hands him who is the most deserving of your anger."

"By Lucifer, explain yourself, Bellido! What would you tell me?"

"I would tell you that the youth loves your sister, and that your sister returns his love."

The count jumped to his feet as suddenly as if a serpent had pierced him with its fangs. Bellido had foreseen his rage, and, in order to lessen it, had intended to break the information to him; he had, however, precipitated it, annoyed by the impatience and the imperious tone of Don Suero.

"Bellido!" exclaimed the count, gazing fixedly at his companion, "perchance you think that I am in such good humour that I can tolerate jokes? Do you believe that the Count of Carrion is so much your friend that you can amuse yourself with him?"

"My lord," answered Bellido humbly, "the vexation you feel grieves me sincerely; but I can only repeat to you that your sister and the page are in love with each other, that they vilely deceive you, and "—

"This calumny will cost you your life, Bellido!"

"If what I tell you is not the truth I am quite willing that you cause me to be hung on the ramparts of your castle."

"What proofs can you give me that you are not calumniating one of the noblest maidens in Spain?"

"My word, which the loyalty and the zeal with which I have served you, will vouch for.'

"Hell, hell! Must I believe what you tell me? No, I cannot believe it, Bellido; it cannot be that a miserable page has dared to set his eyes on the Infanta of Carrion; it cannot be that my sister has opened her ears to so low-born a youth!"

"My lord, I can well understand your incredulity, but there

is nothing more certain than that which I have told you. Silence reigned in the camp of the bandits. I know not what made me suspect that the page was something more than a servant in the eyes of the Infanta; I crept up to the tent in which both of them were lodged, and, as I found that they were awake, I applied my ear to the canvas, and surprised the secret of their love"—

"And if it is a fact that the page loves my sister, why has he voluntarily left her, in order to go to the war in Portugal?"

"Because he aspires to the hand of your sister, and knows that he must be at least a knight in order to marry the Infanta of Carrion."

"Oh, everything conspires against me!" exclaimed Don Suero, falling back into the violent despair which he seemed to have mastered for a moment. "I suffer on earth all the tortures of hell. They deceive me, they sell me; my own kinsfolk and strangers murder me slowly. Whom can I trust? My life appears to be that of the wicked, which my mother often described to me; not a moment of calm; no happiness that merits such a name, enemies on all sides; vain projects; desires never satisfied; sadness, sleeplessness, everlasting despair,—such was the life my mother pictured to me, and such is mine. Oh! am I one that is accursed? No, I am not, I am not. If I have treated my servants and my vassals cruelly, it is because my servants and my vassals detested me, and would have sold me. If I have enemies and plot their destruction, it is because I cannot gain their friendship, because they all insult me and conspire against me. This is to live a life of agony."

And the count, who had bent it down, raised his head suddenly, and such was the appearance of his countenance, and the glitter of his eyes, that Bellido made a movement as if to turn away from him, believing that reason had forsaken him.

"Traitor!" exclaimed Don Suero, "have you come here to take advantage of what I say? My dagger shall teach you to be more courteous."

Bellido arose from his seat, and placing his hand on the pommel of his sword, said, endeavouring to render his words as conciliatory as possible—

"My lord, grief is overcoming you; remember that he who stands by your side is the only loyal friend in whom you can trust."

Don Suero quickly recovered his senses, which, for a moment, had abandoned him, and said, holding out his hand to the traitor—

"Pardon me, Bellido, pardon my burst of passion. Yes, yes, you are right; grief, anger, despair, put me out of my mind. Yes, you are my sole friend, the only one who has not betrayed me, who has not insulted me, who feels compassion for me. But is it quite certain that this miserable page loves my sister, and that she has degraded herself by returning his love?"

"Nothing, I repeat, is more certain."

"And what is to be done, Bellido, what is to be done?"

"Kill the villain who has thus betrayed your confidence."

"Yes, and the Infanta also deserves to die. A hundred lives, taken one by one, would not be sufficient to expiate such treason. But where can I find the page? What a fool I was to let him escape my vengeance! And I have given him arms—perchance to use them against myself, for, I doubt it not, that traitor will proceed to Portugal, he will fight against the Moors, rise from his present low condition, and return, filled with pride and audacity, to insult me, to challenge me, and to impose shameful conditions on me."

"As soon as he returns from Portugal he will come to see the Infanta, and then you will find an opportunity to punish his treachery; but, in order that he may return to the castle, that he may fall into your hands, he must not know that you have discovered his insensate love; you must not let the Infanta know that you even suspect it, for Doña Teresa would be able to discover some means of advising him, and then the traitor would remain unpunished."

"Impossible, Bellido, impossible! Can I look on my sister without my indignation breaking out? Can I put off the punishment, which she deserves, until the day when that traitor may feel pleased to appear in my castle?"

"Certainly, my lord, it would be difficult for you to do so; but you must find some pretext for your annoyance. Say to your sister that you wish to confer her hand on—the first that comes into your head; your sister will oppose your wishes, and then you can give vent to your anger, the real motive of which will not be suspected."

"I shall do so, Bellido, I shall do so. It was a fortunate day on which I first made your acquaintance, for you are the only man who gives me loyal advice, who aids me to fight against that cruel fate which baffles all my enterprises, which upsets all my plans, which does not leave a moment of tranquillity to my soul. Yes, yes, I intend the hand of my sister for the son of the Count of Cabra, and my sister does not yet know of it. The occasion for telling her has arrived."

"But be on your guard, I repeat; do not let her suspect that you know of her love for the page."

"She shall suspect nothing, Bellido. But tell me now, in what condition is the band?"

"I believe that it will totally disappear within the next few days. Although its members are now but few, they are able to defend themselves against the Salvadores as long as they are all together—they can at least escape from them if they cannot conquer them as formerly. I have, however, succeeded in dividing them, under the pretext that such is done for their security, availing myself of the influence which I have gained over the Vengador and Rui - Venablos, from the time I prophesied to them that the band would be destroyed, if they forcibly attacked the Castle of Carrion. After to-day one half of the bandits will be encamped at a considerable distance from the other half, so that they could not rejoin each other quickly, should the two encampments be attacked by the Salvadores, to whom, before I return to the band I shall give full information. You can easily imagine that if the bandits were deadly hostile to you before, they have been much more so since they suffered such a terrible reverse in your castle. For that reason you should be delighted to get rid of them quickly."

"Certainly, Bellido, certainly. I trust that, with your assistance, I shall be able to annihilate those implacable enemies. Continue your efforts in that direction, and count on my liberality."

"Sir," said Bellido, affecting diffidence, "I venture to ask you for some money, which I require to add to the consider-able sum, which I have already expended on the bandits in order to win their confidence, so that I might succeed in realising my plans."

With every coin which he had to give, it seemed to Don Suero that he was parting with a piece of his heart, for avarice was the moving cause of most of his evil actions; however, as it was necessary to secure the aid of Bellido in his favour, he answered, going to the strong chest, in which he had on a former occasion showed his treasures to Bellido—

"Take, Bellido, the money which you require.   Will twenty gold marks be sufficient for you ?"

"That will not be enough," replied Bellido in a humble tone of voice.

"I will give you forty."

"I must have more," said Bellido firmly.

"Take sixty."

"I require as much as a hundred," replied Bellido haughtily.

"Villain !" exclaimed Don Suero in an involuntary burst of indignation ; but a moment's reflection made him recognise that he must be prudent with Bellido, and he added in a more subdued and friendly voice—

"Pardon me, Bellido ; the annoyances to which I have been subjected make me forget myself sometimes, and I scarcely know what I say or do.   Here are the hundred marks which you require."   And he handed them to Bellido, who took them with a joy which he vainly tried to conceal.

They then arranged some matters relative to the business which had brought them together, and Bellido quitted the Castle of Carrion.

Let us see what was taking place in the chamber of Doña Teresa whilst the scene we have described was being acted in that of the count.

When Guillen left the castle, the Infanta took her place at the window of her apartment in order to see his departure, and her eyes, full of tears, followed him until he disappeared behind a cluster of trees which grew at some distance from the castle.   How can we explain what the loving girl experienced at that moment?   It seemed to her as if her soul had quitted her body in order to accompany the handsome youth who was departing from her ; who was going away, perhaps never to return.   It appeared to her that the sky was growing dark, that the fields were losing their verdure and beauty, that the birds had ceased their warbling, that her chamber had suddenly become as gloomy, as dark, and as solitary as it had appeared before she was loved by Guillen ; it seemed to her as if everything was clad in mourning, as if everything was weeping for the absence of the handsome page. Her eyes remained fixed for a long time on that part of the landscape where Guillen had disappeared, trying to catch a glimpse of him, but no, he had disappeared.

Reader ! he who writes this book appeals again to your

recollections, to your experience, to your heart, in order that you may understand that which his pen is not able to explain. Have you ever seen a beloved object disappear from your sight, when going on a long journey, as the poor Teresa saw Guillen? Have you ever walked forth from your native place, accompanying a beloved being, who was about to be absent for a long period, in order to prolong for a short time the sad leave-taking, and when that at last came, did you not ascend an eminence to see the traveller as far as possible on his way, and did you not follow him with your gaze until the horizon shut him off from you; and then, when he had completely disappeared, did not your eyes overflow with tears? If you have experienced all that, as he has done who writes this, you will understand the grief, the anguish, the despair with which Teresa saw her lover disappear behind the distant trees.

The sad girl turned from the window with her heart full of sadness, and kneeling down before an image of Mary, which she had adorned with flowers every day formerly, when she was free and happy enough to go out to gather them in the surrounding fields, now a long time ago, she besought the "Mother of pure love" to protect the brave and handsome and loving youth, who had set out to fight for her love and for the Christian faith, and she felt her heart consoled. In former times, when she felt her soul sad, the tender, the pure, the sweet Teresa sought consolation from her mother; but, as she had been taken from her, to whom could she appeal but to the universal Mother of the afflicted! Oh, what a sweet, beautiful, and consoling religion is that which gives us an immortal Mother, so that we may not remain orphans when she who bore us has departed from us!

Teresa felt consoled; but, her sensibilities being very much excited, she felt the necessity of conversing with some-one whom she loved and who loved her. Who then could that person be but her brother? She was about leaving her chamber to go in search of him, when he appeared before her, and the poor girl trembled when she saw him, for she remarked on the countenance of her brother a certain expression of anger, which she had perceived in it on other occasions. However, Don Suero was restraining himself, and succeeded in somewhat softening that expression; and then tranquillity and confidence returned to the heart of the Infanta.

"My brother," said Teresa in a sweet and affectionate tone,

"accustomed to be so much by your side, I feel lonely when I am long without seeing you, and I was therefore going to seek you."

The Infanta spoke the truth when she said this: from the time she had returned from the bandits' camp she desired to be near her brother, whom she really loved tenderly, for she believed that he nourished the same feeling towards her.

"Hypocrite!" said Don Suero to himself, and he was on the point of breaking the resolution he had made to conceal his anger; but he conquered that instinctive feeling, and answered his sister kindly—

"I also desire to be near you, Teresa, for you are the only being I really love. For a long time I was unjust towards you, but at last I recognised my error, and I wish to repair it by bestowing on you the happiness which you deserve. My sister, I am about to prove to you that I anxiously desire your happiness, that I desire to see you honoured, loved, happy. Have you ever thought on the felicity to which a woman should aspire?"

"I do not understand you, brother."

"Have you never thought that the greatest happiness of an honoured and good maiden, as you are, consists in finding a noble and loving husband?"

The Infanta trembled with fright on hearing this question, and replied—

"Yes, brother, my mother said that to me."

"Well, then, Teresa, your brother is about to bestow that happiness on you."

The terror of the girl came to its height.

"Brother," she said, "I am still very young, allow me to remain at your side, for that is the happiness I desire at present."

"Teresa, at the side of the husband whom I destine for you, you will also have the affection of your brother. Nuño Garciez, the son of the Count of Cabra, is noble, is brave, and loves you now for a long time."

"Nuño Garciez, the son of the Count of Cabra?" exclaimed Teresa, terrified.

"Yes, he shall be the husband who will work out your happiness, my sister."

"Impossible, brother, impossible!"

Anger inflamed the visage of Don Suero.

"Teresa!" he exclaimed, with severity, "do you mean to say that you refuse the hand of Nuño?"

Teresa could not lie; her sincerity conquered her natural timidity.

"Pardon me, brother," she answered, "but I shall never bestow my hand on the son of the Count of Cabra."

"May the anger of God strike you! What is that you dare to say, traitress? Do you repay my affection by opposing yourself insolently and rebelliously to my will? Teresa, you shall be the wife of Nuño Garciez!"

"Have compassion on me, my brother; do not condemn to eternal sadness, to eternal pain, to eternal despair this heart which has suffered so much."

And the Infanta sank down on her knees before her brother, bursting into tears.

"Have you any for me, perchance?" retorted Don Suero. "Have you compassion for me when, seeing me surrounded by enemies, you refuse to procure for me the aid of a family which could help me to triumph over all my rivals?"

"But I could never love Nuño Garciez, and my vow before the altar would be horrible perjury. Brother, have pity on me; remember the promise you made to our mother; remember that she, who gave you life, blessed you when she was breathing her last; for you had just promised her that you would be my shield, my protector, my brother—not my executioner"—

"Hell, hell! Arise from your knees, traitress, for your supplications and tears are unavailing!" roared Don Suero, at the very height of his rage.

And with a violent push he threw the gentle girl on the floor.

Teresa arose quickly, no longer humble and timid, but haughty as a queen whom a ruffian has insulted, and said—

"Listen to me, Don Suero, for you do not deserve that my lips should give you the dear name of brother; perhaps you may be able to escape the justice of men; perhaps God will permit you to escape even His justice for some time; perhaps you will torture me as long as I live; but the Infanta of Carrion will never bestow her hand on the son of the Count of Cabra, nor on anyone whom her heart has not chosen. A woman may be dragged to the steps of the altar, may be calumniated, may be barbarously ill-treated; but if she has courage enough to die without opening her lips, as I have, that vow cannot be dragged from her—that vow which alone constitutes the union of husband and wife."

"Silence, silence!" cried Don Suero, clutching at the handle of his dagger, "or you will force me, at this very moment, to punish your rebellion."

"I have told you already that you may kill me, for death does not terrify me; but my hand shall never belong to any-one who is not master of my heart."

"Then you shall suffer on earth all the tortures of hell; you shall be scoffed at by even the worst ruffians; ignominy and shame shall follow you everywhere."

"Shame shall never humiliate my brow, for in my life there never has been, nor shall there ever be, anything of which I. can feel ashamed."

"Do you dare to speak thus, traitress? Bow your haughty brow to the ground, for the noble Infanta of Carrion cannot raise it proudly when she has become a renegade to her glorious race by loving one who is base-born, one of her wretched menials."

Don Suero repented, perhaps, of that burst of anger which had caused him to reveal to his sister what he had intended to conceal. Teresa trembled when she heard those words, which showed that her brother was aware of her love for Guillen; but both of them now felt that dissimulation was useless, and the masks having been torn off, they made up their minds to fight face to face.

"Well, then," said the Infanta, "I do confess my love for the menial whom you allude to; but I feel no shame on that account, for that menial, that peasant, has a heart as noble as that of the proudest hidalgo of Castile. I shall never feel shame for having loved him."

"That traitor shall die; he shall die, hung up on the ramparts of my castle, and his crime shall be everywhere published; it shall be known that he was the accepted lover of the Infanta of Carrion, and that noble Infanta will be scoffed at by all, and the Leonese and Castilian nobles will spit on her face."

"Be it so, Don Suero; the Infanta of Carrion is resolved to encounter the ignominy with which you threaten her, without ceasing to love Guillen, the miserable page, the humble peasant, whom she does love with all her heart."

"Hell, hell!" cried Don Suero, furious, mad with anger, and he pulled out his dagger to strike down his sister with it; but whether it was that he was not quite cruel enough to commit so horrible a crime, or that he wished to reserve his victim for greater tortures, for a more tedious agony, for a more painful death, he returned the weapon to its sheath, and in order not to fall again into that barbarous temptation, he left the chamber of Teresa, speaking to himself in a loud voice, like a madman, whilst traversing the corridors that lay between his apartments and those of his sister.

When he had become somewhat calm, he took a sheet of parchment, wrote some lines, fastened it up, called Gonzalo, and said to him—

"Start for Burgos at once, and deliver this letter to the Count of Cabra; gallop, do not spare the best horse in my stables. It is now midday; if you are not back by midnight you shall be hung on the ramparts."

"But, my lord," the servant ventured to say, "that time is necessary for the journey thither alone; it is a twelve-hours' journey from Carrion to Burgos."

"Villain! do you dare to disobey your master?" exclaimed the Count, and laying his hand on his dagger he rose from his seat.

Gonzalo retreated a few paces, terrified, and cried out—

"Pardon, my lord, pardon; I shall obey your orders; I shall be back from Burgos even sooner than you say, if such is your desire."

And the servant started from the castle a few minutes afterwards, spurring to a full gallop the very best horse that was to be found in the stables.

CHAPTER XXXVI

THE KING IS DEAD—LONG LIVE THE KING

SOME time has passed since the events which we have narrated in the preceding chapters. Fresh victories gained over the Moors, in the eastern portion of Castile, have raised more and more the glory of Don Fernando, of the Cid, and of the cavaliers who accompanied the latter.

Suddenly, however, both Castilians and Leonese were shocked by rumours which suddenly flew about in all directions: Don Fernando, the great, the noble the brave, the prudent and wise, was about to exchange his crown for a far richer one—one far more brilliant and lasting, for that which God places on the heads of the just in heaven. Years, together with the constant fatigues endured in the defence of the Christian faith and in the government of the nation which the King of kings had placed in his charge, had broken down his health, had weakened his energies, and had brought him to the gates of eternity.

He was in Cabezon, near Valladolid, occupied with the government of his kingdom, when he found that his health was rapidly failing, and he ordered that he should be brought to his Alcazar in Leon, to the bosom of his family, near to the holy temples erected by his never-to-be-forgotten religious fervour. "They carried him," writes Mariana, "in a military litter, borne by hand; the soldiers and exalted private persons were constantly changed, by his orders, on account of the rivalry which was displayed in the work; such was the love that both humble and great felt for him."

As soon as he arrived in Leon, although his disease had become much aggravated, he got himself carried to the churches, and visited the bodies of the saints, where he prostrated himself on the ground, with all the marks of the most ardent and fervent piety. This holy task completed, he was borne to his Alcazar, where he made his will, dividing his estates amongst his children in the following manner:—"To Don Sancho, the eldest," writes the above-mentioned historian, "he bequeathed the kingdom of Castile, as it extends from the river Ebro to the river Pisuerga; all that he inherited of Navarre, by the death of Don Garcia, he added to Castile. The kingdom of Leon he left to Don Alfonso, with the district of Campos, and the portion of the Asturias which extends as far as the river Deva, which flows by Oviedo, together with some towns of Galicia which belonged to him. To Don Garcia, the youngest, he gave the remainder of the kingdom of Galicia, and the portion of the kingdom of Portugal which he had taken from the Moors. All three were to be called kings. To Doña Urraca he bequeathed the city of Zamora; to Doña Elvira the city of Toro. These cities were called the 'Infantado,' a word used at that period to signify the estates left to maintain the Infantes, the younger children of the kings."

Many grandees of the kingdom were gathered round Don Fernando at that time, amongst whom were Arias Gonzalo, Peranzures, Alvar Minaya, Martin Antolinez, Diego Ordoño de Lara, and Rodrigo Diaz de Vivar, and they all urged him not to divide the realm into so many portions, for it was to be feared that his doing so would give rise to sanguinary wars.

"Sire," said to him the honoured Arias Gonzalo, "remember the dissensions and the hostilities which were caused by the division which your father, the King of Navarre, made of his kingdom. Leave behind you one compact and strong realm, and not several poor and disunited states."

Don Fernando gazed round his bed, and saw there, weeping disconsolately, all his children.

"Arias," he answered to the loyal old man, "all those whom you see weeping are my children, all have an equal claim on my affection, and I love them all equally. Why do you desire that I should favour one to the detriment of the others? When I captured a fortress from the Moors, when I conquered them on the field of battle, do you know what was the first thought that entered my mind? I considered that I possessed one jewel the more to leave to my children, and then I saw no difference between them, as I thought on all of them; for, I repeat it, my good Arias, all my sons have an equal right to my love. I now do what both my conscience and my heart prompt, and I trust that my sons shall always live in concord, shall always love each other as they have hitherto done, and shall always be brothers."

Arias Gonzalo inclined his noble and rugged brow, as a mark of respect to the will of his dying king.

His malady became rapidly worse; nevertheless, on the following day, which was the second one before Christmas, he caused himself to be carried to the church of St. Isidore, where he heard mass with great devotion, and received communion.

On the day before Christmas he returned to the same church, clad in the robes and insignia of state, and, having been placed near the sepulchre of the holy Archbishop, he exclaimed in a loud voice, directing his gaze towards the altar—

"Lord! Thine is the power, Thine it is to command, all are subject to Thee, kings are Thy servants, I return to

Thee the kingdom which I received from Thy hand, and I ask from Thee that my soul may enjoy Thy eternal glory."

Having said this, he laid aside his crown and mantle, received Extreme Unction from the hands of one of the many prelates who were present, caused himself to be clothed with haircloth, and got his head covered with ashes, in which condition he left the church.

On the next day, towards evening, feeling that his life was touching on its close, he summoned his sons and daughters, and also his queen, Arias Gonzalo, Rodrigo Diaz, and some other persons.

"You, my good Sancha," he said to the queen, "have always loved me, as the best of wives. In the name of the love which you have felt for me, in the name of God, and in the name of the people whose happiness you have always had so much at heart, I charge you to take good care of our children, to guide them along the paths of virtue; I know the power which a mother, so good as you are, exercises over her children, and in order that I may quit this world with a peaceful soul, it will suffice that you make me the promise which I ask from you."

"I swear to you, my dear husband, that I will fulfil your wishes; I swear it to you by the salvation of my soul," answered Doña Sancha, bursting into tears, and kneeling down beside the bed of the dying king.

He ordered his children to come near him.

"My children," he said to them, "the words with which Christ inculcated love to mankind contain the chief counsels which I desire to give you, 'Love each other.' Obey your mother in everything, so that, guided by her advice, you may never stray from the path of duty. You, my good Urraca, are about to take up your residence in the city of Zamora, you will have near you Arias Gonzalo, who has his house there, and who will return to it as soon as, by my death, he shall be freed from the duties which he at present discharges in my Alcazar; consult him, ask his advice in all difficult affairs, and trust in him, for he is honourable and wise, and will be as a father to you."

"I shall never forget your counsels, my father," replied the Infanta.

"Nor I, sire," said Arias; "I shall serve your daughter with the same loyalty and goodwill with which I always served you."

"Sancho," then continued Don Fernando, "you already know the love which I have always had for the Cid, and the services which he has rendered to faith and country, as an honourable and brave cavalier. It is fortunate for you that you will have him by your side. Love him as I have loved him, honour him as I have honoured him, ask his advice before you come to any resolution, and what he counsels do always."

"Father," replied Don Sancho, "you know the esteem in which I have always held the Cid; I swear to you that he shall have the same exalted place in my heart which he has had in yours."

Don Fernando recommended to Don Garcia the friendship of a Galician cavalier, named Rui-Ximenes, and to Elvira that of another, whose ancestral residence was in Toro, but whose name the "Chronicles," do not mention; he then added, turning towards his children—

"Swear to me, my children, that, content with the possessions which I have given to each of you, no one of you will ever declare war against the other, to take from him any of those states which your dying father has bequeathed."

"We swear it, father and king!" answered all, except Don Sancho, who remained silent.

Don Fernando noted this, and said—

"May the malediction of heaven fall on the Cain who will take up arms against his brother!"

He then ordered the Cid to approach his bed, and said to him—

"Rodrigo, swear to me that you will never draw your sword against a son or daughter of mine, unless you see that such is necessary in order to protect one of them from the oppression of another, and that your strong arm must be used for that purpose."

"Sire, I swear it to you!" replied the Cid, with deep emotion, for his heart was pierced with grief when he saw that his king was near his last breath; he who had been so dear a friend to him, the old man whom he had loved so much, whom he had served so well, and from whom he had received so many proofs of affection.

"Breath is failing my breast!" said Don Fernando in a very weak voice.

Then his queen, his children, all present, indeed, knelt around the bed, exclaiming with sobs—

"Give us your benediction, sire, give us your benediction!"

The dying king blessed all of them; but when he heard their weeping, he made a strong effort to restore to his voice something of the energy which was rapidly departing from it, and said to them—

"Do not weep for me, my wife, my children, my cavaliers, my good servants! No pain afflicts my body or my soul; my spirit is sweetly exhaling itself away like the perfume of the flowers on a beautiful May morning; it is not by physical suffering that my vital forces are weakened, but what is formed from nothingness naturally returns to its origin. I trust in the divine mercy, I trust in God that He will blot out my sins from His recording book, and I go tranquil and even joyous to the gates of eternity. If worldly things can be of any importance to those who are about to leave them for ever, should I not be content to see grouped around my bed those whom I have most loved in the world?"

The king was then silent for some moments, remaining as if in a calm sleep. Then his face became animated, a smile appeared on his lips—a sweet, peaceful smile, like that of a child that, in its sleep, sees itself surrounded by angels.

"What sweet music!" he murmured; "what harmonious singing comes to my ears! What brilliancy surrounds me! What beautiful children, maidens, and youths surround me, all clad in white garments! What a bright throne do I see there —there! . . . They lead me to it. No, no, it is not the throne of Castile—it is more beautiful, more rich. . . . But—what perfumes do I inhale!—what delights!—they intoxicate me!"

And the voice of the monarch ceased—ceased for ever.

And many of those who were in the chamber exclaimed—

"Blessed are the just who die thus! Blessed are those who die in the Lord!"

.   .   .   .

The children of the dead king, Don Fernando, when they took possession of the states which their father bequeathed to them, dedicated themselves peacefully to the government of them, without ceasing to yield obedience to their mother, Doña Sancha, as their father had commanded them, in which task the Cid aided Don Sancho very much, who loved and respected that brave and loyal cavalier.

"The crown became Don Sancho well," writes an historian, "for he was of good presence, and a goodly man; of great prowess, more skilled in the affairs of war than in those of peace. On that account he was called Don Sancho the

Strong. Pelagio Ovetense says that he was very handsome, and very skilful in war. He was well-conditioned, quiet and tractable, if not irritated by some annoying matter, or if false friends, under the pretence of doing him a service, did not deceive him. After the death of his father he complained that, by the division of the kingdom, an injustice had been done to him; that the entire kingdom should have been his, and that it had been weakened by its division into so many parts; he talked over this in private with his friends, and showed it even on his countenance. His mother, as long as she lived, restrained him by her authority, and prevented him from declaring war against his brothers."

Some Moorish kings in Aragon, who had paid tribute to his father, refused to recognise vassalage to him, and he prepared to compel them by force of arms. He collected together an army for that purpose, and, accompanied by the Cid, set out for Aragon. The Moors were routed in several pitched battles; he captured many fortified places from them, and consequently forced them to continue to pay tribute to Castile. He had now only to conquer Almugdadir, King of Saragosa, who, but a short time before, had succeeded Ali, one of the five who had been captured by the Cid in the battle of the Oca Mountains. He encamped before that city, which was of much importance in various ways, encircling it and attacking it with vigour; it was defended by strong walls and a numerous garrison, accustomed to war, and the Castilians were repulsed in several assaults; in the end, however, Almugdadir made terms and yielded, it being agreed that he should break off his alliance with Don Ramiro, King of Aragon, and pay tribute to Don Sancho; the latter binding himself, on his part, to defend him against any power which might wage war on him, whether Christian or Moslem.

Don Sancho was much enraged against Don Ramiro for having aided the people of Navarre, his enemies, who very often made raids and irruptions into the territories of Castile, committing all kinds of depredations; and Don Ramiro, on his side, was very angry with Don Sancho, for he considered that he had humiliated him by having conquered Saragosa, which had been under obedience to him; and the conquest of which, he believed, only appertained to him.

The Aragonese were stationed at the Castle of Grados erected by the Moors on the bank of the river Esera, that it might serve as a defence against the invasions of the Christians, and, quitting their fortified position, they sallied forth to encounter Don Sancho, in order to demand satisfaction from him for the affront which they considered they had received.

Don Sancho asked the advice of the Cid, before replying to the demands of Don Ramiro.

"Sire," answered Rodrigo, "I do not believe that the King of Aragon denies entirely your right to compel to obedience those infidels, who acknowledged vassalage to Castile during the lifetime of your father, or that Don Ramiro denies that the Christian kings of Spain should not have equal right to seize on the territories occupied by the infidels. Explain to him with courtesy, but without in any way lowering your dignity, the reasons on account of which you considered yourself justified in attacking the Moors of Aragon, and if, not satisfied with these reasons, he should take up arms, let you do the same; sustain the general opinion, that Castile should never let itself be made a vassal by either Moors or Christians. It is certainly a painful thing to have to fight against Christians, but it is not less so that Christians should seek to reduce to vassalage Castile, which for centuries has fought against the Crescent. Remember what your father did when the Germans, who were also Christians, sought to impose vassalage on him. If at the beginning of your reign you do not gain the reputation of firmness and bravery, even though you may have to fight against Christians, you will be considered pusillanimous, and even the weakest will dare to oppose you."

This advice of Don Rodrigo was very pleasing to Don Sancho, for both their views on this subject were identical, and the King of Castile answered, in a courteous but dignified manner, the King of Aragon; Don Ramiro, however, who did not want explanations, but rather some pretext to avenge his resentment, would not listen to those of Don Sancho, but at once prepared his army for battle. Don Sancho did the same, and the fight commenced with a fury not often seen.

Don Sancho and the Cid, accompanied by Diego Ordoñez de Lara, a cavalier much devoted to the king and to Rodrigo, and by other good knights, amongst whom were Guillen of the Standard, Alvar Fañez Minaya, and Martin Antolinez, were the first that closed with the army of Aragon.

The battle lasted for many hours, and much blood was shed on both sides, but in the end ·Don Ramiro had to abandon the field in very great disorder. Don Sancho, satisfied with having taught such a lesson to the Aragonese, ceased the pursuit, for to follow up his victory would only cause the shedding of more Christian blood.

The Moors, however, who garrisoned the Castle of Grados, when they learned that the army had retreated, filled with dismay and with its forces much weakened, sallied forth against it and annihilated it; Don Ramiro having been killed in this battle before Don Sancho could come to his assistance, for as soon as he learned that he, whom he had just defeated as his principal enemy, was in great danger, he advanced to the place, rather distant, where the Aragonese and Moors were fighting.

The latter turned back to shut themselves up again in Grados, being much in dread of the Castilians; and, as that fortress was impregnable, and as Don Sancho had not been offended directly by those who garrisoned it, the Castilians did not consider it prudent to remain longer in Aragon, and therefore returned to Castile, satisfied with the success which they had achieved.

The people of Castile, who still deplored the loss of Don Fernando, changed their mourning into gladness on account of those glorious triumphs; hoping to find in Don Sancho a king as brave, as wise, and as great as he was whom they had recently lost.

Don Sancho, desirous of celebrating the propitious commencement of his reign, and wishing to return the proofs of affection which his people had given to him, conceded to them many privileges and favours, and showed himself specially generous to those who had accompanied him during his campaign in Aragon.   This increased the public rejoicings very much.

Guillen of the Standard did not receive the least share of his princely munificence.   Don Sancho had seen him fighting bravely in all the battles, and, as he desired to reward his valour, and knew that the brave youth was ambitious of honours, he gave him such titles of nobility that Guillen could envy few nobles by privilege, a name which was given to those who were ennobled, not by blood, but through the privileges received from the king as recompenses for personal actions.

All the Castilians, however, did not share in the munificence of Don Sancho.   He bore in mind the nobles who, having it in their power to accompany him in the campaign, did not do so, and he took care to manifest his vexation towards them by leaving them unrewarded.

CHAPTER XXXVII

HOW CERTAIN CAVALIERS WENT FOR WOOL AND CAME BACK SHORN

SELDOM was seen such activity and life in the Castle of Carrion, in which, usually, solitude reigned: many cavaliers were arriving at the gates of that gloomy edifice, which, during the greater part of the year, seemed to be uninhabited, as its owner, enclosed almost always within those dark walls, lived apparently without any communication with the outside world.

What event can explain such an assemblage of strangers in the Castle of Carrion? Amongst those cavaliers might be seen the Count of Cabra and other nobles, as well known as Don Garcia for their ungovernable, intriguing, and envious characters.

Let us see what they were occupied with.

In a large apartment of the castle about a dozen cavaliers were assembled, whilst their servitors were talking of love and war in the adjoining rooms, under the eye of Bellido Dolfos, who was moving about amongst them, apparently indifferent to their talk.

Let us listen to Don Suero, who took the initiative in the debates of that assembly.

"The Count of Cabra and I," he said, "have come to the conclusion that the Castilian and Leonese nobility, which has always occupied an honoured position by the side of kings, commenced to see itself lowered and humiliated in the time of Don Fernando I., on account of the favour enjoyed by De Vivar, that ambitious soldier who has succeeded in making himself absolute master of the will of the monarch, so that he will only hearken to his counsels. It was to be hoped that Don Sancho II. would atone for the shortcomings of his father, by letting himself be guided by the advice of his nobles, and not exclusively by that of this soldier of fortune, whom, as he would not quit his side, he should only consult in matters of war—for instance, whether it were better to take a fortress by escalade or by bursting in its gates with the battering-ram. But has the new king done this? No; far from it, he consults the Cid in all affairs of state, and follows his counsels blindly, without admitting to his presence the nobles of the kingdom—such is the contempt with which he treats us, and the distance at which he holds us."

"Yes, yes!" exclaimed all his hearers; "we must assert our dignity by putting an end to the influence and the exclusive favour which De Vivar enjoys with the king, before the evil progresses so far that its cure would be impossible."

"Remember," said the Count of Cabra, "what the king did when he was setting out for the campaign in Aragon : he consulted the Cid as to the prudence of undertaking that enterprise, and he undertook it because that was the will of De Vivar, who, in addition to being ambitious, always seeks for opportunities to increase his wealth by the spoils of war. It was a very ancient custom in Castile to assemble a Cortes before undertaking enterprises of such importance as that of leading an army against another state, and subduing it by fire and sword; but Don Sancho considers the caprice of an individual superior to all old customs, to expedience, and to what he owes to the nobility of his kingdom. If, perchance, he forgets that there are other nobles in Castile besides the friends of De Vivar, let us bring it to his mind, gentlemen."

"And if he pays no attention to the arguments by which we back up our demands," added one of the nobles, "we intend to compel him by means of our men-at-arms; for, if the vassal owes obedience to the king, vassals, on their side, when they are as noble as we are, have the right to demand that the king should respect their honour and the privileges which they, or their ancestors, won by the sword."

"I can count on a hundred lances to help to humble the arrogance of De Vivar," said one of the counts there assembled.

"And I the same number."

"And I two hundred."

"I with three hundred."

"Five hundred stand at my disposal."

And in succession were mentioned all the men-at-arms who could be counted on to dictate terms to Don Sancho, in case he should refuse their demands; the Count of Cabra, however, who, it must be acknowledged, possessed much foresight and skill in hatching conspiracies, objected.

"It is a great and important thing to trust to arms when reasoning fails; but we must remember that the campaign of Aragon has given to Don Sancho and to the Cid great prestige and fame amongst the people; also, that De Vivar has very many friends, and that he is daring, skilful, and strong in battle.

Let us respectfully protest against the excessive favour shown to De Vivar, and if Don Sancho pays no attention to us, let us conceal our displeasure, let us win friends, and let us dispose the people in our favour by letting them see, by skilful management, how undeserved is the incense which they burn before their idol, and when we are in a position to feel sure of success, we shall express our indignation publicly."

All present expressed their approval of the plan of Don Garcia.

"You know already," he continued, "that Don Ramiro owed the destruction of his army and his death to the Castilians, to the injustice of Don Sancho, or rather to the disloyal counsels which the Cid gave to the King of Castile. Well, then, this fact can aid us in carrying out our plans. Don Sancho Ramirez, the new King of Aragon, will aid us, should we require his help, for he is panting to avenge the death of his father."

The views of the Count of Cabra received the full approbation of all present, and filled Don Suero with joy, for he considered himself, even already, freed from De Vivar, who was his everlasting nightmare; and having arranged as to the manner in which they should make their protest to the king against the excessive privileges enjoyed by Rodrigo, and having sworn to go on with their enterprise, the meeting broke up, the conspirators setting out for Burgos, where Don Sancho held his Court.

Don Suero went as far as the gate of his castle to see them off, where he held out his hand to Don Garcia, with all the marks of friendship and gratitude.

"Don Suero," said the Count of Cabra to him, "you do not give me a favourable message to bear back to my son."

"Tell him," answered De Carrion, "that he may trust in my promise to reward the services of the father by giving to the son the hand of my sister."

"Have you already arranged with the Infanta?"

"Yes, Don Garcia; Doña Teresa now knows who the husband is whom I destine for her."

"And she accepts?"

"She is delighted."

"Oh, then I have good news to bring to Don Nuño. When I return to see you I shall bring my son with me, for, as he has loved your sister for a long time, it will afford him the greatest pleasure to see her."

"My sister," replied Don Suero, somewhat disturbed, "is so timid and bashful that, although she longs to see the young man whom she is to marry, she will avoid his presence until the day when she can give him the name of husband. Don Nuño, as yourself, can honour my house when it pleases him; but tell him, that if my sister should not venture to let herself be seen by him, he must not be offended by that."

"Then, Don Suero, I believe that the day is not far distant when your family and mine shall become relations, and we shall defer until then the first interview between your sister and my son."

"Thanks, Don Garcia, for your desire to please both my sister and me."

"Trust in my friendship, and do not doubt, but that with the aid of the cavaliers who accompanied me here, we shall triumph over De Vivar, over that arrogant soldier, from whom you have received so many insults. If fate was against us in the ambush which we prepared for De Vivar when he was going to the Cortes at Leon, and if the Moors, his allies, did not wish to second our plans when they went to his assistance against the allies of the Emperor of Germany, it was because we were fighting alone; but it will be a different thing now, as we can count on powerful auxiliaries, and have arranged a good plan of operations. But you have told me nothing of that treacherous page who dared to set his eyes on your sister."

"That disloyal fellow is so beneath contempt that I would only lower myself by speaking of him."

"And I believe that it would be an insult to your sister were I to ask if you have remarked whether Doña Teresa returns his mad love."

"As to that, Don Garcia, have no uneasiness: my sister was filled with indignation when she learned that the youth had dared to set eyes on her. That traitor forgot for a moment his low condition, and believed that it was allowable to fall in love with his mistress; but she would have got him driven from the castle with cudgels, if she had known to what an extent his audacity went. If we find an opportunity to chastise him as much as he deserves, we shall take advantage of it; if not, let us simply despise him as a madman. What can prevent a rustic from secretly loving, I will not say the Infanta of Carrion, but even Doña Urraca, the Infanta of Zamora?"

"Do you know of the favours which the Cid has lavished on him?"

"That, Don Garcia, is another reason that both you and I should hate De Vivar."

"Certainly, certainly, Don Suero. We shall both be avenged; have no doubt of that."

Thus speaking, the Count of Cabra hastened to mount his steed, and galloped off to overtake his friends, who had already ridden some distance.

Two days afterwards the king, Don Sancho, was conversing with his mother in the Alcazar of Burgos, when Doña Sancha said to her son—

"If the will of your father, if the wishes of a dying man do not suffice to make you content with the kingdom of Castile as your inheritance, the tears of your mother should be sufficient to do so—she who would give a hundred lives to prevent her children fighting against each other."

"Mother," replied Don Sancho, "I swear to you, that if my brothers do not provoke a war, I shall not do so,—but allow me the right to complain here, where none but you hears me, of the injustice which was done me by dividing the kingdom into five parts and giving me one of them, when I should have received all. The kingdom of Castile and Leon, in its entirety, should have gone to the eldest son of Don Fernando I."

"Reason and justice are superior to custom, my son. Why should a father disinherit one son because he happened to come into the world a short time after another? In order that a king may be good, he must be just; he must be guided by reason; for these causes your father gained the name of Great, and only thus shall you also merit it. His brother challenged your father to battle, but your father refused to accept that challenge until his kingdom of Castile was invaded. Don Garcia having been conquered and slain, your father had the right to take possession of Navarre, and he did so. If you desire to imitate your father, how far should you be from declaring war against your brothers, who do not provoke you to do so."

"I shall not do it, mother, I repeat to you, even though I consider myself very much aggrieved."

"Castile is a kingdom which the most powerful monarchs envy, its people are as loyal as they are brave and warlike; the Castilians love you, and a courageous soul beats in your breast. Leave your brothers and sisters in peaceful possession of their states, and enlarge your own by conquering, with the sword, and by the aid of the good cavaliers who surround you, infidel territories, with the possession of which Castile will become so great and redoubtable that powerful rulers will come to offer vassalage to you."

"Yes, yes, I shall do so, mother; I shall thus satisfy that ambition which, in spite of myself, continually disquiets me."

"My son, you do not know how that ambition weighs upon the heart of your mother."

"And do you not know why I am ambitious? Do you not know, mother? It is because I cannot live in a close circle without feeling that I am being smothered; it is because small and petty things are repugnant to my soul; it is because my spirit is only contented with the grand and the magnificent. The title of king is but a mockery when he who bears it only rules over a small state which can be ridden through in a few days."

"Well, then, my son, if mean things are hateful to you, respect the will of your father, and love your brothers, for it would be paltry not to do so."

"My father impressed on me that I should always let myself be guided by your counsels and by those of Rodrigo Diaz; I shall obey him, mother."

"Yes, my son, let not De Vivar quit your side, give heed to his counsels, for none can give them to you as loyally and as wisely as that good cavalier."

"Oh, my mother, you cannot know how much the friendship, which I always had for Rodrigo, has increased, since the crown of Castile first encircled my brow, and especially since, with his aid, I reduced to obedience the Moors of Aragon and conquered Don Ramiro. How invaluable were his advice and his sword to me at that time! It seemed to me that, having the Cid at my side, there was no enterprise that I could not bring to a successful issue; it seemed to me, that if the entire earth declared war against me, I could conquer it with the aid of the Cid."

Don Sancho was interrupted by the entrance of one of his servants who announced to him the arrival at the Alcazar of a deputation from the Castilian nobility, which solicited an audience. Don Sancho gave orders that those nobles should be admitted to his presence.

A few minutes after the Count of Cabra and some more of

those whom we have seen assembled in the Castle of Carrion stood in the presence of the king.

"Sire," said Don Garcia, with all the marks of profound respect, "many nobles, your vassals, have sent us to you to offer their congratulations on the glorious triumphs which you have recently won in Aragon."

"Triumphs," replied the king, "which the Castilian nobility have helped me to win, by accompanying me in the campaign and fighting bravely."

The Count of Cabra and those who were with him perceived at once the reproach which Don Sancho had aimed at them, and were on the point of exhibiting their vexation ; they restrained themselves, however; and Don Garcia continued, as if he had not noticed the irony which was contained in the words of the king—

"Sire, the nobles who have commissioned us to bring you their salutations do not belong to the number of those who followed you to Aragon."

"Who then are they, Don Garcia?"

The Count of Cabra began to give the names of his friends.

"Have you not told me that you come on the part of the Castilian nobility?"

"Certainly, sire, for the nobles I have named are the most exalted amongst them."

"And the most exalted nobles of Castile remained quietly in their castles whilst their king was fighting against the enemies of God and of their country?"

"Sire, the grandees who salute you have given abundant proofs of their valour and of their devotion to their king ; if they did not accompany you to the war of Aragon it was because years, infirmities, or urgent private affairs did not permit it. Besides, sire, they believe that, if the king keeps them at a distance and does not seek their counsels, he does not require their aid when he engages in important enterprises, such as that of making war on foreign states"

Indignation coloured the visage of Don Sancho, who interrupted the Count of Cabra, exclaiming—

"As God lives, I shall chastise the audacity of the subjects who thus insult their lord ! Let both you and those who sent you understand clearly, that the King of Castile will not tolerate any fault-finding from his vassals."

"Sire, it is not our desire to find fault with you, but to beseech you to show that consideration towards us which our exalted position merits, and which was always shown to our ancestors ; we desire that in the Court of Castile there should be favours for all nobles, and not for a few, or rather for one only."

"What is this you say to your king, traitors ?"

"Sire!" exclaimed almost all of the nobles present, in indignation, "what is this you say to us ? You have stained the honour of the most noble cavaliers of Castile."

"No, they are not nobles who dare to impose laws on their sovereign, who dare to speak before him in the outrageous and arrogant way in which you have spoken!" replied Don Sancho, not less irritated than those who were listening to him.

"It would be a stain on our honour," continued the Count of Cabra, abandoning entirely the affected humility with which, at first, he had addressed the king,—"it would be a stain on our honour if we were not to bring our complaints before you with the frankness which befits good cavaliers. You offend us, sire, by keeping us away from your Alcazar, forgetting what is due to us, and the right we have to share in the favours which you lavish on De Vivar and his friends, in order that you may retain their support."

"Silence, silence! and do not dare to profane with your lips the name of the Cid Campeador, or the names of his friends and mine! I understand your desire ; you would withdraw from my side the most honoured cavalier of Castile, the strongest pillar of my throne, the best servant of my father, the terror of the enemies of the Christian faith? Depart from my presence, for anger burns in my heart at seeing before me men with such despicable souls as yours."

"Sire, recognise what we are, and what our rights are !"

"Justice of God!" exclaimed Don Sancho, now no longer able to restrain his anger. "Must I tolerate that traitor vassals should threaten me in my own palace? No, as God lives, no ! there are executioners in my Court who this very day shall make your heads roll in the dust!" Then, turning towards the door of the apartment, he called out in a loud voice, "My guards hither! My guards hither!"

About a dozen archers immediately appeared, to whom the king said—

"Lead off these traitor nobles and shut them up in a prison, from which they shall only come forth to the scaffold."

The archers were about to obey the king, when those men, who had showed themselves so audacious only a few moments before, bent their knees before the enraged monarch, stricken with terror—

"Pardon, sire, pardon!"

Don Sancho made a sign to the archers to retire, and darting a glance at the nobles, which expressed both the contempt and indignation that filled his soul, he said to them—

"Rise, despicable cowards; men as noble as you say you are should not touch the floor with their immaculate brows. Be off from my sight; such baseness afflicts my soul. Depart from my Court at once, and never return to it, for if my eyes rest on you again, they shall be as those of the basilisk, which kills by its glances."

The counts hastened to quit the Alcazar, and even the city, with all the haste which the king had commanded.

CHAPTER XXXVIII

HOW THE PEASANT OF BARBADILLO WENT TO BURGOS, WITH OTHER THINGS WHICH THE READER WILL LEARN

WE must now cast a rapid glance on the mansion of De Vivar, for none of its inhabitants deserve to be forgotten; we shall not, however, penetrate into the principal apartments, for in the entrance-hall we shall meet those who will engage our attention for a brief period. Fernan and Alvar were there, chatting in a friendly manner: we must certainly lend some attention to their conversation, for it is not altogether foreign to the story which we are endeavouring to relate.

"Is it long since you were at Vivar?" asked Alvar.

"I have been there twice since we returned from Aragon."

"And did you go to the house of Pero?"

"Of course; our master and mistress are so fond of Beatrice that they would never forgive me if I were not to bring them tidings of her and her family whenever I happen to be near the dwelling of Pero."

"And what about Beatrice? Is she as gentle and beautiful as at the time when you and I caught fire from the glances of her eyes?"

"More so than even then, brother."

"Anger of God! how fortunate that Martin Vengador is to have won the love of such a splendid girl!"

"And how much more fortunate he is to have gained so much favour in the eyes of our master!".

"Don Rodrigo certainly thinks a great deal of that youth. You saw what a large share of the booty he assigned to him after the campaign in Aragon."

"And his generosity did not stop there with regard to that Martin."

"What? Has he bestowed additional favours on him?"

"He has promised to do so on the occasion of his marriage with Beatrice."

"And what favours are those, Fernan?"

"Don Rodrigo and Doña Ximena are to be groomsman and brideslady at the wedding of Martin and Beatrice; and they are to receive as gifts, for themselves and their descendants, a house and excellent lands on the estate of Vivar."

"Do you know what you should do?"

"What, Alvar?"

"Marry Mayorica, before their wedding, and see if our lord and lady will give you as valuable gifts as they will give to that youth."

"They would give them to me, for they are liberal to those who serve them faithfully."

"Well, if it is so, why don't you marry?"

"I shall do so very soon, Alvar: yesterday I promised Mayorica, who is mad to be married, for she says that if she cannot get me to church now, while she is still young and comely, she won't be able to do so later on. Her complaints almost upset my patience."

"And will you keep your promise to her?"

"I have made it, and I shall keep it, although I was never so much against it as now."

"May the Moors kill me if I understand you! Why should you be unwilling to get married, when you are well off, when you can have a gentle and loving bride, and hopes of rich presents? Is not Mayorica pleasing to you?"

"She pleases me as much as ever, Alvar, but—listen, for I am about to confide a great secret to your discretion."

Fernan looked round to see if there was anyone present who might hear him, and, not seeing anyone, he continued—

"You must know, comrade, that some time ago I saw a girl whose charms would set a heart of stone on fire."

"What? Perchance that girl from Albarracin has come to Burgos, she whom you fell in love with when we were stationed there during the last campaign?"

"No, brother, it is not that one. I should wish indeed that the girl from Albarracin were here, for I think of her night and day. She whom I have fallen in love with in Burgos comes from Barbadillo, and I swear to you that she seems to have come from heaven, so beautiful is she!"

"There is also a girl from Barbadillo for whom I sigh."

"From Barbadillo? I vow by Judas Iscariot that it would be a nice thing if . . . Where did you see her, tell me?"

"At the forge of Master Iñigo"—

"By the soul of Beelzebub I'll cudgel you if you have dared to cast your eyes where I have set mine; it was also in the forge of Master Iñigo that I saw the girl I told you of. What kind is she, Alvar?"

"Dark-complexioned."

"So is mine."

"Black eyes."

"So has mine also."

"A fine figure."

"Exactly."

"Strong hands."

"Just like mine."

"For she made my face smart with a blow, when I began to talk amorously to her."

"My girl did just the same to me! Traitor! How have you dared"—

"But, my friend, if I did not know"—

"You shall know now, if you have forgotten, what my hands are able to do."

And Fernan seized the page by the back of the neck with the force of a pair of pincers.

On hearing the cries of the page, Mayor came out on the top of the flight of stairs, and as she saw that Fernan did not perceive her, so much was he intent on venting his rage on Alvar, she stopped, in order to try to discover the origin of the quarrel, which doubtless she suspected.

"Traitor!" exclaimed Fernan. "I am never to love a woman, but you must needs fall in love with her also? You shall die by my hand!"

And the squire not only plied his hands on the page, but also his feet.

"Let me go, Fernan; I swear to you I shall never speak another word to that peasant girl from Barbadillo, nor indeed to any woman, born or to be born "—

"That oath saves you," said Fernan, letting him loose; "but I assure you, Alvar, that you shall answer for it to me if you ever try to gain the love of that pretty girl for whom I sigh."

"Ah, traitor! oh, false one! This, then, is the fidelity which you swore to me only yesterday!" exclaimed Mayor, no longer able to restrain her anger, and coming down the flight of stairs with two jumps, her hands clenched and her eyes flaming.

Fernan receded a few steps, terrified, as if he wished to fly from that fury, by whose hands he felt himself gripped with almost as much force as Alvar had been by his.

"Traitor! Do you forget me, thus turning your back on me? I shall take care that you remember me as long as you live." And Mayor, with her nails, made the blood run from the neck and face of her faithless lover, who, despite his enormous strength, which he used to its fullest, could not free himself from her.

" Get away from me, wench, or I shall strike and kick you!" cried the unlucky squire, whose strength prevailed at last. Mayor let him go, and, from a shove which Fernan gave her, fell against the bottom of the stairs, receiving a blow on the head which deprived her of consciousness.

Fernan raised his foot to kick Mayor, as he had threatened, but, seeing her motionless, he examined her, and, seeing that blood was flowing from her head, became frightened. His anger suddenly changed to grief and the most violent despair.

"Mayorica! Mayorica! my darling, return to yourself! pardon me!" cried the deeply afflicted squire, endeavouring to raise the young woman; seeing, however, that she was not recovering, he began to tear his hair and strike his head and face, as if he had lost his reason.

"I have killed her! I have murdered her! I am a barbarian, I am a villain! I am a treacherous assassin! Kill me, Alvar, kill me, and kill at once that peasant girl who is to blame for this misfortune."

Alvar, far from killing anyone, was endeavouring to save Mayor's life; he was bathing her face with water, which, fortunately, was near at hand, and bandaging her face with his pocket handkerchief.

At last she recovered consciousness and arose, breaking out, not into abuse of her lover, but into wailings capable of moving to campassion even the stone against which her head had struck.   Fernan redoubled his caresses and promises of amendment, with which he succeeded in consoling her a little, although Mayor knew well how soon the squire usually forgot his oaths.

A moment after, the entrance-hall was deserted, for Fernan and Alvar had disappeared up the staircase, supporting Mayor; however, in a short time a number of persons, who from the commencement of the quarrel had been crowding to the principal gate, approached as near it as possible, commenting on and explaining in their own way what had happened in the hall.

"The girl must have slipped on the staircase and rolled down it," said one.

"No," replied another; "but she was in love at the same time with both Fernan and Alvar, and as soon as they discovered it they knocked the dust off each other, and then settled their accounts with the girl."

"She who got the blow is not the cause of the quarrel; it is a peasant girl from Barbadillo."

"Whoever it is, I swear by all that's holy that women are the ruin of men.   May I be confounded if, from this day forward, I believe in even the best of them."

"All men should do the same, master soldier."

"Yes, they are falser than Judas himself."

"It is men who are false; they fall in love with us, two at a time, and even that isn't enough for them."

"Eh, my good old woman, don't take yourself into the count, for you are out of the running."

"Holy Santa Gadea!   Is there no one to defend an honest matron against the insults of this ruffian of a soldier?"

"This soldier swears that all women are not good for much."

"You insolent, shameless fellow!" cried out a loud chorus of women, who rushed furiously on him who had levelled that insult at them, and scratched and mauled him without giving him time to defend himself.

The men rushed to the aid of the soldier, who, in the end, found himself free from those furies, and went off from the crowd, well beaten, and with a face torn and bleeding.

At the same time a peasant approached the crowd and with very great curiosity asked what was the cause of the assembly; he muttered an execration when he could find out nothing distinctly, for what one said was in complete contradiction to the explanations of another. His chief wish seemed to be to get to the door, around which the people were still crowding, to see if the heroes of the recent fight would again appear in the entrance-hall; he then tried to force a passage for himself with his hands and head, muttering threats and oaths at the same time.

"I swear," he growled, "that even if I'm crushed to death, I'll know what is going on, for it must be something important when it brings so many people here, and I have not come to the city to live in obscurity as I did in Barbadillo."

The execrations and exclamations became more frequent, according as the peasant's efforts to press forward increased.

"Don't push us, you vile rustic!" cried some.

"Anger of God!" exclaimed others, "let us flatten the clown!"

"Don't look on that ass as a rational creature."

"By all the saints in heaven, this fellow is the greatest brute that eats bread."

"Push the pig back!"

"Sit upon the savage!"

"I swear that the insults of those good-for-nothing women are putting me out of patience."

"It's yourselves that are good for nothing."

"Women are never good for anything, and by San Pedro of Cardeña we'll soon come to blows with you."

"Come to blows with us?" cried several of the women, and they made a rush on Bartolo, for it was he who was making such violent efforts to push his way through the crowd, and attacked him with the same fury as they had, but a short time before, exhibited towards the soldier who had insulted them. The peasant, who was very strong, defended himself, knocking down a woman with each blow, and was on the point of triumphing over his furious enemies; they, however, cried out to the men to help them, calling them cowards, and telling them that men are bound to render their assistance to women. The men who were present were but few, for curiosity, in all ages, has been the almost exclusive birthright of women; those who were there, however, ranged themselves on the side of the weaker sex, and attacked with sticks and fists the man from Barbadillo, who at last surrendered at discretion, bruised, scratched, and bleeding, so that he was a pitiable sight to see.

The boy who has been beaten by other boys in a street, which is not that in which he lives, often vents his anger by calling out to those who have maltreated him—

"You'll see how I'll make you pay for this when I get you into my street."

And neither more nor less did the persecuted Bartolo do, for, seeing that he was vanquished, and that there was no possibility of his having revenge then and there, he exclaimed, crossing his arms, moving his head from side to side, and wishing to annihilate them all with a glance—

"I swear by all that's holy that I'll smash you all when I get you in Barbadillo!"

"Oh, the fellow comes from Barbadillo!" said one of those who had been there at the beginning of the quarrel between Fernan and Alvar, and who consequently had had an opportunity of learning something of its cause. "Barbadillo be cursed, for the wench who was the cause of all this row comes from it!"

These words aroused the curiosity of the peasant, who, as we have seen, did not need much to excite it.

"Keep yourself quiet," said Bartolo to himself, "and you'll discover something that will give annoyance to the Barbadillo people, in return for what they have said respecting your going often to the city, that you were outrageously curious, and that you neglected your wife and property to stick your nose into other people's affairs."

And approaching, very quietly, him who was cursing Barbadillo, and who indeed was the soldier whom the women had beaten so severely, he said to him—

"Friend, I am from Barbadillo, but I would rather belong to the country of the Moors than to that wretched village, which, without doubt, God cursed as a punishment for the strife between the Infantes of Lara, which commenced in it. Then she, you say, who caused all this row is from Barbadillo? I swear she couldn't be from any other place."

This agreement in their views gained for Bartolo the sympathy of the soldier.

"What! you know nothing of the cause of the fight? said the latter.

"You will please me much by relating to me what took place; I know you will do so, for you are more polite than this vulgar crew," replied the peasant.

"Then you must know," said the soldier, " that two servitors of the Cid are in love with a girl from Barbadillo, and they have fought and cudgelled each other as the result of a dispute as to which of them should have her."

"I swear that she must be no great things of a girl when she throws eyes at both of them. The women of Barbadillo, my friend, are just that kind; there's the daughter of old mother Valeta, who, they say, fell in love with four."

"According to that, comrade, you should not choose a wife from that place."

"It is from it that I have mine; but I have come with her to live in Burgos, for I am very fond of knowing what is going on in the world, such as one can learn who lives in a city, and I go every day to the forge of Master Iñigo to hear the news that's going round. My wife goes with me, though I find it hard to get her to do so, but wish to polish her up a bit, and it happened the other day that a knave of a squire began to make love to her while I was talking to Iñigo, and she told me, for I saw nothing of it, that she broke the fellow's teeth with a blow of her fist. You see by that what an honest woman my wife is."

"Honesty be hanged!"

"What do you mean, friend?"

"I mean that your wife is the very one that the two men were fighting about."

"San Pedro de Cardeña, help me!"

"And it is quite certain that, even if the first time she received them with blows, she must have shown herself kinder to them afterwards, for, if not, they would not have fought so furiously on account of her."

"I swear I'll kill that false woman!" exclaimed the enraged rustic, tugging at his hair with rage.

As some of the bystanders had heard his conversation with the soldier, all of them knew very soon the cause of his despair, and it was at once intensified by a fearful chorus of hisses, of coarse jokes, and of abuse.

The unfortunate Bartolo faced the crowd defiantly; his words, however, were lost amid the hisses and the loud voices, and then there was no remedy but to open a way for himself and fly, mad, raging, careless as to consequences.

The crowd remained in its position, as those who composed it desired to learn the result of the quarrel between the servitors of De Vivar, for they wished to know for certain, as already began to be whispered, if the waiting-woman of Doña

Teresa had died of the blow which the squire had given her.

The gallop of a horseman was heard, just then, on the road leading from the Alcazar, and it was soon perceived that it was a king's messenger who was approaching the residence of the Cid in great haste ; and he, seeing that the crowd was but slowly opening a passage for him, broke through it, his horse knocking some of the people down.

A few minutes afterwards the Cid was proceeding towards the Alcazar, accompanied by Guillen, Fernan, and Alvar, and the people hastened to withdraw, actuated by a feeling of respect, but perhaps chiefly because they had lost all hopes of satisfying their curiosity, and of seeing the squire and the page engage in a fresh quarrel.

Don Sancho, who, as soon as the Count of Cabra and the other conspirators had departed from his presence, had sent to summon Rodrigo, was awaiting him with impatience, for, although he felt that he should chastise those audacious men, he did not wish to do so without consulting the Cid on such a serious matter. The king also desired to obtain the advice of his mother, and that is why Doña Sancha was at his side when Rodrigo arrived.

"My good Cid," said Don Sancho on seeing him, "the Count of Cabra and other noblemen have but just now left the Alcazar. I suppose you think they came to offer me their swords to fight against the Moorish power?"

"Sire," replied Rodrigo, "that is what nobles like Don Garcia should do ; but neither he nor his friends did so when you set out for the campaign of Aragon, and I doubt much if they have done it now."

"You are right ; those wrongly named noblemen, far from coming to offer their king the aid of their arms, came to insult him, to threaten him, to impose laws on him."

"God's anger ! what traitors they are !" exclaimed Rodrigo, unable to restrain his anger ; but sorry for having failed in the moderation and proper restraint which the presence of his king and of the widow of Fernando the Great required, he bent his knee respectfully and added—

"Pardon, sire ; pardon me if I have been wanting in respect to you."

"Arise, Rodrigo," said Don Sancho, holding out his hand to the Cid, "arise, for your very indignation proves that you are a good vassal and a good cavalier."

De Vivar, emboldened by this kindness, continued, giving reins to his just indignation—

"Tell me, sire, in what way have they offended you; although it is sufficient for me to know that they have done so, and I have a sword to fight with them—to avenge you or to die! Is it not enough that De Cabra, De Carrion, and their partisans should be always in revolt against Castile with their cowardly plots, and never draw a sword against the enemies of their country, but that they should come barefacedly to insult you in your Alcazar?"

"No, Rodrigo, my indulgence does not suffice them; it is not sufficient for them that their king should pardon them their neglect of everything that cavaliers should do: they want me to lavish favours on them; they desire to occupy the best positions in my Alcazar; they wish that Castile should be governed by laws dictated by their caprice and ambition; they demand that all those should be removed from my side who have loyally served and advised me, and you, especially, my good Cid—it is you who are the principal object of their hatred."

"I am not surprised to hear that those counts hate me, for I have known that for a long time. As long as their cowardly attempts were directed against me alone, I despised them. I did not desire to appeal to my king for help to defend myself or for the punishment of my enemies; but now when, to make war against me, they desire to wage it against you also, I feel bound to reveal to you the cowardly treachery of those men, and to urge you to punish them."

Having thus spoken, Rodrigo Diaz put his hand into the pouch which hung from his girdle, and took from it some sheets of parchment which he handed to the king, adding—

"See here, sire, the propositions which the Counts of Cabra and of Carrion made to Abengalvon and to the other Moorish kings, my friends, when we were marching against the allies of the Emperor of Germany."

The king read the letters in a low voice. In them it was proposed to the Moorish kings to get up a plot against the Cid on the first occasion that might present itself, and kill him. In order to induce them to do this Don Suero and Don Garcia employed the grossest calumnies, asserting that the Cid was working in an underhand way, under the guise of friendship, and abusing their confidence, to dispossess Abengalvon and the other Moorish kings of their states. They also promised them liberal rewards.

"Traitors, cowardly counts!" exclaimed at the same time both Don Sancho and his mother.

"Abengalvon and the other Moors," continued Rodrigo, "although infidels, placed these letters in my hands, indignant not only on account of the malice of those counts, but also on account of the insult inflicted on them by supposing them capable of such perfidious conduct towards their best friend—against him, who, having taken them captives in fair war, restored to them their liberty, without imposing any conditions whatsoever on them. And that, sire, was not the first time that De Cabra and De Carrion had endeavoured to disembarrass themselves of me. A short time before the campaign beyond the Pyrenees, when I was proceeding to the Cortes at Leon, Martin Antolinez, Guillen of the Standard, and myself were enticed by stratagem into an ambuscade where ten assassins, in the pay of the Counts of Carrion and of Cabra, awaited us. We fought, and fortune protected us, although we were so inferior in numbers and unprepared for a combat. Amongst the assassins there was one who, before he expired, confessed to us who had put the assassin's steel in his hand."

"With their blood," cried Don Sancho, deeply indignant, "shall those accursed traitors pay the penalty of their crimes. Their heads shall fall on the scaffold, and even that will not be as great a punishment as they deserve."

"Sire," said Rodrigo, "punish them, but do not shed their blood; enough has been shed in the war. Banish them for ever from Castile, and threaten them with heavier punishment if they should ever dare to return."

"Yes, my son, take the advice of Rodrigo," said Doña Sancha; "imitate the generous example of the good cavalier who intercedes for his treacherous enemies."

"If the presence of those counts in Castile were only to my prejudice," said Rodrigo, "I would not counsel you to banish them; but they have dared to threaten you, and they will collect bands together and plot conspiracies, which must be prevented. Cast from the kingdom this evil seed before it has time to germinate; but I swear to you, sire, that even with the price of my own blood I would try to prevent the shedding of that of my enemies."

"Be it so, then, Rodrigo," said Don Sancho; "the Count of Cabra and his partisans shall leave my kingdom within four days, and if they do not go, we shall have no pity for them; in that case their traitorous heads shall roll on the ground. I wish to be good towards the good, but inexorable towards the bad; the Castilian nobles shall have in me a friend rather than a master, if they will correspond to my friendship; but I shall not be subject to them, I do not desire to bear the name of king and allow the nobles to govern the kingdom."

"Thus," said the Cid, "Castile will be powerful and happy as in the time of your father, and like him you will merit the name of 'the Great.' I belong to the highest nobility of Castile, but notwithstanding I maintain that the duty of nobles is to aid their king, not to enslave him and paralyse the hands which should freely guide the reins of the State."

On that same day Don Sancho issued an order that within three days the Counts of Cabra and of Carrion, and about a dozen other nobles, should depart from Castile, into perpetual banishment, as rebels to his authority, traitors, and disturbers of the peace of the kingdom.

CHAPTER XXXIX

HOW THE CID AVENGED HIMSELF ON THE COUNT OF CABRA

DON SANCHO II. had proposed to himself to rise superior to the demands of the nobles; nevertheless, he did not cease to consult them in matters of minor importance, for it was one thing to listen to respectful counsels, springing from loyalty and wisdom, and another to hear interested advice, given, as if it were law, by men who, like the Counts of Cabra and of Carrion, and others, merited the contempt of all honourable men, even though they had descended from the most noble families of the kingdom. His palace, therefore, was much frequented by the nobility, and Don Sancho took great pleasure in being surrounded by the Castilian nobles.

He had invited many of them to his Alcazar in Burgos on the day following that on which he had signed the order for the banishment of the Count of Cabra and his partisans; he made known to his visitors the steps which he had taken, and they all approved of them, agreeing with Rodrigo Diaz that

21

the king should govern, without being plotted against by either nobles or plebeians.

Shortly after the nobles had retired from his presence, the king was conversing in a very friendly way with the Cid, whom he had ordered to remain a little longer by his side, for the company of De Vivar was always pleasing to him; just then the arrival of the Count of Cabra, who solicited a brief audience, was announced.

"Tell him," replied Don Sancho indignantly, "that he must depart immediately from the Alcazar, if he does not desire to receive this very day the punishment which his audacity merits."

The Cid hastened to appease the indignation of the king, by pleading in favour of the count.

"Sire," he said to Don Sancho, "perhaps the Count of Cabra, before leaving the country, wishes to give you some information which may be of importance, concerning the peace of the kingdom. You are justly indignant with him, but what can you lose by hearing him? He is such a coward that he would never hesitate to denounce even his best friend if he considered it to his advantage to do so."

Don Sancho was somewhat mollified by these words, and ordered that the count should be admitted to his presence.

Don Garcia entered immediately after, and, bending his knee before the king, said in a respectful voice—

"Sire, as a good vassal, which I am, I shall submit to the sentence of banishment which my lord and king has passed on me; but, before departing from Castile for ever, I have ventured to solicit your royal attention, in order to explain to you the difficult position in which I find myself."

Don Sancho could not restrain his indignation in view of the cowardice and meanness of that man, who had not sufficient courage or dignity to submit with a calm brow to the sentence which hung over him, as should have done even the least honourable cavalier.

"Depart from my presence," he said to Don Garcia, "and leave Castile within the time which I have mentioned, for I have been sufficiently indulgent in leaving the head on the shoulders of him who not alone dared to threaten me, but who paid vile assassins to strike down the best cavalier in Spain."

Don Garcia was about to deny that accusation, but a glance of the Cid sufficed to close his lips.

"Sire," the count ventured to say, "it would be better for

me to die by a single stroke in Castile, than to die slowly in a foreign country. My estates at Cabra are in the possession of the Moors, and since I lost them I have been obliged to live in very straitened circumstances in Castile, even though I have friends and some little property in it. How shall I be able to live in a foreign land, with no friends there, and no means? Sire, if you have no compassion for me, pity at least my wife and children, who have never offended you; revoke the sentence of banishment which you have passed on me, or if you consider it absolutely necessary that I should quit your kingdom, provide me with some resources which may enable me to procure the absolute necessaries of life."

"Did you not inherit from your father a sword which you have allowed to rust in its scabbard?" replied Don Sancho. "Brighten it again with Moslem blood, reconquer with it your estates, and then you will not find it necessary to beg for the means of subsistence from either your king or your friends."

"My arm is much weakened by age"—

"By age and by inaction, not by exertion on the battle-fields," interrupted the king.

The count, seeing that the king was not disposed to grant him the favour which he had requested, asked another from him.

"Sire," he said, "allow me at least to remain in Castile for the time necessary to realise the small property I still possess, so that I may have something to live on, in the place of my banishment, until I may be able, by means of my sword, to secure the well-being of myself and my family."

Rodrigo Diaz believed that the fears which the count expressed, regarding the privations to which his family might be subjected, were not ill-founded, and, forgetting the just resentment which he nourished towards the count, he resolved to intercede for that man, who invoked the names of wife and children—names which were so dear to himself.

"Sire," he said to the king, "as you denied to the Count of Cabra the previous favour he asked from you, I pray you to grant him the request which he now makes, and that you extend to a month the period within which he must depart from Castile; I guarantee to you that within that time your will shall be accomplished."

Shame and disdain should have been pictured on the visage of the count if he were a good cavalier; but Don

Garcia did not know that noble pride, that dignity which prevents an honourable man from accepting a favour from an enemy. The count would have knelt down before De Vivar had not the king been present.

"Be it so," replied Don Sancho; "I grant the request which you make, but woe to him if he shall not have departed from my kingdom before the end of the month."

"Your will shall be done," replied Don Garcia, with humility; "thanks, sire"—

"Thank the Cid," interrupted Don Sancho disdainfully, "for it is to please De Vivar, and not you, that I have extended the period, before the end of which you are to quit Castile."

Rodrigo Diaz expressed to the king the pleasure he felt in having his request granted, and Don Sancho loaded him with praise and gave him signal proofs of friendship in the presence of the Count of Cabra, in order to humiliate him, by showing how far his intention was from refusing favours to the Cid, as those nobles, who were now sentenced to banishment, wished him to do.

On the same day Rodrigo Diaz said to the king—

"I have another favour to ask of you, sire."

"You know, good Cid, how delighted I always am to please you."

"Happily," continued Rodrigo, "peace reigns in Castile, and we have not to fear that it shall soon come to an end, for some love you, and they are the majority, and the remainder fear you. The sword of the cavalier, who can provide some hundreds of lances, should not lie idle in its scabbard, when there are near his country infidels, against whom he can fight, and countries into which he can carry the Christian faith, which is proscribed by them. You know, sire, that I can count on many brave friends who will accompany me to the war, and that I have a numerous body of men, whom I keep in my pay; well, then, I wish you to give me permission to set out for Andalucia, in order that my friends and I may have an opportunity of escaping from the inaction which is pressing on us in Castile."

"I feel much your leaving me, even for a short time," replied Don Sancho; "but your intentions are so honourable, that if I opposed them I should consider myself wanting in what is the duty of a king and of a Christian cavalier. Go, good Campeador, to the country of the infidels, and fight as you always have fought, for I know that you will gain fame thereby, not alone in Castile, but throughout all Christendom. My father indeed was right when he said, that with a hundred cavaliers like you he could drive the Moors from the entire of Spain."

"Sire, I am only a cavalier, accustomed to conflicts, and I must be excused if from them I hope to win a little honour for myself, and much also for my country and the faith of my ancestors."

"I envy your lot, Rodrigo," exclaimed Don Sancho, fired with warlike enthusiasm; "the throne pleases me, because he who is seated on it is raised above the multitude, because he is always surrounded by splendour and grandeur, for my heart does not feel satisfaction in small things; my soul would desire to rule over the entire world; but I would wish also, like you, to fly to hostile countries, freed from the cares of a kingdom; to sleep in camps, always in armour and girded with my sword; to breathe the air of the fields; to hear the neighing of chargers and the sounds of the trumpets and drums; to see the flags of the enemy floating before me, to close with the infidels every day at the rising of the sun, to fight for many hours without cessation, and to throw myself for repose on Moslem standards, lulled to sleep by the chants of victory, and by the cheers of the enthusiastic people, who crown with laurel the brows of conquerors. Such, Rodrigo, is the liberty and the glory which my soul ardently desires; that is why I envy your lot, for it is in your power to achieve that glory and to enjoy that liberty."

"You also, sire, will gain them," answered Rodrigo, participating in the enthusiasm of the king; "you are young, and have abundant time to devote yourself to a soldier's life. What happiness, what glory, what prosperity may not Castile hope for during the reign of the successor of Fernando the Great!"

"Rodrigo," cried the Cid, with joy and emotion, "you not alone serve your king with the sword but also with the tongue. Your words fill my heart with the noblest ambition and with the sweetest hopes, which must bear excellent fruit."

On the same day the Cid commenced his preparations for an expedition against the infidels; he summoned all the friends who desired to follow him, and very soon he had an army collected, strong both in numbers and in the bravery of those who composed it. In it were Martin Antolinez,

Alvar Fañez Minaya, Guillen of the Standard, Diego Ordoñez de Lara, the cousins of the Cid, and numerous other cavaliers; it is almost unnecessary to mention that Martin, formerly the Vengador, Rui-Venablos, and the bandits who had formed their band, were now in the Cid's army.

On other occasions Burgos had put on mourning when its cavaliers set out for a war; but on the day to which we refer the inhabitants of the city rejoiced, for they felt sure that the army, under the leadership of the Cid Campeador, would return victorious. Even Ximena, whose heart was usually full of grief whenever Rodrigo left the domestic hearth, seemed to share in the universal pleasure and hopes; she trusted that her husband would return from Andalucia crowned with fresh laurels. How love, and generous and noble pride shone in her beautiful eyes when, on taking leave of Rodrigo, she put to his lips the smiling face of a tender baby which she was fondling in her arms. Notwithstanding the universal gladness and the universal hopes, there was a person in the residence of the lords of Vivar who was weeping on account of one of those who was about to set out in the army of the Campeador: it was Mayor, the unhappy sweetheart of Fernan, who was lamenting, in anticipation, over the faithlessness which she feared from him as soon as he left her. Fernan had repented of the rough way he had treated her a few days before, had sworn everlasting fidelity to her by all that was most sacred in heaven and on earth, but—how could she trust in the oaths of one who so many times had sworn similar ones, and so many times had broken them?

The Cid Campeador departed with his army from Burgos. Almenon, King of Toledo, willingly permitted him to pass through his dominions, in order that he might continue in peace with Castile as in the time of Don Fernando; and as he was at war just then with his co-religionists of Andalucia.

When the latter learned that the Campeador was advancing on them, the note of alarm was sounded, and collecting together a numerous army, they hastened to Sierra Morena, in order to oppose the advance of the Castilians. The Cid well knew the advantage he would derive if he could triumph over the infidels in that first encounter, and prepared, therefore, to attack the enemy with greater impetuosity and valour than he had ever before displayed, although his men were inferior in numbers.

When the Moors confidently hoped that the Castilians

would refrain from advancing, if, indeed, they did not retreat, they found themselves attacked with such fury that they had to fall back for a considerable distance. However, the Christians were few in number compared with them, and shame infused sufficient valour into their hearts to prevent them from retreating, so that they swore that they would die rather than abandon the field of battle. Then the combat began anew with fierce determination on both sides. The conflict lasted many hours, and infidel blood, mixed with that of the Christians, ran in torrents; but some supernatural power seemed to aid the Christians,—even though the Moors opposed twenty cavaliers to each of those of the Cid,—and gave the victory to the latter, deciding it in such a way, that but few of the infidels escaped from the weapons of the Castilians.

The army of the Cid collected the spoils, which were very valuable, and having divided them, advanced with stronger resolution, with fresh hopes of conquering in all battles in which they might be engaged.

The Campeador then proceeded in the direction of Cabra. Why should he select the conquest of that place in preference to that of other fortresses nearer to him, and easier to subdue? "The reason," said his cavaliers, "is that he wishes to be able to say to his enemy, the Count of Cabra, 'See, I have been able to conquer what you were not able to defend; with a few hundred men I have taken the place which you were not able to retain with several thousands; you have not, in reality, been Count of Cabra for a long time, but I am so now; give up that title, of which you have been so proud, for it no longer belongs to you.'"

The army of the Cid arrived at last in the territory of Cabra; the frontiers were guarded by watch-towers and garrisoned ramparts; these fortresses fell into the power of the Castilians in a very short time, and although the governor of the town asked for aid from the neighbouring Moors, he asked for it in vain, for they, disheartened by the defeat at Sierra Morena, and others which they had afterwards suffered, were only intent on repairing their fortifications and preparing themselves for their own defence, in case, as they feared, they might be attacked by the Castilians.

The town of Cabra was very strong, both on account of its defences and the number of soldiers who garrisoned them when Don Garcia lost it, but in both respects it was even stronger when the Cid advanced to reconquer it; but that did not cause De Vivar to waver in his resolution to lay siege to it. Having taken their position, the Castilians found that they were unprovided with sufficient warlike machines to break down the formidable walls, but brave hearts never let themselves be foiled by obstacles : such, indeed, were only incentives to the Cid. The besiegers required battering-rams, catapults, and scaling ladders, and they provided themselves with them in a very short time. They then placed them in position, and the place was attacked in many places. Its defenders were brave and numerous, and were supplied with powerful means of defence; the walls of Cabra were always crowded with soldiers, who continually cast forth clouds of death-dealing projectiles; the Cid, however, got his men ready for the assault. The walls had been weakened at four different points; at these four points the Cid determined to assault the town simultaneously, and he did so.

The Castilians and Moslems fought bravely, bloodily, and ferociously on the walls of Cabra; but at the end the army of the Cid poured into the town, and although the infidels, having abandoned the walls, defended, step by step, the streets and houses, the sacred Cross shone, on the same day, above the Moslem minarets, and Rodrigo Diaz could name himself Count of Cabra.

Enormous were the riches which the Moors had accumulated in that town, and consequently the spoils of the conquerors were very great. Rodrigo made the partition of all these valuable things, reserving the fifth part for the king, as was the custom, and only for himself the territory which he had conquered, although by right he could claim not only it, but also the larger part of the spoils. All those, therefore, who had taken part in the victory considered themselves very liberally treated, and broke out into enthusiastic cheers for their valiant and generous leader.

The Cid then put the fortifications of Cabra into a good state of repair, and having arranged that it should be garrisoned by two hundred soldiers, selected from his army, and commanded by Guillen of the Standard and Martin the Vengador, he prepared to return to Castile with the remainder of his army.

How joyful were the Cid and his companions when returning to their own country !

By travelling in a leisurely way four days would be necessary to get to Burgos; the Cid, however, remembered that it wanted but two days of a month, from the time he had set out for Andalucia; and he became very uneasy, and accelerated the march. They went on, therefore, day and night, with but little rest, and came within sight of Burgos before the end of the two days.

"Will you tell me, Fernan," asked Alvar, "why we travelled so leisurely at first, and why our master gives us no rest now?"

"It puzzles me," answered the squire, "unless it is that the Count of Cabra and his partisans have commenced hostilities, and our master wishes to subdue them."

"That cannot be, comrade, for the partisans of De Garcia had to leave Castile almost at the same time as we did; and although the Count of Cabra had permission from the king to remain in it a month longer, his friends being away, he could not venture to attempt anything on his own account."

"You are right, Alvar; but— I swear by Judas Iscariot, I have just hit upon the reason why our master has journeyed so rapidly. On this very day Don Garcia must be off, bag and baggage; Don Rodrigo has made haste to get to Burgos before he leaves, in order that he may throw in his face the loss of his title of Count of Cabra, and tell him a few plain truths which will bring the colour to his cheeks."

"You are right, Fernan; it must be that."

"I doubt whether I most rejoice at having arrived in Burgos to see Mayorica, or to hear th epretty things which my master will say to Don Garcia."

"I would offer four masses to Santa Gadea that my master might find Don Garcia still in Burgos."

"And I the same, Alvar."

Fernan and Alvar had arrived at this point of their conversation when they came in full view of the city.

The army was at but a very short distance from Burgos, when those that composed it saw a number of cavaliers issuing from one of its gates and coming towards them. The Cid, who was riding in the front, was the first to notice those who were leaving the city, and was much rejoiced to find that they were Don Garcia, with some of his friends and retainers.

The Count of Cabra, the time being just completed which the king had fixed for his departure, was leaving Burgos, in order to quit Castile.

The haste with which the army of the Cid had marched

was the reason that his arrival was not known in Burgos, and that the citizens had not thronged out to meet him; but just as Don Rodrigo and Don Garcia met, the city was becoming deserted, as its inhabitants were hastening out in swarms to welcome the victorious army.

Don Garcia, who had already learned that the Cid had taken possession of the states of Cabra, could not disguise his vexation, his anger, his envy, his despair at the sight of Rodrigo. He was a coward, and for that reason would not have dared, on any other occasion, to excite the anger of Rodrigo, but the rage which then burned within him made him reckless.

"You come in good time, De Vivar," he said to Rodrigo; "you continue to clothe yourself in the skin of a lamb in order that none may know that you are a fox."

"San Pedro of Cardeña!" murmured the Cid, placing his hand on his sword, unable to keep in his anger on hearing that insult; but he at once restrained himself, and Don Garcia continued—

"Can he be called a good cavalier who prayed the king to extend the time before my banishment that he might be able to insult me in my misfortunes, by saying, 'Quit Castile, not only without property, but also without the name of your ancestors, for that name is now mine; from this day forward I shall adorn myself with it'? Some day you shall know how terrible is the vengeance of the cavalier who has been so cruelly treated."

"You know, Don Garcia," answered the Cid, still restraining his anger, "that in all Castile there is no cavalier who should doubt of my loyalty less than you. Do not force me to throw publicly in your face the insults with which you sought to stain my honour."

"The day of my revenge will come, and then—beware of me, De Vivar."

"You have abundance of proof of your impotence to revenge yourself on me. I do not fear your vengeance, even if, to carry it out, you use means as base as those which you and your friends have already practised."

"My vengeance can never be as base as yours."

"Don Garcia!" exclaimed the Cid in a loud voice, "you shall now learn how Rodrigo de Vivar avenges himself on those who have injured him, who have hated him, and who have paid assassins to plunge their daggers in his heart. You are leaving Castile, banished, not knowing whither to go in order to weep over your misfortunes. Proceed now to your estates of Cabra, for if you did not know how to defend them, I have been able to reconquer them for you. If you do not consider yourself strong enough to protect them from the Moors, you will find there Guillen of the Standard, Martin Vengador, and two hundred soldiers, who will be able to defend your states against all the Moors in Andalucia. Now do you understand why I besought Don Sancho to extend the time, before the end of which you should go from Castile into exile, from four days to a month?"

The Count of Cabra, stupefied by astonishment and joy, murmured some words of gratitude, and, urging on his horse towards Rodrigo, he held out his hand to him; but the Cid did not hear those words, which were drowned by the acclamations of the multitude, which had been quickly approaching; nor did he extend his hand to take that of Don Garcia, for, as soon as he had pronounced his last words, he set spurs to Babieca and continued his way.

CHAPTER XL

HOW THE COUNT OF CARRION WOUND THE SKEIN AND HOW OTHERS UNWOUND IT

THE Count of Carrion had some friends in Toro, and he proceeded thither, two days after he had received the sentence of banishment pronounced by Don Sancho, leaving his sister in the castle under the guard of his accomplice, Bellido Dolfos.

Doña Elvira, the mistress of Toro, was a young princess, as unsuspecting as she was good, and this being known to Don Suero and his partisans, they determined, at any cost, to make themselves masters of her will, in order to establish at Toro the centre of their operations; for they had resolved to get up a conspiracy against Don Sancho, in order to avenge themselves for the sentence of banishment which he had passed on them. They made the Infanta believe that she was surrounded by dangers, that her brother harboured the design of reigning in all the states of his late father, and that Toro was the first which he had resolved to get possession of, as, being the weakest, he preferred to commence in it his plans of usurpation. "Let us cause enmity," they said, "between Doña Elvira and Don Sancho, and he will at once endeavour to make himself master of Toro. Don Alfonso, Don Garcia, and Doña Urraca will take up at once the defence of their sister, fearing lest Don Sancho would also attack their dominions, stimulated to it by his usurpation of the state of Toro, and then the King of Castile will lose his crown, for he will not be able to resist all his brothers and sisters leagued against him." At the same time they instilled distrust, regarding the intentions of Don Sancho, into the heart of Don Alfonso, and into those of Don Garcia and Doña Urraca, by means of trusty friends whom they had near them. In a word, they were hatching a wide-spread conspiracy, which they felt confident would enable them to avenge themselves on the King of Castile.

The credulous Doña Elvira cast herself blindly into the arms of those men, believing that she could only procure her safety through them ; so that, in a very short time, the Count of Carrion and his partisans were much more rulers of Toro than the daughter of Don Fernando. Such being the condition of affairs, was it not easy for those traitors to force Doña Elvira to declare war against Don Sancho? And having embroiled himself with Doña Elvira, would he not also have done so with all his brothers and sisters? And then, was not his ruin certain?

Don Sancho learned that Toro was now the residence of his bitterest foes, that they were conspiring there against Castile, and that his sister, far from opposing the conspirators, was aiding them by her tolerance, and even openly protecting them. On this account he was very much irritated with Doña Elvira, to whom he addressed frequent protests, threatening her with the loss of her state if she did not change her conduct.

Persuaded by her disloyal advisers, she replied to Don Sancho with much haughtiness, telling him that, if he dared to make an attempt on her state, all her brothers and sisters would side with her, and that they would divide amongst them the kingdom of Castile.

Don Sancho was easily excited to anger, but brave at the same time. That challenge made him very indignant, with the much more reason, as he believed that his brothers and sisters owed the quiet possession of their states, up to the present time, to his affection and generosity—states which, he believed, belonged by right to him. Besides, his mother, whose counsels were the only ones which had very strong effect on him, was not with him ; he held, indeed, those of the Cid in much esteem, but he did not always allow himself to be blindly guided by him.

"My sister !" he exclaimed, filled with rage, when he had read her letters, "thinks that I fear my brothers, but she knows me but very imperfectly. I promised my mother not to proclaim war against my kinsfolk, and I have kept that promise ; but if they declare war against me, I accept the issue. I do not fail in my word. Within a few days the state of Toro shall be mine, even though all my brothers and sisters should unite for its defence."

"Sire," said Rodrigo Diaz and other cavaliers to him, "remember the curse which your father called down on the head of any child of his who would dare to deprive another of them of his inheritance. You should know that Doña Elvira is but a powerless woman, who, instead of being punished, should be protected by you, for, in addition to being her brother, you are powerful."

"I do not incur the malediction of my father by opposing war to war," answered Don Sancho ; "the curse of my father will fall on the head of that sister or brother who insults and challenges me. If I tolerate the arrogance and the provocation of my sister, they will all look on me as weak and cowardly, and some day they will all attack me, anxious to divide my kingdom amongst them. If I let Doña Elvira and all the others see now that I am neither weak nor a coward, they will not abuse my generosity in the future. The state of Toro must be mine, even though I return it to my sister immediately after having taken possession of it."

The Cid endeavoured to dissuade Don Sancho from his resolve, but his counsels were of no avail. He did not persist in them energetically, in order not to act against the principle which he had formerly expressed, that the king should act without being impeded either by nobles or commoners.

Don Sancho then collected a large body of men-at-arms, and was preparing to attack Toro ; but just then Doña Elvira, having sought aid from Don Garcia, who was the most powerful of her brothers, the latter sent one of his cavaliers, named Rui-Ximenez, to Don Sancho, challenging him to attack the kingdom of Galicia instead of the state of Toro, and charging him with cowardice, on account of his intention to fall upon the weak, like Doña Elvira, instead of the strong, like him. The vexation which this message caused Don Sancho was much greater than that which the provocations of Doña Elvira had occasioned.

The King of Castile consulted the Cid as to the reply which he should give to his brother.

"Endeavour," said Don Rodrigo to him, "to avoid war with your brother, but if he perseveres in his provocations, make war against him, without, however, forgetting that he is your brother; but to enter into his kingdom you must pass through that of Leon, and to do so without the consent of Don Alfonso would be only to make another enemy."

Don Sancho and Don Alfonso met in Sahagun, and arranged that the latter should allow the Castilian army to pass through the kingdom of Leon. As a result of this arrangement, Don Sancho sent Alvar Fañez Minaya to challenge Don Garcia.

He accepted the challenge, and collected a large army, with which he prepared to march against his brother, who was advancing in great force towards Galicia. His soldiers, however, who were very much discontented on account of war having been declared against Castile, as they foresaw its disastrous consequences, revolted at the moment of setting out, and killed Rui-Ximenez in the presence of the king, for they believed that it was he who had given evil counsels to Don Garcia.

This occurrence caused the breaking up of the army of the King of Galicia, and thus the Castilians penetrated into his kingdom, and Don Sancho made himself master of several fortified places, and especially of the entire Portuguese portion of the kingdom.

After a time, however, Don Garcia mustered another large army, and sallied forth to encounter his brother. The battle was fierce, the two kings fighting at the fronts of their respective troops, and after a combat, lasting for half a day, the Castilians were thrown into disorder. Don Garcia succeeded in making Don Sancho his prisoner, and having given him into the charge of six of his followers, he set out in pursuit of the fugitives.

"Give me my liberty, cavaliers," cried Don Sancho to those who were guarding him, full of anger at not being able to stop the flight of his disordered army, and of shame at finding himself a prisoner. "Let me free, and I promise you rich rewards, and I also give you my word that I will not cause any further injury to your country."

"For all your kingdom we would not do it," replied his guards, "for we should then be traitors to our lord and king. You must await the return of Don Garcia, and he can act as he pleases."

Alvar Fañez Minaya saw from a distance the capture of Don Sancho, and, spurring his horse towards those who were guarding him, he cried out —

"Traitors, set my lord and king at liberty!"

And as they did not show any disposition to obey him, but were rather preparing to chastise his audacity, he rushed on them, and unhorsed two with the first thrusts of his lance. The other four then fled in terror; and Don Sancho, having recovered his freedom, rode up to the top of an eminence and cried out to his men—

"To me, my cavaliers! Loyal and brave Castilians, rally around me!"

Four hundred cavaliers collected around him in a few minutes, and the others, who were fighting in groups, scattered here and there, recovered courage, and succeeded in also joining the king.

The Cid, who in those wars accompanied the king, without taking part in the conflicts, as he desired to keep the promise which he had made to Don Fernando the Great, never to draw his sword against a son or daughter of his, unless one was oppressed by another and required his aid,—the Cid, we repeat, had remained neutral, at some distance from the field of battle; but when he became aware of the difficult position in which Don Sancho was, he believed that he should go to his assistance, and he appeared, with his three hundred cavaliers, in sight of the king just as he was preparing to descend to the plain, where the battle was continuing, with the troops which he had been able to reunite.

Don Sancho saw him, and joy and hope shone in his eyes.

"Let us descend to the plain," he said to his cavaliers; "for, the Cid aiding us, we shall still be able to recover our losses, the day shall yet be ours."

And he added, approaching the Cid—

"You are welcome, Campeador. A vassal never arrived in better time to serve his king, than you do now."

"Sire," replied Rodrigo, "you can count on winning the

battle. Your brother will be defeated; but you must promise me to spare his life, should he become your prisoner."

"I make you that promise, good Cid," answered Don Sancho.

They then descended to the plain, Don Sancho and the Cid in the front.

Don Garcia, wearied by the pursuit, was returning, well contented, and rejoicing at having defeated his brother, when, on turning a hill, he found himself face to face with the Castilians. The fight then recommenced, all the troops, on both sides, reuniting.

That second fight was as sanguinary as the first, but shorter. The cavaliers of the Cid succeeded in breaking up the ranks of Don Garcia, and the Castilians were victorious.

The Cid took Don Garcia prisoner, and delivered him up to Don Sancho.

"Don Garcia," said the latter to his brother, "tell me, on the word of a cavalier, what fate you had reserved for me when, a short time ago, you had me in your power, for I wish to treat you as you would have treated me."

"Death!" replied Don Garcia, driven to the wildest desperation.

"Your brother does not wish to shed the blood of his brother," said the King of Castile; "your brother would restore you to liberty, and would give back to you the kingdom which he has won from you, if he did not fear that you would provoke a second war, in which Christians would shed the blood of Christians. As you cannot live free in your Alcazar of Oviedo, live a prisoner in the Castle of Luna."

"You do well to imprison me," replied Don Garcia, "as I am now your deadliest foe, since it has been your desire to have in me an enemy and not a brother. But those who will free me from my prison are not wanting. The King of Leon is still free; and the hope also remains to me that your forehead shall be struck some day by the bolt of divine vengeance, with which our father threatened the Cain who would attack his brother."

"It is ye that are Cains, not I," exclaimed Don Sancho, in anger; but, restraining himself, he added—

"Brother, refrain from insults, which can only make your condition worse. Give me your word that you will live far from my states, and I shall see that you want nothing wherewith to maintain your dignity, and in exchange I will now give you your freedom."

"If you give it to me, I shall use it to drag you from the throne which you have usurped."

"Then you shall live and die in confinement, as you so desire!" exclaimed Don Sancho indignantly.

A few days after, the unfortunate Don Garcia was imprisoned in the Castle of Luna.

CHAPTER XLI

FROM BURGOS TO VIVAR

ONE morning in summer, shortly after sunrise, two cavaliers set out from Burgos in the direction of Vivar; both were young and graceful, and rode on, conversing in an animated and pleasant tone, keeping their steeds beside each other.

They were Guillen of the Standard and Martin Vengador.

"What a beautiful morning this is!" said Guillen.

"Yes," replied his companion; "and how pleasant it is to breathe the air of the fields when the sun is rising."

"We, who have passed our lives in the country, smother in cities. See, Martin, how blue the sky is, listen to the singing of the birds amid the trees of that dell, and smell the fragrance of the plants which grow around us."

"This morning reminds me of the one on which we left Cabra, the day following the arrival of the count, whom it cost so little to have it restored to him."

"They say that Andalucia is a fairer land than Castile, and certainly its fields are more fertile and its sky clearer, but may God grant it to me to live and die in our famed Castile, for there is no country equal to one's native land."

"So say I also, Guillen; besides, in our Castile there are abundance of fertile plains, luxuriant woods, and fragrant flowers; we also have a clear sky and a brilliant and life-giving sun. Castile is, above all others, the land of chivalry, of honour, and of glory. If Andalucia has an advantage over Castile in its soil, it has not such with regard to its inhabitants; here we let our souls be seen as naked as our fields; there they show their souls concealed with foliage and flowers, like the fields of that land; as in our land we have permitted scarcely any infidels to dwell, we have preserved pure the blood of the cavaliers of Covadonga and Roncesvalles."

"It delights me to wander along the banks of the Guadalquiver, for on them the trees and flowers are most beautiful; but it delights me more to walk on the banks of the Ebro, of the Tormes, and of the Duero, for they are filled with the memories of brave cavaliers and glorious feats of arms."

"We cannot envy any who dwell in Spain, for God has given us honours, of which we can justly feel proud, and great natural riches which we can enjoy."

"And love adorns all, Martin; for my part, I can say that love causes me to see flowers where others can only see rocks, palaces where there are only huts, and angels where there are but human beings. Does it not seem a great happiness to you to have souls that feel as ours do, and to love so well the land in which we were born?"

"And above all," said Martin, smiling pleasantly, "the love of maidens, so worthy of being loved as your noble Doña Teresa and my humble Beatrice."

Guillen sighed, and there disappeared from his face the joy which, till then, had shone on it.

"Happy you, who can see, as often as you like, her whom you love!" exclaimed the lover of the Infanta of Carrion.

"Guillen, the day is not far distant when your happiness will be as complete as mine. Are you indeed discontented with your lot?"

"No, Martin, no. When I think that I, a poor servitor of the Count of Carrion, the son of a humble peasant, have been made already a member of the order of chivalry, am treated as an equal by the most noble cavaliers of Castile, have won the love of the king and of the Cid, and am richer than many of those who call themselves grandees, it seems that joy should disturb my reason. But why should you be astonished, Martin, that my heart becomes sad when I think of the Infanta, whom I love more and more as days go on, and whom I may not see for a very long time? If Doña Teresa had a mother by her side, or even anyone who could protect her, love her, and cheer up the sadness of her heart, living apart from her would not be so hard to bear; but she is in the power of her brother, nay, even worse, in the power of that traitor Bellido, since the king banished Don Suero."

"But how is it possible, Guillen, that the Count of Carrion can trust the traitor to such an extent, that he not only gives him his friendship, but also confides to him the care of his household? How is it possible that he should have put his sister and his nephews in his charge, during his absence?"

"It appears impossible, Martin, but nothing is more certain."

"But how do you manage to receive news of what takes place in the Castle of Carrion?"

"I hear from Doña Teresa through a domestic, named Gonzalo, who was always devoted to his lady and to me; he is bent on revenging himself on the count, from whom he has received more blows than he has hairs on his head."

"I am astonished that Bellido permits him to absent himself from the Castle long enough to go to Burgos."

"For a considerable time the count made use of him to send letters to his friends; and when he went to Toro, where he now is, he left him in Carrion, in order that he might perform the same services for Bellido, spurred on now and then by a sound cudgelling, which the count advised his friend to apply to him, should he show himself at any time reluctant to do his bidding. Bellido sends him rather often to Burgos, with letters to the partisans of the exiled noblemen, for they have still in Castile some who are desirous to aid them; also to find out what is going on, and to act as a spy even on the king himself."

"It is fortunate for you that you have such means of communicating with the Infanta."

"It certainly is, for if I had them not, I swear by the name I bear, that before this I would have attacked the Castle of Carrion, and have either found my death or removed the Infanta from that prison."

"But I think that even still we should strike a blow against the castle, in order to free the defenceless dove from the claws of the hawk."

"I am thinking of doing so, Martin; and if I have not done so before this, it is because I feared that the attempt might be vain; the castle is very strong in itself, and it is defended by good crossbow-men; but I can now count on friends who will aid me in the enterprise, even Don Rodrigo himself will lend me his assistance, if not personally, at least with men-at-arms, and I hope that before a year passes,

Guillen of the Standard and the Infanta of Carrion will be united before the altar. On the day that I found you in the wood, and induced you to go with me to the wars, if I had said to a grandee, of even the lowest rank, that I aspired to the hand of the Infanta of Carrion, he would have spat in my face and looked on me as a madman; but now even the King of Castile will support my pretensions."

"Blessed was the day of which you remind me, Guillen," exclaimed Martin, thinking of what he had been when he commanded his band, and what he now was, in the service of the Cid. "Blessed also be you," he added, "who, from being a miserable bandit, made of me a soldier, whom the Campeador honours with his friendship and confidence—he who is the best cavalier in the world. You well said that on the fields of battle I would be able to wash away, with infidel blood, the stain which the world sees on the brow of the bandit; that on them I would acquire power to chastise the assassin of my father; that from them I would return a hundred times more worthy to be united to the girl whom I love."

"We have had many glorious days in the wars, and I hope that we shall have many more."

"I pray God that we may be soon fighting once more against the Moors, instead of in those accursed conflicts of Christians against Christians."

"Unfortunately, Martin, I fear that those battles, of which you speak, are not yet terminated. As things are, I believe that, before long, there must be more sanguinary combats between Castilians and Leonese. I would wager the sword which the Cid girt on me, that, within two months, there will be a fierce war between Don Sancho and his brother Don Alfonso. Don Sancho eagerly desires to possess the kingdom of Leon, especially since he has acquired that of Galicia; and Don Alfonso, who knows that, and gives ear to evil advisers, affords every day opportunities for a rupture, by letting the enmity appear which he feels towards Don Sancho."

The two young men were thus conversing when they came in sight of Vivar; they were much rejoiced at this, for the day, fresh and pleasant at its beginning, was becoming oppressive, as the sun was very high, and was shooting down his beams much fiercer than was agreeable. It was not alone the hope of rest, shaded from the heat of the sun, that made them anxious to see the end of their two-hours' journey, for it did not take much longer time to complete it; Martin loved Beatrice deeply, and was returning to see her after a long absence in the war between Don Sancho and Don Garcia, and Guillen was about to see the happiness of his friend and companion-in-arms, in which he rejoiced as much as if it were his own.

In front of the farmhouse of Pero was a beautiful orchard, in which was a great abundance of fruit-trees, which laborious and happy husbandmen had planted, and made to grow and bear fruit with their constant care; in it were standing Beatrice and her parents when Martin and Guillen halted on an eminence which overlooked the farmhouse.

On seeing them, a cry of joy escaped from the lips of Beatrice, who let fall the fruit which she was carrying in her turned-up skirt, and ran to meet the two young men; her parents imitated her, for they looked on Martin as a son, and indeed on Guillen almost as such, for the former seldom went to Vivar without being accompanied by the latter.

Beatrice was soon serving an appetising meal to her guests and her parents under a large tree in the garden, and all were conversing pleasantly together, building castles in the air, and abandoning themselves to a happiness which only good souls can understand.

Shortly after the termination of the meal the gallop of a horse was heard on the road which led to Carrion, and which was only about two stone-throws from the farmhouse. All turned their eyes in that direction, and Guillen uttered a cry of pleasure, for in the horseman he recognised Gonzalo, the servant of Don Suero, who now and then brought him news from Doña Teresa.

Guillen ran across the orchard and went out on the road to meet Gonzalo, who dismounted at once when he recognised him.

"Gonzalo, you are indeed welcome," said Guillen, in whose face pleasure and inquietude were depicted. "Do you come from the Castle of Carrion?"

"I left it during the night," answered Gonzalo, "and I bring you a letter from my mistress. Here it is," he said, and he handed a parchment to the young man.

Guillen hastened to open it, and then read it eagerly.

"To-day," wrote the Infanta to him, "Bellido, my jailer sets out for Toro, and he cannot be back for at least eight days. Guillen, it is a long time since I saw you last, and for a long time I feared to die without seeing you again; ask Gonzalo, when he delivers this letter to you, when he can be back to the castle, for, if you can come to see me, he will facilitate your entrance into it. Have pity on me, do not allow me to die within those gloomy walls without again seeing you—you on whom I place the only hope which I have in this world."

The loving youth pressed his lips on those lines, partly effaced by the tears of Teresa, and felt his eyes moist, as on that night, both sad and joyous, in which he revealed his love to the unhappy maiden in the camp of the bandits.

"Gonzalo!" he exclaimed, throwing his arms round the neck of the messenger, "if I had a hundred lives I would willingly give them in exchange for the happiness which you have brought me, and even then I would consider it but poorly paid ! I am no longer the humble servitor of Don Suero, such as you formerly knew me; I have power and wealth, with which I can recompense your services. Continue in the household of the count, in order that you may watch over Doña Teresa ; and on the day when your mistress shall no longer have need of your care, I will say to you, 'In future you shall not have to go into the employment of any person ; I have wealth which I have won in the wars ; take what you require in order to live free and happy wherever you may desire ! ' "

Gonzalo was not mercenary, but how was it possible for him not to feel happy, when he saw shining before him the hope of being able to live as Guillen had said, instead of being constantly exposed to the outrages and bad treatment to which he was subjected in the service of the Count of Carrion.

"My lady and you," he replied, "can dispose of me, as I am resolved to serve both of you, as far as is in my power, without any recompense but that of being useful to those who need my services."

"Do you believe, Gonzalo, that it will be possible for me to enter the castle during the absence of Bellido ? "

"My lady and I have had long talks on the subject, and we have come to the conclusion that such is possible, by making our arrangements beforehand."

"When can you be in Carrion again ? "

"To-morrow night; I am now going to Burgos with letters, which Bellido gave me before his departure, with instructions to go with them to-day."

"Well, then, to-morrow night, at whatever hour you now tell me, I shall be outside the castle."

"At midnight you must come to the postern very cautiously, although there is not much risk of the crossbow-men hearing you; for, as Bellido makes them keep watch every night, under pain of anyone who falls asleep being hung on the battlements in the morning, they will try to make up for that by sleeping well whilst he is away from the castle. I shall watch for your arrival through the loopholes, and as soon as I see you approach I will open the postern and let you in, and will facilitate your getting through the castle, so that you may see Doña Teresa for a short time."

"Very well, I shall not fail to be there to-morrow night at the hour you have mentioned."

"Take care that you are not surprised by a band of robbers, who, people say, have appeared recently in the district of Carrion, where bandits have not been seen since the Vengador and his men went away."

"All right, Gonzalo, I shall not forget your caution; I thank you for it. What have you to tell me of the Infanta?"

"If her troubles do not soon cease, God will be as unjust to her as men have been."

"No, Gonzalo, God is not unjust, as men often are; God will make up for the sufferings of the Infanta with many years of perfect happiness; tell her that, for you will see her before I can."

After a few more words Guillen and Gonzalo separated, the former returning to where Martin and the Pero family were awaiting him, and the latter continuing his journey to Burgos.

Guillen showed Martin the letter from the Infanta, and told him that he would go to Carrion before he returned to Burgos, with the intention of removing Teresa from the castle.

"I will accompany you, Guillen," said the Vengador, "and I will die with you if necessary."

"Thanks, Martin," exclaimed Guillen, holding out his hand affectionately to his friend; "but I know the danger which threatens both you and me when we approach Carrion; I cannot therefore accept your generous offer, for — what would become of your good and loving Beatrice if she were to lose you?"

"Beatrice," replied Martin, "would look on me as a coward, and would despise me, with very good cause, if I saw you going into danger without accompanying you. Do I not value more than my life the friendship with which you honour me, and the good fortune which you procured me, when you induced me to exchange the vile career of a bandit for that of a soldier? Guillen, let us set out for Carrion as soon as it may please you, for I will follow you gladly to the end of the world, even though there were dangers at every step. I wish that Rui-Venablos could accompany us, but he must remain in command of the Cid's troops during our absence."

Guillen finally accepted the offer of Martin. They spent the remainder of the day and the following night in the farm-house of Pero, and at a very early hour in the morning they started for Carrion.

CHAPTER XLII

FROM VIVAR TO CARRION

At the fall of the evening Guillen and Martin arrived within view of the castle, although they were still at a considerable distance from it; they determined to await the night in a thick grove of chestnut trees, in order that they might continue their journey as soon as it grew dark, and arrive at the castle by midnight, as had been arranged between Guillen and Gonzalo.

The sun was near setting, and was lighting up, with a fiery glow, the distant horizon. Guillen and Martin had dismounted, and, whilst their horses were grazing amongst the chestnut trees, were seated on a high bank, from which they had an extensive view of the surrounding country. Martin had his eyes fixed on the wide and fertile plain of Carrion, the beauty of which confirmed what he had said on the previous day—that the hand of God had been also extended over Castile, when He was distributing the best gifts of nature. Guillen was gazing on the Castle of Carrion, which arose in the distance, veiled by the smoke arising from heaps of burning stubble, like a dark phantom, which seemed intent on filling with terror that calm and enchanting landscape.

"Ah!" he said, with a heavy heart, and with tears ready to break from his eyes, "how near appears that accursed castle, and, notwithstanding, what a distance separates me from her who sighs within it! There—within those gloomy walls—is the dear girl who has, in the whole world, no other hope but my love. Would that I could fly like those birds, which, in the branches of the trees surrounding us, are plaintively singing their farewell to the day! Would that I could fly like them through the clear air and alight on the sill of that window, at which Teresa has so often shed sad tears. Perhaps the poor girl is now standing, full of grief, at that window, thinking of me, and beseeching the Virgin, whose sanctuary is on the neighbouring hill, to guide my footsteps, and to make me brave enough to endeavour to get to her."

Guillen and Martin suddenly abandoned their enthusiastic reflections, for, turning round, they saw behind them about fifty armed men, who came out from amongst the surrounding trees. Both placed their hands on their swords, but before they had time to draw them, those men rushed upon them, with threatening aspect, and seized on them, crying out—

"If you move hands or feet you are dead!"

Guillen doubted not but that these were the robbers of whom Gonzalo had spoken.

"Cowards," he said to them, "you have not courage enough to fight, arm to arm and breast to breast, although you are twenty times as numerous as we are, but treacherously capture us without giving us time to defend ourselves."

"By the glorious San Isidore!" cried out one of the bandits, closely examining Martin, "I have less sense than these horses if we have not amongst us our former captain, the valiant Vengador."

"I am the Vengador," said Martin, examining in his turn the bandits, who hastened to set both him and Guillen free, with evident marks of respect.

"I certainly remember," he added, "having seen some of you in my band."

"We are those who were in it," replied four of the bandits, amongst whom was he who had first recognised Martin, and who appeared to be the leader.

"Do you not remember," said this man, "Juan Centellos, who on the day of the death of the Raposo proposed that you should be chosen as the chief of those remaining of the band, and who said to you that he had a daughter as good as the noblest lady in Castile, and who afterwards cured the wound which you had received on your head?"

"Yes, I remember it well," replied Martin.

"Do you not also remember that after the unlucky attack on the Castle of Carrion, some of the few of us that succeeded in escaping, separated themselves from the band, hoping that, by working separately, they would find it easier to avenge themselves than by remaining with their companions?"

"I do; you were one of them."

"And the others were the three whom you see here. All our efforts were, however, useless, and we therefore made up our minds to rejoin the band. When we went to look for it, we learned that it had marched to Portugal, and since then we have wandered about the district of Carrion, sometimes with good fortune, sometimes with bad. Do you know, Sir Vengador, that Bellido Dolfos, whom you loved so much, was the greatest traitor that woman ever give birth to?"

"Yes; I have since learned that it was he who sold the band in Carrion."

"That is what I was just about to tell you. And, by my soul, Don Suero is pleased with him, for he keeps him in his castle, treating him royally. Anger of Lucifer! if we only lay hands on him, and we are trying to do so for a long time! Don't go too near Carrion, for if that Bellido smells you it will be bad for you, for you must know that he is not so much your friend as you perchance think."

"It is to the Castle of Carrion that we are going, as Bellido is now absent."

"The son of my mother would not trust much in his absences. Do not go there, Sir Vengador; and I give the same advice to this youth, although I do not know who he is. . . . But now that I look closely at him, I think that he is the page who came with Doña Teresa to our camp."

"He is the same," replied Martin.

"What, does he no longer serve Don Suero?"

"Far from serving him, he would plunge his sword in him, and also in Bellido, if he only had them in his power."

"I repeat to you, however, Sir Vengador, that you should not go to the castle, for I fear that some evil will come on you there."

"I thank you for the interest you take in us; but we are resolved to enter the castle this very night, and we would not abandon our intention for all the wealth of the world."

"Well, then, as you are resolved to go on, may God send you good luck!"

"I think," said Guillen, "that we cannot remain here longer, as night is coming on, and we are still far from the castle."

"You are right," said Martin; and he added, turning to the bandits—

"We wish you good luck; and if you don't object, we are going to continue our journey."

"Continue it, with our good wishes," answered Juan Centellos; "but tell me, Sir Vengador, what do you mean by good luck?"

"By good luck I mean that you may escape from the Salvadores, and "—

"And that Bellido and Don Suero may fall into our hands, so that we may pay off last year's treachery; is it not so?" interrupted the captain of the band.

"That is what I was about to say to you," answered Martin.

The two travellers then mounted and continued their journey.

They had left the bandits a considerable time, when they thought they heard the noise of people in their rear; they stopped to listen, but as they heard nothing more they believed that it was voices borne by the breeze from some village in their vicinity; they then silently pursued their way.

They came at last near the wood situated close to the castle, and recognised it by the branches of the trees standing out against the sky behind them. They dismounted there, enveloped the hoofs of the horses with some pieces of cloth, which they had brought with them for that purpose, and, thanks to that precaution, they approached the postern of the castle with scarcely any noise, leading their horses by the bridles.

A white handkerchief, held out through one of the loopholes, and which could be distinctly seen against the dark background of the wall, was waved for a moment, as if summoning them to that spot. They then fastened their horses to trees, and proceeded to the postern, which Gonzalo immediately opened, with the least noise possible.

"Ascend by the secret stairs," he said to Guillen, "and come back soon; I shall await you here, to shut the postern when you go out."

Guillen, who was well acquainted with the rooms and corridors of the castle, mounted, feeling his way, the stairs which Gonzalo had indicated to him, and Martin followed close behind; both had their unsheathed swords in their hands, in order to be prepared in case of a surprise. In a short time they were in the upper storey of the castle, and consequently near the apartments of the Infanta.

The heart of Guillen was beating with violence; against it would soon rest, throbbing, the heart of Teresa, which for so long a time had been sad and solitary.

Both youths reached the door of Teresa's apartment; at that moment it suddenly opened; she rushed towards Guillen with open arms, and fell senseless on his neck, crying out, "Guillen, Guillen!"

And that exclamation was so loud that it echoed through the vaulted passages of the castle.

"Treason, treason! The chamber of the Infanta!" answered, to the cry of Teresa, a voice which Guillen and Martin recognised with terror; it was the voice of Bellido, who had pretended to have left the castle in order to surprise Guillen, who, he doubted not, would be informed of his absence by the Infanta, and would therefore hasten to visit her.

A great din of footsteps, of voices, and of arms followed the cry of Bellido.

The Infanta remained in a faint, notwithstanding the efforts of Guillen and Martin to restore her to consciousness.

"Let us fly from the castle," said Martin. "Take the Infanta in your arms, and I will protect you behind; we shall thus escape, for if Gonzalo did not betray us, the postern is still open."

Guillen took up Teresa in his arms; her weight could not embarrass him much, for the unhappy girl was worn away with grief; then, followed by Martin, he ran to the staircase by which they had ascended. Just as they placed their feet on the first step they were overtaken by Bellido and a number of servants and crossbow-men, who attacked them furiously; the staircase, however, was narrow, and that circumstance favoured Martin, who had only to ward off three or four blows at a time. At last they reached the postern, which Gonzalo quickly opened. He placed himself at the side of Martin, determined to share the fate of the young men, fighting against Bellido and his followers: all the combatants were then outside the castle.

At that moment loud voices were heard amongst the neighbouring trees, and a number of men rushed like lions on Bellido's followers, whilst others entered the postern, in obedience to Juan Centellos, who cried out, "Come on, my brave fellows; let some get into the castle, and let the others exterminate those cowards, who are attacking the Vengador!"

The forces were now more equal; or rather, those who were at first the weaker had become the stronger. The combat was obstinate and bloody, both without and within the castle. Inside, the advantage should be on the side of the bandits, for their opponents were but few, as almost all the men-at-arms, who guarded the castle, had sallied forth in pursuit of the abductors.

At a short distance from the castle was a convent of nuns, to which Guillen made his way, with his precious burden, hearing behind him the noise of the combat.

What a torture was it for the brave youth to hear, at but a few paces from him, the clashing of swords, and not be able to use his! He ran—flew on, as if nothing were impeding his footsteps; and if the question were then asked, What most urged him on with such speed to the convent? whether it was to place Teresa in a place of safety, or to return to fight amid his friends? it would have been difficult to answer.

Suddenly the town and its vicinity was lighted up with a bright glare. The Castle of Carrion had been set on fire.

Guillen arrived at the door of the convent, which was a small building, recently erected to shelter the community which occupied it, until Christian charity would enable them to build another, larger and more beautiful. He pulled violently a rope, which hung outside the door, and set a bell ringing. Some of the nuns ran to this summons, and Guillen hurriedly said to them—

"Fire is consuming the castle of the Counts of Carrion; afford hospitality to the Infanta Doña Teresa, whom I have had the good fortune to rescue from the flames."

The nuns hastened to afford assistance to the young lady, and Guillen left the convent, making his way to the castle, in the vicinity of which the fight was still raging. After proceeding a short distance, he met Martin and Gonzalo, and the three embraced warmly.

"Martin," cried Guillen, "the innocent dove is now free, and saved from the talons of the hawk."

"And the hawk," replied the Vengador, "is in flight, pursued by Juan Centellos and others of our aiders, and the riches of Don Suero are in the power of the bandits."

"To Vivar, to Vivar!" cried Guillen. "God has commenced to discharge the bolts of His justice on the heads of the wicked, and expiation will be completed in the end. Gonzalo," he added, turning towards him who had facilitated his entrance into the castle, "come with us, and you will be with your best friends."

They then proceeded to the place where they had left the horses, which were still fastened to the trunks of the trees.

"My horse is strong," said Guillen to Gonzalo, "get up behind me and you shall see that this horrible spectacle will be soon lost to our view. It is a sight which oppresses and saddens my soul. My God! my God! the fire consumes the apartment of Teresa, which I should like to see preserved, as the sanctuary of my sweetest remembrances. See how the flames burst from the window, at which the Infanta so often stood, sad and broken-hearted! Comrades, let us get away as quickly as possible."

The three of them then made their way towards the Burgos road, whilst the flames, fanned by a strong breeze, roared through the castle, shooting up to the very battlements, and illuminating with their sinister glare the plain of Carrion to a considerable distance.

CHAPTER XLIII

HOW A GOOD CAVALIER WAS CHARGED WITH AN EVIL MESSAGE

It must be confessed that ambition was the ruling passion of Don Sancho; it must also be admitted that the injustice, or rather the imprudence, of his brothers, supplied food to that passion. Don Sancho was haughty and irritable in a high degree, and that character of his contributed also, not a little, to cause him to forget that, in extending his dominions, those whom he attacked were his brothers, and that, whether just or unjust, the wishes of a dying father should be held sacred.

Guillen did not deceive himself when he said that, in a short time, there would be a sanguinary war between Leonese and Castilians. The counts sent into exile by Don Sancho, amongst whom we must include the Count of Cabra, who, not content with the district which the Cid had so generously recovered for him, was working, in union with his friends, to avenge his banishment,—those counts, we repeat, worked on the mind of Don Alfonso in the same manner as they had influenced that of Doña Elvira, so that Leon might provoke Castile to a war, in which Don Sancho might lose his crown, and perhaps his life. It might be that Don Alfonso himself would lose both ; in that case, however, the Count of Carrion and his friends would lose but little, for the worst that could then happen to them would be that they should complete their exile in states held by the Moors, in Aragon or Navarre, instead of in the kingdom of Leon. In that game they might win, but they could not lose.

Don Alfonso knew of the ambitious aims of his brother, and doubted not but that he would very soon declare war against him, in order to dispossess him of his kingdom, whether he were provoked to it or not ; he therefore hastened to put himself in a state of defence, so that he might not be unprepared, should his fears be realised.

Don Sancho, knowing of the warlike preparations of his brother, demanded explanations from him regarding their object. The answer of Don Alfonso by no means satisfied him ; negotiations succeeded, becoming gradually more embittered, and in the end there was a complete rupture between Castile and Leon ; the efforts of the Cid and some other honoured noblemen to prevent it having had no result.

Don Alfonso asked for aid from the kings of Navarre and of Aragon ; but before they were able to afford it, Don Sancho had collected together a good army and hastened to invade the territory of his brother. The two contending parties came to blows near a village named Plantaca ; they fought with great valour, and victory declared for the Castilians. The king, Don Alfonso, being conquered, and his army destroyed, was forced to retire to the city of Leon, where he intended to reinforce himself, with the object of again attacking his victorious enemies.

He encountered them again near Golpelara, on the banks of the river Carrion ; another battle was fought, and, fortune changing, the Castilians were beaten, before the Cid was able to take part in the combat.

Rodrigo Diaz was very unwilling to fight against any of the children of Don Fernando, and he only decided to do so when he saw Don Sancho, whom he had accompanied in this war, quite powerless. On his arrival at the field of battle, he found the Castilian army cut up and in flight, and Don Sancho in despair. He cheered him up, assuring him that he would regain all he had lost, got together again the flying soldiers and before daybreak attacked the Leonese, who, heavy with sleep and wine, as Mariana writes, were far from thinking of such a thing. The most terrible disorder arose in the army of Don Alfonso. Some fled, others took up their arms in a careless way, all were commanding, no one obeying; they were vanquished, therefore, in a very short time. Don Alfonso, fearing that he would soon fall into the hands of his enemies, fled from the field of battle and shut himself up, with some of his followers, in the church of Carrion; the Castilians, however, surrounded it, and compelled him to surrender.

Don Sancho sent him at once to Burgos, and followed up the conquest of the kingdom of Leon. The city of that name and other towns resisted; in the end, however, they yielded, and in a few days the entire kingdom of Don Alfonso was in the hands of Don Sancho.

Many noble Castilians and Leonese, amongst whom were Doña Urraca, Peranzures, and the Cid, interceded with Don Sancho, praying him to make the condition of the prisoner as favourable as possible. The King of Castile consented to his brother going to the monastery of Sahagun, taking the habit of a monk, and renouncing the secular state.

Don Alfonso did not remain long in that monastery. Whether it was that the monastic life disgusted him, that he suspected the intentions of his brother, or that he desired to put himself in a position to recover the kingdom he had lost, whenever a favourable opportunity might present itself,—whatever was the true reason, he fled to Toledo, where he was kindly received by Almenon, who was glad to find an opportunity for fulfilling the promise which he had made to the dead king, Don Fernando, of affording the same protection to his children which he had afforded to his daughter Casilda. He told him that he might remain in his states as long as he desired; that he would provide for all his wants in such a manner that he would scarcely regret the throne which he had lost; and that he would treat him as a son. Don Alfonso entered into a covenant with Almenon to serve him in the wars in which he was engaged with other neighbouring Moors. He was accompanied by Peranzures and other cavaliers, to whom the King of Toledo made allowances, by means of which they could maintain themselves, and his ordinary occupation was the chase. For greater convenience in the pursuit of this, he built a country-house, which was the origin of the town of Brihuega.

There now only remained to Don Sancho to take possession of Zamora, in order to possess all the states which had belonged to his father. The city of Zamora was well supplied with fortifications, munitions, provisions, and soldiers, which were there in order that all emergencies might be provided for. The inhabitants were very brave and loyal, and were always ready to expose themselves to any dangers by which they might be threatened. They were under the command of Arias Gonzalo, a cavalier advanced in years, of great valour and prudence, and whose counsels, in matters of government and war, were much esteemed by Doña Urraca.

Don Sancho desired to possess that city, especially as he now held Toro, which he had taken from Doña Elvira, and, as the two were near each other, he feared that the people of Zamora, who were strong and daring, might fall upon the latter; he, however, desired to live in peace with Doña Urraca, for whom he had always felt a greater affection than for his other brothers and sisters. Hoping that he might be able to obtain Zamora in exchange for some other place, and not by force of arms, he resolved to send the Cid in order to negotiate such an exchange with the Infanta.

"Zamora is worth half a kingdom," he said to Rodrigo; "built on a rock, its walls and citadels are very strong, and the Duero, which runs beneath it, serves it as an admirable defence. If my sister would deliver it up to me, I would hold it in more esteem than the entire kingdom of Leon. I pray you, therefore, good Cid, to go to Doña Urraca, and ask her to give it to me in exchange, or else for a monetary consideration. Tell her that for Zamora I will give her Medina de Rioseco, Villalpando, with all its lands, the Castle of Tiedra, or Valladolid, which is a very rich city, and I, together with twelve of my vassals, will make oath to faithfully keep my promise to her."

"Sire," replied Rodrigo, "you have always found me, and shall always find me, prepared to obey you, for in no other manner could I repay all the favours you have bestowed on me, or fulfil the promise which I made your father when he was on his deathbed; but if I go to Zamora with the message which you desire to confide to me, your sister will believe, the inhabitants of Zamora, and even the Castilians and Leonese will believe, that I am aiding you in depriving Doña Urraca of her inheritance, and that I am breaking the promise which I made to your father. I beseech you, sire, to use the services, in this special matter, of other cavaliers, who have not the same motives as I have to keep entirely out of the matter."

"I do not send you," replied Don Sancho, "to threaten my sister, but to make amicable proposals to her. What Castilian cavalier is as respected as you by the inhabitants of Zamora, or whose words would have so much influence as yours on Doña Urraca? Or do you fear that the promises which you might make in my name would not be kept by me?"

"You insult me, sire, by imagining that Rodrigo Diaz could have any doubt regarding the promises of his king."

"Then go to Zamora and endeavour to induce my sister to yield up her inheritance to me; I beseech you to do so, as a friend, and I command you to do so, as your king."

On the same day the Cid set out for Zamora, where, for some time, embassadors were expected from Don Sancho to demand the submission of the city. When the Cid came near it the Infanta was in her palace, listening to the counsels of Arias Gonzalo and other noblemen.

The inhabitants of Zamora, when they saw from the walls Rodrigo Diaz and his retinue, who were proceeding towards the ancient gate in order to enter the city, they began to utter loud cries and lamentations, seeing that the time had come which they had so long dreaded; and the guards at the gate prepared to resist the entrance of the Castilians. Doña Urraca heard the loud cries and the alarm, which had now extended through the entire city, and when she inquired, and was informed of the cause, she went to a window which overlooked the exterior of the gate, although the nobles who were with her tried to prevent her, fearing that some weapon might be cast at her from the outside. It was then that, seeing the Cid at the foot of the wall of the city, she addressed to him those bitter reproaches, which have been preserved, thanks, perhaps, to the metrical form which, at a later period, was given to them—

> " Leave me, leave me, Don Rodrigo,
> Haughty Castilian cavalier!
> Well should you remember
> The good times that are past;
> When a knight you first were made
> Before St. James's holy altar;
> My father gave to you your arms;
> My mother gave to you your steed;
> I buckled on the spur of gold;
> That more honoured you might be."

Rodrigo raised his face on hearing that reproof, which he was so far from deserving, and felt his heart wounded, not so much because those words accused him of being disloyal and ungrateful, but on account of the grief which Doña Urraca showed by still wearing mourning, both for the death of her father, and for the death of the happiness which had reigned for so many years in her family. The face of the Infanta was pale and haggard, and from her eyes flowed abundant tears.

"My lady," replied Rodrigo, "calm yourself, and admit me to your presence, for I do not come as an enemy; Rodrigo Diaz de Vivar will never bear arms against the daughter of Don Fernando the Great."

Doña Urraca became calm on hearing those words, and gave orders that the Cid should be permitted to enter the city.

A few minutes later the honoured Castilian was in the presence of the Infanta. He kissed her hand, bending his knee respectfully before her, and repeated to her the message which Don Sancho had entrusted to him. Doña Urraca then broke out afresh into lamentations.

"Woe is me!" she exclaimed; "what is this which Don Sancho demands of me? How badly has he fulfilled the wishes of our father!—of our father, who called down the wrath of Heaven on the brother who would attack his brother. Our father was scarcely dead, when Don Sancho took all his territories from my brother, Don Garcia, and made him a prisoner; then he deprived Don Alfonso of his kingdom, who, finding himself so badly treated by Christians, had to take refuge amongst the Moors. He took Toro from my sister, and now he desires to take Zamora from me. Don Sancho knows that his brothers and sisters are not strong enough to fight against him face to face; but where the sword of the loyal is not able to do its office, the dagger of traitors can work; if Don Garcia is a prisoner, Don Alfonso, on the other hand, is free and is in the country of the Moors."

Doña Urraca was weeping inconsolably whilst thus speaking; and neither the words of Rodrigo nor those of the other cavaliers were able to tranquillise her.

"Dry up your tears, my lady," said old Arias Gonzalo, whose words were those which had the most authority with the Infanta; "it is not with tears that troubles are remedied. Consult your vassals; inform them of that which Don Sancho pretends to, and if they think it well, deliver to the king the territory of Zamora; but if they consider that you should not do so, we shall all defend it for you, as brave and honourable men.   Don Sancho asks you to give him Zamora, promising to hand over to you other places in exchange for it ; but how can you trust him to keep his promise, who has so badly carried out the will of his father?   For my part, I advise you not to deliver up the city to your brother.   We shall die in it, rather than surrender it in a cowardly manner, and I believe that all its inhabitants will be of my opinion.   Do you wish to know at once, my lady? Do you wish to learn now, whether the people of Zamora are resolved to defend your inheritance or not?   Crowds swarm at the gates of this Alcazar in order to learn what resolution you may come to.   Let me ask your people whether they prefer to bring on them the anger of Don Sancho, or to see their mistress despoiled of that which rightly belongs to her."

When he had thus spoken, Arias Gonzalo went to a window which overlooked a small square which lay at the front of the Alcazar.   Crowds were indeed swarming into it, anxious to learn what the message was which the Cid had brought, for no one doubted but that it was a very important one for the people of Zamora, when that famous cavalier had been entrusted with it.

"People of Zamora!" cried out old Arias Gonzalo, whose first words imposed a hushed silence on the assembled multitude. "The king, Don Sancho, wishes to take from our lady, Doña Urraca, the city of Zamora in exchange for other places which he promises to give her.   Do you desire that the Infanta should yield to those demands of her brother, or are you prepared to fight, as brave men, in the defence of her inheritance?"

"We will die fighting within the walls of Zamora!" was the universal shout which answered Arias.

"Zamora for Doña Urraca! Zamora for Doña Urraca!" the multitude continued to cry; and then the old man turned to the Infanta and said to her—

"Now you hear, my lady, the opinion of your vassals."

"Well, then," replied Doña Urraca, assuming a masculine haughtiness, "good Cid, say to Don Sancho that his sister and all her vassals will die in Zamora, rather than yield it up to him."

"I shall bring that answer to the king, my lady," said the Cid; "permit me to kiss your hand once more, as a pledge that I shall fulfil my promise not to bear arms against you."

"I know already, Don Rodrigo, that you are an honourable cavalier," replied the Infanta, holding out her hand that he might kiss it.   "Tell him that it sullies the reputation of the strong to attack the weak ; tell him that he should remember the affection I always had for him ; tell him that, however great his ambition may be, he should be satisfied with the states which he already possesses ; tell him that the malediction of his father will fall on him ; and tell him, finally, that I am his sister."

Rodrigo went forth from the Alcazar of Doña Urraca, followed by the Castilian cavaliers who had accompanied him. The people who still crowded the square, raging with fury against Don Sancho, became silent when they saw him, and respectfully opened a passage for him. Such was the esteem in which that brave cavalier was universally held.

Whilst going through the crowds he saw cavaliers and peasants, young men and old men, people indeed of all ranks and conditions, and he thought he saw amongst them the Count of Carrion and some others of the nobles who had been banished by Don Sancho.

Shortly after the Castilians had left the city, they turned their looks towards it, and saw the walls crowded with men, preparing for the defence ; they heard the sounds of the implements which they were employing to repair the fortifications.

"Alas !" then exclaimed Rodrigo, "how much Christian blood must flow by reason of the ambition of Don Sancho and the wickedness of those who have stirred up those discords !"

CHAPTER XLIV

THE SIEGE OF ZAMORA

RODRIGO returned, sad and downcast, to give the answer of Doña Urraca to Don Sancho, for he knew that ambition and anger had more effect on him than the voice of relationship and reason. The king was awaiting him impatiently, for he did not wish to delay the addition of Zamora to his dominions, either by arrangement or by force of arms. As soon, therefore, as Rodrigo appeared in his presence, he hastened to ask him what the reply of his sister was.

"Sire," answered the Cid, "the Infanta fears that, once having taken from her the city of Zamora, you would not give up to her the places which you offer in exchange for it."

"As God lives," interrupted Don Sancho in a rage, "I have

been very foolish to make peaceful proposals to one who has so little faith in my promises! But does my sister consent to yield up her territory to me?"

"On the contrary, she is resolved to defend it at all costs, for such is the love that her vassals have for her, that I myself have heard them swear that they would defend the inheritance of Doña Urraca, even were they all to die with their arms in their hands."

"Then they shall die, and Zamora shall be mine."

"Sire, give ears to reason; consider that you are about to fight against a weak woman, and, above all, that she is your sister."

"She, who rejects the peace which I offer her, is not such; she is not my sister who insults me by doubting my promises, who denies the justice which urges me on to recover the states which have been usurped from me, taking advantage of the wishes of a dying man, whose reason at the time was clouded by the near approach of death."

"Zamora is so strong, both in its walls and its defenders, that, before you can take it, Christian blood will swell the current of the Duero. Leave, sire, that paltry speck of earth with your sister, and increase your kingdom by other conquests, richer and more glorious: you are brave, and have good soldiers, go to the lands of the Moors and fight there; you can thus enlarge your dominions and gain honour, the worth of which no one can ever place in doubt."

"Rodrigo!" exclaimed Don Sancho, irritated, "you plead the cause of my sister with such warmth, that one might well imagine that you were one of her partisans."

"Pardon me, sire, if I depart somewhat from the respect which a vassal owes to his king; but it is my duty to tell you that all good cavaliers are bound to defend the weak, and I only comply with the demands of chivalry by pleading the cause of your sister."

"I wish to spare you the annoyance of being present at the humiliation of Doña Urraca, by causing you to absent yourself from Castile. Leave my kingdom, banished from it, within nine days; for, if up to the present you have been a good vassal, you are such no longer, since you oppose the wishes of your king, instead of assisting him to augment his states."

"It is my duty to obey your orders," replied the Cid, with humility.

And on the same day he set out from the Court, in order to

go into exile, followed by several cavaliers, who voluntarily went to share his disgrace. The lamentations of the Castilian people accompanied him everywhere, and all showed by their demeanour, and by their words, the indignation with which the conduct of Don Sancho filled them.

It was not long before he repented of his ingratitude; his conscience and the words of the nobles who were present at the Court made him see at once how unjust he had been towards the Cid, and what evils the banishment of such a good cavalier might bring upon Castile.

"Go," he said to Diego Ordoñez de Lara, "overtake De Vivar, and pray him, in my name, to return; tell him that I revoke the sentence of banishment, and that my greatest happiness will be to see him return to my side, free from all resentment."

Diego Ordoñez de Lara hastened to obey the king, and at two o'clock in the afternoon he overtook the Cid, to whom he delivered the message which the king had entrusted to him.

Rodrigo returned with the messenger; and the king, instead of giving him his hand to kiss, opened his arms to him, with all the marks of affection, and besought him to forget his unjust severity.

Nothing, however, could induce Don Sancho to abandon his determination of taking possession of Zamora, although many cavaliers, amongst whom De Lara was one of the most prominent, joined their requests and prayers to those of the Cid, that the Infanta might be left in peaceful possession of her city. Don Sancho enrolled a good army and all the war-like instruments necessary for the siege of a strongly fortified place, and set out for Zamora, accompanied by the Cid, who, however, was resolved not to break his promise or unsheath his sword against Doña Urraca.

Having arrived before Zamora, he again demanded its surrender by the Infanta; but the inhabitants, crowding on its walls, replied with loud cries and threats, that they were resolved to die rather than yield it up, and Doña Urraca answered to the same effect. Don Sancho then hastened to commence the siege, which, from the first day, was prosecuted with great ardour. It was not much to the taste of the soldiers of Don Sancho to be obliged to attack the inhabitants of Zamora, but the cries and insults such as usually are exchanged between besieged and besiegers made the Castilians forget the bad cause for which they were fighting, and they soon regarded the people of Zamora as enemies and nothing more.

The siege of Zamora was now definitely commenced.

The Castilians made an attempt to take the walls by assault; they were, however, repulsed with heroic valour, and the defenders of the city were filled with renewed confidence by this first triumph. The assaults were frequently repeated, and always with unhappy results for the besiegers, which intensified more and more their anger, and especially that of Don Sancho, who had not expected such a stubborn resistance from the weak woman who had opposed his ambitious plans.

The tent of Don Sancho was pitched on a hill, a few hundred paces distant from the city, opposite one of the large gates which afforded entrance into it. From it Zamora could be plainly seen, the walls and turrets of which were always crowded with men who defied those outside with shouts and waving of their arms. The Castilians attacked the walls three times during one night, and Don Sancho was at their front, in the most dangerous positions: all these attacks were, however, unavailing, for the walls were almost impregnable, both on account of their solidity and height, and of the great bravery of the people of Zamora. At sunrise on the day following that sanguinary night, Don Sancho was standing before his tent, gazing on the haughty city and thinking out new plans by which to take it. His cavaliers, heavy with sleep and fatigue, were lying in all directions throughout the camp; but he, Don Sancho the Strong, had not taken any repose, for the energy of his soul was superior to all physical weaknesses. His eyes remained constantly fixed on the proud city, which he would have wished to reduce to ruins by his glances. In his mind no project was so impossible that it could not be carried out, but the taking of Zamora now appeared to him, if not impossible, at least very difficult, as the flower of his warriors had perished at the foot of those walls, and in proportion as his soldiers became discouraged, the confidence of his opponents had increased. The proud monarch was thinking of the shame which would come upon him on the day when he should have to abandon the siege, and all the world would know that he had not been able to conquer a woman; at that moment he would have accepted death itself, if it were only accompanied by the surrender of Zamora.

When he was deeply immersed in those reflections, he heard loud sounds of voices in the direction of the city, and he saw, coming through the gate, which was opposite his camp, a number of cavaliers behind a man, who was advancing about forty paces in front of them. Don Sancho believed that the soldiers of Zamora were making a sortie for the purpose of attacking the camp, and the sentries thought the same. They began to spread the alarm amongst the Castilians, when they ceased suddenly, on seeing that only he who was in advance of the cavaliers came towards them, and that the others returned into the city through the postern by which they had issued from it.

"King Don Sancho!" a voice called out from the walls, just at the moment that this man was approaching the camp of the besiegers,—"King Don Sancho, beware of Bellido Dolfos, for he is going to your camp, plotting some treachery against you. If he deceives you, do not blame us, for Arias Gonzalo and all the honourable men of Zamora warn you."

Bellido heard that voice, and coming up, panting, he prostrated himself at the feet of the king, exclaiming, "Sire, do not believe those men of Zamora. Arias Gonzalo and his followers calumniate me, for they fear that you may conquer the city if you hearken to my words, for they know well that I can point out a position to you from which you can take Zamora."

Don Sancho held forth his hand to Bellido and raised him up kindly, saying to him—

"I believe you, and I should be considered stupid and an idiot if I were to trust in those who insult me and oppose my authority, instead of in him who comes to my camp to receive orders at my feet."

"Thanks, sire!" exclaimed Bellido. "Zamora shall be yours within two days if you let yourself be guided by my counsels, for not far from here there is a gate, through which you can enter it; but I fear that, having heard the accusation of treachery, which Arias has directed against me, you will distrust me, and that my desire to serve you shall be in vain."

"No, it shall not be in vain, Bellido; I do not distrust you, and if you wish that I should prove that to you, tell me where I must assault the walls, and you will see that, this very day, I shall fight there in front of my troops."

"Well, then, my lord, come with me, and just beyond that rampart, which you see to our right, I will show you the

Cambron Gate, through which you will be able to enter Zamora, provided you do not forget the instructions which I will give you."

"Let us not lose time, my good Bellido, let us now proceed to reconnoitre the gate of which you tell me, and this very day we shall enter through it, and humble the insolent pride of the defenders of Zamora."

Don Sancho mounted his horse, in a joyous state of mind, and prepared to set out with Bellido. The cavaliers who surrounded him, amongst whom were the Cid and Diego Ordoñez de Lara, were preparing to go with the king, but when Bellido noticed it he hastened to say to Don Sancho—

"My lord, it would much please me if you and I alone went, in order not to attract too much the attention of those in the town, for they would fortify at once the abandoned gate if they surmised that we were going to make an attack on them through it; but as you have just reasons for distrusting me, it is but right you should bring your cavaliers as a guard."

"Bellido," said Don Sancho, somewhat vexed at seeing that the deserter was not quite convinced that he trusted him, "I repeat to you that I have the fullest confidence in you, and I assure you of that on the word of a king and of a cavalier."

Then, turning to those who were preparing to accompany him, he added—

"Remain in the camp, for I do not need to be guarded."

"Sire," said the Cid, "we shall go with Bellido; either remain in your tent, or permit us to accompany you."

Don Sancho, however, did not pay any attention to the words of the Cid, but set out with Bellido, both of them proceeding cautiously around the walls of the town, and doing their utmost to conceal themselves amongst the trees, so as not to be seen by the enemy.

In a short time they were at a considerable distance from the royal camp, but not so far that the cavaliers, who had remained in it, lost them entirely to view.

Don Sancho was mounted on a spirited horse, the impetuosity of which he felt it rather difficult to keep in control; and when Bellido informed him that they were near the Cambron Gate, he advanced some paces, not being able to curb his impatience to see that road which he believed was to lead him to the goal which he so anxiously desired to reach. Bellido took advantage of that opportunity in order to carry out the hellish plot, for the purpose of which he had gone to the Castilian camp; he took a javelin in his hand, and darting it with all the force he could command, buried it in the breast of the unfortunate king. Don Sancho uttered a cry of agony, and seized the javelin, not so much to free himself from it as to use it against the assassin, but his strength was insufficient, as it was quickly leaving him, and it was only with very great difficulty that he could keep himself on his horse.

"Quick, my cavaliers!" cried the king, struggling with death, which was now stopping his breath; "pursue the traitor who has wounded me!"

The Cid hastened to mount Babieca in order to pursue the assassin, who was hurrying off to seek refuge in Zamora, whilst Don Diego Ordoñez de Lara and other cavaliers quickly proceeded to the spot where Don Sancho was lying. The Cid, in the haste with which he had mounted, had forgotten to buckle on his spurs, for which reason the horse could not be got to gallop as fast as the enraged cavalier desired. Bellido was rapidly nearing a postern, and although the Cid urged on Babieca by striking his flanks with his heels and the butt-end of his lance, he was not able to overtake in time the treacherous regicide, who arrived at the postern and entered it without any opposition. Rodrigo, blinded by anger, would have rushed into the town after him, but the gate was shut in his face, and the Cid exclaimed in despair—

"May God curse the knight who rides without spurs!"

Don Sancho had breathed his last just at that moment, and the loud lamentations and cries of fury, which were uttered by the Castilian cavaliers around him, rent the air, and filled with fear and dismay the entire camp of the besiegers.

Diego Ordoñez de Lara left the dead body of the king, weeping with grief and rage, and ascended a hill which commanded the town and sloped down towards it.

"People of Zamora!" he cried from it, with a voice of thunder, "you are all murderers and traitors, for you have received into the city Bellido Dolfos, who has assassinated Don Sancho, my good king and lord. Those are traitors who protect traitors, and as such I, Diego Ordoñez de Lara, brand you. As traitors and murderers I challenge you all, great and humble, men and women, living and dead, born and to be be born, the fish and the birds, the flocks and the waters, the plants and the trees, everything, in fine, that is in Zamora, and all shall be exterminated by our anger!"

Arias Gonzalo, who heard the challenge of De Lara, answered from the wall—

"If the people of Zamora were capable of committing the treacherous act of which you accuse them, De Lara, Arias Gonzalo and his sons would serve Moors rather than fight for Doña Urraca. Remember that we cautioned Don Sancho that Bellido was going to the royal camp for some treacherous purpose, and that caution frees us from any blame. But if you persist in your challenge, I accept it; for if I myself am too old to fight against you, I have sons, honourable and valiant, who will take my place."

"That is what I desire," said De Lara. "On the field of battle I shall prove that the people of Zamora are vile traitors and assassins."

Arias Gonzalo turned to those who crowded the ramparts of Zamora, and to those who filled the square which was opposite the palace of the Infanta, and said to them—

"Men, great and small, nobles and commoners, if there are any amongst you who have taken part in the treachery of Bellido Dolfos, speak out at once, for it would be better to go as an exile to Africa than to be vanquished on the field as a traitor and murderer."

"No, no!" cried out all, "may there be no salvation for our souls if we had any part in that act of treachery!"

"Hear, De Lara," cried Arias: "Zamora accepts the challenge which you have given to it, and Arias Gonzalo and his followers will fight against you."

On that same day many Castilians left the camp and set out for Castile, with the dead body of Don Sancho, which they brought to Oña, where it was interred.

On that same day the people of Zamora and the Castilians arranged the date, the place, and the conditions of the duel, for which the challenge had been given by De Lara.

On that day, also, active search was made in Zamora with the object of finding Bellido Dolfos, and delivering him up to the fury of the townspeople, who were enraged by his crime, even though it had been committed on their enemy.

The assassin, however, had succeeded in scaling the wall, which overhung the Duero, without being seen; and having done so, he hastened away from the town.

And finally, on that day, the Count of Carrion and his friends celebrated the death of Don Sancho by a banquet given in the lodgings of Don Suero.

CHAPTER XLV

IN WHICH IT IS PROVED THAT ONE CAN FIGHT WITHOUT CONQUERING OR BEING CONQUERED

SOME days after the death of the king, Don Sancho, great excitement could be noticed in Zamora and its neighbourhood. The cause of it was that, on a plain beside the Duero, the combat was about to take place which was pending between the Castilians and the men of Zamora, or, as their champions, between Diego Ordoñez de Lara on the one side, and Arias Gonzalo and his sons on the other.

Doña Urraca was in her palace, bathed in tears, on account of the death of her brother, on account of the accusation which De Lara had hurled against the people of Zamora, and on account of the risk which the sons of Arias ran, for she esteemed them very much, as, although very young, they were loyal and brave cavaliers. Just then Gonzalo appeared, followed by his sons Pero, Diego, Fernando, and another, whose name the Chronicles do not give.

The old man and the youths, throwing back their large cloaks, appeared clad in coats of mail, and they all knelt down at the feet of the Infanta, whose hand they kissed with marks of the greatest devotion and respect.

"Noble Infanta," said old Arias, "you know already that Don Diego Ordoñez de Lara, one of the best of the Castilian cavaliers, has challenged Zamora, and I have accepted the challenge in the name of your subjects. The lists are open, the judges of the combat are appointed, and the hour for it approaches. I would be the first to commence the fight if I did not know that my age makes me feeble, and that De Lara might be able to boast of the first triumph; my sons, however, whom you see here, are young, and moreover, skilful and brave combatants, and they will defend your honour and that of your subjects as long as they have blood in their veins. If all my sons should fall in the struggle, I shall then use, in the defence of your outraged honour, the little strength which yet remains in my arm."

Doña Urraca broke out into fresh tears on hearing old Arias.

"Do not weep, my lady," he said to her, "for good cavaliers are born to conquer or to die in the fight. My sons and I will go to the lists if you grant us your consent; give us no thanks for doing so, for it is the duty of good vassals to sacrifice their lives and their property for their sovereign " ."

"Go then, noble old man, and you also, loyal and brave youths; God will protect those who defend their honour, and He will have compassion on me, for if I should lose you I shall ever weep for you."

Arias Gonzalo and his sons left the palace of Doña Urraca and proceeded to the place of combat, accompanied by the prayers which all the inhabitants of Zamora offered to God, that He might give His divine aid to such good cavaliers.

An enormous multitude was collected around the lists; but there were not reflected on the faces of those present the animation and the joy which we have seen on those of the spectators of another combat, that between Rodrigo Diaz and Martin Gonzalez the Aragonian. Both the people of Zamora and the Castilians were filled with grief by the death of Don Sancho, for if the late king was ambitious and unjust when he let himself be led away by his haughty and irascible character, he was, on the other hand, valiant and passionately fond of difficult enterprises; such qualities constituted the chief merit of men in that specially warlike age.

Around the enclosure had been erected platforms for the ladies and the judges of the combat, and the latter already occupied their places when Arias and his sons received permission to defend her cause from Doña Urraca; the places reserved for the ladies were, however, unoccupied. That combat did not awaken female curiosity, on account of the way their minds were affected by the disastrous death of the brave King of Castile, and by the infamous accusation which weighed upon the people of Zamora. At the same moment, also, Arias, with his sons and Don Diego Ordoñez de Lara, arrived in the lists; he was accompanied, as his second, by Martin Antolinez, in the absence of the Cid, who had departed from Zamora, going with the corpse of Don Sancho to Oña. He was desirous of accompanying his king to his last dwelling-place, and of fulfilling his promise not to take any part against the inhabitants of Zamora. When the spectators saw those honoured and brave cavaliers, they broke out either in lamentation or in maledictions on the treacherous regicide, on account of whose crime such esteemed combatants had to risk their lives.

All the preliminaries having been arranged and the ground

measured by those appointed for that purpose, Pero Arias appeared at one end of the lists, and Diego Ordoñez de Lara at the other. Both were mounted on fiery chargers, were clad with shining armour, were girt with swords, and were provided with good shields and strong lances.

The judges gave the signal to the heralds, and they sounded their trumpets. On hearing the first blast, the champions prepared for the charge, and scarcely did they hear the second when they drove their spurs into the flanks of their horses, which rushed forward as swift as lightning. The meeting of the combatants was terrible; the lances, however, struck the shields, and, glancing off them, left the champions uninjured. They then made ready for the second charge, and starting with even greater speed than in the first, the lance of De Lara pierced the helmet of Pero Arias, who felt himself seriously wounded in the head. The champion of Zamora reeled on his saddle, but, holding on by the mane of his horse, he had strength enough to deal a furious blow at his enemy. The sight of Pero Arias was dimmed by the blood which flowed over his face, and, for that reason, his lance only wounded the horse of De Lara; the young man then fell to the ground, breathing his last.

A cry of lamentation was heard on all sides, and many of the spectators burst into weeping. Diego Ordoñez brandished his lance in the air and cried with a voice of thunder—

"Woe to the people of Zamora! Arias Gonzalo, send out another son, for the first is settled with!"

Diego, the second son of Arias, went into the lists when the body of his brother was removed, and when De Lara had mounted a fresh horse, instead of that which had been badly wounded by the lance of Pero. The cuirass of Diego Arias was strong, but the lance of Diego Ordoñez struck it with such force, that it went through it, and came out, with its point so abundantly covered with blood, that the shaft and pennon were stained by it. Diego Arias, mortally wounded in the breast, fell to the ground, like an inert mass, and fresh cries of grief and fresh wailings accompanied the death of the second champion of Zamora.

De Lara again brandished his bloodstained lance and cried out—

"Woe to the people of Zamora! Send out another son, good Arias, for Diego's fighting days are over."

Fernando Arias was awaiting the blessing of his father

before proceeding to the lists, when the old man said to him—

"My son, go fight for our honour, as a good cavalier should: imitate your brothers and avenge their deaths, washing off at the same time the stain of treachery, which De Lara has cast upon us."

"Father," replied the young man, "do not insult me by reminding me of my duty; I trust in God and in my arm that Zamora and my brothers shall be avenged."

And Fernando Arias went out to the lists, anxious to pierce with his lance Diego Ordoñez, who seemed to wish to devour him with his furious glances.

The champions rushed on each other with a fury seldom witnessed, and the lance of Fernando entered the shoulder of Diego; he, however, far from losing courage on account of the intense pain which the wound must have caused him, hastened to charge again, and aiming at his adversary's head, carried off his helmet, and wounded him, though but slightly. Fernando, when he felt himself wounded, directed his lance against De Lara, blind with rage and desperation; he, however, only succeeded in wounding the horse.

The animal, feeling the blade of the lance of Fernando in its neck, gave a great jump, which disconcerted its rider, then, darting off, Diego not being able to control it, jumped over the barrier, trampling down the crowd which was outside.

The judges ordered the herald to give the signal that the combat was suspended, for according to the laws regulating the duel the cavalier who quitted the lists was considered conquered.

Don Diego de Lara wished to resume the fight, for he said that his horse had crossed the barrier, he not having been able to control it; but the judges did not permit it, and began to argue over that unforeseen occurrence, without being able to come to any decision.

Whilst the judges were deliberating, Arias Gonzalo said to De Lara, not having sufficient mastery over himself to repress his anger and the grief which he experienced on account of the loss of his two sons—

"You are more arrogant than courageous, De Lara. You have conquered beardless youths; but I maintain that you could not overcome men, such as I formerly was."

De Lara replied, without becoming irritated—

"Good Arias, I could well recount to you acts of valour,

which would contradict your words; but to prove my prowess it needs only to say that I have fought with your sons and have vanquished them."

The old man recognised the fact that grief had made him discourteous, and he could not but appreciate the moderation of the Castilian who paid back insults with flattery. He was about to hold out his hand to De Lara, but he restrained himself when he saw that the judges were about to announce their decision. This is how the heralds made it public :—

"The judges of the combat declare that both the champions of Castile and of Zamora have acted as good and true men in this contest, for if the Castilian champion quitted the lists, it was not of his own election, but through the fault of his horse. Both sides should consider themselves victors—the Castilians satisfied, and Zamora freed from the charge of treachery which was imputed to it."

This decision changed the lamentations and the consternation of the crowds of spectators into joyous cheers ; and Arias Gonzalo extended his hand to De Lara, and said to him—

"You have taken from me two sons, give me your friendship in exchange for them, as I consider it as valuable as the short tenure of life which remains to me."

"My friendship and my arms I give to you, honoured Arias," replied Don Diego, pressing the old man to his breast.

Some hours after the Castilians raised the siege of Zamora, and Doña Urraca, by the advice of Arias and other nobles of the city, wrote to Don Alfonso, shedding at the same time copious tears, to inform him of the death of his brother, and to advise him to take immediate steps to place his father's crown upon his head, before ambitions could break loose, and rival factions inundate the country with blood.

Eight days afterwards, Don Alfonso arrived in Leon, and again took possession of the kingdom which his brother had usurped from him ; the kingdom of Galicia then spontaneously placed itself under his sway, for no one desired the liberty of Don Garcia, who was detested on account of his ungovernable, tyrannical, and foolish character. He was then preparing to set out for Burgos, to take possession of the kingdom of Castile, but when this became known, the Castilian grandees assembled together, at the earnest request of Rodrigo Diaz, who thus addressed them :—

"I have always considered Don Alfonso an honourable

man, and Castile by right belongs to him; but as connivance in the death of Don Sancho can be attributed to no one with greater probability than to him, I am of opinion that the Castilian people should demand an oath from him that he had no part whatever in the treacherous crime of Bellido Dolfos. Castile is held in the highest honour, and for that very reason it has a right to know if he is an honourable man, whom it proclaims its lord and king. It is necessary, then, that Don Alfonso should swear that he had no part in the death of his brother."

All the nobles approved of the views of the Cid, but all trembled at the idea of the vexation which the demand of an oath, that implied a highly offensive suspicion, would cause to Don Alfonso.

"And who will dare to draw down upon himself the indignation of Don Alfonso by exacting such an oath from him?" many asked.

"I!" answered the Cid, with generous pride. "In addition to being a subject of Don Alfonso, I am a Castilian and a cavalier, and it is my duty to risk death, in order to preserve immaculate the honour of my native land. I have always looked upon Don Alfonso as an honourable and good man; but I also know to what extent men are blinded by ambition and the thirst for vengeance. I would venture to swear by all that I love most in the world that it was the Count of Carrion, with his partisans, whom I saw at the time at Zamora, that spurred on Bellido to assassinate Don Sancho; but how can I have complete confidence that they were not, beforehand, instigated by Don Alfonso, especially when Doña Urraca reminded me, before the commencement of the siege of Zamora, that Don Alfonso was free, and that, if she was too powerless to fight face to face with Don Sancho, daggers could reach where swords could not avail? Let Don Alfonso come to Castile; I shall exact the oath from him, and when he shall have taken it, I shall be the first to kneel before him, in acknowledgment of the vasalage which I owe him. The land which was ruled over by the Count Fernan Gonzalez, and by Don Fernando the Great, must only have as its king a man as loyal and honourable as they were."

In a short time the resolve of the Cid had spread through Burgos, and even through the entire of Castile, and this gained for him, in the eyes of all the Castilians, a title to their love, as great as that which he had ever gained by the most glorious of his triumphs on battlefields. On the same day on which he had arranged with the nobles to demand the oath from Don Alfonso, the brave and loyal cavalier was surrounded by his family, delivering himself up to domestic happiness, which for him was the sweetests of delights. Rodrigo was born in an age when, in order to be a good son, a good husband, and a good father, it was also necessary that a man should be a good soldier; for the latter quality figured amongst the greatest virtues. For that reason he passed the greater portion of his life in the din of combats; but how can it be conceived that a man could prefer the barbarous charms of war to the sweetnesses of domestic peace, who always appears in history with the names of his spouse and of his daughters on his lips, weeping when separating from them, and loading with gifts and affection those who protected his Ximena, his Sol, and his Elvira? A Castilian artist, an enthusiastic admirer of the Cid, the popular hero of Castile, has painted Rodrigo Diaz in the following manner: the Cid has his left arm thrown around the necks of Sol and Elvira, and his right arm around that of Ximena; from his belt hangs his formidable sword, and before them stands Babieca, ready caparisoned to set out for the battlefield.

That picture is the complete history of the Cid Campeador. It is as interesting as the one which Rodrigo Diaz and his family presented on the day which we have mentioned. It was a beautiful evening in spring: the background of the enchanting picture was formed by the modest garden belonging to the mansion, in Burgos, of the lords of Vivar. Rodrigo was seated under a tree covered with foliage, and was caressing a golden-haired child, that was jumping on his knees, whose name also was Rodrigo, and was his first-born. By his side were Ximena, Teresa, Nuna, Lambra, and Mayor, occupied with work suited to their sex; opposite was the venerable Diego Lainez, who had been entertaining all of them, for a considerable time, with a curious story of chivalry, connected with one of his ancestors; and finally, was to be seen Gil, the Moorish boy, adopted by Rodrigo in the mountains of Oca, who was now approaching manhood, and was the idol of the family, by reason of his discretion, his beauty, and the generous instincts which he displayed.

"It is good," said Diego, "that the remembrance of deeds, such as those which I have just related, should pass down from father to son; that is why I have often recounted to you

those of Lain Calvo, who was my father. Would to God that
we had in Castile some that were capable of chronicling the
heroic deeds of those who wielded lance and sword, but in
that we are less fortunate than the Greeks and Romans."

"You are right," replied Rodrigo. "Oral tradition easily
distorts real facts, and it is a sad thing that the deeds of a
loyal and valiant age of chivalry should traverse the centuries,
confided to the folly of the ignorant crowd."

"Then it must not be the ignorant multitude that shall
perpetuate your brave deeds; if God permits me to become
a man!" exclaimed Gil, he who afterwards composed the
Chronicle of the famous cavalier, Rodrigo Diaz de Vivar.

"Rejoice, O Cesar, for you have already your Suetonius, to
write your history," said the old man, laughing, and all the
others joined with him.

"Good Gil," said Rodrigo, "wait until we return to Vivar,
and there I will teach you, if not how to write histories of
cavaliers, at least how cavaliers should act, so that their
memory may never die."

"And when shall we return to Vivar?" asked Ximena;
"when, Rodrigo, will you forget arms, in order to consecrate
yourself entirely to our love?"

"It appears to me that that day is not very distant,"
answered Rodrigo. "Don Alfonso is about to assume the
crown of Castile; Castile and Leon will then form but one
kingdom, and peace will be the result of the union of both
crowns. The day on which they hang up banners in Castile,
to honour Don Alfonso VI., will be that on which we shall
leave the Court and return to Vivar, where all of us will enjoy
the tranquillity which the anxieties of courts banish."

CHAPTER XLVI

THE OATH IN SANTA GADEA

THERE is unusual excitement in Burgos; very many persons
crowd in from the neighbouring villages on all sides of the
city, and streets and squares are thronged by the crowds, on
whose visages both fear and curiosity are expressed. The

place, however, where the crush is greatest, is outside the city, in the direction of the Leon road; many thousands of people of all ages and conditions hasten thither, and direct their looks, with avidity, towards a road which, at about half-an-hour's walk from the city, becomes lost on the summit of a hill, which limits the horizon. Whom do those people of Burgos expect? Let us see if, amongst the crowds, we can find any of our old acquaintances, who may be able to fully satisfy our curiosity. Men and women, nobles, peasants, and townspeople are everywhere, in the centre of the road, and on the raised banks beside it, on the trees and on the adjacent hills, all impatient, and all weary already of waiting; however, we see no one that we know, not even the peasant from Barbadillo, whose curiosity is as proverbial in Burgos as that of his friend Iñigo, and whose conjugal affairs amuse so much the townspeople, since the day they saw him disown his wife at the door of the mansion of the lords of Vivar. But is not that his wife,—the wife of Bartolo,—that handsome peasant woman, who is walking with a young man on the summit of the low hill? Yes, it is she. And is not Alvar the youth who is in such good humour, and who is laughing with her? It is Alvar, no doubt of that. She does not now seem disposed to refuse, with blows, as she used to do at the smithy of Iñigo, the flowers which the daring page presented to her.

"It is a long time now," said Alvar, "that I sigh for you and bear the insults of your husband, and you have not rewarded me even with a little embrace! Tyrant! Does a lover, as faithful as I have been, merit such poor pay? Does my love, perchance, displease you?"

"I only wish I were not a married woman, as you are such a gentle youth, and not a fool like my husband; but, as long as Bartolo lives, your efforts will be in vain, and those also of the squire, Fernan, who makes love to me, as well as you."

"Accursed be my ill fortune!" said Alvar, stamping on the ground. "It is on account of that Fernan, and not on account of your husband, that you respond so badly to my love."

"I respond to Fernan just the same as to you."

"So, you are pleased with his graces?"

"Why should not his please me as much as yours?"

"But don't mine please you? Reward me, if it is so."

"But those of Fernan merit an equal reward."

"Oh, how unfortunate I am with the women!" said Alvar,

despairing of ever seeing his love requited by the peasant woman.

Whilst she and the page were thus conversing in a field beside the road, Bartolo himself was struggling to make his way through the crowd, looking anxiously in all directions, as if he were seeking someone.

"Oh, Señor Bartolo, come here, as I have great news for you!" cried out a man, who was resisting the rushing of the waves, formed by the multitude, firmly planted against the trunk of a tree. That man was the soldier who, on a former occasion, had so courteously explained to him what was going on between the servitors of the Cid; but Bartolo either did not hear him, or paid no attention to his words.

"Señor peasant, come here, and I shall relate strange news to you," persisted the soldier.

"I don't want your news," replied Bartolo at last. "I am looking for my wife. The jade has escaped from my house, and I swear that, if I catch her, she'll have to bear more wood than a miller's ass "—

"But what I have to tell you is about your wife."

"About my wife? Where is the slut?"

"Look at her over there in the field, amusing herself with one of her lovers."

"San Pedro de Cardeña, preserve me!" exclaimed the peasant, looking in the direction which the soldier had pointed out to him.

"Ha, ha, ha! I stick to what I always said—that is, that women are no great things," said the soldier, laughing maliciously.

"I swear by all that's holy!" muttered the rustic, breaking suddenly through the crowd in the direction of the hill. "My wife was a simpleton in Barbadillo, but no person ever said a word against her honour. A curse on this city and all the news that can be got out of it! Since I came to Burgos I have never had an easy day. Treacherous women! my wife is a deceiver! I swear that, this very day, she shall return to Barbadillo, with more blows than she has hairs on her head, and neither she nor I shall ever leave the village again."

At last he arrived at the little hill, and making a short circuit, in order to take at the rear his wife and the page, who were still talking, to all appearance, very confidentially, he fell suddenly on them, and with a stick, which he had provided himself with, he began to belabour them furiously, his wife specially. Alvar only received one good stroke, for he managed to escape through the crowd as soon as he felt the peasant's stick on his back.

"I swear I'll kill you, traitress!" exclaimed Bartolo, without ceasing to chastise his wife.

"Woe is me, woe is me! this brute of a husband will kill me!" cried out the peasant woman. "Is there no one to defend me against the savage?"

"You barbarian!" cried the surrounding people, "do not maltreat a defenceless woman in such a way."

"I'll kill her, she is a jade!" replied Bartolo. And seizing his wife by one arm, he went off, dragging her along and exclaiming—

"To Barbadillo, to Barbadillo! May Heaven's curse fall on cities!"

This incident had amused the impatient crowd for a short time; but, as soon as it terminated, all turned their gazes again towards the hill on which the Leon road was lost to view.

"If Don Alfonso learned that no banners would be hung out in his honour until he takes the oath," said one of the bystanders, "he has certainly stopped on his way to raise men to accompany him, and aid him in imposing his will on the Castilians."

"What Don Alfonso has to do," replied another, "is to swear, if he can do so with a good conscience; if not, he must only rest content with the kingdom of Leon which he already possesses, for honourable men will not be wanting to govern Castile, as in the time of the Judges."

"There is one thing certain, and that is, if Don Alfonso tries to put down Castile by force, he engages in a bad business; and let him beware lest he have neither one kingdom nor the other."

"God's anger! If the Cid raises his Green Standard and cries, 'Castilians! we are honourable, and he who governs us must also be honourable; we shall have no king suspected of having shed his brother's blood. Rise with me to defend the honour of our native land!' you will then see how all Castile will spring up and seize on the kingdom of Leon, and Don Alfonso will have to go and demand hospitality from the Moors."

"I believe that he will not refuse to take the oath, for it is impossible that he can have had any part in the death of Don Sancho. Don Alfonso was always a good cavalier; he may have wanted prudence, he may have lent his ears to evil councillors, he may have been weak, but fratricide—I can't believe that."

"What I believe, and what all believe, is that he will reject the oath, not on account of his conscience, but through pride; for, you see, the great always resent having conditions imposed on them by their inferiors."

"And especially when those conditions imply so infamous a suspicion as fratricide. But listen! What cries are those which arise? Is Don Alfonso approaching already? It must be, for all the people are crowding up on the hill."

Indeed, a body of men had been seen on the eminence which bounded the horizon, and on seeing them, the multitude became agitated, a prolonged murmur arose, and the people who were scattered in all directions began to make their way towards the main road. The strangers, who were in reality Don Alfonso and about a hundred horsemen, who formed his escort, were rapidly nearing Burgos. At last they came to the place where the crowds were awaiting them, and which then accompanied them, moving on at both sides of the road. They were about one hundred paces from the city, when, at its gate, the Castilian nobles appeared, bearing the Standard of Castile, veiled with black gauze. The nobles made a sign to Don Alfonso to halt, which he and his followers did: Rodrigo Diaz then advanced, and, having saluted, addressed Don Alfonso, not as a king but as a cavalier.

"Don Alfonso!" he said to him, "you are heir to the kingdom of Castile, and no person has any intention of disputing your rights. Castile is an honourable land, which always venerated and defended its sovereigns; but how can it venerate and defend them if it has not the fullest faith in their honour? We have always, in Castile, looked upon you as good and honourable; but now an infamous suspicion weighs upon you, and it is necessary to destroy it before this country, always loyal, raises its standards for you. You know already that the hand of an assassin deprived your brother of life at the siege of Zamora; although your antecedents justify you, circumstances cast upon you a terrible suspicion, which never should rest on him who wears a crown and who is called upon to rule an honourable and generous people. Well, then, in order that Castile may love and respect you, in order that the world may know that he who occupies the throne of Don Fernando the Great is worthy to occupy it, you must swear in

Santa Gadea, with your hand on the holy Gospels, that you had no part in the death of Don Sancho."

Indignation had been colouring the visage of Don Alfonso whilst the Cid was thus speaking, and all the spectators, except Rodrigo, were trembling, seeing that he was about to burst out into anger.

"God's justice!" he then exclaimed, "who is it that dares to speak thus to me? Who is it that dares to demand of me this shameful oath?"

"Rodrigo Diaz de Vivar!" answered the Cid, not with haughty insolence, but respectfully and firmly.

"I would renounce, not only the kingdom of Castile, but even the empire of the entire world, rather than submit to the humiliation which you propose to me, Cid! Does any good cavalier suspect my loyalty to such a degree that he can suppose me to be an accomplice in the death of my brother? I cast in your face, and in the faces of all who think as you do, the infamy with which you desire to sully me!"

"Sire," replied the Cid, "by refusing to take the oath you afford fresh motives to those who suspect you"—

"Well, then," exclaimed Don Alfonso, interrupting Rodrigo, "let us get on to the church. But woe to those who insult me! Woe to those who dare to humiliate me, in a way that a king was never before humiliated!"

"After the oath," humbly replied Rodrigo, "you will be my king, and it will be in your power to dispose of my life and of my property as it may seem well to you; now, however, I willingly risk both in order to comply with the dictates of my conscience and of my honour."

Castilians and Leonese then proceeded to the Church of Santa Gadea, around the gates of which thronged the multitude, scarce able to repress the admiration with which they were filled by the abnegation and heroic firmness of the Cid.

He and Don Alfonso approached the altar, at the foot of which the prince knelt down, placing his hand on the Book of the Evangelists, which Rodrigo supported on his, whilst Don Diego Ordoñez de Lara held the Standard of Castile at some distance, and all the nobles, wondering and timorous at the same time, contemplated the imposing scene. The populace, who crowded up to the entrance of the church, endeavouring to see what was taking place within it, kept silence, anxious to hear the oath of the prince, for whom, a moment after, they were about to raise their standards.

"Don Alfonso," said the Cid in a loud voice, "do you swear, on the holy Evangelists, that you had no part in the death of Don Sancho, your brother?"

"Yes, I swear it!" answered Don Alfonso.

"If you swear truly, may you be always happy and prosperous on this earth, and may you be safe from the torments of hell; but if your oath is false, may rustics of the Asturias of Oviedo kill you, and not those of Castile; may you die by shepherds' crooks and not by lances; may those who kill you be such as wear coarse sandals, and ride on asses, instead of mules or horses; may you meet your death in fields, and not in towns or villages; may your heart be dragged out through your left side; and may you descend to hell, to suffer there for ever!"

"Thus let it be," replied Don Alfonso, without, however, concealing the irritation which the daring of the Cid caused him.

Rodrigo then placed the Book of the Evangelists upon the altar, and when Don Alfonso arose, he bent his knee before him and kissed his hand; all the nobles who were present imitated him.

Don Diego Ordoñez de Lara then pulled off the black gauze that had veiled the Standard, and went out with it to the porch of the cathedral, where he cried out three times—

"Castile for Don Alfonso!"

The populace repeated that cry with joy and enthusiasm, and in all quarters of the city standards were raised and proclamations issued, announcing that the throne of Castile was now occupied.

How different was the spectacle which Burgos offered on that day, compared with that on the preceding one, when all was uncertainty as to the future, sadness and mourning; now there were strong hopes of a prosperous, peaceful, just, and powerful reign; for Castile would be a large and powerful kingdom, as it had been in the time of Fernando the Great, and not limited and surrounded by rival states, as it was under Sancho II.

On account of that propitious event, the Castilian people were preparing to give themselves up to joyous festivities; enemy was disposed to hold out his hand to enemy, the rich to mitigate the hardships of the poor, and the king to grant liberal gifts to both nobles and civilians.

The rainbow, rich with brilliant hues, showed itself after the storm, and filled with gladness the souls of all the good Castilians.

CHAPTER XLVII

IN WHICH THIS BOOK ENDS, PROVING THAT GOD GIVES IN THIS WORLD, BOTH TO THE GOOD AND TO THE BAD, A SAMPLE OF THE CLOTH WHICH THEY SHALL WEAR IN THE OTHER WORLD.

SOME days have passed since the Castilian people raised their standards for Don Alfonso VI.

It is the morning of St. John's Day. The sky is azure, and the stars which sprinkled it are gradually disappearing, for the brightness which precedes the rising sun is beginning to illumine the east; the breeze is so gentle that the leaves of the trees, in which the birds sing, scarcely stir, and the golden corn, amid which is heard the plaintive cooing of the turtle-doves, is also motionless. That light breeze has, however, sufficient force to extract the perfumes from the thyme and hundreds of other herbs and flowers, and to bear them on its wings, filling the air with sweetness. The white, misty clouds which veiled the river Carrion, like a web of white and transparent gauze spread over the plain, had entirely disappeared, and the morning light was reflected from the tranquil surface of the stream, like the light of a lamp from a string of diamonds. What a beautiful sight the banks of the Carrion present! Here, the ripe corn, the colour of which shows that the golden dreams of the labourers are realised; there, trees, the branches of which are bent to the ground by the luscious fruits, as if they wished to cheer the passer-by with their sweetness and perfume; farther on, a meadow covered with flowers, the various colours of which are made still more varied by the mild breeze, as it gently agitates them whilst passing along; and finally, a hundred white villages scattered over the plain, like flocks of pigeons which have alighted on the cornfields. Singing is heard in all directions, and a thousand joyful cries fill the air. Who are those that walk across the plain, singing and shouting? Are they the young men and women of Carrion, going to gather vervain on the banks of the river? How is it that, so early, white columns of smoke arise from the houses scattered over the plain? How beautiful is St. John's morning shortly after sunrise!

The sun ascends, shooting torrents of light upon the slopes

and inundating with splendour the plain of Carrion, already filled with flowers and perfumes, and to the shouts and songs of the multitude are united the peals of the bells of the town, in which some festival, much above ordinary ones, is about to take place. But those bells which cheer up the inhabitants of the town and of the plain are not those of the Virgin of Belen, or those of Santa Maria del Camino; they are those of a new church which rises to the east of the town, of a church which did not exist on the night during which the count's castle was devoured by the flames; the blackened walls of which, half-destroyed, rise on the eminence which looks down on the town,

Immense crowds pour indeed across the plain from all quarters. Men and women, people on foot and on horses, peasants and nobles. Let us listen to the conversations of some of those who flock to that festival, the object of which is still unknown to us.

"By the soul of Beelzebub, even at the battle of the Oca Mountains there was not such a multitude as there is to-day on the plain of Carrion!" exclaims a dark-complexioned man, who is amid a group of men and women, standing on an eminence beside the Burgos road, looking down on the plain.

By my life that man is Fernan, mounted on Overo, although just now he does not carry the accoutrements of a squire! The woman who is at his side, mounted on a donkey, is Mayor, and in the same group are other persons, not unknown to us: for instance, Martin Vengador, Rui-Venablos, and Beatrice, who are riding, the latter on an ass, like Mayor, and the men on horses.

Let us listen to Fernan, who, to judge by the attention which the bystanders are bestowing on him, must be intimately acquainted with everything concerning those festivities.

"The tournament which is to take place on the plain of Carrion," he says, "will be the most famous that has ever been seen or heard of in Spain. They are going to celebrate, in magnificent style, the coronation of Don Alfonso, as King of Castile and Leon."

"Can you tell me, friend," asked a bystander, "why Don Alfonso has taken it into his head to have those famous festivities on the plain of Carrion instead of in Leon or Burgos?"

"I will tell you, brother," replied Fernan; "as Carrion

stands in the centre of the two kingdoms, now united again, as in the time of Don Fernando, and as the country is so beautiful and level, Don Alfonso has desired to celebrate the festivities in a place to which it is an easy journey for both Castilians and Leonese."

"And do you know who are to take part in the jousts?"

"The most noble cavaliers of Leon and Castile, and it is even said that the king, Don Alfonso, will break a lance with De Lara, the Campeador, and other distinguished cavaliers."

"Those festivities, then, will be worth seeing."

"Of course they will; there will be ring, wand, and other games, and finally a passage-at-arms, which Guillen of the Standard will defend, not alone to celebrate the coronation of Don Alfonso, but also to celebrate his own marriage."

"And to whom is that youth going to be married?"

"This very day he marries the Infanta of Carrion, in the convent which Doña Teresa built at her own expense for the nuns of San Zoil, who are going to it to-day. She did that to repay the hospitality which she received from them on the night that Guillen rescued her from the burning castle. The Campeador and his wife, Doña Teresa, my lord and lady, will give them away, and for that purpose they are in Carrion since yesterday. Just listen how the bells of San Zoil are pealing! I would lay a wager that at this very moment they are uniting for ever the hero of the Standard with the Infanta."

"The marriage of Doña Teresa and Guillen must be great happiness for them; people say that they love each other very much."

"Brother, there is one here—ay, more than one—who can speak with certainty regarding such happiness. This honoured lady, who is beside me on the donkey, and I have got married, for love only, a few days ago, and also that brave youth and the young woman, over there, who are talking so lovingly to each other."

"I wish joy to you all, for you must be happy when you love so sincerely."

"We love each other, and are now well off, for the lords of Vivar, our masters—may God bless and prosper them!— have given us very rich gifts."

"It does not astonish me that the Campeador has been liberal to his servitors, for Don Alfonso has given a good example to all. It is said that the favours which the king has bestowed are enormous; and, being so, I am surprised that he has not shown himself indulgent also towards those lords whom Don Sancho exiled, by pardoning them and allowing them to return."

"Far from doing that, he has taken their estates from them, in order to bestow them on their next-of-kin; and he has imposed the penalty of death on them if they should set foot in Castile or Leon. And, by my soul, Don Alfonso has done well, for those counts deserve it richly. The king has strong suspicions—and those also who are not kings—that those accursed counts, and especially De Carrion, were the persons who paid Bellido to assassinate the brave Don Sancho."

Those who were thus talking had now descended to the plain; they ceased their conversation, for the crowds that were about them absorbed their attention, presenting to them a thousand different scenes. A minute afterwards they were amid the animated multitude, and joined in the general rejoicings.

An hour after, King Alfonso, accompanied by Castilian and Leonese nobles, arrived on the centre of the plain; the platforms which had been erected, as if by magic, were occupied by a thousand noble and beautiful women, and the games were commencing to the sounds of numerous musical instruments, the sounds of which filled the air and increased the enjoyment of all the spectators.

Whilst the plain, rich with light, harmony, flowers, and happiness, offered such enchanting scenes to the sight, another scene, entirely different, was being enacted in a wood filled with briars and ancient chestnut trees, situated on the slope of one of the hills which bound the plain, and at a short distance from the road.

About fifty men were in it, some tranquilly sleeping, stretched on the grass, others viewing with delight the magnificent spectacle which was offered by the plain, which from that point could be seen to its fullest extent; and others still, under the spreading branches of the trees, watching the approaches to the wood.

These men were bandits; they were Juan Centellos and his band, whom the Salvadores were pursuing in vain; for they laughed at their efforts and baffled them, sometimes by their cleverness and sometimes by means of the money which they possessed, especially since they had sacked and burned the Castle of Carrion.

Juan Centellos and another bandit, who seemed to be his

second in command, began to speak in a low voice, as soon as the former had sent away a peasant, who, shortly before, had entered the wood and conversed with Juan for a few minutes.

" Have we good news ? " the lieutenant asked.

" The spy has indeed brought good news from Carrion," answered Centellos. " The bird will soon fly into the net."

" How so, comrade ? Tell me all about it."

" Don Suero has taken refuge in an ancient castle which he possesses in Senra, a solitary valley in the Asturias, despairing of being able to conquer his opponents there, and fearful of dying on the gallows if he sets foot in Castile or Leon. It appears that, desirous of having someone to amuse him in his solitude, he sent to seek out, by means of Bellido, that wench whom we found in the castle, but did not kill, as we did not wish to stain our hands with the blood of a woman ; and this very day Bellido is to pass along here with her."

" Anger of hell ! what a fortunate day we shall have if that traitor, who sold the band of the Vengador, falls into our hands ! We also will celebrate the coronation of Don Alfonso, and will not leave it altogether to those down below on the plain."

" Bellido shall not escape us on this occasion, as he did on that night some time ago. I once swore to hang him on the ramparts of the Castle of Carrion, in which, through his vile treachery, so many of our comrades perished ; and if, as I hope, we capture him to-day, he shall appear to-morrow as a scarecrow on the blackened walls of the burned edifice. We must keep our eyes open, comrades, for I have been told that the Salvadores are in this neighbourhood ; doubtless to see to the safety of all those who have come to take part in the festivities."

The officers of the band had got thus far in their conversation when they were interrupted by a whistle, which was a perfect imitation of that of a blackbird.

" People are approaching, and the lookouts are giving the signal," said Juan Centellos ; and he added, looking towards the road, " It is a man who is carrying a woman behind him on his horse. May the demon carry me off if it is not he of whom we are in search ! To the road, to the road, comrades ! "

And Juan Centellos and some of his men took up their arms and hurried in the direction of the road.

The man indeed whom they had seen was Bellido Dolfos

and the woman he was carrying behind him on the horse was Sancha, the daughter of the blind lute-player, the mistress of Don Suero.

Bellido put spurs to his horse, but the bandits barred his way. He then drew his sword, resolved to defend himself obstinately. Vain, however, were all his endeavours, for in a few moments he was disarmed by the bandits and dragged, together with Sancha, into the wood of chestnut trees.

Bellido indeed deserved to suffer on earth all the tortures of hell, and the wretched woman, who accompanied him, was not worthy of compassion, for she had become degraded to that extent that she avoided her blind father, who was seeking her all over the country; and it was she also who had aided Don Suero and the Count of Cabra to allure the Cid and his escort, when going to the Cortes of Leon, into the ambush, where, almost by a miracle, their lives were preserved; notwithstanding all this, it is repugnant to us to mention the cruelties of which they, especially Bellido Dolfos, were the victims when they fell into the hands of the bandits.

"Comrades," said Juan Centellos to the members of his band, "let this woman go and bring the news to her noble lover; we shall take good care of Bellido."

The bandits then seized on the traitor and dragged him to a very large chestnut tree, the trunk of which was hollow, and into which a man could enter through an aperture which was almost on a level with the ground. They shoved him into the hollow trunk notwithstanding the furious resistance which he made to avoid it; they then closed up the hole with a large flat stone which they carried to it, and against this they placed others, so that no man's strength, exerted from within, could push them away.

It was but a short time since they had restored freedom to Sancha, when the whistle of the blackbird was again heard, and those who were watching the approaches to the wood, hastened to descend from the trees, crying out—

"The Salvadores! the Salvadores are approaching!"

All the bandits made preparations to take to flight, for, indeed, a large body of Salvadores was coming from the direction towards which Sancha had gone.

"Let us kill Bellido before we go!" cried several, and they were about to remove the stones which closed the entrance into the trunk of the chestnut tree.

"Let no one touch those stones!" said Juan Centellos; and

he added, with a sinister smile, "I should like Bellido to get accustomed to fire before he goes to hell."

He then applied a burning torch to the bushes and brambles which grew round the chestnut tree, and cried—

"Now, comrades, let us get away!"

The bandits dispersed themselves through the wood, endeavouring to get to the rear of the Salvadores, for in that direction the ground was more broken and the trees closer together. The Salvadores were following the principal body, composed of Juan Centellos and about twenty of his men.

"Comrades," said their chief to those bandits, halting on an eminence, now almost safe from his pursuers, "through a foolish act we were near falling into the hands of our enemies, for it was a great piece of stupidity to let the companion of Bellido go free; it was she, doubtless, who gave information to the Salvadores. But—justice of God! Is it not she who is walking along the road down there?"

"Yes, yes, it is she!" cried all the bandits.

"My good crossbow," said Juan, descending towards the road, "aid my revenge as thou hast always aided it!"

The leader of the bandits shot an arrow, and Sancha uttered a cry of agony and fell, mortally wounded.

At the same time immense columns of smoke and flame arose from the wood, and horrible cries, becoming weaker by degrees, were heard proceeding from the place where the fire had commenced.

Those cries ceased altogether in a few minutes, and an hour after there were neither chestnut trees, bushes, nor anything else left but heaps of glowing ashes and a few calcined stones, where the bandits had enclosed Bellido Dolfos in the hollow tree.

The following morning was as beautiful as that which had preceded it: the sky was azure, the air was full of perfumes, the birds were singing in the trees, and everywhere were exhibited the animation and pleasure of those who were returning from the festivities that had taken place at Carrion.

The Cid, Ximena, the Infanta, Doña Teresa, Martin, Beatrice, Rui-Venablos, Gonzalo, Alvar, and, last, Fernan and Mayor, were travelling together along the road to Burgos; all joyful, all content, all happy, except the two last-mentioned, who had had a serious disagreement on that morning. Fernan, remembering the pretty girls whom he had seen on the previous day at the festival, was bitterly lamenting the tyranny of matrimony, which, among Christians, does not permit more than one wife, when, according to his infallible calculations, two, at least, should be allowed to each man. Those complaints and those calculations naturally irritated Mayorica; Fernan cursed the wrong-headedness and stupidity of women, of his wife especially, and the quarrel ended in scratches and blows, Alvar receiving some of them as he had endeavoured to pacify the combatants.

Some hours after they had left Carrion, on arriving at a cross-roads, they heard the sounds of a lute, which an old man, seated by the wayside, was playing, and, at the same time, was asking charity from the passers-by.

The Cid and Ximena sent one of their servants to give alms to the mendicant, and Guillen and Teresa did the same. The old man began, just then, to sing a ballad which commenced thus—

> " Cavaliers of Leon,
> Castilian cavaliers !
> Haughty with the strong,
> But gentle with the weak."

"By St. James of Compostela !" exclaimed the Cid, pulling up Babieca when he heard those lines. "It is the old man who, in the name of God, told me on the road to Zamora that I should conquer in all my battles, and that my honour and my prosperity would ever increase."

The blind man continued his ballad, calling for vengeance on him who had stolen his daughter.

"You have already been avenged !" said solemnly some of the listeners, amongst whom was Rui-Venablos, for all of them knew of the tragic end of Sancha, and of the unhappy life to which Don Suero Gonzalez was condemned.

The Cid approached the mendicant and said to him—

"Old man, if the sword of a cavalier has not struck the head of the Count of Carrion, the justice of God has sentenced him to misery, to infamy, to loneliness, and to despair, which are worse than death. Your daughter disowned you, and ceased thinking of you almost as soon as she was separated from you ; but she also has suffered the chastisement which her crimes deserved. Do not weep for her: she merits oblivion and not your curse. Have you not a family which will console your grief and support your old age? Yes, you will find such in my castle. Get into one of the litters, and come to share the happiness which smiles on the lords of Vivar."

The old man then got into a litter, weeping with gratitude and joy, and the travellers continued their way, all joyous, contented, and happy, for even Fernan and Mayor were beginning to make peace.

THE END.

M. H. GILL AND SON, DUBLIN.

www.ingramcontent.com/pod-product-compliance
Lightning Source LLC
Chambersburg PA
CBHW032143110726

47902CB00003B/668